The Island of Dreams

Gregory James Clark

Clink
Street

London | New York

About the Author

Gregory James Clark was born in Lancashire, England, in 1962. Educated at the Reading Blue Coat School he gained a BSc Honours in Maritime Studies (International Transport) from the University of Wales (Cardiff) in 1988 and an MBA from Manchester Metropolitan University in 2008. He was Editor of the *Quality Matters Newsletter* from 1989 to 2000, which was later compiled into the book *'Quality Matters: The Decade of Quality 1989 - 2000'*. He has recently worked as a teacher/trainer in Quality Management for the Chartered Quality Institute Certificate and Diploma in Quality Management, and helped to design and present The Programme for Global Quality Promotion (PGQP) in Russia and the African nations from 2005 to 2010. He also assisted in the publication of *'Deming and Juran: Gift to the World'* at Bradford University in 2007. He is currently Editor of *The Electron* Newsletter for the Institution of Electronics. Recreations have included ice dancing, ballroom dancing, golf, chess and snooker. Languages spoken include Dutch, German, Portuguese and Swedish.

This book is dedicated to my late father Wilfred Neville Clark and his good late friend in Australia, Aub Roberts, after whom two of the characters have been named. My late father's contribution, the character Kathleen, has also been retained in the story.

Chapter One
Rejection

It was 10.30 p.m. on the last Friday in March, 2107, and Singles Night once more at Reading's prestigious riverside venue, the Caversham International. At the far corner of the ballroom Gary Loman, twenty-four, sat at a small table sipping a half litre of stout and gazing out of the window over the moonlit Thames toward Rivermead.

He paid little attention to the half-familiar faces that leered at him from a distance, save but to perceive the falseness that lurked behind the half-grins and pretentious swaggering that drew a fine line between arrogance and confidence. The expressions conveyed all to him, making it be known that he existed in a climate of tension, excessive competition and fear.

A few of the attendees smiled and greeted each other politely, including Gary, and with each person supposedly present with the objective of discovering the perfect soulmate, it could only be expected that one should be entitled to request dances from the ladies, and to make efforts to generate friendships that would lead to further things. To Gary this appeared to be obvious.

After some minutes, during which he contemplated the results of his latest job interview at Longroads Haulage in Witney, the youthful Victoria greeted him and presently sat down opposite. She had circulated freely and was characteristically bubbly and effervescent, seeking neither to harbour grudges nor to ignore those who might appear to have ended up sidelined and peripheral to the various cliques that had assembled themselves week by week. Smartly dressed, she remained aloof to the subtle pecking orders that permeated the chattering groups and formed the basis for the numerous unwritten rules that dictated the way in which interactions were to be permitted.

"Hello again," she remarked. "How did the interview go?"

"I don't know," Gary replied. "I just can't seem to impress the interviewers though. They always seem to be these personnel types, asking questions that rarely appear to have relevance to the job."

"How do you mean?"

"Well, if the vacancy is for a storekeeper, why ask questions about whether you can thrive on stress or enjoy team sports? Surely a better question would be 'what's a buffer stock?' or 'what does Pareto Analysis mean?' This would at least be relevant to stock control."

"I can understand you might see it that way," said Victoria. "but I have worked in human resources and that is not the way recruitment officers are trained to select their candidates. Recruitment is conducted according to a formula, and the first thing an interviewer wants to determine is whether you are confident, and sharp, so as to be responsive to training. Knowledge such as you have described would be acquired during training. Also you need good body language and dress sense, and you need to learn to be less hesitant. It is a competitive world out there and you really do have to learn to compete".

"What about being methodical and thorough, and being able to contribute ideas? Don't these things count any more?"

"They probably do, but those attributes are not those that the interviewers are trained to seek out. Unfortunately they are neither instantly visible nor simple to assess. Poor body language and hesitating incessantly are dead easy to see and assess."

"Just like those bloody exams at school," said Gary. "Working hard for a long time and acquiring knowledge counts for nothing if you can't pass an exam at speed. Don't you ever feel that quality and reliability are unnecessarily and wrongly compromised for speed?"

"Yes," replied Victoria. "But it's the way things are. You have to learn to adapt to the society of which you are a part, not the one that you may prefer to be in. Anyway, where's your next interview?" " Meridian Circuits in Slough next Tuesday."

"Well, I hope it goes good. But remember, look cheerful not forlorn. See you later."

As she rose the music began.

"Take your partners for the Carousel Waltz," the D.J. announced.

As Gary had invested a considerable amount of his time and money over the years in perfecting the steps, style and technique of dancing, it was only natural that he should seek to make use of such an investment in an appropriate environment. Unfortunately, the task of requesting a dance from a willing partner was somewhat more onerous than the mere learning of steps by rote. It required more than just a little tact, and the threat of rejection was ever-present. Hardly, if ever, could he expect to enjoy the luxury of being asked for a dance. That was a privilege reserved solely for the ladies. Also, in addition, once he had been refused once, and been seen to have been refused, experience had shown that it was subsequently more likely that the refusals would continue, and hence provide a strong disincentive to make further requests.

The intense strains of the Argentine Tango presently resonated through the hall. Gary knew that it was time to tout, but by not being in a clique it was a fact that the odds of him being successful at the first attempt would be slim. However, he was willing to try, even if it meant dancing the first few chords without a partner. Then, if after a couple

3

of minutes he had not been joined on the floor, he would retire. This often happened, but not on this occasion.

Victoria for once was not taken. He had danced this dance with her before and, unlike many of the other women, she was prepared to disregard the long accepted custom that men must ask the ladies first – the very aspect of social etiquette that had given rise to the multiple rejections that Gary had grown to hate.

The dance went well, in fact possibly too well. As it was not the simplest of dances, it afforded Gary the opportunity to practise with the accomplished Victoria unopposed by other suitors, and with space on the floor to fully utilise the talents which he had mastered.

"I see you have had more lessons," Victoria said quietly. "Where did you learn all those steps?"

"The Forbury School of Dance," replied Gary. "And you?"

"Bulmershe".

"Maybe we could get together sometime?" he suggested. "Learn together as a couple."

"I'd like to, but I don't think my boyfriend would approve."

They danced on, Gary fully aware that he had to make the most of his opportunity because when it came to the somewhat more casual smooch it would be a different matter entirely. Now the emphasis changed from being a test in performance of a routine to one of social intimacy, the type of intimacy that Gary all too openly craved.

In the hope of attracting at least one loose person, Gary had, the previous week, taken to the unorthodox practice of floating between couples during the smooches and the slow waltzes, staring from time to time at the stroking hands from which closer relationships latterly had the chance to blossom. There was the occasional whisper of filthy talk, together with a half-look of sympathy from Victoria. From others there were a range of expressions, from the red look

4

of outrage to the quiet snicker of mockery, the occasional shake of the head and the aloofness of those who pretended not to notice him. To all but Gary there was a general acknowledgment that this type of behaviour infringed just about every unwritten rule in the book. It simply was not done.

"Excuse me sir," the club secretary remarked to him. "But must you dance solo to these slow dances? I have noticed you a few times doing this and feel it is time that I asked you to refrain. These are couple only dances."

"Then why doesn't someone help me to become a couple?" Gary replied.

"You have to go and ask the ladies," said the official.

"And if I get turned down? I come here to dance not to stare at the riverbank."

"That's your problem, sir. As far as I'm concerned if you persist with this ridiculous conduct I shall have to ask you to leave the club permanently."

Gary heeded the message and returned to his former place, for a moment turning his back on the throng and gazing at the swans that congregated on the towpath outside. Then he turned around and began to contemplate his options. One was to try to pre-book the next smooch with Victoria and at least make certain of having that dance with her once. It was worth a try, he thought.

"Victoria, may I dance the next smooch with you? I would so much like to do it," he asked when she had returned to her table, careful to wait until her boyfriend was off-guard at the bar.

"Alright, I suppose once wont hurt. I'll have to ask Ivan first though".

The plan might have worked were it not for three unfortunate facts. The first was that Ivan was not the most tolerant of boyfriends when it came to the issue of other men, as he saw it, muscling in on his relationship with Victoria. The second was the fact that it was invariably

Victoria with whom Gary was seen to be dancing to the exclusion of all the others, and the third unfortunate fact was the manner in which Gary set out to exploit the dance.

Ivan reluctantly agreed to allow Gary to dance the second smooch with Victoria. Unfortunately, however, the way in which Gary had decided to dance with her tested Ivan's patience to its limit. For three whole months, since joining the club, Gary had wanted to smooch, and this longing was very evident. As he took to the floor his hands clasped hers and Gary began to dance closely and intimately, as if he were an equal to the other couples on the floor, which of course he wasn't. Kissing and intimate stroking in the rear quarters were not within Ivan's scope of permission.

The dance lasted all of six minutes, but it was sufficient for the alienation to show. As the dance ended Ivan seized Victoria abruptly, pushing Gary aside with obvious disapproval. This may have been the end of the matter were it not for Gary's unfortunate propensity to stare, albeit subconsciously, at Victoria.

At the end of the evening, as the crowd began to disperse, and Gary made his way toward the towpath, Ivan and one of his associates intercepted him.

"Look mate," he said. "I don't want to spoil your fun, but I must insist that you stop making advances towards Victoria."

"And you look," said Gary. "This is a single persons club and we all have the right to ask for dances and look for partners".

"Perhaps. But she's with me, okay? Now you just keep your distance do you understand? I saw you there on the dancefloor pressing yourself against her and slipping your hand somewhere where you shouldn't. Now you just lay off her, otherwise you will be ending up in that deep water over there".

Gary sloped home, crossing Caversham Bridge, then through St. Peters churchyard and on up St. Peters Avenue until he reached Upper Warren Avenue, with its dip and incline, which led to his residence where he lived with his mother and father.

As he walked Gary recollected the advertisement which had attracted him to The Caversham International in the first place. 'There's someone for everyone', the advertisement had said, inviting people to join for a subscription of 4,000 euros. What nonsense, he thought as he rounded the drive which led to the house. Then he recalled what his father had said to him about looking to the day ahead rather than the one that had passed. So, Friday had been none too good, but just maybe Saturday at the ice dance club would be better?

*

The club met at the newly rebuilt Ice Stadium in central Oxford and Gary was fortunate enough to have use of his father's former company car, an ageing Ford, in order to complete the half-hour drive north through the undulating Oxfordshire countryside. At noon he arrived at the rink, and the dancers were already warming up, some singly, some as couples, waiting for the two resident coaches, Timothy Browne and Patricia Sandwell, to summon them to the centre.

Gary quickly put on his kit and warmed up with two laps of the rink before joining the others. Then the group lesson began, as usual, with a recap of the basic technique for forward and backward skating.

"Try to gain momentum not so much from the initial push as from the rise which follows," Timothy advised. "Imagine that you are being drawn upwards by an invisible string that connects your head with the roof."

Presently Gary caught sight of Deirdre Atherton, a forty-five year old manageress at The Defence Research Establishment, as her head was carefully adjusted by Patricia so as to provide her with a more upright posture. Talented

7

youth passed her with speed and precision, dodging the ageing hobbyists, who distinguished themselves with their scratching and scrapings of worn toe-picks upon the smooth glassy surface.

Deirdre was a godsend to Gary, freeing him, in some respects the same as Victoria, from the monotony of being forced to dance solo for practically the whole of the two or three dance intervals that served to bring ice dancing as a social pastime back to life. The forward and backward chasses and the change of hold, which Deirdre practised with him, provided the essential ingredients of the Fairyhouse Waltz, which was today's subject of study.

"What do you think about entering for club competitions?" Deirdre asked him.

"Rather pointless," replied Gary.

"I agree," said Deirdre, slightly to Gary's astonishment. "All that judging and ranking of individuals is quite unnecessary."

"I still strive for excellence in everything I do though," Gary added. "I'm not into giving up simply because the going gets tough. I love skating for what it is, not for the medals or the competition."

"You also told me a while back that you did ballroom dancing."

"I do."

"At what level?"

"Level Six, the old Third Gold Bar".

"Don't tell me, you haven't got a partner for that either?"

"Afraid not," said Gary.

"I can see we will need to do something about that," Deirdre responded slowly, in her Anglo-Russian accent.

They continued to practise the remainder of the dance, the continuous three turns around the end of the rink and the synchronisation of the change of edge which followed the intervening chasses. The dance interval followed and for most of it Gary stood on the sidelines, past the point of rushing to break the protocol that dictated who should dance with who. The Tango Alcantara provided one exception as, with its higher degree of difficulty, it tended to receive fewer takers than the other less complex dances, affording Gary the opportunity to attempt a solo dance without having to continually give way to couples ad infinitum. The Fairyhouse Waltz, danced with Deirdre, provided the other exception.

"How many times a week do you skate?" Deirdre asked.

"About five," said Gary

"Quite good really. Then again to tackle the Tango Alcantara must take at least that. Tell me, am I right in understanding that you are now twenty-four, have no brothers and sisters and have never had a full-time job?"

"I'm afraid that is true, yes. But I am doing something about it. I am going to see a psychiatrist next week to find out what's wrong with me."

"That won't do much good," Deirdre suggested. "When a system lets a person down the only cure is usually a change of environment".

As the dance session progressed Gary thought for a moment about this comment, but quickly forgot about it as the dance club disbanded and the public streamed in, screaming, pushing and shoving, with scant regard for anyone or anything that might happen to be in their path. The heavy beat started and the mob took to the ice, racing, turning, swerving and spraying each other with ice. The odd ice ball was thrown and, as for skating the time for dedication had well and truly gone for another week, save for the handful of new beginners who crept round, hugging the barrier, and one lone girl, who sought, with difficulty, to master a spin somewhere toward the centre of the rink.

At the far end of the rink, Timothy and Patricia prepared the cones that would seal part of the rink off so that the children who were lined up could collect their small badges in exchange for performing a sequence of moves. There was joy, initially, for these keen boys and girls, until it eventually became tempered by some judge on some day, and in most cases killed off in time as a consequence of multiple failure. It was inevitable, though, in a profession that was determined to accommodate no more than two per cent of its would-be entrants. The tears on one girl's face told it all. No wonder did so few children even bother to attempt the learning process.

*

Sunday passed, and there was nothing unusual about Monday other than that it was the day that Gary had to go into Reading to continue his registration as a jobseeker, and the small matter of a strange card which had somehow found its way onto the floor behind the front door.

The card was seemingly hand-delivered, lacking any kind of postmark or other clue as to where it had come from. Upon it were merely printed the words:

'Gary Loman,

You are kindly requested to dine at the Home From Home restaurant in Benson, Oxfordshire, at 20.00 hours, tomorrow evening (Tuesday). Please do your best to make yourself available unaccompanied as this is a once in a lifetime opportunity to begin a new life in a new land.

Signed,

A Friend.'

Gary showed the card to his parents.

"Why unaccompanied?" his father asked

"Seems a bit odd, I don't think he should go," his mother advised.

"Maybe someone's playing a practical joke," said Gary. "Or trying to set me up for something, like that Ivan for example."

"Who's he?" asked his mother.

"Victoria's boyfriend. You know, the girl that dances with me on Fridays. He warned me this week to stop touching her up."

"So you ought," said his father. "I always said that one day this strange behaviour of yours would get you into trouble."

"Oh, he mustn't go," his mother urged.

"Give me that card," his father demanded. "Let me see what it says."

His father scrutinised the card carefully, noting particularly the gold on blue imprint of Saturn in the top right-hand corner.

"Promise me you won't go, Gary," insisted his mother. "It's not safe."

"Hang on," said his father. "This could be something interesting."

"Why's that?" asked his mother.

"That logo on the top right-hand side. I'm sure it means something. I have seen a picture of it somewhere, I know I have, and I've read something about it as well. I swear it's supposed to be lucky if you get one. I don't somehow think that a practical joker or a disgruntled boyfriend would be likely to know about or use that symbol. It's too obscure. In fact that could even be why it's kept obscure, to stop it from being misused."

"I don't think I would have much to lose by going, would I?" Gary concluded. "I couldn't see that Ivan going to all that trouble to lynch me. If he were going to do that he would have done it there and then on Friday night. Besides, I don't think he knows where I live anyway."

"I see whoever it is has provided directions on the reverse of the card," his father said, handing the card back to Gary.

"Well, if you do decide to go, for God's sake be careful," advised his mother.

Chapter Two
Home From Home

The next evening Gary drove out to the Home From Home. It was a quaint old coaching inn which lay along a remote country lane not too far from Benson airfield. There was no doubt that he needed the directions which had been supplied. When he arrived, however, he did wonder if he really should have come all that way, as not only was the car park deserted, but also the building itself was in total darkness.

He strode towards the entrance and tried the front door. It was locked. Then he knocked three times. There was no answer. He knocked again and waited for a couple of minutes. Still there was no answer, and after a further two minutes he decided to make his way back to his car. It was only when he arrived back at the car and turned round briefly that he noticed the appearance of a small candle alight behind one of the downstairs windows. He turned around and began to walk back toward the inn. It was at that instant that a jet black cat sprinted across his path before slowly advancing to the door. As it mewed the door gradually creaked open and the cat shot in. Then a woman's hand beckoned Gary to enter.

"Gary," whispered a voice, as he entered the pitch-dark passageway.

He crept forward, puzzled by the lack of light and total absence of people. Then he saw the dark-haired woman, who was about twenty-two years of age and wore a black dress to which was attached a distinctive badge which bore the same logo as that which was embossed on the card.

"We've been expecting you, the table is set," the woman said in a soft voice as she led him into the candlelit dining room, where one table only was set for two and a short, dark-skinned waiter stood expectantly.

"Please," said the waiter, pulling one of the chairs out and directing Gary to be seated.

"As you can see, we don't open to the public at the beginning of the week," the lady commented as she sat herself opposite him.

The waiter, who also wore the distinctive badge, handed them menus.

"*Boa tarde,*" he said in Portuguese.

"*Boa tarde,*" replied the woman.

Gary scrutinised the list of dishes and the accompanying wine list. There was nothing especially unusual about the menus, except for the absence of prices, but, as it was not in Gary's nature to commit himself to any good or service without being assured of its cost, he felt honour bound to ascertain just exactly what the costs were.

"I see there are no prices on either the menu or the wine list, so can you tell me what the prices are?"

"No is prices," replied the Portuguese waiter. "Here we have Non-Capitalist Economics".

"I'm sorry, I don't understand," said Gary.

"Don't worry about it," the lady reassured him. "All will be revealed. You can make your choice."

"Seafood roulade looks nice, and then the Bacalhau grelhada."

"Good," said the lady. "And I will have the Beignets dos Legumes and the Pescada com Arroz and Batatas do Dauphin."

"And for you some wine?" the waiter asked. "Vinho regional do Ribatejo branco goes well with the fish. I recommend it."

The woman nodded.

"So, you are Gary Loman, birthdate May ninth, 2082," the woman said, as she produced a file from the black bag which she had placed between her chair and the wood-burning fire which the waiter presently tended.

"Yes. How do you know my name?"

"And you have been skating now for almost seven years, never worked, left school a year late and rather fluffed it when it came to examinations," she continued.

"Yes, but how do you know all of this? I have never even seen or met you before. I don't even know your name. Who are you and where do you come from? And what does the emblem on that badge signify?"

"That would be telling," replied the woman coyly.

"There must be some reason why you asked me to come here."

"There is. Let me just say that someone who is in an influential position has put in a kind word for you."

"But why me?"

"Because we think you are a deserving case and would respond well to what we have to offer. Your background and character would suit our society well, and would be far more productive for both us and yourself than for you to stay in what really is an inappropriate place for a person like yourself. In other words, we need you."

"Society, what society?" Gary asked.

"I represent a place, an organisation, you could say a nation," the woman explained.

"What nation?"

"Collectively and historically we are known globally as The Island. It's actually been going for some time, seventy years in fact, but in recent years it has opened its doors a little so as to provide more opportunity to people like yourself. People who deserve a choice rather than being made to have their lives sub-optimised as a consequence of being domiciled in a capitalist world which is quite unsuitable for certain types of individuals."

The waiter presently arrived with the starters and uncorked the wine. He filled the two glasses.

"Thank you," acknowledged Gary.

"*Obrigado*," replied the waiter.

"So, where is this Island?" Gary asked

"We operate throughout the world," explained the woman "But our original site was a small island that was once part of the Azores. That is where you will spend your first year, meet your contemporaries, and learn about how our society functions. For whilst you may be well suited to our ways, they are very different to those here and you definitely have to be shaped to fit, as we say. New ways of working and new ways of thinking are always needed. After a year you and your contemporaries should be ready to join our society in full in the main territory of Kamchatka."

"I thought that was part of Russia?"

"To the outside world it is, but it is fully owned and managed by The Island and has been since 2077. Tell me, have you ever heard of Non-Capitalist Economics?"

"I have heard of the theory," answered Gary. "But as far as I was aware that was all it was, just a theory that has never materialised."

"Well, I can tell you that it has evolved into far more than just a theory. It has been well and truly put into practice. Money is not used at all but everything is privately owned. Goods and services are distributed according to need, but the driving force is to reduce waste and improve quality rather than to apply targets or quotas. It is a system that trades with the capitalist world, but does not use capitalism. There is no such thing as credit control and the only bank account that exists is the single one that The Island maintains in Switzerland for the purpose of maintaining its import and export balance of payments. There are no wages, but also no taxes. There is full employment, but nobody is overworked."

"But how do people get what they want?" Gary asked

"A feedback and control system combined with high mobility of labour and multiskilling matches supply with demand. Believe me it does work."

The main courses arrived.

"More wine, *senhor e senhora?*" asked the waiter.

"*Sim*, Jose," replied the woman.

The waiter topped up the two glasses.

"I still don't understand why I have been selected for this".

"The places are highly prized, and in the opinion of our pre-selection committee you have the qualities that are required to be able to adapt to our way of life."

"Such as?"

"A creative mind and a determination to persist even when things start to become difficult. Then there is the methodical approach to tasks and challenges, a negative reaction to competition, a corresponding positive reaction to cooperation, no excessive striving for monetary rewards, and an integrity that displays an unlikely probability that you would be inclined to cheat in any way. These attributes are by no means as common as you may think. We need people who are keen to learn and work hard, so of course we would be looking to harness your talents in exchange for giving you a better life than you are likely to get here. On top of that you can skate, not perfectly, but reasonably well. You will be well trained to enter into a way of life that is fast becoming the envy of the world."

"Who is in charge of this Island, nation or whatever it is?"

"We are a Queendom," replied the woman. "That is all you need know for the present."

"And this Queen decides who gets what and when?"

"Not at all. People are free to claim whatever they wish as long as they feel they have need of it. It's very relaxed. In fact, it's a lot more relaxed than capitalism. People are trained not to waste things needlessly, and as long as they keep to that in spirit and just take what is generally regarded as reasonable the system remains stable, unless of course there is some natural disaster, then that's different, but so it would be under capitalism."

"What kind of work would I do?"

"We have planned initially that you be trained as part of a highly talented skating team to tour the world representing the automobile manufacturer Kamchatskiy Auto, located just outside Petropavlovsk Kamchatskiy. Not only that you will form a skating partnership with a compatible person for your personal life also."

"How do you know that we would be compatible?"

"Because we have compiled a file detailing both your and her characteristics. You will be compatible, believe me."

This sounded to Gary like a dream come true, to have the chance to become a skating celebrity and actually meet a compatible wife. Was it too good to be true though? He pondered a moment.

"What if I don't like The Island when I get there?"

"Highly unlikely. I don't know of anyone who has ever wanted to leave. It may feel a little strange for you at first, but I'm certain that once you are there you will never want to go back to as you are now."

"But if I wanted to come home I could?"

"Of course. But if you did you would have to accept that there would be no readmission."

"So if I accept, what happens next?"

"The plane leaves Benson at ten tomorrow morning. You will stay here overnight. Any personal belongings that you require can be forwarded on, once your next of kin have been informed that you have decided to accept a place on The Island."

"*Para sobremesa?*" interrupted the waiter.

"He's asking you if you would like a dessert," said the lady. "I can recommend the apple strudel."

Gary nodded

"*Dois*," she said, before asking Gary if he had any more questions.

"You know I am willing to give anything a try if it sounds reasonable," Gary said.   "And I feel that if I were to turn down this opportunity I could quite possibly live to regret it. So I am going to accept."

"Therefore I need you to complete a few documents for our records. Then, if you would make your way upstairs, Jose will show you to your room. Overnight kit is provided, breakfast is at eight o'clock and the chauffeur will be outside ready to take you to the airfield at half past nine. Good luck with your new life. *Adeus.*"

"*Adeus*," Gary replied, as the lady bid him farewell and he sat quietly contemplating his new future.

Chapter Three
Departure

Gary awoke at 7.30. A breakfast had been laid out for him, but there was no sign of the woman in black whom he had met the night before, nor of the Portuguese waiter Jose. As he helped himself to it, he wondered again if he had made the right decision. Was this promised land of The Island of Dreams going to live up to expectation? Only time would tell.

The chauffeur arrived exactly at the time stated. He was then escorted by the well-built, pale-skinned driver to the awaiting limousine which transported him to the nearby airfield. Gary made one last glance at his own car as he left, contemplating the new future which awaited him, and the life that he was leaving behind. He noted particularly the gold letter K on the bonnet and steering wheel of the limousine which confirmed the fact that for the first time in his life he was riding in a Kamchatskiy.

"You might as well give me the keys to your old vehicle," said the chauffeur, who had a strong Russian accent.

"Will I get another?" Gary asked.

"You will not need a car on The Island," the chauffeur explained. "When you leave and go to Kamchatka you will have shared cars with your setmates."

"What are setmates?"

"Principals and secondaries. You will learn all about these when you arrive on The Island. We do our best to match people together who are compatible and to join them in union with others who are like-minded and share the same ideals in life. In that respect our society is much less random than is the case here."

"Do you have setmates?"

"Of course. All of our citizens do, unless they choose to contract out. You do not have to accept the partner or the set that has been found for you, but experience has shown that most people would rather be in a set than not, and one in which they feel they can belong without frustration or conflict. You'll settle in okay. Trust me".

"What will happen to the old Ford?"

"The keys will be returned to your father of course."

A few minutes later the car drew up alongside the plane. At first it looked just like an ordinary small jet aircraft, but on closer inspection he could see that, like the limousine, it was not a standard type, but a supersonic design, something like a miniature Tupolev or Concorde.

"That my dear friend is your plane," the chauffeur said, pointing to it. "A Kamchatskiy Aerospace Hebden Three".

"Never heard of them."

"Made in Opala in Southern Kamchatka. They are made to order by Kamchatskiy Aerospace for the top of the bizjet market. We also use them internally for a few of our inter-island services. Like most things in our society quality takes precedence over cost. We believe in making things to be as high quality and reliable as possible. Most capitalist manufacturers would consider such a model to be totally uneconomic from a marketing perspective, but the world is slowly changing."

The limousine drew up alongside the steps that led up to the flight deck, from which a petite oriental hostess emerged. She bowed to the chauffeur, who responded in kind. The chauffeur then opened the car door for Gary, for him to make his way up the steps.

"Enjoy your flight," said the chauffeur.

*

The hostess, like the lady at the inn, wore the obligatory gold on blue Saturnian badge on her cream-coloured jacket. She shook Gary's hand then led him inside the plane, its luxurious interior with wide leather seats serving to impress.

"This first class only service," explained the hostess. "So plenty of legroom. Normally only carries up to thirty-six passengers on. Also can go supersonic, but not today. Here, enjoy extra wide seat. Then I get you Bucks Fizz to celebrate your joining of our nation. You will be pleased to know you are only passenger today."

"I take it I don't need a passport," Gary remarked, as the hostess returned with the drink.

"Passport not needed. New one will be issued when training completed".

"What if I don't pass the training?"

"Everyone always pass training. No one ever fail on Island."

The cabin doors closed and the engines started. Then the plane began to taxi. Gary instinctively fastened his safety belt as the plane accelerated quickly but quietly into take-off.

The hostess sat with Gary for the duration of the flight. When the ascent was complete she removed a remote control from her inside jacket pocket and activated a screen at the front of the cabin.

"Now I show you something of our Island," she said, pressing a button to commence the half-hour film which described The Island from its beginnings in 2026.

The film began with an aerial view of The Island with its distinctive Dome and Bell Tower overlooking an extensive sandy coastline with an oval shaped swimming pool and Stone Boat clearly visible in the bay. Other buildings were dotted about, though with less distinguishing features.

Then the voiceover commenced:

'Welcome to The Island of Dreams, which for the next year will be your new home from home. We are pleased that you have decided to accept our offer of a place here and the opportunity to train to become a citizen of The Island and its territories.

Every year for the last eleven years, 240 young people have been specially selected from around the world to join with us to train to be skating celebrities for one of four companies that comprise The Kamchatskiy Corporation, the world's greatest transportation company.'

The images then changed to show the rugged volcanic hills of Kamchatka, followed by other scenes from around the globe to match the soundtrack. The voice continued:

'The Island, as it is still affectionately known, is the world's newest constitutional monarchy and is in itself a nation state within nations. Kamchatka is by far its largest acquisition, along with the adjoining territories of Sakhalin and the Kuril Islands. Progressive agreements with Russia enabled the entire territory to be owned by The Island in 2077, yet without compromising any of Russia's sovereignty. Since then The Island has continued to provide its unique alternative to capitalism in islands throughout the world, from The Falklands and South Georgia in the South Atlantic; to the offshore Brazilian islands of Trinidade, Noronha and Rocas; to Kerguelen and the Crozet Islands in the Indian Ocean; to Cheju-do, Tsushima and Izuhara in the Far East; and finally the Aleutian Islands which have now been fully purchased from the Government of the United States forming a continuous territory that now stretches from Kamchatka to the Alaskan Peninsula. But it is on one small island where our history really began.'

The images changed from modern snapshots of territories to a shot which showed an ageing unusual luxury yacht which was reminiscent of a small high-class eighteenth-century sailing ship moored in a harbour. The name of the ship, the *Katie* was clearly visible on the side, and next to it a thirty-something man stood, dressed in an old admiral's uniform that pretty much matched the style of the vessel. The narration continued:

'In 2026, whilst en route from Rio to Cardiff, an eccentric thirty-five-year-old shipowner by the name of Ken David, sailed accidentally past what is now our beautiful Island after being blown off course in a storm. He was a master of the sea and a genius at building and adapting unusual vessels for specialised tasks, but even with all of his skill occasionally the weather combined with a technical problem, such as a damaged rudder, can throw the unwary off course, particularly in the notorious waters of the equatorial Atlantic. But he fell in love with the island as soon as he saw it and figured that his fiancee would too. Two years later he and his fiancée Kathleen visited it again in the odd-looking vessel which you see here. He named this, his personal ship, which he himself built, the Katie after her.'

The scene changed again, this time to another, even older film this time showing a lady in her early thirties gazing eagerly at the stars through a large telescope. Presently the reflector's image focused on the planet Saturn.

'His fiancée on the other hand was an opera singer whose main hobby was astronomy. Both were exceedingly rich and in 2030 they purchased the sixteen-square-kilometre uninhabited island from the Portuguese government.'

The narration ceased for a while as the gold on blue Saturnian logo was pieced together on the screen. Then it resumed:

'Ken was at heart a revolutionary and he and Kathleen already had plans for what was to be their new island enterprise. Their dream was, with the help of friends, to lay the foundation for a new world order that would continue long after their lifetimes. For this they decided that they wanted a logo so she suggested the splendour of Saturn's rings at which she always marvelled.'

Three still colour scenes followed showing the thousands of blue flowers that grew wild over large stretches of the island.

'The flowers led Katie to suggest the gold of Saturn superimposed on the blue of the flowers.'

Three more scenes of 'The Island' as it had looked in 2030 followed, and the narrative continued:

'This is The Island as it had looked when Ken and Kathleen had purchased it in 2030. It was once a Portuguese garrison where sailing ships would call to take on fresh water on their way to South America. In Victorian times, however, it fell into disuse and no one really had much use for this picturesque, but redundant, island of peace and tranquillity. These were Kathleen's personal photographs.'

The images of photographs of dilapidated buildings overgrown with trees, weeds and wild flowers slowly gave way to colour shots of the semi-completed Island as it appeared in 2037. This commenced with an aerial shot, followed by further still photographs.

'We now move forward to the year 2037 when The Island as we know it today began truly to take shape. There are at this point one or two buildings still requiring finishing touches, but it is virtually complete after almost seven years under construction. The photographs which you now see show the Colonnade and Gloriette. We then see the Buddha and Japanese garden, reflecting the strong Japanese influence, and the Stone Boat, built by Kai-San, one of two Japanese engineers who were engaged in the construction. The Stone Boat was, in fact, a joke aimed at Ken David and his reputation for restoring ships in his Cardiff boatyard, with Kai-San famously saying to him "David san, please, show us if you can put to sea in that!"'

The singer reappeared, taking applause from her adoring fans in Cardiff's St. David's Hall. Then the commentary resumed:

'It was planned that Kathleen would be crowned Queen of The Island, but she was never crowned as she died prematurely in a car crash whilst on holiday in Colorado with her trusted friend, the somewhat younger Justine, who survived and was honour bound to take Kathleen's place as Ken's fiancée.'

Justine was then seen being crowned at a small ceremony in an underground cavern with Ken at her side.

'It was therefore Justine rather than Kathleen who became the first Queen of The Island. The royal wedding took place shortly before the coronation in The Island Church. As you can see it was a very small and private affair, as was the next. It is only now, after seventy years that things are set to change.'

Scenes from this were briefly shown before the focus changed to that of a stout man in his fifties who had been visible at the both the wedding and coronation, but was now seen striding past the Houses of Parliament in London.

'Ken was greatly assisted by Leo Harvey, his banker, who was head of the multinational Harvey Banking Corporation. One could be forgiven for thinking that you can't get more capitalist than that, but it was precisely because he reached such a position and had been able to view capitalism from every angle possible, that he became convinced that it was a system that desperately needed a completely new and viable alternative. To him the world deserved a choice, but that choice had to be something other than communism.'

The faces of two other gentlemen then appeared, namely those of the twentieth-century philosophers William Edwards Deming and Joseph Moses Juran.

'Both Leo and Ken were inspired by the two twentieth-century philosophers W. Edwards Deming and Joseph M. Juran, who had led the quiet revolution in quality that had made Japan prosperous after World War Two. Together Leo and Ken used their theories to shape the blueprint for the world that was later to become known as Non-Capitalist

27

Economics. The teaching of Deming and Juran was very much integrated into The Island's economic and political planning.'

A picture of the book *Non-Capitalist Economics* by Leo Harvey then gave way to a more light-hearted sketch showing games played on ice in elaborate costumes.

"Every year we have our annual fun and games contest 'Games Without Frontiers' where teams from different Island territories come together once a year to do battle in our magnificent Non-Olympic Stadium.'

The scene changed quickly again to show a human chessboard on ice.

'Then we have our long-standing human chess matches played on ice on giant curls in the world's most exclusive ice rink. Two of the world's experts sit at each end of the rink and play against each other in an exciting competition showing that competition can be fun if it is applied in the right way.'

As pieces were taken they were pushed by pushers into a specially created ditch that surrounded the ice surface, whilst the knights were lifted in and out of position by means of an overhead lifting device.

Next, it was Carnival on Ice.

'Each year we have our carnival with a celebration of dances performed on ice.'

"Pretty costumes," Gary remarked.

"Island people always love to dress in costume," said the air hostess.

Skaters were shown performing elaborate routines around cars, airborne craft, small yachts and moving cranes, trains and lifting equipment, specially built to size so as to serve as props.

'The climax of the show is our demonstrations by our chosen recruits for the senior executives of the four Kamchatskiy companies Kamchatskiy Auto, Kamchatskiy Aerospace, Kamchatskiy Maritime and Kamchatskiy Logistics.'

"This what you will be doing," remarked the hostess.

"As good as that? I don't think so," remarked Gary.

"You will be," the hostess said, encouragingly. "Island skating teacher world's best."

From the elegance of ice dancing the documentary switched to the sound of a steam locomotive chuffing up a gentle incline with its train of four luxury carriages into the grounds of a palace that strangely resembled that of Versailles.

'Built in the centre of The Island and completed to the Versailles specification The Royal Palace is accessible by steam railway and lies in the centre of The Island approximately four kilometres from The Town. It is now home to our present queen, Queen Katie of Kamchatka, and on the tranquil lake behind one travels in style on the steam yacht Gondola, which is a replica of the one that Her Majesty Queen Justine had fallen in love with on a holiday to Lake Coniston in England in 2050.

Beyond the lake is the cable car that leads up the mountain to the north side of The Island and the Non-Olympic Stadium, which used to serve as the centrepiece for our four-yearly sporting extravaganza for amateur sports. Now the events are held elsewhere. As you can appreciate, under Non-Capitalist Economics all sport is amateur sport. Engineers, led by Kai-San and Endo-San, carefully constructed the Colosseum-like stadium by carving away part of the volcanic mountain on the north side of The Island furthest from The Town at a distance of some eight kilometres.'

Next, it was back to The Town where small- and medium-sized blue bullet-shaped taxis, each bearing The Island logo, sped around giving periodic blasts of their horns to warn pedestrians of their passing.

'Getting around The Town in the daylight hours is never a problem. The traditional Kammies can always be flagged down for a free ride.'

The film concluded with a short scene which began with a shot of the roof of The Great Dome that was situated in the centre of The Town. A strange screeching sound was heard as a section of the roof slowly began to open and the gold metallic head of a giant mechanical bird emerged, taking Gary by surprise. It climbed onto a purpose-built perch from which it launched itself into the air over The Town before flying out to sea for a few minutes, its twenty-foot wingspan dominating the skyline.

'For the last eleven years The Eagle has become a familiar sight, as it provides a unique way of both maintaining security around our beautiful Island and of rescuing those in distress either at sea or in the mountains. A fabulous sight you have to agree and just one of several wonderful pieces of engineering that you will find in this remarkable wonder of the world that is The Island of Dreams.'

"Now Su-Lin bring you snack," said the air hostess, revealing her name.

"You are Su-Lin?" Gary asked.

"Yes," she answered, shaking his hand. "Su-Lin from Korean island of Chejo-do, now part of Island's many territories".

When she returned with a tray of assorted vol-au-vents and two more glasses of Buck's Fizz Gary asked her how Chejo-do had come to be part of The Island's territory.

"The Island purchase land over many years," she explained. "People who supported Non-Capitalist Economics, and were Korean nationals and who had money to invest in property, were asked to put their investment into a special fund until they had enough to purchase Chejo-do completely and were in a majority in local government. Then in 2073, Non-Capitalist Economics was introduced by consensus, and rights to visit other Island territories were granted by the Island monarchy and council in 2074. Everyone on Chejo-do celebrated as they knew the change would be very good for them. In 2075 Tsushima did same, but they are Japanese.

That is the route I fly most. Chejo-do to Tsushima. I have lots of friends there, because we all think alike of course".

"So how did you finish up in Benson?"

"This is a roving plane, not scheduled, so it just flies where needed to no specific timeframe. Now, out of window you can see Island."

Gary looked out of the starboard window and could just make out a cluster of islands that lay to the south and east of The Island.

"See Island," said Su-Lin, pointing to a single island that was somewhat detached from the main group.

The plane turned sharply to approach it. As it descended he was able to spot some of the major features which he had seen in the film. The Bell Tower dominated the skyline and he could just make out The Great Dome, the mountains on the north side of The Island and the lake in the centre, but these features quickly disappeared as the plane touched down on the tiny coastal runway on the south west side of The Island, which could only just accommodate the Hebden Three.

As Gary stepped out he bade farewell to the young Su-Lin and gazed at the seemingly deserted runway, which was surrounded by sand dunes and was strangely silent. There was no terminal building nor any immediate sign of life. The steps which led from the aircraft had obviously been placed alongside upon landing, though the attendants who had brought it were nowhere to be seen.

Gary descended the steps and waited. The weather was fine with the noonday sun beaming down from overhead. He waited for several minutes and looked all around. Then a voice called to him.

"Gary," called a man's voice.

He looked behind him, but saw nothing.

"Gary," came the voice again.

He looked around again, scrutinising the dunes, then the sea to the other side. It was not until he turned to face

31

the plane that he was to get a surprise, for emerging from behind it suddenly appeared an open topped black Landau carriage hauled by two jet black stallions and steered by a gentleman dressed in top hat and tails.

The coachman stopped beside him and dismounted from the carriage. He opened the door for Gary and he stepped inside, pondering for a moment the remarkable scene of the supersonic jet in which he had just flown and the Victorian carriage in which he now sat. He had just transferred from the world's most modern mode of transport to its oldest, but both forms had one outstanding feature, and that was that they were both unmistakeably best in class.

Chapter Four
Lunch with Connie

The carriage sped south east from the airfield along a single track road from which the dunes quickly gave way to more arable pasture where crops, fruit trees, vines and marketable flowers grew irrigated by carefully routed streams which flowed down from the hillside beyond. The road meandered through fields in which a handful of farmhouses and outbuildings were dispersed, but the coastline was never more than a few hundred metres away.

It took about ten minutes for the coach to enter the grounds of The Town from the north side through the small wood that marked the boundary, followed by The Japanese Garden and on through The Triumphal Arch. Then the coach descended the hill until it came to a large building by the shore. The carriage drew to a halt outside with the oval swimming pool to the left behind him and the Stone Boat to the left in front across the lawn that separated the building from a narrow promenade.

The coachman opened the door of the carriage and Gary stepped down.

"Lunch is served in the restaurant, sir," he said. "Table number five."

Gary entered the building, pausing for a moment to scrutinise the Deming Memorial that was set into the rock face to the right of the entrance. He read the inscription on the plate below the bronze statue upon which were engraved the words 'W. Edwards Deming 1900–1993' followed by the list of the Fourteen Points by which he was perhaps best remembered. Then Gary entered, drawn toward the dining room by the sound of chattering. The Usherette greeted him at the door and showed him to table number five, at which a twenty-three-year-old casually dressed auburn-haired lady sat expectantly.

"Gary," said the lady, shaking his hand.

"Who are you?" asked Gary.

"I'm Connie from Anchorage, Alaska," she replied. "I am your fiancée by the way, or principal, as they prefer to call it here."

"Principal? Yes I heard that term when I left England. What does it mean exactly?"

"Something known as The Set Formation Act defines it. It's broadly similar to a wife or husband. There's no difference really, apart from the fact that should a relationship get into difficulties your secondaries will be on hand to help you sort things out. I've got a booklet I can give you later on which explains all about it simply and concisely. Basically now that you have arrived here you have automatically become a member of a twelve member conventional set which will live and work together in Petropavlovsk Kamchatskiy, home of The Kamchatskiy Auto Company."

"So I believe. I was told that I would be transferred there after a year."

"Yes. After we have done our year's training here that is where we will go. Then we do five or six years in the skating troop, depending on whether or not there is an intake next year. After that we work on the shop floor and later in management. It's self-service here by the way."

They made their way past the light vegetarian and fish servery.

"How does it work?" Gary asked.

"You point to the items that you want and the server puts them on the plate," Connie explained. "It seems pretty efficient. They don't serve meat though. The Island believes in trying to minimise animal cruelty so it's just fish and veg. Apparently that was arrived at by consensus right across The Island and its territories five years ago, so The Usherette told me. Most people, including myself, don't seem to have anything against it."

"So, there's no meat anywhere?" Gary asked.

"No. Five years ago a decision was made to close down all the abattoirs everywhere in every Island controlled territory. Queen Mary, now the Queen Mother, decreed it after popular consent, though seafood continues to be caught, farmed and served according to strict environmental criteria. Not to fish would apparently disturb the world's ecosystems, but we still have to be careful not to overfish. Like everything else, supply has to be exactly matched with demand."

They sat down.

"I'm still curious to know how this system of Non-Capitalist Economics actually functions," said Gary. "Until last night I thought it was no more than a theoretical concept."

"It's a lot more than that I can assure you," Connie explained. "It is tied in very closely with the political system. I found out yesterday that The Island and all of its territories operate as a one-party state. There are no competitive elections."

"So, what is it then? A dictatorship?"

"Oh no, it's definitely not a dictatorship," said Connie. "It's what is known as a One Party Democracy. We are governed here by a team of scientists, statisticians and engineers in Kamchatka who serve the queen and her prime minister here. Politicians are not programmed to fight elections. Instead technical people are trained and educated to make the system work and continually improve on it. And as long as that continues to happen they have nothing to fear with regard to elections. I am looking forward to experiencing an election here though. It is rumoured to be something quite special."

"You say you are from Alaska?"

"Sure am. And I'm glad I am because it has allowed me to find out about The Island at an early age. I had the good fortune to go to a school in Alaska that has a long association with the philosophy of W. Edwards Deming, the guy whose statue stands at the entrance to this training centre."

"Yes, I noticed that as I walked in," said Gary.

"Well, he had an influence at my school way back towards the end of the twentieth century before he died. Little did I know that there was a whole society growing and thriving within Alaska and indeed the world that based its workings upon exactly that philosophy transposed at every level. I kept an eye on the local papers and became inspired to learn more about the system that had steadily made its way east from Kamchatka without anyone hardly knowing. Every few years I would find out that another island had been bought out and converted to this new system. Yet there was no change of sovereignty, just a complete change in the way in which society is organised. But it was always little by little, nothing dramatic. This has gone on for pretty much as long as I can remember. Once an island has been converted, however, it shuts its doors rigidly to outsiders. Now the territory extends as far as Fox Island, which is just off the Alaskan Peninsula. Rumours abound that the Alaskan Peninsula itself could one day be bought up, though it is likely that Nunivak and Kodiak Island will be transferred first.

I knew ever since I was at school that I wanted to be part of the non-capitalist community of the US and not the capitalist one that still dominates the US so shamefully."

"So how did you manage to get here?"

"I revisited my old school. I felt sure that someone in that school would know something about how I could do it. An appointment was set up for me with my old head who said he thought he could do something as he had a few contacts. If I waited for a chance otherwise I would be unlikely to be successful."

"So your old head fixed it up for you to end up here?"

"He arranged for me to meet a Kamchatkan who worked for the Kamchatskiy Auto Company and gave me the prized opportunity to come here and then go to Kamchatka, the place that in my heart of hearts I knew I wanted to be but never thought that I ever could. Fortunately my skating served me well. I never thought I would get to be a skater either, but I was told, after he had taken a look at me down at my local rink, that my skating was good enough for the car company. So, how did you end up here?"

Gary told her his story. Then Connie explained the programme for the day.

"At five o'clock you must go to The Great Dome for Joanie's address," she said. "She's the prime minister and dame in charge here. One step down from the queen you could say, and in charge of all political and day-to-day operations associated with The Island. I heard her address yesterday so I do not need to hear it again."

"So what do we do between now and five?" asked Gary

"Well, we could go and look at our home for the next year. We will be sharing a room in a cottage known as Angel. When we have finished we can go up there. After that there should be time to visit The Wax House."

Connie led Gary back up the hill, pointing out Anchor cottage to the right where another set of new recruits were installing themselves.

"That's The Town Hall on the left," she said. "And The Wax House is next to it with its blacked out arched windows. The entrance to our cottage is round to the right, by Atlas' statue. I suppose we are quite privileged having a residence that is right in the Town Square. That rectangular piece of water in the middle is called Leo's Lake."

The door to the cottage opened automatically, and then closed automatically behind them.

"The whole set isn't here yet," explained Connie. "Me, Carl, Jose and Graca arrived yesterday. Carl is from

Newfoundland, which, like Alaska has strong ties with The Island. Jose and Graca are from Lisbon. Carl has a background in engineering, but as he couldn't pass exams too good so he wasn't going to be able to make a lot of his talents in Canada."

"So how did he get his passport here?"

"Family contacts. His dad knew of The Island and some of the local landowners had links to The Island. He thinks, and so do I, that the island of Newfoundland is a target for The Island for conversion to Non-Capitalist Economics. It won't happen soon, though. His dad thinks it won't turn non-capitalist for at least twenty years. Carl is already twenty-nine, so unless he was given a chance now he would have had to accept that he would have to live the rest of his life under capitalism. The landlords held a secret meeting and somehow fixed it for him to have that prized Queen's Ticket."

"And what about the Portuguese couple?" Gary asked.

"They are Catholics, but they belong to a very special church called The Church of The Founder Mary in Lisbon, not to be confused with the Church of Saint Mary, which is quite different. The Church of The Founder Mary, I learnt, has nothing to do with the Virgin Mary, but with a far more recent person by the name of Mary, who established our multi-religious faith to which all other religions of the world would one day subscribe. No more wars caused by religion. A noble aim, most would agree, but she received little support in her time, especially in her native England. She was an obscure woman, just like that church where Jose and Graca worshipped is a very obscure church with a very private congregation. It contributes to the Catholic Church and, for so doing, is not criticised for its existence, but it is definitely not a conventional Catholic Church, and its weddings are not recognised officially as being Catholic. Its priests and priestesses are likewise not recognised as being officially Catholic. I guess it is more than a matter of coincidence that the ice rink where Jose and Graca practised their ice dance routines is situated exactly opposite the church, and that every year it is accepted that two of its twenty-somethings are selected to come here and start new lives in a place where this multi-faithed religion is the norm rather than the exception."

"Where are the others now?"

"Up at the rink I guess. There should be more of our set arriving today or tomorrow. I know there will be twelve of us in all."

Connie showed Gary around the cottage, which consisted of a living room, study room, kitchen and two bedrooms downstairs, and a further four bedrooms upstairs. Connie and Gary's room was one of the upstairs ones. Once inside Connie handed Gary a little red book.

"What's this?" he asked

"Something you'll need to get used to using. It's called a requisitions book. You can use it for requisitioning all of your standard personal items, such as basic clothing, toothpaste, basic food items, in fact anything that is classed as basic and unrestricted. There's a different system for what under capitalism would be classed as more expensive items. They are more tightly controlled but aren't rationed or subject to rigid quotas. Excessive consumption could give rise to what is known as a demand irregularity, but usually there would have to be an error of some kind or something very out of the ordinary to invoke that. It is what is known as a fault tolerant system."

Gary looked closely at the various categories of basic goods.

"How do I apply for these things?" he asked.

"You either fill out a form and have them delivered or you present yourself at a place of release, that is, a shop, and get an entry made in your requisitions book. A lot of things will be requisitioned collectively, so there is joint responsibility for ordering meals for the week, for example. You can also requisition online."

"What about pubs and restaurants?"

"Depends on the place. In a basic pub or restaurant it is sufficient just to present your ID number."

"And higher than basic?"

"Higher class places often require a ticket for which you have to apply, unless you get it as a merit award. Applications are usually granted, but you can't abuse it by always going to a posh place and never to a basic one. I'll try and download a factsheet if you like. The Island website is easy to log onto here, although outside Island territories it is impossible. The only way anyone ever hears of this place is by word of mouth."

"So it seems," acknowledged Gary. "Shall we go to The Wax House then?"

Chapter Five
The Wax House

A set of steps led to the entrance to The Wax House. Outside a dozen recruits were already waiting to be escorted inside. A sign at the door read 'next tour at 3 p.m.'

As the clock on the Bell Tower struck three, the door opened and a dark-haired lady in her late forties beckoned them to come inside.

The hall into which they stepped was darkened to protect the delicate wax exhibits, which were arranged in two lines of six pairs with a platform at the far end upon which one further waxwork stood, dressed entirely in white, set on a pedestal behind as if looking over them from above.

"Good afternoon, ladies and gents," said the lady. "I am Maria Salvatore and have the honour of being The Curator of this our fine Wax House museum. Allow me to introduce The Founders of our Island. If you will follow me round I will move to each pair of figures in turn and then give you a brief description of each couple and what their role was in the establishment of the fine community which you have been invited to join. These are the great and glorious men and women who, over seventy years ago, shaped and constructed our Island. Many of the people who live and work on The Island are direct descendants of these Founders.

All in their thirties, they were men and women with means who shared a common vision of a better world that would be achieved not by violent revolution, but by popular consent that would ensue over many generations in territories that would be acquired through a long-term strategy of progressive acquisition. The acquisition of islands would form the basis of this strategy, but other territories, notably peninsulas, would also be earmarked for purchase under opportunist conditions. Kamchatka, with its previously low rate of economic growth, yet considerable geothermal energy reserves and cheap land, was a special target for acquisition at an early stage.

All of these individuals were wealthy, but at the same time they all recognised the unfairness, injustice and suffering that capitalism created. But whilst they all had a quiet despising of capitalism, they all agreed also that communism was a worse rather than a better economic model and that at some point it would either collapse, as happened in eastern Europe, or would be forced to slowly revert back to capitalism, as happened in China. In the view of The Founders the world needed a completely new third theory to rival capitalism and that theory is the one that we know commonly today as Non-Capitalist Economics."

The Curator presently stepped toward the first pair of exhibits.

"The first Founder that we see is Eric, The Journalist, and architect of our political system which functions under the title of One Party Democracy. Next to him we see his principal, Rachel, who had served alongside him during his years of media reporting researching and studying different systems of government throughout the world, as well as different systems of management. He took particular interest in the techniques of quality management that had been adopted by the Japanese in the twentieth century and believed that some kind of system that removed the competition and wastefulness of multi-party systems was needed, but without creating a dictatorship. Eric was duly appointed Minister for Democracy.

Facing them, we see the all-female partnership of Mary, The Priestess, and her principal Norma. They believed in the need for a single unified world religion, which, whilst not being a religion in itself, would provide an umbrella for all other religions. Mary became the Minister for Religious Affairs and shared a close affinity with the queen for ice dancing, which increasingly became part of our culture. She also managed gay and lesbian affairs, against which The Island does not specifically legislate, although everyone is expected to remain faithful to their set.

Diagonally opposite we see David, The Publisher, and his principal Valerie. He was a strong campaigner for the anti-gun lobby in America, which didn't exactly make him popular in some quarters in the US where he did much of his work and campaigning. His experience of world affairs, however, gave him sufficient expertise to take on the role of Media Minister, freeing up Eric to concentrate on the political side.

Opposite David and Valerie we see John, The Barrister, otherwise known as Big John, with his principal Angela, whom John had met at law school. John was the legal expert who was responsible for all aspects of law and order. He was dismayed at Britain's legal system as well as the current state of policing in all countries. In his many papers he likened policing to inspection on the factory floor, but his ideas were not readily accepted by either the British media or academics. Much of his work fell on stony ground until he met the two Japanese gents Endo and Kai at a Deming conference. These two men, whom we shall see later, were very interested in his ideas and, following a meeting with Leo and Ken, invited him to join The Island and take on the Home Secretary role. Building on the third of Deming's Fourteen Points, namely to cease dependence on mass inspection to achieve quality, John constructed what was later to become the Self Policing State. Our Greencoats as they are called now test for social defects by looking for common and special causes that could potentially lead to dissatisfaction and address those rather than attempting to police by inspection.

Moving on, the next waxwork on the left is Colin, The Analyst, who was quite a different character. He was the Minister for Education and Information Technology, and, with the help of Clifford, whom we shall see in a moment, and Endo-san, developed our intranet system known as Commander, as well as revolutionising education and learning. He was a computer expert from Wales who worked closely with Leo and Ken to ensure that their computer systems were always ahead of everyone else's. His expertise made him very rich, not that Sheila, his principal, was aware. She loved him for his desire for continuous learning. As a schoolteacher in the Rhondda Valley she was as dismayed at Britain's education system as Big John was at the legal system. Both Colin and Sheila's condemnation of the UK examinations system especially led them both into conflict with the Department for Education costing them their jobs. Ken immediately rewarded them both with a place on The Island.

Opposite these two is Peter, The Sportsman, with principal Rosalie. He amassed a considerable fortune by acquiring and managing sports and leisure facilities throughout Europe. He banked with Leo and was a great advocate of amateur rather than professional sport, and often expressed concern at the increasing pressure of competition in sport which he said was driving people to cheat and discrediting the Olympic movement. Following his invitation here he set to work establishing the so-called Non-Olympic movement under the umbrella of Non-Capitalist Economics and was charged with the responsibility for ensuring that everyone on The Island took an interest in sport and fitness, as well as organising a universal training system to make skating, dancing, and chess features of The Island's culture. He also designed The Island's championship golf course, The West Links, and thanks to his and Rosalie's efforts boredom and depression have never really existed on The Island.

We now move on to Anton, The Magician, and principal Jane. Together they made an impressive partnership, achieving great success as renowned comedians, psychics and illusionists. They were favourites of the queen, whilst their expertise in the field of health and safety also impressed Ken who became convinced that he needed a Minister for Health and Safety, as well as someone to ensure that a first rate national health service was both set up and well managed. Today our health service is the envy of the world and brings in huge revenues from capitalist nations. In the course of their work they had witnessed many accidents and had to perform emergency first aid and even operations using only the most basic of materials, so they had a lot of skill of a rare kind. The other Founders also voted by consensus to appoint Anton as Deputy Prime Minister, a post which the Health and Safety Minister still enjoys to this day.

Facing Anton and Jane are Patrick Carmichael or 'Paddy', The Actor, and his principal, Georgina. She had had a troubled life at the hands of a tyrannical husband. He had suffered also at the hands of bullies in his childhood. They were close associates of Anton and Jane and, like Anton and Jane, were popular with the queen. Paddy was a keen Shakespearean actor, as well as an accomplished director of stagecraft, opera and film, producing several blockbuster movies. Georgina, whom he had met on the stage, was a talented musician and opera singer, whom both Queen Justine and Kathleen, who we shall see in a moment, liked immensely. Both felt the need to give her a new life free from the husband who was threatening her life, and to provide him with a role in the new society. Queen Justine decided therefore to appoint Paddy as Culture Minister. He believed strongly, in line with the Deming philosophy, that pride and joy in work were important counters to bullying and, if successfully instilled at an early age, could greatly help to eliminate it. He and Georgina actively promoted artistic pursuits alongside sports as an integral part of the Island's development.

Moving diagonally again, we see Darren, The Merchant, with his principal Annette. He was the Foreign Secretary who was appointed by Leo to act as an interface between The Island and the outside world, both with regard to trade and issues of national security. He became known to Leo through his banking of substantial revenues which he raised through the transportation and sale of diamonds and other precious gems on special safe routes which he established between his base in London and sources of supply in Russia and South Africa. Annette's father owned a chain of hotels and also banked with Leo. These hotels provided safe and inconspicuous accommodation to people from The Island whenever they travelled abroad and it was at one of these hotels that Darren and Annette met. These hotels are still owned by The Island and you will probably find yourself staying in one of them when you visit a capitalist country.

Turning round we have Clifford, The Scientist, and his principal Zena. He was a government scientist who worked on many pioneering projects, but became infuriated with the interference and bunglings of politicians to such an extent that in the end he resigned. His name was Clifford Hebden and was a brilliant aviator and aircraft designer. He was a compatriot of Ken who famously reconfigured Concorde in miniature to make a unique new aircraft, known as The Hebden, or Hebden One, which was the forerunner to the modern Hebden Three which brought many of you here. The British Ministry of Defence was glad to see the back of him. The Island welcomed him with open arms, as Minister for Projects and founder of what is now Kamchatskiy Aerospace. His pioneering work with Endo and Kai led the production of designs that would one day harness the vast geothermal resources of Kamchatka to provide cheap, clean energy to the world, which it now does. Latterly he became keen on brain research and The Clifford Institute for Brain

Research here on The Island, home to the legendary Dream Machine, is named after him."

"The Dream Machine," whispered the group curiously, as they advanced to the top of the line where Leo and Ken faced each other with their principals. The Curator turned to face the pair on the left and continued with her commentary:

"So we come to Leo, The Banker, and first Prime Minister of The Island, with his principal, Nora.

As head of a multinational banking corporation he was a somewhat lonely and insular character, and Nora, an intern, succeeded in opening up his eyes to possibilities, particularly if he was going to resign and throw everything he had into The Island and his and Ken's dream for the world. The son of a banking tycoon, who had devoted his life to the pursuit of wealth, Leo was groomed to take over and expand his father's business, with an education at Harrow, Oxford, and latterly Lucerne. Over the decades his father had built the business up acting as banker for royalty, large corporations, and even governments. He frequently advised governments on aspects of financial policy. Yet the more he saw, the more he hated capitalism, which, in his opinion, rewarded all the wrong people for all the wrong reasons. Nora taught him what it was like to be happy, which in his highly stressful life he had been unable to appreciate, from his harsh childhood in boarding school, through the perpetual pressure to perform well at college and university, to his later years running his father's banking empire, forever compelled to watch his back for fraud, insider dealing, sabotage, and threats to his personal life. He was not a happy man until he met Ken and Kathleen and heard of their plans for The Island. His bank still manages The Island's one bank account with which it trades with capitalist countries and he is widely regarded as being the father of Non-Capitalist Economics. It is said that he had a very distinctive laugh and some people on The Island claim to have heard this laugh as, ghost-like, he watches over it.

Opposite Leo and Nora we have Ken, The Mariner, and first King of The Island, with principal Justine, who of course was our first Queen. Ken was a shipping tycoon who specialised in all kinds of transportation by sea. His father had helped his son to get established by seeing him through university, where he displayed great talent as a maritime engineer, and on to a shipping career. When he graduated his father gave him £100,000 to invest in a couple of ships, but before long he was buying far more and converting them to specialised uses such that whenever there were unusual cargoes or combinations of cargoes he was the expert. I suppose you have already heard the story of the Stone Boat down at the training centre?"

There were nods from the group.

"Ken was retiring, but firm, having little tolerance for people simply followed orders without thinking about what they did. Above all, those who worked for him were expected to be creative and have a capacity for innovation, just as he himself was adamant that The Island King 'must demonstrate a unique set of outstanding capabilities to justify holding the Crown'. With this proviso, the world's newest monarchy was formed with its unique structure whereby the Crown passed down the female line, with each new King selected by The Queen and then subsequently trained so as to be able to raise standards throughout the world, including the capitalist world, in accordance with the teachings of Deming and Juran. Above all, according to Ken, The Island King must be 'strong, innovative and pure', and only hold the rank of Prince Regent until all senior parties, whom the Queen's father, the outgoing King is to select from among his Ministers, are satisfied that the new monarch is fit to take on the role. The Queen may choose a Prince, with her father's help, once she has attained the age of eighteen."

The Curator now turned to face the low stage, upon which stood the single wax figure of the woman in white.

"At the back of the stage, watching over the scene we see the figure of the deceased Kathleen. She was an accomplished singer, dancer, skater, comedienne and actress. Less is known about her than the other characters, but archive materials, especially interviews with Ken from the early forties, have provided us with a pretty good picture as to what she was like as a person. The Founders all admired her and were deeply distraught when they learnt of what had happened to her that fateful night when she drove home from a gig in Jackson Hole. In the end it made them even more determined to make this fantastic project a success and in exactly the manner that she laid out in her will, that is a Queendom, with Justine as Queen, and a King that both she and the others wanted, equipped with all the skills needed to lead and govern wisely under the system of Non-Capitalist Economics that Leo had devised. As you can probably guess Kathleen was a keen advocate of women's rights, but with a strong sense of fairness and an eye for talent."

At the far corner of the hall an open door led through from the first hall to the second. In this hall there were more waxworks, although this time they were placed singly around the room. At the top there were the present King and Mary, The Queen Mother and former Queen, Queen Katie, who has been our Queen for the last five years, and her two siblings. The Curator presently led the group in.

"In this hall we see an array of figures which show some of the key support staff from the early days followed by more modern figures including our present day royals about whom you can read at leisure.

First though we see the two Japanese engineers Endo and Kai. Kai was the Chief Civil Engineer who designed and built The Town, the hamlets of Sabfelt, formerly Kai Endo, and Aldebaran, as well as The Royal Palace and The Non-Olympic Stadium. Endo, the Chief Mechanical and Electrical Engineer was responsible for other features such as the hydro-electric plant on the north east side of The Island, the steam railway and the small Kammies. He also founded the two companies Kamchatskiy Auto and Kamchatskiy Logistics, with his friend Hiro Mitsumoto. The King himself of course founded the oldest company, Kamchatskiy Maritime."

The group then moved on to two more wax figures, the first of which was of an elderly gent in a blue suit.

"This figure is one which you may have seen before, at the entrance to our Training Centre. The statue was placed there early in 2037 in memory of the man and his message. He was renowned for his teaching, particularly in Japan after the Second World War. His Principles for the Transformation of Western Enterprises were very readily assimilated into Leo's Blueprint for the Future of Humanity and Model for Non-Capitalist Economics. This waxwork was made from a still photograph of Deming taken in the 1970s, and made, like the others, by the Island waxmakers, who still have their workshop up in the hamlet of Aldebaran, which lies two kilometres to the north of The Town, where you will also see monuments to the memory of Ken, Kathleen and Justine. Aldebaran was named by Kathleen after the red-eye star of Taurus, which was her starsign. There Kai-san built both an opera house and an observatory in her honour.

Opposite Deming we see Joseph Moses Juran, who also has a statue in his honour outside the Deputy Prime Minister's residence. He was born in Braila, Romania, on Christmas Eve 1904 and his Universal Sequence for Breakthrough was also integrated into Leo's Blueprint for the Future of Humanity, upon which our modern policy and strategy is based, and which looks forever towards quality improvement and beating the best capitalist performers on quality in every sector wherever in the world they may be.

Between him and the modern royals you may note our present Prime Minister Joanie Carmichael, great granddaughter of Patrick Carmichael, her Deputy Hamilton Francis, her Chancellor Simon de Havilland and two other figures, our Concierge and Reverend whom you will meet later during your stay here and who have done much work abroad to improve the world in line with the wishes of our present King, King Neville.

I will leave you to study these exhibits at leisure. Please come and see me if you have any questions about our fine history. I think you will agree never before has so much been achieved by so few."

Chapter Six
The Great Dome

When Connie and Gary returned to Angel Cottage three more of their set had arrived. Anne Clancy introduced herself, explaining how she had arrived from Coniston in the English Lake District, and had skated at the newly refurbished Lancaster Ice Theatre.

"I'm twenty-three and have been skating for just under three years. I thought of applying for a place at university to study economics and politics, but my exam results were poor so I gave up on the idea. I nearly thought of giving up on skating as well and just emigrating to Canada, not knowing what I would do there of course."

"Then of course all of your skating talent would have gone to waste. Why Canada?" asked Connie.

"A land of opportunity, and Newfoundland particularly appealed to me. I knew that it was slowly detaching itself from Canada."

"That would explain why The Island Authorities have matched you with a guy from Newfoundland," Connie replied.

"Have they?" said Anne. "I haven't met him. That's odd because I always had a strange feeling that I would meet someone from there."

"He's called Carl. He arrived yesterday. You presumably flew from England today?"

"I did, although I am still unsure of how I came to be given one of those precious tickets. It just arrived hand delivered. I know everyone here skates, its clearly part of the culture, so there must be a connection somewhere with the Lancaster Ice Theatre, but I can't guess what. I did say that I was thinking of quitting skating and one man said he didn't think that I should. He knew I wanted to go to Newfoundland, and he just said 'oh', and gave me a strange look. I think he worked for the armed forces."

"I don't suppose it really matters," said Connie. "The main thing is you're one of us."

Connie then turned to the other two newcomers and asked them their names.

"I'm Michael from Berlin," replied the tall fair-haired gent. "I'm twenty-five and have skated for four and a half years. I received my card by hand on the rink, almost as soon as I told her I had no job and was about to give up skating. I was told to go to Cuxhaven where I met a lady friend of hers who said I could transform my life if I was willing to put my faith in her. When the lady said 'how would you like to skate for Kamchatskiy?' I was sure that it was what I wanted."

Connie then turned to the other newcomer, a dark haired twenty-three-year-old Austrian girl and obviously Michael's principal.

"My name is Claudia, I am twenty-three and I am from Vienna. I was fascinated with the Kamchatskiy company, especially the wonderful cars and the aircraft, the Hebden Three, which is so lovely to fly in compared to a normal plane. I have only seen a few of the cars and, until today, only read about the planes, but the thing I most liked was the very different culture that was so good in its concepts. I saw the skaters once at an exhibition in Salzburg, and, like many in the audience was captivated. I knew that I wanted to work for them."

"And you obviously impressed someone enough to get the prized ticket to come here," said Anne.

"Obviously. But I don't know who. I met several people there, but one man said he thought he had seen me skate in

Vienna. He knew that I would be too old relative to my ability to become a skating professional by the conventional route. Then he said he had contacts in Kamchatskiy, one of which was a close friend of Queen Katie of Kamchatka. I never knew the man, or his name. The next thing I knew was that there was a ticket hand-delivered to my parents' house. I was told on the ticket that if I were to go to the landing stage for the hydrofoil to Budapest late last night I would have the chance to change my life as the Kamchatskiy company was interested in me. A little Japanese man then escorted me to a special hydrofoil that took me to an airfield just outside Bratislava where a Hebden Three was waiting to take me to The Island."

"Well," said Anne. "As The Island Authorities have been kind enough to provide us with some tea and biscuits, I suppose we might as well make use of it. There are a few ready-meals in the fridge and everything we need for breakfast, but tomorrow we will need to make out our first Requisition Notes."

"I think it will be quite a challenge getting used to a system that does not use money," Michael replied.

They continued to talk for a while. Then, there was a knock at the door.

"I'll answer it," said Claudia.

When she arrived at the door she found a small oriental girl of about eight clutching a bouquet of flowers.

"Kiri bring you special message from Jobine," said the girl. "She is skating mistress at rink. She want you have these flowers and asks you all to be at rink at eleven o'clock tomorrow. She look forward to seeing you."

The girl bowed her head, then curtsied and then left.

"Who was it?" Connie asked

"A small girl brought us these flowers from our new skating teacher. She wants us to be at the rink at eleven o'clock tomorrow. Now I think its time for The Prime Minister's address. I have already heard it, so I don't need to go."

*

The new arrivals, including Gary, freshened up quickly, then prepared to make their way to the Great Dome where they waited, along with several other sets consisting of people from many lands. Gary recognised some of them from the museum. Others were new, including the final four members of his own set. These were Lars from Norway, his principal Elena from Sweden, Terry, from Hong Kong, and his principal aboriginal-Australian Yvonne. They greeted each other briefly. Then the great white door opened to reveal the prestigious circular, marble floored entrance porch of this fine working building. At the far end a pair of sliding glass doors remained closed until they were all assembled. Beside these the tall, stocky, middle-aged Chancellor, Simon de Havilland, The Prime Minister's personal assistant, stood dressed in top hat and tails. Then the white door closed and the glass doors opened allowing the hundred or so attendees to descend the half dozen steps to the main theatre, where a large brown leather armchair backed them on a stage, beyond which there was a large screen that was slightly offset to one side. A hundred and twenty black leather seats faced it. The Chancellor ushered the crowd in, and the lights were dimmed with the spotlight focused on the chair. It slowly turned to reveal a slim, dark-haired lady of about forty.

"Greetings," she said, in a mild Anglo-Russian accent. " I am Joan Carmichael, Prime Minister of The Island and its territories, but you may call me Joanie for short. Welcome to The Island. Some of you are probably wondering how you have come to be here, and I can tell you that it has, like many other things, resulted from a combination of good luck and hard work. Good luck because by some coincidence one of our senior representatives from around the world has watched you over a period and decided to pick you out and give you the chance at least to make the bold decision to leave your old world behind. Hard work because, despite your difficulties in adapting to the competitive capitalist world, you have all exhibited a sufficient degree of talent for us to be assured that shaping you for our society will be both beneficial and worthwhile for all of us. The philosophy is one that the eminent W. Edwards Deming would have called win–win. That means that everyone wins and nobody loses. That is the very essence of our society, which depends for its survival on total trust, both between individuals and between individuals and groups and those who govern us.

As Prime Minister I have both the responsibility and the authority for the day-to-day management and running of The Island and its territories and for the management of its affairs of state on behalf of Her Majesty Queen Katie of Kamchatka. She is our constitutional monarch, and I will now display a picture of her on the screen behind me. She resides on The Island at the Royal Palace, which you will all have an opportunity of visiting during your time here.

Some of you may already know a little about our history. As you know this small island is where it all started, some seventy years ago. It has expanded since then, gradually acquiring mostly small islands under the sovereignty of different countries. The one exception is the peninsula of Kamchatka which was slowly purchased in stages in the sixties and seventies. It now supplies around a quarter of the world's energy, which is of course our main export along with healthcare, transport, scientific research and financial services to name but a few. This energy is clean, efficient and low cost energy derived geothermally from deep within the earth's mantle. Over the years our scientists researched the geology and pioneered new ways of harnessing this incredible resource from what is probably the optimum place on the planet to try to harness it. In addition our Founders set up the Kamchatskiy Auto Company, the Kamchatskiy Aerospace Company, Kamchatskiy Maritime and Kamchatskiy Logistics, the four companies that collectively are your new employers.

The Island is unique on the world stage in that it is partly a nation and partly an organisation. It possesses features that are common to both. We have a government, a monarchy, and a parliament, and in this respect we are a nation, yet we possess no sovereignty, only an entitlement to manage the land which we have lawfully acquired, and a flag, which could be regarded as being as much a company flag as a national one. Our government pays taxes to the appropriate nation state on all profits made through our legitimate trading within capitalist countries. We have one bank account, which is still managed in Switzerland by the Harveys Banking Corporation. We have the protection of the law of trespass with regard to the territory which we own, but have no army nor any conventional defences. We are an organisation in that we have a political structure that is more reminiscent of that of a company than of a country, and we welcome and support globalisation. We endeavour as part of our strategy to transgress nations without challenging their sovereignty, but, at the same time, we are committed to a course that will, over time, render the sovereignty of nations less and less relevant to the world and the way in which it is managed.

We are a democracy in that those who hold office have to be approved by the people in order to continue the job which they do, but at no time in our history have any of these officials ever been asked or encouraged to compete for office against any opponent. We do not therefore have a government that consists of politicians, but a government of technicians, statisticians, analysts and tacticians with a remit to manage the system of Non-Capitalist Economics in a stable fashion with an objective for continual improvement built in, to which the people have a remit to provide an input. I will now show you a picture of these people at work.

As you can see it looks a bit like the floor of the stock exchange, with lots of observers keeping watch over trends and movements in supply and demand so as to ensure that there are no discrepancies other than those that are small, manageable and self-contained. Where necessary workers can be loaned from one organisation to another for a short time at the request of one of our ministries in order to keep the system in balance. Its guiding principle is one of continued feedback and control. The people play their part by keeping their requests for requisitions within normal, predictable bounds and avoiding unnecessary waste. This is where the trust comes in, but once educated we have found that the right sort of people, like yourselves, see the logic and are fully committed to maintaining this system, which you should all find to be both kinder and fairer than the one you have left behind.

It goes without saying that The Island and its territories have stable, full employment. Everyone is expected to work to the best of their ability in their chosen field, and in return for this commitment the state is committed to ensuring that each and every citizen is satisfied with their quality of life. Your happiness is our desire, as a contented workforce is a loyal workforce.

As a society, although we practise Non-Capitalist Economics and use neither money nor credit to allocate resources, we do not have the policy of nationalisation or collectivisation that characterises communism. All property, goods and services are privately owned, as are all processes and tasks. Property, goods and services are requisitioned, with trust placed in the people to take or consume only that which they feel that they need. We call this The Psychological Contract. People work and the state provides.

We do not use targets, quotas or rewards in our organisations as we have found that they do not work. Neither will you be subject to performance appraisals or ranking. In selecting you for our society we have taken great care to ensure that none of you are the type of individual that would look to the establishment of pecking orders, as we have found this to be detrimental to teamwork. The pressurising of others to secure one's own advantage is not a feature of our society.

I will now turn to the matter of housing. On the screen you can see a collection of houses in the southern Kamchatkan town of Opala. As you can see they are large and spacious with some innovative designs. One is shaped like an old fashioned telephone, whilst another has the appearance of a large golf ball. There is some variance between the housing stock, with houses graded according to their standard. Each set can select any house of their choosing within their allotted band. This is determined by the level within the organisation in which the set is placed. There are six bands of housing in all, with band one being the typical starting point for young sets starting out, and band six being the highest for senior executives and their families. You will start in band three.

As for families, it is allowed for and expected that each couple within a standard set will have two children. This, however, is not a hard and fast rule. Occasionally a couple may have more, particularly if there are twins, for example. By the law of averages the number of excess children above two per couple tends to be offset by others that, for one reason or another are below. It is not expected that any couple will purposefully seek to have children above the recommended two.

Vehicle ownership, like housing, is usually done on a set by set basis. Individuals are encouraged to share vehicles wherever possible. If a clear need exists for vehicle acquisition, then it can be simply chosen, again from one of the six bands that follow the same principle as the housing. Usually sets are expected to run their cars and larger carriers for a minimum of ten years, and Kamchatskiys rarely fail within this time.

The next picture is one of a school. It looks like a school, of course, but there are no examinations or tests. Instead each child compiles a log-book of projects successfully completed. Again there are no targets or quotas for schools. Each school will seek to develop its own specialism, and each child is free to choose a school anywhere in The Island territories except for The Island itself. The school will always accommodate every child that chooses that school, even if it means requisitioning extra accommodation. Our education ministry will always make sure that no child is disappointed. Set formation is also encouraged in schools, with natural bonds of cooperation reinforced by teachers when they are identified. Particular attention is given toward encouraging boys and girls to work together so as to remove any unwanted barriers to social integration as a result of gender. The talents and make up of all have to be fully respected.

Health, like education, is also free from targets. Here you see inside a hospital, and, as you can see, it looks more like a luxury hotel than a hospital. This is because it has been long accepted that those who are sick deserve the very best service that can be provided. It is not like a hospital in a capitalist country that is under pressure to meet targets and cut costs. This particular hospital on the island of Kunashir is currently the subject of a benchmarking exercise for both Russia and Japan. The governments of both countries are observing its standards and practices with a view to implementing them in various hospitals of their own, particularly the privately owned ones. As I said earlier, everything in our society is privately owned and managed. Hospitals, schools, and even public conveniences are privately owned and those who own and run them do so with pride in their work as their prime motivator. Politicians in capitalist countries rarely seem to be able to accept this, yet scrapping management by targets, quotas and performance appraisals is the only way that they will ever hope to match our standards.

Next up is a job centre. Here we see school leavers receiving advice and presenting their log-books for scrutiny so that they can be matched with batches of vacancies. No time is wasted in the matching process, and competition between applicants is minimised as much as possible. Where possible the employer will tailor or fine tune a vacancy to the applicant that wants it, and may even create extra posts in order to ensure that all applicants are taken in right away so that training can be commenced and the log-book made continuous between school and work. Further education is always there as an option, and there is no competition for entry to colleges and universities, nor any exam targets. Instead the applicant submits the log-book and gives a presentation outlining the projects that they have completed, and a plan for research, demonstrating that they have the skills that they need to conduct that research. If an applicant is not granted a place at the university of their choice they will always be given a course of action which is within their capabilities to follow in order to pursue their goal. Nobody ever fails in our society, but this is not because there are serious penalties for failure, it is simply that the system has failure programmed out of it.

Another key principle of our system is to remove dependence on inspection to achieve quality, and this applies to law and order as much as to anything else. On the screen you will now see two of our so-called Greencoats. To some of you they may have all of the appearance of old-fashioned Redcoats from a holiday camp, only dressed in green. They are not there to entertain, however, but to practice management by walking about.

We do have crime, but, of course, with all money related crime eliminated, it is on a much smaller scale than in capitalist states. Most crime relates to nuisance, such as drunkenness, but even this is less serious than in capitalist states because we are so much calmer and contented by nature. The Set Formation Act has likewise had a big impact in reducing so-called domestic crime which is now, fortunately, rare in our society. It also has, incidentally, helped to completely eradicate sexually transmitted diseases in all of their forms from all of The Island's territories.

Applause briefly rippled around the room, prompting Joanie to pause for a moment before continuing.

"The Greencoats are therefore more akin to health and safety professionals in an organisation and are there to preserve and ensure that safety is maintained at all times. I might as well say now that you all have a duty by law to keep up to date with safety legislation as it applies both to your work environments and to the community, and to report any unsafe situations to the local Greencoat office. Please note here and now that I have told you this.

That leaves only defence and international relations. Our defence system does not rely on any military forces or units, but on an internal system of grapevines. We do have an early warning system that would warn us of any potential attack from outside, which would give us the time to prime up our internal system. You will learn about your roles in this when you are enrolled with your respective Kamchatskiy companies. We do seek as a strategic objective to work towards, and assist others to work towards, the end of war and conflict that stems from the sovereignty of nations and religion, which all too often is used as a smokescreen for politics.

We continue to seek to maintain good international relations with all nations of the world. We have, notably, good relations with Russia, Japan, Portugal and the United Kingdom, largely from our historical connections. Investment in Kamchatka has been repaid to Russia multi-fold.

The revolution is happening, ladies and gentlemen, at a pace that is well under our control. It is a revolution which, when it reaches completion, in about another 130 years, will transform the world forever for the better. I therefore ask you to join with us, have fun and become lifelong learners. I will now take any questions which you may have."

The Chancellor stood beside The Prime Minister ready to take questions. A few hands were raised, and an American gent stood up.

"Why, Madam Prime Minister," he asked. "is it that if this system is so good and it has so many followers as it appears, do you not open your doors to the world and allow more people to learn about and join this great society? Why all this secrecy and restriction on entry?"

"I take your point. It is unfortunate, but true, however, that if we were to try to do that there is every chance that we would not survive. We have learnt the lessons of history in the sense that if revolutions move too quickly they will not produce the desired outcome. You good people have been very carefully selected. It takes a lot of effort on our part to find people like yourselves, and even more effort to train you as adults for the roles that you will have in our society. Most people in the capitalist world are too far gone when it comes to the way they have adapted, and if we were to allow too many entrants the chances that we would allow in undesirable elements would increase enormously. Our system would then be undermined and probably revert backwards into a competitive and violent society, or else become totalitarian as with the accession of Stalin in the Soviet Union. So, I hope you can see why the slow pace must be maintained. Next."

"How do we keep in touch with families and friends that we have left behind?" asked an Australian girl.

"Good point. Commander allows for messages to be sent and received. Although Commander only functions within Island territories, and can be used to send and receive messages directly to any location within it, it can be used indirectly to contact approved individuals outside. You provide the approval, and your message is then sent to an Island representative who then relays it. Similarly that same representative can be reached from the approved contact, who will then relay that person's message to you by inputting it to Commander. You will also have an opportunity to receive and send a message by hologram. Next."

The girl raised her hand again and she was permitted to speak.

"Okay," she said. "But what about actually meeting them. Is that going to be possible, or are we never to see our relatives again? I am delighted that I have been selected to be here, and will stay, so long as you promise me that there will be some way or another that I can meet my old family at least once in a while."

"That's no problem. We have a system that allows for that, the only restriction is that we choose the place and time, and also ask that relatives and friends respect our privacy by not talking to the press or television about our activities. Relatives and friends, though, can be granted small discretionary periods of time in Island territory in exchange for a payment. Likewise Island citizens may be granted time and money in a capitalist country as part of their annual leave. Free hotel passes are granted so long as you agree to stay in a hotel that is Island owned. Next."

"I agree with Non-Capitalist Economics," said a German man. "but I would like to know how something like tickets for a major sporting event or something that was very limited in supply would be allocated. Under capitalism these things would go to the person who offered the most money. Here it cannot. So who or what decides?"

"Good question. Thankfully it has a simple remedy. Most of these sorts of allocations are made by the organisers of the event, who also are the owners of the event, and are made according to a formula that is related to the degree of effort and support that various people have given to the particular sport or activity in question. Most people think that this principle is fair. All applications for such tickets have to be approved by a range of people who then must agree on the application. Those who are unlucky can apply again in the future and the fact that they have not been lucky the first time will be taken into consideration. People thus tend to select the event they prefer on the basis of opportunity cost. In other cases, things like art treasures automatically become the property of those who own and manage the place where they are housed, as with our museum. There is no incentive for theft as there is no market, and smuggling items out of Island territory is virtually impossible, as the movement of all exports is tightly controlled, and, apart from in Northern Kamchatka, all our borders are sea borders, and these are all monitored for unauthorised movements. Next."

A French girl then stood up and asked "Why would anyone choose to manage the public loos as a career? Surely everyone would choose much more rewarding careers given all of the training and opportunities that you are saying? Who would want the most unpopular jobs?"

"What we have found over the years in our society is that there are people who leave school and do not necessarily want to join organisations or go on to further education. That isn't because they can't, it's because they want to do something different. There are teams of people who want a particular way of life, like regular soldiers in the old days, and these task forces as they are called will undertake to complete those tasks that others leave behind. These people are highly respected and certain privileges are granted to those who join up, set at a level to attract a sufficient number of volunteers as to ensure that such services are undertaken to the same or higher standards as would be the case in the most highly benchmarked capitalist society. We benchmark a lot around the world to make sure that we not only meet but surpass the highest standards that we find. Money is not an issue. Quality is. As for the public loo case, however, some years ago a girl called Linda left school and observed that there was a deficiency of public conveniences in her town and reported this to her local council. She then made a proposal to maintain a string of conveniences so as to improve the situation and, naturally, this was accepted as it would both improve local facilities and relieve the burden on the local task force, or Directed Labour Volunteers, which had the things she was proposing well down on their list of priorities. More loos were built, and a few existing ones transferred to her ownership, and she began her work with pride and dignity. There are now several thousand of Linda's Loos. Linda herself is the Managing Director and she employs several hundred staff. Others have since followed her example by taking otherwise unpopular tasks and running small enterprises based on them. It can be more rewarding than you might think. Next."

There were no further questions.

"I thank you for your attention, and invite you each to collect your information packs as you leave."

*

The sets dispersed and Gary and the others returned to Angel. For the first time they were all together as a complete set. Gary looked carefully through the information pack. He read with interest the opening section on Non-Capitalist Economics, taking in its theoretical background which began with basic economic concepts such as opportunity cost, utility theory and comparative advantage. Then there was the conventional theory of supply and demand and the price mechanism which controlled it, followed by The Island's feedback and control system which effectively replaced it. This was derived from engineering concepts and used circuit diagram representations to illustrate the various ways in which supply and demand were manipulated and regulated using interventions such as resistances, damping components, storage loops analogous to capacitance in an electrical circuit and smoothing devices made possible by the easy transfer of labour through which variations in supply and demand in one area of production or location could be offset with opposing variations in another. A section on bartering explained how, limited though this concept was, it could still work in certain cases as a means of exchanging commodities and reducing wastage, especially of used and redundant materials for whom others may have a use. Exchange centres were therefore set up as places where bartering could take place and people could obtain some of the things they needed without requisitioning them as these centres were the one place where requisitioning did not apply.

Amplifiers, as they were called, could be introduced to step up production, whilst dampers acted to suppress demand by encouraging substitution effects to replace adverse variances. Resistances slowed down production to prevent over supply and reduce unwanted variation, and the study of variation was used to identify common and special causes that were liable to affect demand so that the appropriate advance measure could be put in place to prevent the adverse variance from taking hold. It did not take long for Gary to realise the enormous responsibility that the management of this nation, organisation or whatever it was had in order to ensure that there were never any shortages and that all citizens were able to enjoy the happy and contented lifestyles that their leaders had promised. No way could such people provide this if they were constantly burdened with the need to fight elections and defeat opponents in order to stay in office. Competitive democracy was undoubtedly inferior to the One Party Democracy that was described in the handbook.

Goods and services flowed like current in a circuit with 'voltages' used to denote the 'potential differences' between supply and demand that needed to be smoothed. Waveform diagrams showed patterns of supply and demand as they occurred over time and extrapolation was used to forecast future movements using trend analysis and the theory of variation. Consumption data provided the key input for stability in the absence of special causes that had the potential to disrupt it. Aggregation of consumption data allowed for the requisitioning system to be moderately fault tolerant in that the specific needs of one person were different from those of another and any excesses in consumption of one good by one person would tend to be offset by an under average demand for it by another. A simple example was provided by showing that the child that liked a little extra apple pie may not want as much banana custard, solely as a result of personal preferences. It was easy to see that under such a system there was clearly no need for quotas or rationing. The only thing that the system would have trouble in coping with would be a large influx of people and that, Joanie had explained, was not going to happen with a snail's pace revolution that had been programmed to last for over two centuries.

When Gary went upstairs to his bedroom he found Connie freshly showered. He then noticed the neatly folded skating suit which had been placed at the end of his bed, along with a brand new pair of ice skates. Connie had the same, except that her costume was different and her skates were white instead of black, which was conventional for ladies.

*

As it was their first evening on The Island the setmates decided by consensus that they would investigate The Island by night and try to take in some of its romantic character before the novelty wore off.

"It is a strange, quiet and enchanting place by night," Connie said.

"Are there any places to eat out?" asked Anne.

"There are three bars," Connie explained. "There's The Cat and Fiddle over the road just up from the museum. I think that's the oldest, and bar meals can be requisitioned there on a fairly frequent basis. There's another more modern one in The House of Cards, near the archway that leads to The Japanese garden. That serves bar meals on a similar basis. That's an interesting place full of amusements and games. You can even gamble with tokens for small stakes and prizes. Then there's a nice little restaurant down near the harbour, but I think you have to book for that. Bookings are at the owner's discretion, unlike the others, and as it is upmarket they would not expect any sets or groups to visit it too often. Tonight there's a welcoming in night at The Cat and Fiddle, so I expect everyone will be going to that."

The sound of the jazz band echoed out into the street from The Cat and Fiddle, which succeeded in attracting all of the newly arrived sets. The entrance to the pub was small, but inside it was deceptively spacious with a moderately sized dance floor which was of sufficient size to allow it to be used for dinner dances for up to 300 people. Inside the sets relived the big band era, with classic music played along with some more recent compositions and tracks from later periods that had been adapted to the big band sound.

Large twelve-seater tables had been laid around the dance floor, complete with menus. As more sets entered more tables were laid. It did not seem to matter how high demand was there was always room for one more. The drinks selection resembled that of any ordinary public house in a normal capitalist state. Only the makes were different. The large variety of Russian wines was striking, especially those from the newly cultivated Caucasus region, along with various Portuguese makes, which had clearly been imported from the mainland. The house wine, Twos Company, was bottled locally. Then there were the ales, the draught Number Six, several Russian and Portuguese types, and the Falkland Ale, which was imported from the Island owned Falkland Isles.

Over the drinks and the meal the set began to get to know each other a little better. Yvonne's story of how she came to be on The Island evoked some interest. She was a black Aboriginal girl of twenty-one from Darwin in the Northern Territory of Australia.

"I couldn't believe what was happening to me," she explained. "I travelled to Sydney for a conference on excellence in public services. I had been intending to study management at the Macquarie University, but didn't get accepted. I did, however, skate at the Macquarie rink where I met this guy called Aub Ryman, who had spoken at the conference and who said he had seen me skate in Darwin and had been impressed. I said I had been impressed with his talk. He was the leader of the Deming Followers Society in Australia, and also the Australian Defence Minister. His talk was all about the life and work of W. Edwards Deming and how public services in Australia desperately needed to apply the teachings of this man. I think he was a little disappointed at the lukewarm response that he got from the audience, as was I. I suspect that most of the others saw Deming as being someone who lived so long ago that his theories were pretty much meaningless nowadays. How wrong they are."

"So how did you come to be here?" asked Claudia.

"Aub took me on one side and said that he had been given 240 special invitation cards from the young Queen, which didn't make sense at the time, but it does now. He said that he had one left, the rest had all been sent to his representatives around the world. Then, he said that he wanted me to have the last one. Then he handed me the card and said that he trusted that I would be someone that would use it wisely. He said that if I went to a small pub just outside Darwin on my return all would be revealed. An old man from Bathurst Island met me there then told me about the new life that I could have as a skating celebrity for Kamchatskiy Auto, and with a principal that I could trust. I trusted him because I had heard from my family about life on Bathurst and the legendary place where money didn't

71

matter and people worked to a much better system. I flew from Bathurst Island yesterday morning on the Hebden Three."

"It's interesting," said Connie. "that he admitted to having had in his possession, at some time, all 240 of those cards".

"And that they were given to him by The Queen," added Anne.

"It means that every one of the cards that enabled us to be here are traceable to him," said Michael.

"And he declared who he was also," Lars commented.

"He must be close to The Queen in some way," Connie deduced. "How old was this Aub Ryman?"

"About thirty," said Yvonne.

"I have a strange feeling that that name is going to come up again sometime," Connie added.

"He was a very intriguing man," Yvonne continued. "with a strange piercing shine in his eyes that appeared oddly mystical when he looked at you, yet you knew you were dealing with someone with good intent. Inside, though, he gave the impression of being just a little troubled. My Aboriginal background taught me that a person can often gain an insight into the character of another by looking into their eyes as they talk to you. And I think you're right, Connie, we probably haven't seen the last of this man. I think he has some powerful influence here".

"If you want to talk about mystery, my path to The Island certainly had plenty of that," said Lars. "I finished up meeting a girl on a white horse up near a remote Norwegian fjord".

"What?" said Graca.

"That's right. I went to skate one day at the open air rink near my home in Tromso, just as I had done many times before, then I came back to find this card telling me that I could change my life. Tromso is a nice enough place, but there wasn't really anything there for me. I had never heard of Deming or anything connected with him until a few weeks ago, but when I was told about him I knew the way I lived life was in accordance with his principles. The card directed me to this small sort of cave near a remote fjord. I thought someone was having me on. I certainly didn't think that this cave would have so much inside. It was like a kind of mini hotel. I stood outside it for a while, as directed, because, like you, Yvonne, I had heard rumours about a society where there was an entirely different way of life going on in the world. Then this girl on a white horse arrived. She was something else. She invited me in for dinner and told me all about The Island, explaining how that cave had actually been used long ago by a man called Darren for the smuggling of diamonds. Now it was a quaint little Island-owned guest house."

"Had you ever seen her before?" asked Claudia.

"Never," said Lars. "But she acted as if she knew me. The experience was just so bizarre, then again my principal Elena also has a bit of a bizarre tale to tell."

"Go on, Elena, tell us about your experience," said Graca.

"I'm from Umea in the north of Sweden. I got the card after skating on my local outdoor rink, purely for fun of course. It told me to go to a little craft shop about ten kilometres up in the hills. An oldish lady greeted me, like some sort of soothsayer or clairvoyant. She knew that I was bored with my dead-end life and told me that I could change it and go and live in Kamchatka with a well-matched man. This craft shop also was an Island-owned guest house used for diamond smuggling years ago, but now sold all kinds of crafts from the Kuril Islands – Russian and Japanese dolls and the like. She said that I should stay the night with her. I was unhappy at home and at least what she said about Kamchatka did sound as if it was true, being a part of Russia that had its own way of life that was different to everywhere else, and I liked the sound of Non-Capitalist Economics. When she said that I had been chosen to train to be a skating celebrity with Kamchatskiy Auto, I couldn't believe my good fortune. In the morning I went with her to the small airport at Umea, and was led to this strange looking plane, astonished to be told that I was its only passenger."

"The Hebden Three?" said Michael.

"The Hebden Three," said Elena.

The evening continued with light drinking and dancing, with the pub staff keen to see that everyone enjoyed the evening. It was designed to make the setmates feel at ease, and to encourage them to interact. For Gary this was a wonderful and refreshing experience compared to what he had experienced in Caversham. All were unaware that back in The Great Dome Joanie was watching them on her screen, noting the variations in dancing knowledge of the various participants and observing their drinking habits so as to add to her portfolio of knowledge about the newcomers.

At half-past eleven the sets drifted out. Gary and the others walked for a while around the Town Square. They passed the House of Cards pausing briefly to look inside at the array of games such as bar billiards, pool, snooker, table tennis, chess, table soccer, Mah Jong and pinball that some of the staff members were playing. These were games of skill where competition could be enjoyed at a trivial level.

Slowly they made their way to the Colonnade where they sat and continued to talk and exchange their experiences alongside a few others. Otherwise The Town was silent. As the clock on The Bell Tower struck twelve, a small man dressed in a black cloak and carrying a lantern made his way up from Atlas' statue.

"Who is that man?" asked the French girl from the neighbouring set, whom Gary had remembered from The Great Dome earlier.

"Good evening fine people," said the Welshman. "You aren't supposed to see me".

"Why not?" asked Gary.

"I be the Night Watchman, see?" he said, looking at his watch. "Nobody is supposed to see me. It's my job to look after The Town and see that there is nothing untoward during the night hours. If this lantern goes out there will be an alert. So I must keep this lantern alight until I knock off at dawn."

"Have you ever had a problem here at night?" Lars asked.

"A few times I have. One night a few years ago I smelt smoke and discovered a small fire down near the Training Centre kitchens. A faulty switch was the cause of that, proving that even our quality isn't always perfect and there's no such thing as zero defects. Another time we had a storm and it caused some superficial damage to structures. Another time we had a storm combined with a high tide. That did a bit of damage down at the harbour. A similar storm about ten years ago destroyed the old swimming pool. Next time you go in the museum, look at the old photographs. You'll see that the swimming pool is in a different place. Not the oval-shaped one you see down by Anchor Cottage. I know it's your first night and everyone's a little bit excited, so I'll be on my way, but don't leave it too late will you? "

The man moved on, but his message was clear. It was not normal to be out and about after midnight unless there was a reason. The two sets said goodnight and left the Colonnade for their residences. All was still except for the slight rustling of leaves. Then Elena thought that she heard something.

"What is that sound?" she asked.

"What sound?" replied Anne.

"I thought I heard someone laughing".

They all stood still for a moment.

"Listen there it is again," said Elena. "It's a strange deep laugh, very faint, but discernable."

"I think I hear it," confirmed Yvonne.

"Me too," said Michael.

"Sssh," said Connie.

Some heard it, some did not.

"I swear that this place is haunted," said Anne.

"Wasn't it Leo who was supposed to always have the last laugh?" Terry asked.

"Yes, I believe it was," said Claudia.

"Maybe he is laughing at us for being here," Michael suggested.

"I think it's just the rustling of the trees," said Gary.

Chapter Seven
Ice Dance

The next morning as The Bell Tower clock struck nine and the setmates were having breakfast there was a knock at the door. Anne rose to answer it.

"Requisitions delivery to Angel Cottage," said the stout man holding a box.

"Now we haven't ordered too much, have we?" Anne asked, tentatively.

"Oh no," said the man. "You would soon know it if you did. As long as you order whatever you actually need, or think you need, over a reasonable period of time, Non-Capitalist Economics will not be a problem for you. Our Government always trusts its people each according to their needs. You really would have to be excessively wasteful to fall foul of it. Anyway, here are your provisions. The Kammie will be here in half an hour to take you to the rink."

"Now we've got more than just toast and jam and a cup of coffee," she announced as she brought the items into the kitchen and breakfast area.

The twelve-seater Kammie duly arrived and with their skates and kits the twelve setmates scrambled excitedly into the awaiting vehicle. The driver gave his usual three blasts of his horn before the battery-propelled vehicle quickly accelerated up the road past The Cat and Fiddle and on towards The Triumphal Arch that led to the Japanese garden and beyond.

"What's that strange looking graveyard?" Elena asked as they passed a group of small tombstones at the far end of the garden.

"It's a dog's cemetery," said the driver of the Kammie. "A little bit unique, no?"

"I have never seen one," Elena replied. "That's very thoughtful."

The Kammie ascended further up a gentle incline before shortly arriving in the small piazza where the regency style ice rink faced the mock Victorian railway station, separated from it by the small Fountain of Peace, for which a glossy marble statue of two ice dancers formed the centrepiece. The Kammie stopped outside the ice rink as a small, thin man of about sixty unbolted the large Medieval-style wooden doors and opened them ready for the setmates to enter. Momentarily the set was distracted by the sound of the stationmaster's whistle, followed by the chuffing of a steam train as it left on the line which headed north to the hamlets of Sabfelt and Aldebaran, and eventually The Royal Palace.

The set stood briefly in the entrance porch of the rink, pausing briefly to admire the convex ceiling upon which was painted a medley of skating scenes which included the classic Bolero, the Capricchio Espanhol featuring the matador and his cape, the jugglers of Barnum and the magic of Mack and Mabel, the artwork being a testimony to the performers who were its subject.

At the other end of the square entrance hall two plane glass wooden doors led through to the rink itself. The lone figure of a thirty-something fair-haired woman watched from the centre of the rink as the twelve setmates entered. The mixed changing room on one side of the rink was clearly identifiable and the woman pointed toward it. Each of the new recruits quickly changed into the red lycra training suits that had been provided and pressed their feet into the firm boots which they would have to break in over the next few days. They then stepped tentatively onto the ice and approached the centre where Jobine was waiting.

"Greetings," she spoke in a soft Dutch accent. "So, here we have another new team hoping to join Kamchatskiy Auto. I am Jobine van der Eyck, and during the next twelve months I shall be teaching you to skate as you have never skated before. Then you will be ready to tour on behalf of the company as its representatives at exhibitions and the numerous skating fairs that the corporation organises. As such, each member is expected to attain a standard of skating that would pass for professional in the capitalist world. The responsibility has now fallen to me to ensure that over the next year you reach that standard to the satisfaction of the company executive. You will have to work hard at your skating, there is no doubt, but I am under no illusion that it will be a great experience with a rewarding life ahead.

You will, in the coming years, develop a portfolio of skating routines, which you will be able to reuse as part of your ongoing programme of advertising and demonstrations. You will need to get used to using the Kamchatskiy car as prop. This year for your demonstration it will be the new executive version, The Silver Shadow, but on tour you may get the taxi or minibus Kammies, family saloons, sports cars, dormobiles and jeeps. The prop should be regarded not just as a car, but also as a work of art.

The routines which you will choreograph as a set will be unique to you, but as your trainer I will be endeavouring to ensure that all sets reach a common level before being handed over to the respective company trainers of Kamchatskiy Auto, Kamchatskiy Aerospace, Kamchatskiy Maritime and Kamchatskiy Logistics.

During your time here you will learn to develop complete trust in each other and in this regard skating is such a wonderful aid to development.

To begin with I shall be taking you for three two-hour sessions each week, although this will increase later as we approach Carnival and you become more proficient. Sometimes I will be training you in the morning, sometimes in the afternoon, or occasionally in the evenings. On some days I will be training just your set. On others you may be working jointly with one or more others. On the remaining days you will be attending seminars and practicals in the Training Centre, as you learn more about work at Kamchatskiy or else undertaking special assignments under the direction of Joanie Carmichael, The Prime Minister, so that you will know all of the essentials regarding our society, how it functions and how you will be expected to integrate into it.

I know you can all skate and have all demonstrated the fact that you are prepared to work hard and unsupervised. My challenge is to change you from working as individuals to working together as a team. You must be able to do much more than perform moves by rote. They must be synchronised and in time.

For Carnival, all sets will be expected to perform a four-minute routine that is innovative and impressive. You will also be expected to learn your company's dance and one set from each company will be selected to demonstrate it. The steps of the company dance are different for each company, and change every year, but the music is always the same.

I am a great believer in ensuring that all of my skaters master their school figures well so that they not only perform the figures, but also perform them in unison. That means that you all turn at the same time, your free legs swing through at the same time and your arm and head movements are coordinated.

Other essential skills such as use of the harness we will deal with later.

If I require your attention I will give one single blast on my whistle to summon your attention like this."

Jobine blew her whistle and then resumed.

"Now, I am sure you are all eager to get started and to break these new boots in. To make it easier for you I will start with basic forward and backwards skating and simple turns with the emphasis on technique."

The setmates were thus directed to perform first forward runs in a circle.

"Try and keep a fixed distance apart," Jobine urged. "And try to synchronise your rise and fall. When I clap my hands you should all rise and I should see your heads being drawn up towards the ceiling. Try to gain momentum on the rise."

Gradually the skaters became more synchronised and when she was satisfied that the exercise had been productive Jobine summoned the setmates together and moved on to the back crossovers.

"The same applies," she said. "You should all be crossing in front at the same time, not at random."

Again she continued with these for about ten minutes before moving on to some more specialised adaptations.

"You will often be required to skate in chains of three," she explained. "That is, either two girls and one man or vice versa. These formations with their associated partner changes are a favourite with the Kamchatskiy Auto trainers. You won't need them for Carnival, but the Kamchatskiy trainers will expect you to be familiar with the style. As with the forward runs you will need to all rise and fall together. Normally the left arm is in front and you hold the person behind by the right. The third person in each chain will have the right arm free. These are skated in serpentine fashion with the front person leading the chain randomly around the rink."

This type of skating, although basic by Kamchatskiy standards, was new to the setmates, having its roots in historical dancing, but the style lent itself easily to transposition onto the ice. Jobine watched as the setmates grappled with the style.

"Now try it with closed chasses in place of the runs," she ordered, smiling as her recruits became more confident.

This sorted them out. Now the movement suddenly became much more difficult as the cross behind element made it far more difficult to maintain the hold and gain speed.

"This needs much more polish," she concluded. "You should gain speed on the cross behind not lose it. And tuck your hips underneath you as you cross behind, Gary. Your head is tilting far too much. And Anne you are prone to the same. Keep your heads raised and your free legs straight as you cross behind. Lars and Graca you are bending your knees to bring the free leg behind and it is spoiling the movement."

She watched for a few minutes as the chains meandered around the rink out of time and straining to stay to stay together.

"Enough," she said as she blew her whistle. "This will get better. Now I would like to see what your variation is with regard to turns. Carl, can you show us an inside closed Mohawk?"

Carl duly performed the turn from a forward inside edge to a backward inside edge.

"Quite a clean turn. Well done. Now, Yvonne, let's have one from you."

One by one Jobine examined the setmates' Mohawk turns until they had all demonstrated the move.

"I see you all perform the move slightly differently, and it does not come naturally to any of you. The Mohawk can be used to give character to a routine. It's primarily a linking step that can be performed in many ways. Most importantly it should flow and look elegant. I will now show you a flowing Mohawk turn."

Jobine presently demonstrated the turn, which she embellished with arm movements, taking care to present it rather than simply execute it.

"Can you see a difference?" she asked the setmates.

They nodded.

"Make your skating flow," she said, as she unexpectedly took hold of Gary and whirled him around the ice, a look of partial terror appearing on his face.

"Too much tension in the arms, though I accept you were not ready for that. And, yes, occasionally at Kamchatskiy the girls do perform lifts, even if they are only small ones, and the turning Mohawk is often used in these shoulder height lifts. So, guys and girls, you all have to be able to lift and be lifted, and when you are lifting or being lifted your arms need to flex to give you control and you need to be expressive. Gary's look of fear was not a good example here. It's got to look effortless and it will. Now, let's see some jumps and spins. You will be pleased to know that as dancers your jumps need only be small, and your spins need only be of five or six revolutions, but the jumps do have to be landed cleanly and the spins do have to be correctly centred, every time that they are performed. Kamchatskiy doesn't like inconsistency."

Again she observed the setmates performing one by one and again she same the same level of variation in both the three jump and the upright spin.

"The good news is you can all do it. I don't have to waste time going back to square one, but it's no good having a free leg that is only sometimes straight or a spin that is only sometimes centred," she commented after they had all demonstrated. "But I know, because you are who you are, that you will all practise religiously over the next year so that you can show me and the Kamchatskiy trainers that you can perform all of these basic moves not only consistently, but also consistently between each other so that everything matches. Good show. Now there is one more basic type of skating style that you will not have come across and that is the Quadrille style, which derives from the figures that were popular in the Victorian era. The Kamchatskiy trainers, and especially the Kamchatskiy Auto trainers, often like to incorporate these figures into their routines. Again, you don't need it for Carnival, but you do need to know of it.

Basically, the Quadrilles are danced in squares with four couples facing one another. They consist of five figures separated by a chorus figure. The skating style, however, is totally different to all of the others, as I will now show. Michael, let me take your hand, arm nice and straight."

Michael duly assumed the starting position.

"Now, I am going to ask you to do something that a skating instructor would otherwise never ask you to do, and that is to skate forward onto a flat with the skating leg straight. That's because the Quadrille figures are skated almost entirely on flats rather than edges, and the steps are very small. You may glide but the glide is slow and short, such that there is hardly any requirement to perform a stopping action. The glide uses only friction between the blade and the ice in order to come to a halt. So, Terry and Yvonne, I want you to stand as we are opposite us, and when I blow my whistle I want you to skate exactly as we do on four small flats, almost as if you were just stepping, so that we meet half way, that's a distance of about three metres."

She blew her whistle and Terry and Yvonne did their best to copy Jobine and Michael. They met in the middle, but not without a small collision.

"Not as easy as it looks is it?" she said, half expecting the newcomers to gain a surplus of momentum as a consequence of automatically skating forward as they had been taught as opposed to adapting to the alien compact style that was to apply here. "Never mind. You will get used to it. The most difficult thing about these figures is remembering them. They do contain some quite intricate turns and controlling your speed is a challenge. Usually the Quadrille figures require another set to practise because we need three squares for a demonstration, and as that requires two sets we will leave the Quadrille for now. Great to watch, though, Quadrilles on ice, and a speciality of Kamchatskiy. You won't tend to see them in any conventional skating shows.

I will now turn lastly to your demonstration dance, which you will be performing here on this rink at our annual Mardi Gras Carnival.

For the demonstration dance all sets are required to compile an original routine to a theme. The idea is that you create a four-minute long routine that tells a story or represents something, like you may have seen on the ceiling of our entrance hall. This is what our training sessions will be working towards so that you can all be true celebrities. As Ken once said 'today's innovation should be tomorrow's standard'. So, you must all learn to be inventive on the ice.

For this you will need an ability to choreograph skating routines and develop an original centrepiece that will show that you can cope with a high degree of difficulty that will distinguish your skills from those of the others. Each set will have its own centrepiece. In your case it will be a complex lift as opposed to an advanced proficiency with the harness. Study the archive material from past years and you should soon get an idea of the standard that is required.

Kamchatskiy skaters have a reputation for not only acquiring exceptional skating ability, but also for being good all-rounders when it comes to academic and managerial skills. I will leave it to my friends in the Training Centre to teach you the other half of what it takes to be a Kamchatskiy employee. All work and no pay, but it's a great life. You will travel the world and have fun and be celebrities in your own right with five or six years on the world tour before you become managers.

I will now leave you to practise for the last half hour. Help each other. See how much more quickly you improve when you do. On Friday I will see you all again and we can begin work on our school figures."

Jobine then performed a quick twizzle and whizzed off the ice leaving the set to practise. The six couples then practised for a while, mixing and matching, each helping the others to improve. Unlike in their previous environments, it was possible for each member of the set to assist each other member to maximise the standard that was achievable collectively. With this approach, along with collaboration with the other sets, they would all in time be able to take their skating into a new dimension as a matter of course.

The practice continued until a hooter sounded and the base of the barrier rose. When they had cleared the ice a single ice scraper and resurfacer emerged from one end of the rink and made its way to the other in twenty seconds, leaving behind a smooth glassy surface.

"That beats the old Zamboni," said Gary.

Chapter Eight
A Question of Quality

The set lunched in The Training Centre along with the four other sets who had also been invited to attend the first afternoon lecture from the training school of the Kamchatskiy Auto Company. These sets had also been selected to train for work at the Petropavlovsk Kamchatskiy factory and had an itinerary that was similar to that of Gary's set. Their skating and training programmes had different timings, although there would be times when a lecture or skating period may overlap so that more than one set could be taught at a time, for example as Jobine had stated. This lecture, however, was an introductory lecture that was common to all of the Kamchatskiy Auto sets.

With lunch over the sets made their way upstairs to the lecture theatre where a stocky seventy-three-year-old man of oriental appearance awaited their entrance.

"Good afternoon," he said, once they were all assembled.

He was then silent for a while as if to invite a response.

"Good afternoon," returned the voices of the sets when they had sensed that this was what the man was waiting for.

"My name is Mitsumoto-san," he continued. "Grandson of Hiro Mitsumoto, friend of Japanese engineers Endo and Kai who were instrumental in establishing this wonderful historic Island, as well as our great company. Behind me you will see a screen on which I will show you some of our proud history.

Kamchatskiy Auto was founded on the traditional excellence of Japanese engineering. Following the teaching of Deming and Juran Endo-san determined to set up world-beating car company to surpass all others. Bit by bit his company would build up a reputation for excellence of the highest order.

In the following photograph from 2041 you can see a Rolls Royce Silver Ghost from 1910 which Queen Justine had purchased and given to my grandfather to use and re-engineer so as to design a new breed of car that would look and feel like no other. Later, in 2045, you can see the finished version, which looked nothing at all like the standard cars of that time. It was strictly for the connoisseur, and the collector. A couple were even built so that they could fly, and here you can see a photograph of one of them, which was built to order for a Russian billionaire's daughter. It could take off and land on a small runway or an open field. Occasionally we still receive such bizarre requests, and, if it is at all possible, we will always honour the request, for a price, of course.

The cars which we made before 2056 were not called Kamchatskiys, but Mitzies after our family name. In our car museum beside our original Island workshop, you will see three Mitzies, each with a unique design, and the original M logo with Samurai coat of arms, which has since been replaced with a K. Our Island workshops are now, of course, used purely for training purposes. By the fifties they had already become much too small for the scale of production we required, so we invested in new factories in Petropavlovsk Kamchatskiy, and in 2056 we renamed ourselves The Kamchatskiy Auto Company.

Over the next twenty years we gradually expanded so that in addition to making special cars to order, like Ken had done with ships, we were also able to make high class vehicles for ourselves as well as for other markets.

In 2076 we introduced a new idea, that of training all of our workers to skate. At first we had just forty-eight skaters, one for each of the Kamchatskiy companies, drawn from the families of the Kamchatskiy workers. This was at the joint suggestion of the newly crowned Queen Mary and Justine, The Queen Mother. Here you can see our first skating team, skating to their routine 'Girl with the Sun in her Hair', as requested by a certain blonde popstar for whom a special sports model had been built. Following this, in 2077, sports cars were added to our portfolio of designs, but not for racing. These were showpiece cars for those who did not just want style and elegance, but also speed and performance at the top of the range.

In 2079 you see the more modern Kammie. These were small metallic blue bullet-shaped vehicles, slightly larger than the two-seater Kammies which you see on The Island today. The Kammie has become popular in a number of cities and towns around the world, and you will see plenty when you are in Kamchatka, not so much in the cities as in the small towns for which they are best suited. They are particularly suited to old towns with narrow streets, as in Italy, for example, and were our first mass-produced vehicles opposed to old-fashioned batch production, which was high quality but slow.

Nowadays we have many more such designs, but unlike other auto manufacturers, we have still retained all of our batch production expertise and are determined to stay as the world leaders in batch production. Some cars are therefore just standard, whilst others are made to order. We also make buses, minibuses, vans and commercial vehicles, in fact any kind of vehicle that is built to be driven along a road or across country. We pride ourselves in making the stylish and the unusual, and are determined like all Island-owned companies that we will never be beaten when it comes to the price-quality combination. We will always be ahead of every capitalist producer. Any kind of vehicle may be your skating prop depending on the exhibition or fair, or purpose of the demonstration.

So this explains a little about our background. I will now say something about our training programme, which will complement your skating tuition. I will begin with our management strategy, which, like all others on The Island, is a question of quality. Unlike in capitalist countries cost is not a factor in our production programme, although waste minimisation is. Our Government, with the backing of The Queen, has decreed that quality, not quantity, should be what drives us forward, with the teachings of W. Edwards Deming and Joseph M. Juran forming the managerial framework to which we all should work. We will therefore be teaching you the theory which they left to the world, along with our method of applying it.

We benchmark quality in auto manufacture, as well as other industries, religiously, so that any example of good, better, or best practice, can be studied, refined, and, if appropriate, implemented. We benchmark internally with all Island owned organisations, both capitalist and non-capitalist, and with others that are keen to learn from us. This helps us to drive up standards everywhere in the interest of the whole world not just ourselves. We ensure that everything we do is of a win–win nature. Win–lose relationships are not acceptable, as they invariably degenerate into lose–lose. That is the first and most important of Deming's laws.

We will train you to work as teams and in how to adopt and practice different team roles according to your ability. In short, we will be training you to make the most of your skills, and to become self-motivating. All motivation is intrinsic. Joy and pride in your work is essential to us. This is the second of Deming's important laws. There can be no such thing as a discontented workforce. It never happens at Kamchatskiy.

As a policy we engineer our designs so that they have the very highest possible standards of reliability. We do not, for example, use cheap components or materials to cut costs. Only the very highest standards of quality input and processing is acceptable. Our reputation stands by it. Equally, we do not subject our workforce to unnecessary controls, bureaucracy or competitive measures that otherwise would be likely to cause suboptimisation of performance, and we certainly do not practice the performance appraisals that so much damage the employee satisfaction of other organisations. There are no targets, no quotas, just a very high degree of trust both within and between the sets that work for us.

In our design shop you will learn all about our design philosophy, which is based very much on individual innovation and creativity. King Ken was adamant that anyone and everyone who comes to The Island would be driven by the need to innovate, otherwise they should not remain. We have kept to this principle and therefore we will be looking for each and every one of you to supply a constant input of suggestions for improvement as a matter of course. Continual improvement and Breakthrough improvement should both be considered, with Juran's Law of Managerial Breakthrough applied throughout.

Once you have begun working for us it is expected that you will continue indefinitely. Even retired people, such as myself, are expected, but not demanded, to continue to have an influence and a role in the future development of our company. We do have retirement, but not apathy. Apathy is not acceptable either on The Island or in any organisation that works for it.

There are no examinations or marked assignments for your studies here, and nobody ever fails. As W. Edwards Deming recommended, we will always spare time for the beginner, and offer special help to anyone who needs it or feels that they do. I am therefore instructing you to ask myself or one of my staff if you feel that there is anything in this course that gives you difficulty. It is in everyone's interest to make sure that everything is right first time, even if it means taking a short while longer to complete.

So, this is our company, which is as of now also your company. There are no wages, but also no taxes, just a way of life from which you will draw contentment. We are certain that you will all fit well into our organisation and are committed to your ongoing success. Our society and our company need you. That is why you are here. We are giving you a chance because we feel that you deserve it, where others have turned their backs on you. So I ask you to work with us and for us in the name of Kamchatskiy, The Island, and the whole of the non-capitalist principle. Viva Kamchatskiy."

The lecture had now finished, but, as at the beginning, he stood and continued to face the audience to invite a response.

"Viva Kamchatskiy," he repeated, raising his right arm in the air.

This time the audience knew that he was waiting for them all to repeat the company motto.

"Viva Kamchatskiy."

Chapter Nine
By Royal Command

The ninth of May. Gary's set had just had breakfast and Connie was reading extracts from Leo's book '*The Sovereignty of Nations*' which had been provided for all sets to study during their time on The Island.

"What does Leo's book tell us?" asked Lars.

"Leo states quite clearly that in the late 21st century the concept of the sovereignty of nations was going to undergo substantial change, and I quote 'As the 22nd Century approaches it is quite to be expected that a New Game will emerge whereby the sovereignty of nations will become a notable trading commodity to the extent that governments and entire nations may be bought out by the bidding powers of wealthier nations and other parties, such that weak and poor governments that have no idea how to manage may rapidly become replaced without recourse to war or conflict'.

Now this is something about which I had no knowledge until I arrived here and began to delve into this book. In his *Blueprint for the World*, Leo clearly states that it shall become a matter of fact eventually that wars and conflict shall one day be ended on the floors of stock exchanges, with The Island providing a crucial lead. He also envisaged that during this same period there would become an ever-decreasing distinction between organisations and nation states to the effect that the distinction will become ever more blurred until eventually a point will be reached when there will be no distinction at all".

Connie passed the book to Claudia who then read out the relevant paragraph.

"The Island, in time, shall develop the potential to instigate major change to the sovereignty of nations, proving that it is both possible and desirable, as well as in everyone's interests, to operate a nation state as if it were a well run and sensibly managed organisation. Indeed it shall be demonstrated that in the long-term this is a far more sustainable manner in which to manage nation states and to maintain the sovereignty of nations. Lines on maps shall not be set in stone, but shall be entirely negotiable between governments, landowners, and major players in each respective region of the earth."

"Leo speaks throughout of management by consensus using the Deming principles," Michael added. " Systems, including his own conception, must grow according to popular demand. If it proves to be a success then it should be allowed to expand at a controlled rate, by the consent of the people who are affected or who desire to be affected. Leo's message was simply that the world deserves a choice. He said that communism was no longer a viable alternative to capitalism, and then goes on to present his case for an alternative to both communism and capitalism to be made available to the world so that people still have the chance to choose something other than capitalism. He then refers the reader to his other book '*Non-Capitalist Economics*'".

"But '*The Sovereignty of Nations*' is all about how Non-Capitalist Economics is to be implemented, rather than the theory itself," added Yvonne.

"Here," said Michael, "turn to page 273".

Yvonne then read from the book.

"The world deserves a choice, not just between communism and capitalism, but also between good management and bad, between competition and cooperation, between improvement and stagnation, between construction and destruction, and between conflict

94

and peace. Our revolution shall be slow, but sustained, and we shall not be afraid to spit in the eye of those who seek to ruin the world with sham incentives and political dogma."

In the sanctuary of her Dome Joanie listened with interest to the discussion as she focused briefly on this set, satisfied that the set was making good use of the materials that had been provided. She then watched the courier as he delivered three packages to them.

Anne answered the door.

"Special delivery sign here," said the courier.

Anne duly signed on behalf of the set for three packages.

"Gary, these are for you," she said, handing Gary two of the packages. "One is from England, the other is from us."

"And the third?"

"The third is our weekly shopping requisition."

Gary proceeded to open the overseas packet which contained a birthday card and letter from his parents along with two gifts of a wine goblet with a small bottle of red wine and a wristwatch. He read his father's message on the card which said 'Many Happy Returns, here's so you can tell the time and have a drink on us'.

Memories of home flooded back, but he was encouraged by the letter in which his parents clearly stated they felt that he had made the right choice by accepting Queen Katie's invitation to go to The Island. 'There is no doubt you will be on a winning team there' his father wrote.

Gary then turned to the other package which contained five luxury gifts and a large birthday card which had been signed by each of his setmates. Gary opened these one by one, starting with aftershave, then luxury chocolates, a new shirt and tie, a gold plated pen set, and a blue jersey with The Island logo embossed.

"I don't know what to say. I have never had a birthday like this before," Gary remarked.

"Joanie has also sent you something," said Anne. "It's in the kitchen. I will now go and fetch it."

Anne returned a few moments later with a birthday cake and a letter marked 'private'.

"Georgina's Finest Birthday Cake," said Gary, reading the words on the box.

He then opened the cake upon which there were twenty-five candles.

"We must light these," said Elena.

They then sang 'Happy Birthday', after which Gary extinguished the candles, opened the letter and read the words aloud.

"What does it say?" asked Connie.

"Her Majesty Queen Katie kindly requests the pleasure of the company of Gary Loman and set at The Royal Palace at 1 pm today, the ninth day of May, signed H.M. The Queen."

"We obviously aren't going skating then," said Terry.

"Obviously not," said Connie.

"How do we get to the Royal Palace?" asked Gary. "The letter says nothing about being taken there."

"We must have to go on the noon train," Elena suggested.

*

At half past eleven a twelve seater Kammie arrived which duly took the set to the railway station to connect with the twelve o'clock train. At the station another set was waiting to board the same train. They had also been summoned to the Royal Palace as a certain Scottish gent, otherwise known as Hamish, also happened to have a birthday on May 9.

The set boarded the train along with one extra person, a fair-haired lady in her early thirties.

"Who is that strange lady with the laptop?" asked the French girl from the other set.

"I don't know," replied Connie. "I guess all we can do is ask her."

After they had boarded the train the two sets sat with the lady.

"Excuse me," said the French girl. "but who are you? It's not your birthday is it?"

"No, not at all," said the lady in a softly spoken English accent as the whistle blew and the engine hissed. "I am actually a reporter, Sylvia Smith, and very privileged I have to say, to have been granted permission by your Queen and Prime Minister to compile a documentary for British television about The Island, its people, its territories and its strategy. Ms. Carmichael kindly gave me an interview yesterday and Her Majesty has kindly granted me an interview this evening. I can't wait to meet her, but I am also keen to talk to people like yourselves. I understand that you are among a group of 240 people who have been fortunate enough to receive the coveted invitation to experience life in this truly fascinating place, which anyone and everyone just simply falls in love with the minute they get here. My job is to somehow present a true and accurate picture to the world of just exactly what is going on here without being too conspicuous. In coming here I have sworn my allegiance to The Queen and I shall only present to the world information that The Island is happy for me to release. The Island is happy because they are keen that their philosophy is shown to be good for the world in the eyes of the world's media. Information can be released in controlled amounts, but you have been here how long?"

"Just over a month," replied the French girl. "And you are right there is an intake of 240 most years at the end of March."

"And how do you all find life here?"

"We are all very happy," answered Jose. "None of us were doing too well in life before we came here. We are pleased that we have been given a rare chance to live happy and fulfilling lives that otherwise we would not have had. We are therefore all very grateful to the people, whoever they are, that nominated us".

"Indeed," said Sylvia. "And you are right to be. But I have to show you something, and I am perfectly entitled to show it to you, as Joanie Carmichael has already agreed. Tell me, have you ever thought that a place and a system could in fact be too good?"

She pressed a button on her laptop then continued:

"I will show you something from the other side. This is a piece of filming that was done a few weeks ago near the town of Vyvenka which lies just south of the current border between Island owned Kamchatka and the Russian state of Koryak. What you see is a small girl crying as a supposedly friendly Island Greencoat holds up his hand and says '*Niet*' to her and her parents. She is crying because she knows that she must return north to her poor life in Koryak, and people are upset. They feel that The Island territory should be open to them.

Five years ago house prices in Vyvenka soared when it was announced that The Island had negotiated with Moscow to have the border moved by twenty kilometres. Quite a lot of people made a lot of money when they found out that Vyvenka was soon to be acquired by The Island and the lives of its citizens transformed with no more unemployment, a guaranteed end to poverty in the region and a lot of prayers answered. The local council in Vyvenka was delighted, and so were the people that lived there. The ones who were less happy were the ones from further north who suddenly saw a once run down place made into a relative paradise whilst their town stayed run down. Furthermore, they were now to become trespassers if they so much as dared to venture into a town that they had always known and saw no reason to be excluded from. So you see, even a really good system, and there is no doubt that it is good, can appear to be not so good to some people, even though for those people life has not really changed, and could, in time, get much better, for there is no doubt that for those who live close to the border there is every chance that one day it will be moved favourably for them also. There are four more towns in that area, namely Korf, Tilichiki, Vetvey and Novoolyutorka, where house prices are now beginning to rise substantially in anticipation that The Island could acquire them within the not too distant future, but this can have a downside for some local people who could well be priced out. In our documentary we feel obliged to show the effect that being close to the border is having on the local population. In fact I want to make a point of showing this to that beautiful young Queen of yours because she really needs to know about it. I think it will bring tears to her eyes. "

"Are you sure that she doesn't already know?" asked Connie.

"Perhaps she does, but there is always a chance that she does not know the full story, as I'm sure you don't."

"But do you really think that there is a problem?" Gary asked.

"There is if it starts to create civil disorder and unrest, which neither The Island nor the Russian authorities want. That is why I have been granted permission to be here. Her Majesty wants the potential for unrest to be averted. Lots of people like The Island and applaud its methods, but nevertheless are reserved about its closed and secretive history. Most people are unaware that The Island even exists, and even those who are see it merely as a collection of landowners. They have no idea of just what kind of a phenomenon this creeping entity has become as it nibbles away at islands, peninsulas and towns insidiously and pretty much without opposition. This could be interpreted as a very subtle form of economic warfare as opposed to what you see as a benevolent Queendom out to improve the welfare of the world".

"The world deserves a choice," said Yvonne.

"I am aware of Leo's theories," said Sylvia. "The problem is they can be interpreted in different ways by different people, and at present there is nothing to stop parts of the world's media from drawing its own interpretation of The Island being more of a threat than an opportunity. It's wrong, but it's happening, and soon The Island will have to act to prevent these beliefs from delivering a false impression. I had to ask a lot of questions at the highest level before I even found out about the existence of The Island. I am staggered at the length of time that it has been going."

"I remember seeing a documentary in Alaska about the acquisition of the Aleutians," explained Connie. "There was a lot of hype at the time, but then it all just died down and everyone pretty much forgot about it. Sure the price of land rose on the islands that were being earmarked by those who were willing to pay over the odds for land and properties on them, but everyone accepted that in a capitalist country that was just the law of supply and demand taking its course."

"I appreciate that," replied the lady. "But the power of the press to whip up fury over the potential for a dictatorship, the potential for rationing and for Non-Capitalist Economics to ultimately revert to communism cannot be ignored. If you choose to mention the Aleutians you will remember what the papers said about the islands not being American in the end and how Alaska was going to be taken over by the Russians."

"And you will remember how all of that was defused a week later when the press finally confessed that these fears were totally unfounded, as all the owners were American and that it was the absolute right of these Americans to do as they pleased with the land that they purchased fair and square," Connie added.

"I know. I was the journalist who did the report. I have fortunately since become respected as a reliable correspondent acting on behalf of The Island whilst at the same time interfacing with the outside world. I along with a few others make it our business to expose lies and falsities at source and to warn of intended mischief, which is certain to occur as The Island continues to gain power and political influence. The point is the Russian authorities are very much in league with The Island. Those Island Greencoats will collaborate with the local Russian authorities to enforce border law so like it or not without paying over a lot of money those who live on the capitalist side of the border will not be able to go to Vyvenka and experience the high quality of life that has recently emerged there."

The train stopped briefly at Sabfelt station and the setmates looked at it whilst the train was stationary. Particularly prominent was The Gun Inn, which had all the appearance of a traditional Irish pub.

"Gosh, they've even got an Irish pub here," Gary remarked.

Some of the other set then began talking to Sylvia, who was keen to learn how they had come to be nominated for a place on The Island. As with Gary's set the interest in skating and in ice dance in particular formed a common thread amongst them.

"I love the Kamchatskiy skaters and so pleased that The Island gives opportunities for people like yourselves to have a dream come true rather than giving the reward to those who have already been successful in life. It's nice to see effort rewarded as I know you all worked very hard at your skating well before being invited to come here."

Sylvia explained a little about her background at British Television as the train chuffed on to Aldebaran, where again it stopped to take on provisions bound for the royal household. On the return journey the train would stop again to take provisions back to The Town. The setmates gazed briefly at the distinctive Opera House, a miniature version of that in Sydney, that was the centrepiece of the small hamlet, along with the statues of Ken, Kathleen and Justine that stood in a triangle facing the entrance. Beyond there was the vegetarian delicatessen, The Island bakery, the waxworks and beyond those an astronomical observatory.

The train steamed on toward the Royal Palace until it finally ground to a halt at its terminus, The Palace Gates station. This stood at the southern end of the east garden of The Palace, through which a path wound its way through rose gardens and shrubberies before opening out onto a patch of ground with well-kept lawns beyond. The train driver directed the sets and the reporter up the pathway to the south entrance of The Royal Palace where The Queen's Butler was ready to greet them.

He escorted them across the parterre, then through the billiard room to a large entrance hall upon the walls of which were hung portraits of The Founders and their partners which they all recognised. Beyond was the dining room where twenty-six places had been set on a long table for lunch. Here The Queen stood to greet the arrivals.

On the walls of the dining room were hung portraits of the royals, including her parents Mary, The Queen Mother, and King Neville, and various cousins. On the ceiling was painted a mural of 'Fire and Ice' whilst above the Victorian style fireplace was hung a large oil painting of 'Barnum on Ice', reflecting Queen Justine's admiration of the legendary British skaters and from which the inspiration for The Queen's Tickets had originally come.

With The Queen's position at the head, the remaining places were then named such that the two sets faced each other with the final place at the other end of the table, facing The Queen, marked Sylvia, reserved for the reporter.

"So," declared The Queen, "it is a pleasure to welcome you all today to this our fine residence. I know you were all expecting to be doing other things today, but, in accordance with Island tradition, I have taken this opportunity to get to know you all personally. I use the first birthday in each set to invite the whole set, so Happy Birthday to Gary Loman and Hamish McEwan.

As you no doubt know, I am twenty-three this year and we are coming to a very exciting period in our history. This

Island is our cosy retreat, but this does not mean that we do not go out and meet our people, as you will discover. We often visit towns, countries and islands and meet people old and young, as does our Prime Minister.

I know you all have a story to tell about how my Ticket led you here. I am naturally keen to know what path the Tickets have taken since I gave them to The Prince when he stayed here over Christmas. I have a little treat for you all this afternoon and maybe as we talk informally you can let me know something about your little secrets as to how you got here. First, however, we invite you to try our food, which has been lovingly prepared from the finest ingredients by our resident Head Chef Bob, who heads a team of four top chefs on The Island."

The Chef entered accompanied by two waiters who served the tiger prawn starters to the table.

"We now wish you to enjoy our royal fare, so you may leave refreshed ready for your afternoon ahead."

At the end of the meal The Queen rose to explain the details of the afternoon's programme.

"My compliments as ever to The Chef for a superb culinary experience. I would now like to invite each of you to join me on the steam yacht gondola which will take you from the jetty on the lake to the north of The Palace to the other side of the lake where a cable car will convey you up the mountain to The Non-Olympic Stadium, which these days, apart from New Year's Day, I tend to have all to myself. This is a must-see for you all. Coffee and petits fours will be served on board the gondola."

The sets and Sylvia were escorted from the dining room to the entrance on the north side of the palace, observing the three tapestries depicting the history of The Island that hung on the walls of the drawing room through which they passed. A love of skating was prominent in all three, as was transport in all its forms from The Stone Boat to the Hebden Three.

Elsewhere photographs showed various stages of The Royal Palace under construction, more personal scenes of the royals over the years, and setmates from years gone by who had been previous recipients of The Queen's Ticket from Mary, The Queen Mother during her reign. As the setmates ambled past these Yvonne spotted the picture that she had been looking for, that of The Queen and Aub in a fond embrace beneath a large pine tree decorated with Christmas lights. Her suspicion of an engagement was thereby confirmed.

Bob led the setmates out to the awaiting Steam Yacht Gondola beside which the Queen's parents and younger brother and sister of The Queen stood to shake hands with the setmates and Sylvia.

On board Bob served the coffee and petits fours before taking to the helm. Then, steam powered it soon built up speed across the still lake allowing the sets to view The Royal Palace from the north side for the first time, and showing the clear resemblance to Versailles that the deceased Kathleen had stipulated should be a feature of her Royal Palace when it was finally completed. Looking the other way they could see the outline of the mist covered mountains that lay before them.

Chapter Ten
The Non-Olympic Stadium

The gondola meandered around the lake for about half an hour before finally coming to rest at the jetty on the north side of the lake, at the foot of the mountains. The rocky slopes rose steeply from the shore of the lake presenting a contrasting view to that which existed on The Island's south side, which was mainly grassy and cultivated. On the slopes there were some trees, but for the most part there persisted only barren rock.

Bob ushered the setmates and Sylvia into the awaiting cable car, which was then set into automatic motion so that it rose above the woodland below before ascending sharply over the steep grey mountainside.

After about ten minutes the cable car stopped at an intermediate station. From here a large waterfall could be seen flowing down to the hydroelectric plant on the north east side of The Island. Here the thirty-seater cable car remained stationary for a while before it continued rising to the next station from which five or six ski slopes led off from a hut some fifty metres below, not that there was any snow covering. The climate of The Island was much too warm for natural snow. Only the snow generator would make the slopes fit for skiing when the Christmas season arrived. The cable car stopped this time for a slightly longer period. Just when it seemed as if it would go no further another cable car could be seen rising up along a parallel wire at a somewhat swifter pace. This cable car was somewhat smaller, black rather than blue and in place of The Island logo was a gold crown signifying that this was The Queen's cable car.

Presently The Queen's car drew level with the other one, but did not stop. Instead it passed on slowly through the station overtaking the setmates, so that it would obviously arrive at the summit ahead of them. From the window The Queen waved and the setmates waved back, surprised to see that she was evidently going to join them.

When The Queen's car had passed the other car continued its more leisurely ascent, rising into the mist until it eventually came to rest inside a grotto that had been carved into the rock. A long corridor then led to a portcullis which opened revealing behind it a large open air ampitheatre which was surprisingly mist free. It was deserted, although at one end a large dish could be seen, whilst the centre was concreted and about the size of a football pitch.

"Hello, is anybody there?" Hamish shouted, his voice echoing in the silent stadium as the setmates stood gazing out across this Colosseum-like construction. Then The Queen appeared.

"This way please," she ordered, waving the setmates and Sylvia out into the stadium. "So, bet you didn't expect to see me again. You will be pleased to know that I shall be your tour guide for this afternoon around this magnificent stadium. As you can appreciate, the Non-Olympics is our counter to the Olympics and this Stadium was built by Kai-san in 2040 under the direction of Founder Peter, The Sportsman to promote amateur sport following the original Olympic principle.

The Stadium is situated right at the northern tip of The Island, and as such is the furthest point of The Island from The Town. It has been carved out of the mountain in a remarkable feat of engineering which has made the most of its natural volcanic features. Beyond us to the north lies only sea all the way to Greenland.

The Non-Olympics is different from the Olympics in

two important respects. First of all, as you can obviously guess, in our non-capitalist society there is no such thing as a professional sportsman, so all of our participants are strictly amateurs. So whilst we may have trainers, coaches and performers our performers are not professionals, as they are all required by law to have some other form of occupation, just as in the old days with the Olympics. For many years the Non-Olympics was largely just an elite sort of club for friends of The Island and those with close ties to it. Since the end of the last century, however, amateur sport has really taken off with lots of interest from outside and even from the Olympic movement itself. This led to four new Non-Olympic Stadiums being built in Kamchatka, Sakhalin, the Falklands and latterly Groznyy. Since 2093 therefore this Stadium has become redundant for its original purpose, The Island being much too small to host what is now a very popular Games that have become renowned for their fairness and integrity.

The second important feature of the Non-Olympics is that the emphasis is much more on the taking part than the competition, which makes them much more relaxed and informal, a bit like me really. The emphasis is very much on displaying talent and exhibiting excellence. Also, unlike with the Olympics, a platinum Merit Medal may be granted by myself in consultation with trainers and participants for an individual who has not necessarily won, but made an outstanding achievement at or on the run up to the Games. These Merit Medals are as much prized as the Victory Medals.

I say there is less competition, but that does not mean that there is no competition. Competition can be fierce, but there is a different approach towards it. Yes, everyone likes to win, but it is not the end of the world if one doesn't. Joy in work Deming style ensures that everyone respects everyone else. There is simply not the incentive to indulge in drug misuse and other cheating methods that have so ruined the Olympics for many decades. No wonder the Olympic Committee is starting to look at us.

You will observe above the west stand the dish which used to hold the Non-Olympic flame, whilst opposite us on the north stand is the Royal enclosure. Behind us is the participants' entrance to the stadium.

The surface upon which we stand will be ice covered for New Year's Day, and our annual fun and games contest Games Without Frontieres, which we hold every New Year's Day here for specially invited participants, and to which you will all contribute. Now, in your own time, if you can please follow me I will show you a bit more of Non-Olympic history."

The Queen led the party back through the entrance to a room which contained memorabilia and artefacts from the Non-Olympics. Here viewers could watch playbacks of events that had been built up over the years as archives, as well as listening to commentaries about the Non-Olympics and its origins. Most notably one could observe a critique of the Olympic movement and why The Island considered it to be flawed. It stated:

'The Olympic movement was a great inception. The idea of involving the youth of the world in a single prestigious event, stressing the importance of taking part, and of maintaining the amateur ethic, was a noble achievement in its day. Unfortunately, however, this ideal has, over time, fallen into deeper and deeper disrepute. First there was the political interference of Berlin in 1936. Then, later, there were the endless endeavours of certain individuals to cheat any way they could in order to secure victory at the expense of others. This has continued to such a point that today, with ever more sophisticated means of disguising performance enhancing substances, even the rigorous testing regime of the Olympic Committee has been tested to its limit. The old noble ambitions of the Victorian era have long gone, superseded by a contest that promotes only victory and the demarcation of competitors. It is true that it remains a great honour to compete for one's country, and to win a medal, but one should not be labelled as a loser simply for being shaded out of the medals or not being precisely on form on that critical day when one's event is called.

The modern day Olympics has not only fallen into disrepute by rewarding those who succeed in dodging the doping, it has also become a theatre in which winning can almost mean the difference between life and death. Yet winning can often be as much a matter of chance as merit. The fact that a child lives close to a facility, or has parents who are able and willing to fund the years of training that are required for one to become an Olympic competitor, is often not down to the talent of the child, but a consequence of fortune.

The Non-Olympics do not contain these chance elements, but instead reward effort and merit that is sustained and within the reach of everyone. Winners receive recognition, but this never replaces one's true commitment to society. We invite you to observe our archive materials and contrast it with what you see and hear of the Olympics.'

The party was guided past photographs of the four Non-Olympic Stadiums in Yuzhno Sakhalinsk, Petropavlovsk Kamchatskiy, Port Stanley and Groznyy, then on to a section which faced a screen. The commentary to the film began thus:

'Throughout history the human species has been obsessed with competition. The Romans raced chariots. Men and women have raced against each other in every way possible, and pushed themselves to jump and throw longer and longer distances. They have strived to defeat their opponents in rink and ring, and they have maintained their honour by gaining the coveted gold medal that has come to mean so much. Our question, however, is this: do we have to endlessly drive ourselves to defeat others simply to preserve honour, satisfy our ambitions and raise standards?

Our Founders and friends back in the 2030s believed

that the answer to this question had to be no, and in the decades that have followed we on The Island have set out to demonstrate to the world that it is not only unnecessary to focus our aims on defeating others, it can be quite harmful as well as grossly unfair.

Our Non-Olympics has grown from strength to strength, so much so that now the rest of the world wants to join in. In fact so great has been the interest in our approach that we are now in the process of planning a merger with the Olympic movement within the foreseeable future. There is no doubt that the Olympic Committee want and need a cleaner and fairer Olympic Games, and there is no doubt on our part that we would like our philosophy to be more widely adopted. The new games, if they occur will have to be a combination of both movements with our contribution relating to a greater recognition for the amateur ethic, and the Merit Medals, which our Games are pledged to maintain. We love sport. It's healthy, it's entertaining and it's fun, but it's not if it falls into disrepute and destroys morale.

We believe, as in other areas, that the world deserves a choice when it comes to sport. Contrary to popular belief we want to preserve and enhance the Olympic movement, not simply maintain ourselves as a rival to it. We do not hate competition as some would believe, but simply state that it has its place within sport as in other areas. In particular it should not be so intense as to drive people to cheat or to crush the morale of those who have worked hard and long in the hope of gaining recognition and achievement.

The chariot race, which you now see is an old favourite that started life on our beach and is about as competitive as it is possible to get, and we are pleased that this is being seriously considered for introduction at the next Olympic Games. As you are listening to this a new Non-Olympic stadium is already under construction in Groznyy, outside Island territory for the first time, although naturally under our management. When the Non-Olympics are held there in 2109 attendees from all over the world will be able to purchase tickets for these Games rather than the Games being open only to Island citizens and wealthy individuals who last time had to pay extremely high sums for the two-week Falkland Islands entry visa.

On ice there can be no doubt that the standard achieved by our participants at least rivals that achieved at the conventional Winter Olympics. Skiing likewise is focused on personal achievement, as are the ever popular bobsleigh events.'

Scenes of these were shown on the screen as the commentary continued.

'We are not short of world records as you can see. Over the years we have built up an impressive list of amateur world records. Take, for example, Ivan Pskov's famous long jump of 2097, the now famous marathon run by Ernie Hammond in Yuzhno Sakhalinsk in 2101, and the many track and field achievements of the eighties. Here we see Olga Chalnikov breaking the women's amateur 5000 metres record in Stanley in 2105. There are more should you wish to view them. As for the chariot race, this started as a fun race as you can see from this old clip from the very first Non-Olympics held here in 2041. Few people were here then and the Non-Olympics was really a non-event, except for those on The Island and a handful of specially invited guests.

The chariots of course are all of standard design, made of course by the Kamchatskiy Auto Company, which has a world copyright for their design. Maybe you too will have your own chariot and take part in one of our Sunday afternoon rallies.

Like the Olympics the Non-Olympics have their own para-equivalent. Here we see their coxless pairs rowing event from 2093, the last ever event to be held on the lake at The Royal Palace. That was a landmark year, as in 2097 the Stadium at Petropavlovsk Kamchatskiy was completed for the first modern style Non-Olympics as we know them today, marking the end of this Stadium's fifty-two years as a sporting venue.

Now we look to the future and the merger with the Olympics. What can the world expect? The Olympics will still be there of course, but amateur sport will be given a new lease of life, not just for us non-capitalists, but also for amateurs in the capitalist world. Come and join us at Groznyy 2109."

The music of Vangelis's 'Chariots of Fire' ended the filmshow, with scenes of the beachside chariot race of 2041. Outside The Queen was waiting in the executive lounge by the cable car station where both cable cars were parked. Inside the lounge the Queen talked informally to the two sets to learn about what had happened to her Tickets as she had said over lunch, and to Sylvia who was particularly interested her life and personal experiences.

"Being a Queen is not as easy as it might appear," Her Majesty said quietly. "Often there are tight schedules and a very great sense of duty. One must never let one's subjects down and one is always in the public eye. Then there is the responsibility of maintaining one's appearance and quality of judgment. It is not about living a pleasure bent lifestyle. It is about fulfilling a very important role for one's country, whichever one it happens to be. I had to grow up very quickly when I became Queen."

"Do you see yourself as being the same as other world monarchs?" Sylvia asked.

"In terms of role and duty, yes," she said. "But in terms of history, no. We are definitely different, much newer and with a quite different structure. The set system is unique to us, and of course there is no money. We are the only royal family in the world to have no money at all. Not that that affects our status or quality of life. In fact we probably live better and more comfortably than any other royal family. When I have met other royals around the world I often leave feeling so fortunate to have the nation state and territories that I do, and subjects who are always loyal and kind and think cooperatively. Human psychology in some places really does have to change and I feel sorry for some of the monarchs who have to rule over territories where terrible atrocities are occurring. I would hate to feel responsible, as I would, if some of those things were to occur in any of my territories."

"What are your relations like with The Prime Minister?"

"Always very positive," replied The Queen. "The Queen, The King, my mother and my Prime Minister all have specific roles at the head of a very well balanced system. We do share political decision making though, perhaps rather more than in other countries where the monarchy's political influence has been diminished, largely through a history that we, thankfully, don't have. We try to be approachable to the people, and to be seen. We do not spend all of our lives in this cosy retreat, but it is true that The Island itself does provide a level of privacy that I know some royals around the world do envy."

"True," replied Sylvia. "I know that for a fact. A little bird also tells me that The Island is soon to have a new King. That's causing some excitement amongst the world's media as more people are aware of The Island's existence than ever before. Can you give us any indication as to how long it will be before we have a King?"

"Oh it will be soon," answered The Queen. "I know the people always begin to speculate as soon as a new Queen is crowned, but it will be soon, shall we say this year?"

"And is there any truth in what I have heard that a dozen or so of your Ministers as well as the outgoing King have to be fully satisfied in your choice before The Prince can become a King?"

"Absolutely," said The Queen. "He has to be trained for the job and be totally outstanding in his political capabilities. Our Kings don't just inherit a throne, they have to be thoroughly competent to manage the world, almost like the Samurai tradition."

"So what sort of training does a Prince have to undergo here?"

The Queen and Sylvia talked for about twenty minutes, the setmates listening with interest about what was soon to transpire.

"I can't believe that from where we all were just over a month ago here we are now rubbing shoulders with Queen Katie of Kamchatka," Anne remarked to her setmates. "She just seems so ordinary, yet she is going to be a phenomenon on the world stage very soon and hardly anyone has ever heard of her. Unbelievable."

"But then this is The Island of Dreams," said Gary.

Chapter Eleven
The Self-policing State

Four weeks later.

It was four o'clock in the afternoon and Gary and the others had just returned from the ice rink. Anne was making tea in the kitchen whilst the others were sitting in the living room discussing the latest refinements to their skating routine as they eagerly awaited a television announcement from Joanie. On cue the television switched itself on at four o'clock.

"Good afternoon setmates," she said. "I now have some important things which I wish to say to all sets, so please listen carefully. As you can appreciate it is my duty as far as is reasonably practicable, to maintain equilibrium of the social system. It follows that it is also my duty to ensure that all newcomers to our society are able to understand and apply the procedure for recognising and dealing with forces that may tend to act to disturb that equilibrium. In order to do this I have to disturb the equilibrium intentionally and, having done so, seek to ensure that all of you are able to subsequently restore it yourselves.

This exercise is designed to demonstrate to you how our legal system operates. In your study manual entitled 'The Self-policing State' you will find a diskette and a description of the history of our system for law and order as defined by Big John, our first Home Secretary.

When Big John examined the failings of the British judicial system from which he resigned he concluded that many of its misgivings could be attributed to the state's dependence on mass inspection to secure law and order. The police, he said, were like inspectors on the factory floor, and, by having such a role, they were unlikely to be able to optimise on justice. Instead their role undermined justice and generated pecking orders within society, with a system that was adversarial and blame ridden. The policeman, like the factory inspector, was there simply to bring to book those who stepped out of line, irrespective of whether individual laws were seen as good, bad or indifferent. He did not see a positive role for the police at all in this regard, although he did accept that in order for their role to be changed there would have to be a dramatic reduction in the scale and nature of crime within society as a whole.

In Big John's view the nature of policing should be reappraised in line with Deming's Third Point, which requires that we cease being dependent on mass inspection to achieve quality. Having considered this carefully and looked at parallels between the policing function and the role of inspectors on the factory floor Big John came up with his own unique interpretation of what we now know as the Self-policing State.

In Deming's vision, workers would achieve a higher level of quality if they were empowered to take responsibility for the quality of their output rather than placing all of the responsibility on inspectors. Big John's view was that the quality of life in an entire society would improve if everyone were empowered to police everyone else, rather than placing all of the responsibility on police, the courts and the prison service. In a capitalist society such a change was possible, but difficult to apply because of the high levels of crime that existed in some areas. The Island, however, was fortunate enough, through its people and the way its citizens were carefully selected and trained, to be able to start from a standpoint of a virtually zero crime rate. This was largely because all money related crime was eliminated and domestic crimes equally reduced to a very low level thanks to the Set Formation

Act and its provisions, which place a duty on secondaries to intervene should signs of a breakdown be evident.

Traditional policing methods, Big John said, were unacceptable as they do nothing to prevent law abiding citizens from falling foul of pecking orders, often tragically early in life, leaving them frequently with the stark choice of either remaining at the bottom or of forcing themselves up by pressurising others. Therein lies the problem, as the ensuing pecking orders do not benefit society, but suppress talent as dominance is by aggression rather than wisdom.

The fact is that traditional inspection based policing fails to detect the presence of deviants, and fails to apply the appropriate corrective action through the criminal justice system until it is much too late. This is in contrast to our system which aims to prevent crime before it happens by removing the cause, which is known as deviance. Big John asserted that if the status of a deviant can be diagnosed before the crime occurs, then the danger of a disturbance to the social equilibrium can be averted. Sometimes certain conditions, such as the existence of internal competition within a group, were found to increase the probability of deviance and so develop the pecking order. Without deviance the desire to pressurise others is eliminated. In other cases a latent defect may be triggered, for example through access to firearms or offensive weapons, which give the holder a strong and immediate sense of power that can be very destructive. A case of the latter is that of Dunblane 1996, which is featured in your study packs. I leave it to you to decide whether you think that under our system the shooting of the children would have been prevented.

The tradition of shared responsibility on The Island has led to a culture of shared responsibility for the actions of deviants. It is not purely the deviant that is responsible. It is everybody.

It is now my duty, in accordance with my terms of reference as Prime Minister, to declare each and every one of you deviant until further notice. It is your duty as prospective citizens to study and enact the provisions of the Self-policing State so that this status can be effectively removed, leaving you with a secure knowledge of how this system operates."

"Well, what do you make of this one?" Anne asked.

"I guess the first thing we need to do is ascertain why we have all been declared deviant," said Lars. "It has to be done with a reason. That's clearly stated in the study module and its odd that the PM hasn't stated it."

"We must have to find out the reason," suggested Graca.

Connie made her way to the computer.

"What are you doing, Connie?" asked Michael.

"I'm going to key into Commander for some ideas. It usually has solutions for most things. I'm going to start with the definition of a deviant because although we have read about the Self-policing State, I feel we need to go back to basic definitions if we are to complete the task that we have been given."

Gary joined her as she entered the study module. He then read aloud the two definitions that Commander provided.

"Definition one, person incompatible in time or space with others with whom he or she interacts through neglect of social principles. Definition two, a state of mind of an individual which has exceeded its bounds of stability to the extent of presenting a social hazard."

Connie then clicked on to the related term of deviance and obtained the definition for that term. Again Gary read this definition aloud.

"Deviance is the condition arising from the presence of one or more deviants which results in a disturbance of social equilibrium."

The same was then done for the term deviantism, which yielded the definition of 'conceptualisation of the condition of deviance into a theory that is governed by natural laws'.

"Natural laws sounds interesting, I think I will dig a bit deeper into that," said Connie.

She keyed in to the section on theory as the set gathered round. Gary read the theory.

"All sets are presumed to be non-deviant when a state of contentment exists as defined by the psychological acceptance limits of their members as indicated by their social, emotional and physical parameters. The social system of a community and the nation will remain stable so long as all sets are non-deviant."

"So where do we go from here?" said Jose.

"I'll try deviance, remedies for," replied Connie.

This output revealed that there were three legal remedies for deviance, namely Reversal by Testimony, Social Reconstruction, and Grounds for Dissent. Gary read the procedures for each of the three methods.

"Reversal by Testimony. Should a person of known good character be satisfied that the underlying cause of the deviance in question has been addressed and rectified to such a point where there was unlikely to be a recurrence, then the defendant may apply for Reversal by Testimony. The defendant must publicly revoke the Declaration of Deviance before the Social Standards Committee.

Social Reconstruction. For more serious cases or where there are repeated complaints made against a citizen, such that mere Reversal by Testimony is deemed insufficient, then the Social Standards Committee may apply for a further investigation of the offence or intended offence or habit, and, if deemed appropriate, may recommend a course of Social Reconstruction, which, if successfully completed to all concerned, will provide the necessary evidence for the Declaration of Deviance to be overturned by the Social Standards Committee. In such cases the Social Standards Committee must agree to address the underlying cause of the deviance on behalf of the defendant should the defendant accept the cause but consent that he or she needs help in order to remedy it.

Grounds for Dissent. Any person who is served with a Declaration of Deviance may contest that the Declaration is unfair or illegitimate before the Appeals Division of the

Social Standards Committee should they have grounds to believe that the said Declaration has been wrongly applied, applied maliciously or applied for political rather than social reasons. The Appeals Division will then rule as to whether the Grounds for Dissent will be accepted."

"So where does that leave us?" asked Lars.

"Reversal by Testimony presumes that we know the reason why we have been declared deviant," commented Yvonne. "But we don't so I can't see how we could apply for Reversal by Testimony, and the same would be true for Social Reconstruction."

"I don't think anyone actually applies for Social Reconstruction," said Connie. "It has a section all to itself and exists in many forms, mostly educational, requiring a regular attendance by the defendant. Prison is the next step on from Social Reconstruction, but it looks as if there is no such thing as a prison sentence here. Social Reconstruction merely leads on to prison through a succession of failures, which would only happen if the convict adamantly refused to take the course, treatment or whatever seriously. It never happens, however, because we are all trained to think in such a way that it never would. It looks like there is at least one prison though, as it has to exist by law even though there may be nobody inside."

"So the Island has one prison somewhere in Kamchatka with nobody in it?" said Michael.

"That's what it looks like," said Connie. "Although there are records of people going into detention as part of Social Reconstruction, like a sort of sin bin. The other remedy that is more common is that of Directed Labour, which has its own Ministry that is attached to the Ministry for Law and Order. It's all explained in the study module."

"What's Directed Labour?" asked Elena.

"There are three types," explained Connie. "According to the online study module there are Directed Labour Volunteers, who voluntarily agree to sign up for a fixed term of Directed Labour, a bit like old-style regular soldiers. Then there are Directed Labour Convicts, who are sentenced to a fixed term of Directed Labour, usually for short periods as part of Social Reconstruction for public order offences like drunkenness. These are under the control of the D.L.V.s. Then there are the Directed Labour Conscripts, who are aged 16 to 18 and expected to serve one year as a form of national service. These are also under the D.L.V.s, but are separate from the convicts. All of this Directed Labour is required in order to ensure that one way or another all of the less popular tasks that people do not otherwise choose for their employment, and are not absorbed into job descriptions, do actually get completed."

"So I suppose they will work mending the roads or cleaning things?" said Elena.

"That sort of thing," said Connie. "Quite a lot of people apparently do sign up for it for the lifestyle and the comradeship that it offers, as well as knowing that they are making a valid contribution to society, a desire that pretty much seems to be indoctrinated into The Island's citizens."

"Useful to know about, but leaves us no further forward with our assignment," Anne commented. "I can only see Grounds for Dissent to overturn the Declaration."

"Then," said Terry. "We must decide what grounds we have and to whom we must apply. Who is in charge of the Social Standards Committee?"

"I could key in to Grounds for Dissent and find out what the procedure is," suggested Connie.

The set nodded and Connie pressed the appropriate key. Gary read the text.

"An application for Grounds for Dissent should be made to the Social Standards Committee Appeals Division within fourteen days of receipt of the Declaration. The Application may be submitted in person at the local Council Chambers or applied for online. The application must state clearly who issued the Declaration and whether the Declaration has been issued singly, jointly or *en masse*. Careful consideration should always be given, especially with *en masse* cases, as to whether the issuer has acted within or outside his or her authority. Grounds for Dissent will always be granted where the Social Standards Committee Appeals Division rules that the Declaration has been made for strategic or political gain."

"That sounds as if it could be relevant," suggested Claudia.

"It's about the only thing that is," affirmed Anne.

"The text goes on to say that no one is above investigation," added Gary.

"That means even The Prime Minister?" said Graca.

"Right," said Connie.

"So that means that whoever is in charge of the Appeals Division of the Social Standards Committee can, at least sometimes, even override The Prime Minister in certain circumstances," Terry added.

"Who is in charge of it though?" asked Elena.

"That's what I mean to find out," continued Connie. "I'll key in to Social Standards Committee Appeals Division and see what it says."

"The Social Standards Committee Appeals Division is a division of the Social Standards Committee that is responsible for the handling of all appeals on behalf of the Social Standards Committee," Gary said, as he read from the screen. "Both Committees are appointed to ensure the continued wellbeing of the community and are jointly a responsibility of the Welfare Ministry and the Health and Safety Ministry."

"Health and safety, that's it," shouted Lars.

"What do you mean?" said Anne.

"The Deputy Prime Minister is next in line to The Prime Minister," Lars continued. "and he is responsible for health and safety on The Island. I think we should go and have a chat with him. His is that big grey building that is set back from the road at the bottom of the hill from The Great Dome".

"And his door is always open, like the PMs," Elena said.

"And he can override anyone if he thinks health and safety might be compromised," added Michael.

"Then let's go," suggested Carl.

The set left Angel Cottage and they made their way to The Deputy Prime Minister's residence. They had no need to ring as the white regency-style door opened automatically. The Usherette greeted them expectantly, leading them into an entrance hall where two other sets were also waiting to see the same person.

"So at last you have come to see me," said the square faced, slightly balding fifty-year-old man. "Well you three dozen had better come into my office."

The thirty-six setmates sat around the large oak table ready to be briefed.

"Well," he continued. "I am pleased to tell you that you have come to the right place, but for the wrong reasons. I know that you are here to tell me that you have Grounds for Dissent against the Declaration of Deviance which The Prime Minister has conferred on you all. You would be right in alleging this except for one thing, and that is that technically you are in practice deserving of a Declaration. It is unfortunate that none of you conducted a thorough enough examination of your own status of learning to recognise this. Only one set appears to have done so and I will be contacting them shortly to congratulate them.

I have to tell you that there is quite a lengthy list of offences for which a Declaration of Deviance can be served. One of these I can state is a failure to update one's health and safety training on a monthly basis. Had you been working for Kamchatskiy today the Health and Safety Officer would have been well within his rights to issue a Declaration of Deviance *en masse* to all of those who had neglected this important duty. This does happen, as to neglect one's health and safety training is deemed to be a neglect of social principle and it is an easy offence to commit. Do nothing and you will automatically commit it.

I am, however, prepared to accept that you are fully and openly willing to put right this deficiency forthwith. I therefore, in the absence of the full Committee, am prepared to grand to each of you a Reversal by Testimony for the Declaration that has been served upon you by my superior. Arrangements have been made for you to ratify the Testimony before Mitsumoto-san in the boardroom when you next attend for training.

This is not, however, the end of the matter, because there is one other thing that no sets actually appear to have spotted, and that is that when a Declaration of Deviance is issued the issuer, especially if he or she is a senior member of the community as The Prime Minister is, is required by law to give a reason for the issuing of the Declaration. Failure to do this is also breach of social principle, and therefore there is a case to be answered by her also. In a real situation she could expect to be heavily criticised for this.

You should now go back to your cottages and decide for tomorrow how you propose to serve a Declaration on The Prime Minister to remind her of the protocol that she herself should be obliged to follow. For the purposes of this exercise you should assume as from now that the Social Standards Committee has suddenly become corrupt and is no longer approachable, and also that The Prime Minister has become power-crazed and is behind the corruption, which is in need of exposure. I will remind you that Deviantism is a mechanism that is intended to prevent accidents and disharmony by revealing unsatisfactory behaviour, not an instrument for power or control. You should network with other sets so as to collectively contrive a solution."

The three sets dispersed as three more entered to receive the same message from The Deputy. Armed with the knowledge that had been given to them all of the sets now began to converse through Commander. They later met in the bars to consider what they had come up with. The networking process quickly led all of the sets toward a common understanding of what Deviantism was and what the legal remedies were for it.

The next day Connie and the others again gathered around the computer. Connie sent all of the observations that her set had made and these appeared to correspond with those that other sets had pinpointed and sent to them. They brainstormed online for solutions to the final problem which they had to solve collectively.

"Our set believes that the media should be involved to expose the corruption," said Carl reading an incoming email.

"We thought of that, but ascertained that the media is also corrupt," Gary said, reading another.

"It's a clear abuse of power on the part of The Prime Minister," he continued, reading another. "So no one set can act independently. We must all act together. This is obvious if the Social Standards Committee has effectively been taken over."

This networking exercise was designed to introduce the sets to a method of policing abuses of power, and to the grapevine that formed the basis of The Island's defence system. By acting in unison they would effectively be able to restore social equilibrium following the disturbance that The Prime Minister had introduced.

"What about contacting some of the staff for their suggestions," another email suggested.

"No good. We have ascertained that all of the staff are corrupt," came another. "The PM has a complete stranglehold on power. A police state is being formed."

"The staff will turn more on our side as this situation progresses," another email suggested.

"The PM has to be isolated," Connie said as she fed this suggestion into the twittering.

"Agreed," came a response. "We need a way of doing this."

"We have watched the diskette of Big John," came another message. "It states that in such cases the despot has to be brought out into the open."

Other messages affirmed that there was support for this, but no consensus as yet on how to bring the corrupt leader to face the people. When the time was right the PM, reverting to her old teaching role, unlocked the concluding section of the diskette so that they could use the prescribed method to displace the corrupt leader.

This decreed that each set would send one setmate to The Great Dome to request that The Prime Minister make an appearance at the Gloriette at four o'clock the next day. The method stipulated that every set had to do this. These selected setmates would then draw lots in order to ascertain which of them should actually make the formal request to The Prime Minister to convey the message that all of her people had turned against her.

"No animosity must be used, just a plain request. We must use gratitude rather than animosity to coax her to the stand," a further email stated.

"She cannot refuse to go public because all actions taken by Deviants to remedy Deviance have to be acknowledged by law. If we are required to act, then so is she," came another.

"The staff have agreed to be ready with the drums at the end," another stated.

The draw decreed that French girl Marie would thank The PM formally in The Great Dome and request her public attendance. Brazilian Mario would then accompany her to the Gloriette and make the stage-managed announcement.

*

At half past three the next day the twenty representatives from each set entered the Great Dome to deliver their

126

ultimatum to The Prime Minister. Naturally she was unresponsive to any requests to see her, given that her role at this point was to mimic the role of a dictator rather than to be the benevolent Joanie that they all knew.

The representatives, including Anne from Gary's set, who waited to see her naturally represented the voice of the people and once the people had turned there was no way back for a dictator as many examples in history had demonstrated. With the exceptional levels of trust and cooperation that existed amongst The Island's people, superior to that of any other in the world, it was obvious that The Island was not the sort of place where a despot could emerge and hope to survive. So, in the end she had to concede.

"Enter," said The Prime Minister, as she turned to face them with a defiant expression. "So, what have you come to tell me?"

"We have come to thank you," answered Marie humbly as she stepped forward and bowed her head.

"To thank me?"

"Yes, to thank you for bringing to our attention our lapses in updating our training requirements. Now, in accordance with our rights we would like to thank you publicly."

"You need not do that. In fact I would prefer it," said Joanie, still acting the part.

This placed Marie on the spot, Joanie secretly, and for the training purposes, eager to see how she would handle it.

"Yes, we appreciate that, but I believe protocol allows for us to thank a person in authority such as yourself in public in such cases?"

"You are right. It does. So what? I'm the dictator. I'm in charge. What can any of you do?"

Marie now had to use her improvisation skills

"Your people have turned, not just some, but each and every one. You have no choice but to step down. Your orders have become meaningless. Your presence before the people is awaited."

"As you have stated your case in such a way, protocol gives me no choice. I congratulate you," said The PM, as she suddenly reverted back to her old role.

Marie and Mario led The Prime Minister out to the Square. Mario was ready with his speech, which he had specially adapted from the diskette and the study module. Staff and setmates intermingled and the representatives who had been in attendance to back up Marie and Mario returned to the throng. Their presence was to demonstrate that every set was behind the scheme that was about to unfold.

"Fellow citizens," said Mario. "Please applaud our Prime Minister. Through her astute judgment she has brought to attention a very important omission, a lapse on our part, that of updating our training in health and safety matters. Thanks to her we have secured Reversal by Testimony for everyone for this. For this we are truly grateful as until this point we were all Deviants endangering this our fine community. But her methods have done us a disservice. Her departments have turned on the people. For this they must be exposed. We stand united. We will not fall. The Prime Minister is deviant."

At this point there was silence for a few moments before Joanie, now back to her old self, concluded the test by holding Marie's and Mario's hands aloft.

"So, good people, this is how it is done," she said. "This is how you can take it upon yourselves collectively in small groups to prevent opportunists from getting a grip on power. Yes, we still have crime, mostly petty, mostly insignificant, and the system has been found to work well in preventing people from becoming negligent or reckless in what they do, but it can never be taken to excess as long as we have our checks and balances, as you have now learnt through this exercise. Social disorder, drunkenness and the like are well controlled by Big John's system, The Self-policing State, removing the need for mass inspection to police the streets and secure harmony within sets and families.

From time to time you may see our equivalent of a police force, namely the Greencoats, who can be contacted should people need some reassurance or advice on matters that relate to health and safety, the environment or procedures for remedying problems that you may encounter in everyday life. Their role is mostly advisory and their inspections tend to be confined to buildings and equipment. You would call them, for example if you suspected a gas leak or were concerned about the safety of a building or piece of machinery. They also conduct routine maintenance inspections on plant and equipment in accordance with schedules and investigate accidents. So you see the Greencoats are safety inspectors, advisors, solicitors, firemen and the police all rolled into one, designed to be approachable, friendly and competent, giving peace of mind to citizens without having the hard hand of the modern day policeman, who, in other countries, has no choice but to show strength with decreasing compassion as criminals become tougher and crueller in the sharp decline that the 21st century has now brought into the 22nd and that we are trying to reverse.

I will now ask our two Island Greencoats, man and lady, to come forward so that you can all see them. You will note the distinctive lime green almost theatrical uniforms with gold buttons and tapered jackets. Do feel free to talk to them. Now I will leave you all to continue your work, and don't forget, always keep your health and safety training up to date."

Chapter Twelve
All the King's Men

Another month passed.

Spring passed into summer and a new staff member had appeared on The Island, although the setmates did know of him.

He was in his late forties and was broad and stocky, like The Chancellor. His accent was part Irish, part Russian, and his first task with the setmates was to provide tutorials in chess, for he was a Grand Master after all, as well as being a highly accomplished golfer.

Outside the Training Centre, on the lawn, tables had been laid out with chessboards with setmates encouraged to compete during the long summer days as part of a broadening of their all-round skills that was expected for all future employees of the four Kamchatskiy companies.

This Grand Master, who was otherwise known as The Concierge, was always on hand to offer tips, as well as to offer special help to those who tended to lose initially, so that they may learn and come on strong. This way, as with the skating, the overall standard of all of the recruits would rise as they all achieved a common level of ability that could then be subject to incremental improvement. The Concierge therefore was determined that none of the setmates was going to be left behind when it came to developing the thinking and analytical skills that chess demanded.

During these games The Concierge was assisted by another, taller and slimmer gent of about the same age who also spoke with an Irish accent mildly combined with Russian. His accent, however, was distinctly Northern Irish. In contrast to the somewhat casual dress of The Concierge this man had the appearance of a clergyman, and was easily recognisable to the setmates as The Reverend whom they had seen in The Wax House.

Like The Concierge The Reverend was also a Grand Master, but was additionally the head of The Church of The Founder Mary and was responsible for ensuring that The Island faith was promoted as widely as possible throughout the world as a means of securing religious tolerance on a global scale in the name of The Island King.

By July all of the setmates had achieved a moderate proficiency at chess. There was no overall champion and no overall award, but there was a satisfaction from winning matches that The Concierge and The Reverend had purposefully engineered. These two men were exceptionally talented in enabling teams of individuals to achieve high standards in a relatively short time.

By tradition on The Island the chess season lasted two months, culminating in the celebrated contest between The Concierge and The Reverend, on ice, with special guests invited to sit upon the specially designed curls that represented the pieces. On July 10th, however, the game was to take an unexpected twist for the setmates.

That morning The Concierge, under instruction from The Prime Minister, addressed all of the setmates from The Gloriette:

"Now that you have all become acquainted with the wonderful game of chess, and will naturally improve as the season progresses, my colleague and I have decided that we are going to make your experience a little bit different. Between us, over the next six weeks we are going to turn you all not just into accomplished chess players, but also into leaders.

During this time, one by one, you will be called to The Great Dome to receive your instructions for an exercise.

For this, each year, we invite a team of sixth formers from a school in one of our territories to play a game with you. This year our chosen school is The Karaginsky School, which is just outside Opala in southern Kamchatka.

Every setmate will have the opportunity to play the game, but I have to ask you all, in order that the test is fair to everyone, that you do not discuss your game with anyone, including your principals, until every setmate has played the game. As these games are taking place, for everyone not involved, life will go on and, when you are not otherwise engaged, we will continue on the boards outside the Training Centre, weather permitting. Enjoy."

*

The next day began as usual for Gary's set, as did the next and the one after, although they all could not help but notice the comings and goings of the students, a few on horseback performing the role of knights, the others on foot, dressed for the parts as other pieces from the chessboard.

It was not until five days had passed since The Concierge's announcement that Gary's set began to be summoned to The Great Dome. Claudia and Michael were first, then Connie and Gary. As one setmate completed the test the next was called until eventually all 240 setmates would have an opportunity to play the game and see how they fared.

"Gary Loman, step this way," said Joanie as she turned to face him. "Welcome to your game. Do sit down."

Gary duly sat on the chair as Joanie began to explain to him the rules.

"Outside, in The Town, the students are divided into two sides, black and white. Your task for the day is to locate the goose that lays the golden eggs. It is up to you to decide whether you play black or white and in this connection you should not be afraid to question pieces from either side about matters relating to your assignment. It is up to you to decide for yourself as to the reliability of the information that is fed back to you. I can tell you that this is a test of leadership skills and that your ability to supply accurate information and unambiguous requests or commands will be carefully scrutinised for inclusion in my report to the Kamchatskiy Auto executive.

Once you have chosen one side, you can hardly expect favours from the other, and they will be out to take your pieces should your leadership prove to be inept. The players on both sides are, however, at liberty to persuade you to change sides. You should think carefully before accepting. I cannot disclose to you which of the two sides is the stronger, or which may be when subject to your own personal form of leadership. What I do advise is that you do not delay in making your choice for too long, for if you do you will be in danger of being perceived as indecisive, with neither side wishing to be led by you. Difficulty will then be experienced in commanding respect in the ranks. The fine line which separates confidence on the one hand from arrogance on the other, must be negotiated with care. You may now begin your game. The students are all wearing headsets so that messages can be relayed instantly. Good luck."

As Gary left The Great Dome he was immediately confronted by two pawns, one dressed in a black costume, the other in a white.

"What be it for which ye be a searchin'?" demanded the white pawn.

"The goose of course," replied Gary.

"There be plenty of geese about 'ere," the white pawn replied.

"Plenty," repeated the black pawn.

"They be that way," said the two pawns in unison, as they both pointed in opposite directions.

Gary hesitated.

"Follow me," said the white pawn.

"Follow me," said the black pawn.

Gary could not decide from words alone, so he studied the expressions on each of their faces. The students tried to make the decision a little easier by presenting different expressions to the candidate. The white pawn who, by tradition, always answered first, had adopted a sterner appearance. This could suggest that the white team would be the stronger by first impression, Gary thought. On the other hand, black could be more calculating and more cooperative, and therefore a better team to lead.

"Follow me," demanded the white pawn again, this time with a greater sense of urgency in his voice.

Then, before he had had any further opportunity to choose, the white pawn shook his head and walked off. This left Gary with Hobson's choice of black.

A black knight then quickly joined the black pawn.

"He's gone. He must have seen you coming," said the black pawn to the black knight.

"Greetings, o noble one," said the black knight to Gary. "To whom do I owe the honour?"

"'Tis our noble majesty the black King," replied the pawn. "He be lookin' for a certain goose."

"A goose? A goose?" replied the knight. "What manner of goose?"

"A goose that lays golden eggs," answered Gary.

"Then that be a very special goose," said the knight, who turned to the pawn and asked, "Did he tell you that he was looking for a goose that lays golden eggs?"

"No sire, he just said a goose, and I said I knew where there were lots of geese. I know that makes things more difficult, but his information was unclear. Ambiguous."

"It certainly does, my lord," replied the knight to Gary. "Now I must keep a stronger lookout for danger. You go with my friend."

"This way," urged the pawn, as he guided Gary down the lane past The Deputy PM's residence and spoke of his delight that he had chosen black.

"Did I choose you or did you choose me?" asked Gary.

"Well you didn't choose them, did you? Anyway, we will help you find the goose."

"How will you help?" asked Gary.

"In this world you have to fight for what you want and what you believe in. I have a plan"

The pawn pointed to the Triumphal Arch that now lay in front of them.

"It's alright," the pawn continued. "The black rook is guarding the Arch offering safe passage behind enemy lines. The knight will provide protection from the rear. Once we are through the Arch we will make haste to the chapel for there the white Queen is vulnerable as she is alone in prayer, and may be made to confess the whereabouts of that most precious of geese. We must beware though, as her knights are known to lurk in the forest. Also, she is protected on both sides by her two bishops, but remember we have two also. Sadly our own Queen is imprisoned betwixt the two white rooks. Should she take one, she will immediately be taken by the other."

When they reached the Arch the black rook approached Gary and told him that he was in need of reinforcements.

"Fine," said the pawn. "But I have to advise that if we choose here to call upon the services of another piece it could leave us dangerously exposed elsewhere on the battlefield and potentially diminish the resources that are available to us later."

"Without reinforcement though checkmate in the chapel is a real possibility as well as heavy casualties," advised the rook. "So I suggest you be decisive, lest we should be taken by surprise. You may summon the bishop, his pawn or the King's knight from the rear."

"The bishop's pawn," Gary replied, cautiously.

A second pawn now joined the first and the black rook displayed an expression of relief as they entered the wooded area.

"My line of sight will cover you to about halfway between here and the chapel," explained the rook "After that you will have to manage without me, lest I leave my post and expose you to check from behind from one of those white rooks. It's your choice. Of course, I will come with you if you order it."

"What is to be gained in having you come with us?" Gary asked the rook.

"A new line of sight, which may allow me to give early warning of impending danger."

"Not advisable to let a rook leave his post," suggested the King's pawn.

"Let's get halfway, then decide again," Gary commanded.

At the half-way point the rook was lost from view and their path was immediately blocked by a white pawn. Gary's pawn drew his sword and froze for about five seconds, after which he was struck down by his opposition as he waited for Gary, the black King's orders.

"I don't understand," said Gary. "It's our move surely?"

"He was afraid to take action without orders," explained the bishop's pawn. "So much for working in a company where people are used to doing as they are told. I would have done the same. Strong leadership can also be weak leadership if people are afraid to act for the good of the team because they have to wait for orders. We need more authority to act without orders. You do not have to compromise strong leadership for a culture of empowerment. Quite the reverse. In the meantime, I think the opposition will exploit our weakness, or should I say your weakness, your majesty."

"Okay, we will have more empowerment," said Gary

The challenging white pawn was quickly joined by another.

"Check," shouted the second white pawn.

"Take him with the knight," Gary's remaining pawn whispered to Gary.

Gary nodded, and the offending white pawn was taken, but a white knight then arrived on the scene.

"Oh dear. I forgot about him," said Gary's bishop's pawn.

"Now what do we do?" Gary asked the pawn.

"Don't assume that all information that you receive is accurate," replied the pawn. "But you can assume that some information invariably will be accurate, like the fact that we have been protected from the rear by our own knight by virtue of our policy and strategy."

"Policy and strategy?" questioned Gary. "What policy and strategy?"

"A component of business excellence which tends to result in improved accuracy of information when properly communicated," explained the pawn. "Fortunately we are one up on white in this respect, as they have been trained to demand faster responses than us. That's why in the end you were denied the opportunity to lead them, but also why we are able to outscore them on reliability sometimes. It's a trade off."

The remaining white pawn now turned theatrically violent and a makeshift duel ensued between Gary's bishop's pawn and the white knight's pawn. Gary's bishop's pawn fell, but Gary still had his rook's pawn as well as the knight and, though he didn't know it, his own rook for protection. This did not, however, prevent the white knight's pawn from also taking Gary's rook's pawn in the absence of action from the black knight. The black rook's pawn therefore fell, as the two opposing knights stood glaring at each other.

"You can take this pawn yourself you know," shouted the rook's pawn as he fell.

Gary assumed that his rook's pawn was now lost, but wasted no time in taking the challenging white knight's pawn, who dropped to the floor with a stroke of his plastic sword. Now the chapel lay ahead. The white knight retreated as the black rook came forward to threaten the knight and join his apparently slain pawn. Outside the chapel Gary met one of his bishops.

"I have grave news, sire," said the bishop. "I'm afraid one of your knights has been taken by a white rook."

"And they still have the Queen?"

"Yes. It's a shame. You threw that knight away. You really shouldn't have allowed the rook to come forward like that. In doing so the knight lost his only protection."

"But what could I have done?"

"Ordered the rook back to his post," explained the bishop. "He would have stayed there, but he presumed that he was now empowered to come forward, given what you said to my pawn. The rook thought that the knight could defend himself, but against that white rook he didn't stand a chance. Empowerment can be both misused and misdirected. Anyway, it's your move."

"What's the situation in the chapel," Gary asked.

"The white Queen is in prayer. But beware as you enter, as you are liable to be checked on entry by her bishop."

"Can't you take this bishop?" Gary asked his own bishop.

"Sorry, different squares old boy. You should have asked me about that one. Where there is doubt a good leader always makes certain. Your problem, old boy."

"Where's the other bishop?"

"Covering the white Queen's retreat."

"And the other rook?"

"Making sure the coast is clear on the other side of the chapel."

"And the other knight?"

"In reserve for later."

"So what are my options?"

"We could think of freeing our Queen."

"At what cost?"

"I could take one rook out and put white in check. I would be lost of course, but your Queen would then be free and she would certainly get the second white rook. The net result would be you losing a bishop and them losing two rooks. It's a gamble with the odds in your favour. First, however, we have to get you out of check. It's quite easy. You can just step round him."

139

Gary stepped round the opposing bishop as he entered the chapel.

"Now I am sorry to advise that the black Queen has been taken," said Gary's bishop. "I would at least take the opposing bishop as a consolation."

"I thought you said we could free her?"

"I did. But I forgot that that white bishop had a clear run at her. You were in check, though. You had get out."

The way to the altar was now clear and before him the white Queen deep in prayer.

"I wouldn't let the white Queen see you or you could be in check," said the bishop. Oh, and by the way, look out for her other bishop. I'll be off now."

The bishop disappeared, leaving Gary with just a pawn for company.

"Not very reliable that bishop," said the pawn.

"I thought the bishop was on our side," said Gary.

"He is, but he's not all that sure that you're that strong a leader. He now thinks that he can simply come and go as he pleases."

"Can't we get him back?"

"He's gone back behind our rook for safety. But I wouldn't worry about him."

"Why?"

"Well, perhaps our rook wasn't so silly after all."

"What do you mean?"

"Well, his pawn was merely wounded in that skirmish earlier on. He wasn't taken."

"I thought he was taken."

"Things are not always as they seem. It can pay a leader to make sure, and sometimes the good leader must rely on others. The rook didn't return to his post because he knew he could protect his pawn all the way. And now, if the pawn makes it to the chapel bell he will have reached the end of the board, and we will have a new Queen, right here in the chapel. The white Queen will have to take her. Then our rook can take the white Queen, wipe her clean off. He'll spare her of course, so long as she directs us to the golden goose, which gives us a chance of checkmate."

The bell sounded and the black Queen duly entered, guarded by her rook. The white Queen then rose from her deliberations and took her but, at the black rook's mercy, she was forced to confess the whereabouts of the golden goose.

"It's at the centre of the corn maze, protected by the King."

"I think you can trust our rook better than the bishop to do a good job," whispered Gary's pawn. "You were right to empower him and now he has rewarded you with a chance to win."

"How do we know that the white Queen is being truthful with him?" Gary asked.

"Because he can hold her until we have verified it. If she lies she knows that she will be taken by your empowered rook."

"How do we reach the maze?"

"Up the coast road, where we will have our second rook's protection, plus the protection of that old bishop, for what it's worth."

As they set out on the coast road they were quickly ambushed by three white pawns.

"It's that damned bishop," said Gary's pawn. "He has given us away. Someone needs to be firm with him and give him a direct order. He's the sort of person who will follow it to the letter, but if left to his own devices he will let you down."

"Alright," said Gary. "Tell him to go out and take the white rook."

"Now I think you'll find him quite reliable," said the pawn. "Sometimes you have to tailor your leadership style to fit the personality of the employee. The empowerment that the good leader gives to one employee may be entirely inappropriate for another."

The second black rook disarmed the three marauding pawns and joined Gary and his pawn on the journey up the coast past the harbour. Soon they were in the maze. Inside they were joined by the one remaining black knight and his pawn.

"Beware the King be guarded by his knight," warned Gary's knight's pawn, as he led them toward the centre of the maze. "Lucky I have already sussed the way to the middle."

At the centre the white King stood in the shape of The Concierge. Next to him was the large wooden goose that candidates were instructed to locate. The white knight stood beside the King accompanied by two pawns. It was now up to Gary to use his skill and judgment at directing his team, to end the game by gaining access to the goose.

White, typically, was quick to act and the white knight wasted no time in taking the black knight and subsequently threatening Gary.

"Check," said the white knight.

"That means that you have to concede a move," whispered his bishop's pawn.

The white knight then removed this pawn and called check again, forcing him to concede another move. Gary now had to think because he could not afford to simply allow this knight to keep placing him in check. Eventually he would run out of pieces. Furthermore, the white knight was driving him further from his pieces.

"You can summon one more piece to join us," his rook advised. "But you will have to choose quickly. You can bring the bishop, but, as you know, he can be unreliable and may not arrive in time, or you can call your other rook, who is reliable, but will have to sacrifice his chance to take the white Queen. If you choose him she will be in hot pursuit to the maze, so you must be confident that you can get checkmate before she arrives. Good luck."

"It's a trade off between speed and reliability," whispered Gary's other pawn. "If you were playing as white I would have gone for speed, but as our strength is reliability I would say that the rook was trustworthy and can be relied upon to be here promptly and checkmate the King. In the meantime I suggest you step aside from that pesky knight."

Gary duly moved to face his pawn.

"If I summon the bishop, he will come immediately, won't he?"

"He will, but don't expect him to act on his own initiative when it comes to checkmating the King."

The white knight then took that pawn but there was no call of check so the move could be made.

"I call the rook," ordered Gary.

The rook arrived by Kammie.

"You called, sire."

"Yes. I thought I could rely on you to checkmate the white King."

"Sure, mate in two moves," said the chapel rook.

"Check," the white knight shouted again.

"As I was saying, it's mate in two moves as long as you sacrifice me to get out of check. Think carefully, but don't dither as the white Queen is already in the maze. You will have to move one more square from me I'm afraid."

The white knight took the black rook, but Gary trusted the taken rook's words. Now he had to think of two moves that he could make to end the game. Without his second rook he deduced that he would need to have a bishop and a rook for checkmate to be possible.

"You may tell me your move," said the white knight.

"Call the bishop," ordered Gary.

The bishop arrived exactly as ordered and the white knight withdrew to his King's side. Now Gary could see how mate was possible.

"What colour is your square?" Gary asked the bishop.

"White, old boy"

"And the white King?"

"Black, and his goose."

"Can our last rook take the knight?"

"Yes."

"Can you take the knight?"

"Yes."

"Then who should take the knight?"

"I should," said the bishop.

"No, I should," said the rook.

"You will have to choose one or other of us and look sharp about it," advised the bishop.

It was now a question of trust. Both pieces expressed the desire to be the one that took the knight, but only one could. Gary chose the rook.

"Wrong, I'm afraid," called the white Queen from behind him, as she removed his rook from the board. "And now it is checkmate to us."

"How do you explain that," Gary asked The Queen.

The Concierge then advanced to Gary and explained all.

"Your trustworthy rook," he said. "Was right in telling you that it was mate in two moves, and it could have gone your way if you had disregarded your bishop's advice to choose one or other piece to take my knight, or at least questioned it, as you knew his information was suspect. The pawn could have taken my knight, then I would have had to move and it would have then been checkmate to you if you had then ordered the bishop to act. He betrayed you though because he did not like your air of authority toward him.

Knowing how to read the character of people is no easy matter and it takes time. You may have lost the game, but you, like the others, have won by the knowledge that you have gained. Leaders are made, not born, and in our society everyone must know how to lead. Children act out this game with their teachers at school. The teachers always win of course, because they can manipulate the outcome of the game. I was in communication with your pieces and mine throughout the game, so, of course I was able to control it so that you learnt exactly what I wanted you to learn.

The good leader is the one who never allows his or her

subconscious arrogance to get the better of them, and whose mind is always focused on possibilities, with the ability to weigh up and devise a range of possible outcomes. All leaders will be influenced by track record. Your bishop was highly efficient in carrying out orders, but he was evasive and economical with the truth. There are people like this in real life. In your old world these people could easily be alienated. In ours they are not. If they are the type that need to be handed orders for everything then this is accepted, but it is not done with arrogance or the threat of discipline.

I can tell you that Connie played a very different game, having chosen white quickly enough to be accepted by them. Her problem was the question of deciding which rules one is allowed to break and which rules one is not. This too is never an easy question, and is something that has to be learnt. Favouritism for one side at the expense of another cannot be allowed to stand, and it creeps in once one starts to break or bend rules, or allows results to stand that have been achieved by such bending or breaking. Claims of unfairness then abound and a leader is quickly discredited. Yet, at the same time, there can sometimes be very good reasons for not conforming to a specific rule or set of rules. Each time one must consider who wins and who loses, and what the possible consequences will be every time a rule is bent or broken. Often a system has to be fault tolerant when it comes to rules, as ours is. Nitpicking is no better than favouritism and can also lead to a leader being discredited.

You will receive your feedback reports from The PM in due course. Meanwhile, keep up the good chess because you're doing just fine."

*

By the end of August all of the 240 setmates had played the real-life chess game. There was then just one event left to bring the chess season to a close, and that was the annual duel of the supremes that took place between The Concierge and The Reverend on ice.

Thirty-two of the sixth formers that had played the game with the setmates were then selected to take their places on the giant curls that were in place on the rink, now resurfaced with curling ice, upon which dark and light squares had been superimposed with the aid of the lighting system. The barrier that surrounded the ice during skating sessions had gone and the floor that surrounded the perimeter of the ice had been partially removed so as to create a ditch into which the curls would be pushed by one of two boys from the school, or else lifted and placed by a crane that the rink engineer had, under supervision, permitted one lucky girl to operate for the knights both to move and be taken.

At the commencement of the game The Concierge and Reverend faced each other at either end of the rink mounted on high chairs. Meanwhile, in the royal enclosure, Queen Katie sat along with Joanie, her Chancellor, The Deputy and the other royals.

The rink was full to capacity as the entire population of The Island, consisting of 1,200 inhabitants and 240 staff took their seats to watch this annual event. When everyone was seated The Queen rose.

"I hereby declare this year's contest open," she said. "Let battle commence and may the best man win."

Chess games are rarely quick and this one was no exception, although a maximum time limit of four hours had been set such that if not completed within this time the game would be declared a draw. This ensured that the game, having started at 6 p.m. would at least be over by 10 p.m. As it happened this game was over by 9.30 with The Reverend, playing as black, victorious, following a closely fought contest. The spectators were kept entertained throughout as both players proved their ability to take calculated risks and both, although of virtually matching standard, refused to accept the possibility of the draw.

At the conclusion of the game the taken pieces were pushed along the ice covered 'ditch' to the far corner of the rink where a wooden partition lifted allowing them to be pushed, minus the students, into their closet ready for the next year. Then, under the control of Commander, the side of the ditch nearest the ice rose vertically to form the ice rink barrier once more, whilst the other side folded horizontally to reform the perimeter floor. The two Grand Masters meanwhile dismounted, met halfway along the side of the rink that housed the royal box, then shook hands before climbing the steps up to it.

The Queen held in her hand the twelve-inch high glass trophy, shaped in the form of a King from a standard chessboard, and presented it to The Reverend.

"It gives me great pleasure to present the annual 'Duel of the Supremes' trophy to our one and only Donald McIlroy," she declared as she handed him the trophy. "Now it is eight victories each in our annual joust. But we must not forget our runner-up, also one of the world's finest players, our very own Master of Ceremonies, our Concierge Mr. Patrick O'Rourke."

The audience applauded again as The Queen reached for the six-inch high glass pawn that was the runner-up trophy. The Reverend then said a few words:

"As this year's champion I thank you all, but I especially thank my good friend Patrick for making this such a wonderful event each year. Like other things chess takes two to make a game. I also thank the ice rink staff and our resident engineer Alexis Childas for doing a great job with the ice, the lighting and the overhead equipment. Also, last but not least the sixth formers of The Karaginsky School for doing such a marvellous job helping to train our new recruits. So, for now, it's goodnight from me and it's goodnight from him."

So the game was over for another year, but, as the setmates were soon to discover, there was far more to these two men than just chess.

Chapter Thirteen
Sabfelt

The first of September.

Joanie was up bright and early, the lengthy chess assignments finally completed. The Chancellor stood beside her as she placed the last of her completed feedback reports onto the pile beside her.

"Now," she said. "I am going to ask you to send these forms out to each setmate, but first I need you to fetch me those new identity cards and place the correct group of cards in each pack along with the details of their next assignment. You will find the cards and the assignment sheets in the cupboard marked C over in the corner."

"Yes Ma'am," replied The Chancellor.

"And whilst you are doing that I will see about letting them loose on the supermarket. Use of the cards at the checkout will greatly simplify their shopping task, reducing the need for all of those Requisition Orders. They should all be fully conversant with our system by now, with concepts like deviance quite fully understood. You will find the instruction sheets in the cupboard marked D. If you could place one instruction sheet in each twelve pack I would be much obliged. I'm sure they won't have any difficulty now in adapting to standard shopping for each of the basic classes of goods."

"I'm sure they will each take only as much as they know they will need," said The Chancellor. "As soon as they realise that all they need do is take as much as they would need for ordinary consumption that is what they will do."

"Good. Then I will let them see their new store today on a set-by-set basis. Then they can prepare to take a trip to Sabfelt. It shouldn't take quite as long to get through as it did with the chess, as there are only twenty games of this rather than 240, but it will still take a couple of weeks I'm sure. I'll make sure The Concierge and Reverend have been fully briefed as to their timings, along with those of the sixth formers."

An hour later during breakfast the post arrived for Gary's set.

"The feedback reports have arrived," said Anne

"Let's have a look," said Carl.

Carl scrutinised the reports.

"Looks like we are all ok on leadership," he said. "Though it's interesting how all of those games turned out so differently. I never knew that leadership had so many different aspects to it. There's certainly quite a lot to remember."

"There looks to be a few other things in the pack," said Anne.

"What?" asked Connie.

"Well, it looks as if we have all got these ID cards with our number on and we can use them to shop in the supermarket which will be open from tomorrow morning. The store manager will call us when he is ready for us to start shopping there."

"Hooray," said Yvonne. "I wondered when that place was finally going to open down by The House of Cards."

"Looks like The PM has finally come round to trusting us," Connie remarked.

"Instruction sheets seem simple enough," said Anne. "Excessive removal of items may be subject to a Declaration of Deviance. But who would?".

"I suppose she had to be sure that we all know what a Declaration of Deviance is and what a Deviant Act is," suggested Terry.

"At least now we know that these things are not something to be afraid of," added Elena. "A person would have to be really feckless to fall foul of such a set of rules."

"Great. So now we can go and do our own shopping without everything having to be approved by the authorities first," said Graca.

"There's more," continued Anne. "On Friday morning we have to report to the train station at eleven. Another special task it looks like, and like the last one sets are not allowed to discuss it until all sets have had a chance to complete it. Special uniforms will be provided."

"Anything else?" asked Connie.

"It doesn't seem so," replied Anne.

"I'd love to know who devised these tests," said Carl.

"I guess they have been adapted and handed down ever since the days of The Founders," said Connie. "Part of the history of the place. At least we can say when we get to Kamchatka that we have been to the place where it all started. I have noticed these games are normally taught to children growing up under Non-Capitalist Economics. We, on the other hand, have to completely readjust our thinking patterns. Fortunately we are all the sort of people who are willing and able, and The Island authorities know it."

"I'm really looking forward to Kamchatka," said Gary. "Though I know we will all miss this place. It's just so enchanting in every respect, and to think that so few people from the capitalist world have visited it in all these seventy years."

"I think it's mainly only VIPs and the like," added Michael. "Government House looks as if it has been frequented by a few top politicians and business people for trade deals and so on for some time. According to yesterday's *Island Times* a combined Argentine and Chilean delegation are expected to sign a deal on Tierra del Fuego very soon."

"I know. The Island near enough owns it outright now," said Connie. "I can't see it being more than a couple of months till the handover."

"The power of this place is unbelievable," remarked Yvonne. "Practically every country in the world is involved with it in some way, and yet The Island hides itself neatly away, carefully concealing itself from public knowledge. The media never speaks of it. In Australia not a word is spoken of it, and, apart from myself, hardly anyone seems to be aware of what is going to happen there."

"And how do you know?" asked Connie.

"Because Aub told me. You know, the guy who gave me the prized invitation to come here."

"Who exactly is this Aub?" asked Connie.

"A landowner with strong connections to the Australian armed forces. His parents made a small fortune buying up and managing ex-servicemens' clubs in Australia. He then went into politics and rose quickly to the post of Defence Minister, but he voiced his disappointment at how the nation's political strategy toward defence is progressing. He thinks that all of Australia's politicians are behind the times and lacking in vision. He sees The Island as a much more viable future for both Australia and the world, run by people like us who have no desire to compete for power, just willing to work hard to reform bad systems. Unfortunately the people around him are totally blinkered."

"And to think it all started with just a handful of people," remarked Jose,

"Incredible."

*

On Friday morning the costumes arrived.

"These are Greencoat costumes," said Lars. "complete with stripes".

"The instructions state that we are to change into them and await the twelve-seater Kammie to take us to the station," Anne stated.

"Nothing more about the assignment?" asked Graca.

"It says that we have to go to Sabfelt, which it points out is an anagram of Belfast, and maintain order there as if we were acting as Greencoats. The police, you could say. That's it."

Joanie watched the set as they boarded the train.

"Well, at least the weather is set fair," she remarked to The Chancellor. "Not like the washout we had last year. Let's get Sabfelt on the screen."

Sabfelt station was a short walk from the Gun Inn, to which the set was drawn by music, in this case a piano version of 'Orange Coloured Sky'. An artificial population, played by the sixth formers of The Karaginsky School, went about their daily business in the hamlet that was traditionally home to The Island's engineers, except for these two weeks when they were on holiday and it was transformed into theatre.

As soon as the set entered the hamlet they were struck by one single unmistakeable fact, namely that everyone was wearing orange. They gazed awhile at the scene before it was suddenly interrupted by the dragging of a girl dressed in green from the saloon to a makeshift jailhouse. Then, they entered the inn. Surely there were some questions to be answered there.

Inside, the set recognised a few familiar faces, most noticeably that of The Reverend. He, like the others, was dressed entirely in orange, with an orange shirt, jacket, tie and trousers. He did, however, preserve his priest-like image.

"First one's on the house," shouted the barman, as he poured each one of them a glass of orange juice.

"Don't we get a choice of drink?" asked Connie.

"Sure, as long as it's orange," the barman laughed.

The crowd laughed. Then The Reverend turned to the set.

"I think you should change those uniforms," he ordered. "They don't go down too well in these parts."

"Yeah, come on, get those uniforms off," yelled another.

"We can't. We're Greencoats," replied Michael.

"I don't care. Here we have Orangecoats," The Reverend ordered. "Here you do as I say. You become one of us or else."

"Suppose we do as you say. What would happen?" asked Jose.

"Then you'll be part of our good honest police force, serving the majority for the majority."

"And if we refuse?" said Connie.

"You can't refuse," said The Reverend. "You just can't."

"The woman who was dragged to the jail. Did she refuse?" questioned Claudia.

"What do you think?" laughed The Reverend. "Now you just surrender to us and you'll be just fine. We'll look after you. We're a civilised and democratic society. We don't believe in the gun and the bomb."

"So why is he wearing a gun?" Connie asked, noticing that one of them was wearing one.

"Because the greens insist on carrying guns," The Reverend explained. "And, as they won't accept democracy, we have to defend ourselves."

"Yeah, that's right," added the man with the gun. "Full of hate those greens. And if you insist on staying green we will have to turn our guns against you."

The set conferred, then Anne, on behalf of all of them, asked if they might speak to the woman in the jail so that they might hear her version of events in Sabfelt.

"Of course," replied The Reverend. "She's your prisoner. You're the police."

"They are wicked people," explained the girl, whom Connie recognised from her chess game.

"What is your crime?" asked Connie, through the bars of the cell in which she had been placed.

"Not changing my clothes," she said. "We won't surrender to them nor they to us, so there is but one option open to us. You, unfortunately, are in a no-win position. As it stands it is your duty to police a minority in the majority's

154

state. But things are repeatedly rigged against us. That is our grievance, and it is your job to decide whether you want to betray your own colour and join those heavy-handed rulers, or stay with us and take up arms, or find some third solution, if you can that is."

The set conferred.

"Suppose we keep our colour but don't take up arms?" asked Anne.

"Then we will deem you to be serving the orange regime," replied the girl.

"I think our visitors should be placed in protective custody, don't you?" said The Reverend to one of his sidekicks.

The orange guards were duly ushered in and encircled the set before presently herding them into an adjacent cell.

"Let me know when you're willing to change that uniform of yours," laughed The Reverend.

"Don't listen to them," urged the girl. "Once a green always a green. Keep to your principles. Be Greencoats, not turncoats."

"Go on. Work for us and be free," The Reverend tried to persuade them. "Lots of fringe benefits you know, once you're confirmed into the orange force."

The set conferred again.

"We've decided," said Anne. "We're staying as Greencoats."

"So be it," said The Reverend, leading his men outside.

This decision left the set imprisoned alongside the girl.

"So you have decided to remain one of the imprisoned minority," she said. "Even though you have a system that is biased against you in so many different ways. But don't worry. Together we can change the system."

A few moments later a tinkling noise came from the small opening in the makeshift cell wall. As Lars peered out he saw a hooded man dressed in green throw a set of keys into the cell. Free to unlock themselves the set first freed themselves and then the girl. Outside the man in green stood before them and removed his hood revealing himself as none other than The Concierge. Then he mounted an old grey mare, his gun clearly visible around his waist. Behind him six further hooded men stood, each dressed in green and each holding a rifle aloft ready to fire into the air over a makeshift coffin draped in a green cloth mounted on a cart.

"To the martyr," shouted The Concierge, as they each fired two shots upward. "Now to avenge the martyr's death."

The six men then hauled the cart away before returning a few minutes later with another cart, which this time was loaded with imitation rifles, grenades and other armaments including handguns and explosive devices.

"Now we must fight," said the girl. "We must fight the orange regime for it is the source of our misfortune The politicians who attempted to solve a political divide by drawing a line on a map are now long gone, but still the divide remains. Negotiations have failed for the orange regime justifies itself forever through the excuse of majority rule. They call it democracy. We call it tyranny. Go on. Get your guns. Throw those stripes away and join us in the struggle to expel the conquistadors."

The set conferred again.

"The orange side also has guns. We know that already," whispered Claudia.

"And we know that they are as determined to defend their principles as the greens are theirs," Jose added.

"I think we should call both sides together," suggested Terry.

"Negotiations?" said Yvonne.

"Yes," said Terry.

"Now what are you going to do?" The Concierge asked.

"Call both sides together to negotiate," replied Anne on behalf of the set.

"There is another problem with the orange regime,"

explained the girl. "And that is that they always need a few of our colour to defend their interests against our people. As long as a few of us are coaxed into joining their force they can never say that we are not represented in their orange force. I dare say that if you decide to negotiate they may allow you to keep your green uniforms provided that you agree to serve them. I warn you to tread carefully down the well-worn path of negotiations."

"But if we don't negotiate what do we do?" questioned Lars.

"My boyfriend was innocent," continued the girl. "But the orange regime took his life simply because one of our people took one of theirs, and so it goes on. My boyfriend, however, was special because he had one thing that the opposition desperately wanted, but knew that they could never have. This, of course, made him a target."

"What did he have?" asked Connie.

"The Golden Harp," said the girl. "It's our heart and soul. It's something that's kind and gentle and carefree, but sadly at odds with the orange ideal of the glorification and celebration of ancient conquest. Wars are not won they are merely ended by one side or the other. Throughout our lives we have sought to keep the Golden Harp and throughout theirs they have tried to take it away. They may march and beat their drums, all to intimidate and preserve their pride at the expense of ours, but our Golden Harp is immortal, because it is spiritual not temporal. I advise that in the course of your negotiations you resist the temptation to sign up to their demands. Now I must go. They must not see me."

The orange delegation, led by The Reverend, duly arrived as all of the greens retreated, except for The Concierge.

"So you have decided to talk," said The Reverend. "Surely though you must know that there will be a price to pay for any kind of agreement?"

"I know. The green lady told us," said Anne.

"So, do you accept?"

The set huddled again to confer.

"If it is to avert war, how can we avoid having to pay at least some price?" whispered Michael.

"I don't see that we can," said Gary.

"But we also have the right to demand something from them in return," suggested Lars.

"Such as?" asked Connie.

"An agreement to disarm maybe," Lars suggested.

The set nodded and Anne spoke.

"We accept provided that you agree to start decommissioning your weapons."

"Good. Then you can start policing the streets of Sabfelt with our consent as of now," said The Reverend. "But remember this. We will only decommission beyond a token gesture so long as we see evidence that the greens are doing likewise."

"Well as long as nobody spies on us then perhaps we might," added The Concierge. "I tell you what. We'll offer you a cease-fire. That will allow time for you and your good officers to agree to end your attempts to rob us of our pride by marching only on your own turf and not on ours."

The Concierge left with the Greencoats now having no alternative but to join forces with the orange guards, who outnumbered them by a factor of five. They would now receive their orders from The Reverend.

"Here, take these," urged The Reverend, offering them a set of handguns.

"No thanks," said Connie. "We agreed to be an unarmed police force in our own colours."

"Okay, but you'll find it hard without a gun," The Reverend warned.

The Greencoats patrolled their allotted territory, which consisted of a collection of stables and cowsheds with a dunny behind. After about two minutes two unarmed hooded greens approached them and removed their hoods.

"Hey, brothers," said one young gent. "I see you are trying

to police Sabfelt. You stood up to The Reverend. That is to be applauded. We also know we could not achieve peace by ourselves. So, though we are but two in number we are willing to become your allies."

It was not long, however, before three orange representatives were also on the scene.

"And what do you think you are doing?" one of them asked. "This is a very serious breach of confidentiality."

The two greens replaced their hoods and fled.

"Now what are you going to do?" laughed the second orange gent.

Moments later the two hooded greens returned, this time wearing guns.

"If I were you I would get yourselves armed," suggested the third orange officer.

"And if I were you I would discard those Greencoat stripes and then get armed," advised the second green. "You may not need to use the guns mind."

The set conferred.

"By the sounds of this we have no option but to accept the offer of guns either way," Claudia whispered.

"We could always call for another negotiation," suggested Gary.

"But what would we ask for?" said Graca. "Another ceasefire?"

"Neither side is going to back down," said Michael softly. "It's obvious. We are going to have to accept the arms."

"But with which side?" questioned Connie.

"I think orange, because the greens are just outlaws when all said and done," whispered Jose.

"But I think we should just suggest it first," Elena suggested. "Give them a chance to change their minds."

"Are we all agreed?" said Anne.

They nodded. Anne then turned to face The Reverend.

"We have decided," she said. "We will arm ourselves with orange, but we take the arms with reluctance."

With this outcome the greens retreated as reluctantly the set took the guns that orange offered them and strapped them to their waists.

"Now we have a result," said The Reverend. "Joanie now knows that there is at least one set of circumstances in which you as a set would be willing to take up arms. Now we must examine the consequences."

The Reverend led the set to the undertakers opposite The Gun Inn from which a coffin was wheeled out mounted upon a gun carriage. This time, however, there was no flag. Then, all of the characters disappeared. For a moment there was silence. Then, without warning, there was a loud bang, which startled the setmates, giving all the appearance that the mounted coffin had exploded. Smoke surrounded it. Then it cleared and the lid creaked open. A few seconds later The Concierge rose up from within and spoke to them.

"Both sides suffer as a result of this so-called democracy," he asserted. "For a majority that imposes itself upon a minority for whatever reason will invariably incur that minority's wrath and so induce conditions of strife. Equally, those who live by the bomb and the bullet can one day expect to die from them. Thankfully my home nation of Ireland is now at peace, but the problem is still not fully resolved. This is now the end of your assignment, but I will address you all at The Opera House when all of the other sets have had a chance to play the game. There I will tell you a little bit more about how world peace can be created and sustained, even though every individual and set has some definite point at which they will take up arms. Your train now awaits."

*

Twelve days later The Prime Minister assembled all of the sets inside The Opera House in Aldebaran where Kathleen's Golden Harp, which The Island used as its symbol of peace and harmony, stood elevated in the centre of the stage. The girl from the jailhouse gently played as the setmates entered. A few minutes after they were all assembled she stopped playing, allowing The Concierge to take his place at the lectern below. His short address then followed.

"A big round of applause for Katarina," he said, beckoning her down from her instrument. "As top musician at Karaginsky she has the honour of playing this wonderful instrument that once belonged to Kathleen, The Island Queen that never was. It's of fourteen-carat gold you know, so it's not surprising we want to guard it well, but it is played, and a more beautiful sound you will never hear. It's as beautiful as the girl that plays it. Thank you very much Katarina."

Katarina bowed to the audience.

"Now to my short talk for tonight," he continued. "You will be pleased to know that afterwards there is wine and a lovely buffet full of vegetarian goodies supplied by our very own vegetarian delicatessen here in Aldebaran. I won't keep you from that for too long, but what I have to say to you tonight is, I feel, quite important and does have a serious side.

Over the last couple of weeks you have all had an opportunity to act out a game that is based on the thankfully now historic Irish troubles. At the turn of the century Donald and I renamed the original hamlet of Kai Endo Sabfelt so as to reflect the Irish slant that we have given to the test and the fact that it is where Duncan and I reside when we are not out in the world conducting our peace campaigns. Like the other tests it has an educational purpose, in this case to teach the principles for world peace along the lines proposed by our Founder David Stoneman.

During the course of your assignments Duncan and I, with the help of all of our kind volunteers, sought to demonstrate to you that there is some point for every man, woman and child, no matter who, at which they will agree to take up arms. It may be by persuasion, compulsion, peer pressure, or some other reason, but it will happen. We also sought to teach you that a terrorist of any colour cannot love peace, for peace and terrorism are mutually opposing. With these concepts understood, I will now explain to you Stoneman's solution, which has been progressively refined and applied across the world, responsibility for the implementation of which now rests with Duncan and myself.

As you know, my family is originally from Ireland and back in the twentieth century, like many Irish families, my ancestors suffered in the days of the troubles. I was somewhat more fortunate in being born here of Irish parentage. In 2070 my father left The Island for, of all places, Groznyy in the Russian Republic of Chechnya. He did this in the knowledge and belief that something really great and exciting was about to happen there, and it was.

Most of you, even before you came here, know Groznyy as that dream city down in the Caucasus where that lovely Russian wine comes from and classy people zoom off to enjoy something different. I am proud to tell you though that if it hadn't been for The Island and a handful of entrepreneurs, of which my parents were members, as well as Donald, grandson of our Founder Anton, it may never have been so. I will show you some pictures of Groznyy before the transformation, which will astound you. It was wartorn and shattered, and may well have remained so if The Island had not intervened to restore peace.

The game which you all played is, in fact, a child's game in Chechnya. The children play it to learn about and remember the sacrifices that their forefathers made. In the twenty-minute film which follows my talk you will be guided through each of the stages of the transformation from the initial talks with the Russian government and the dissident Chechen leaders, through the investment and construction of the new Groznyy, and on into the boom years of wine, women and song. We will invite you to take a tram ride through the streets of prosperous suburbs like Donegal and Tralee, enjoy a scene from Riverdance on

Ice, and see Chechen children riding on the little narrow gauge steam railways that run at the bottom of back gardens collecting them as they make their merry way to school.

The effort and investment that The Island put into the project has been well rewarded, not least because it enabled a struggling Russian regime that had been very cooperative with us in Kamchatka, to regain its popularity by ending the problems in Chechnya and neighbouring South Ossetia, where our work continues to be ongoing. Having allowed them to take most of the credit for the achievement and to stay in office as a result, they have helped us ever since, and it has to be said that seeing the smiles on those children's faces, as well as those of the elders, Russians and Chechens both, enjoying life playing chess in quaint old beer gardens, Guinness in hand, is extremely satisfying, knowing that it is something on the world stage that we created. The honour is ours and we know that it can never be taken from us. That is The Golden Harp proper, the way Kathleen would have wished it.

Many cultures are represented in Chechnya today, as it is seen as one of the more attractive parts of the world to visit, work in and study in. Groznyy is very cosmopolitan, unlike the city of old, and as you will see in the film the people are happy. Joy in work and pride in a job well done are the norm not the exception. It is still capitalist, but that does not matter so much when we have a population that is basically content, a gun free zone, and a virtual absence of serious crime. So, how was this miracle achieved?

For a good part of the last century poor, devastated, traumatised Chechnya was beset with problems. The Island needed the help of the Russian regime. The Russian regime was desperate to solve the problems that it had in the region. Nobody at the time had the means to solve it, or so it seemed.

Ken's lost wife Kathleen adored harp music and contrasted especially the music of the fabulous instrument that we have just heard with the discords of guns and bombs. She in particular wanted to teach children that individuals and groups, once induced to take up arms, invariably concede to enter a zero-sum game, that is to say a game in which there can be only losers and where harmony is never accomplished.

Often the zero-sum game results from the outcome of an election which then places one group of citizens in a minority with their chances of succeeding in life automatically prejudiced by the majority. There is then a discord as what is perceived as democracy by one group is seen as being tyranny by another.

The Island has always opposed electoral systems which give rise to such discords. As a result as part of our foreign policy we ask all businesses with whom we trade to sign a declaration to the effect that they will join us in our efforts to end minority repression around the globe. This had a particularly profound effect in Chechnya and South Ossetia when The Island began to invest there introducing both wealth and a culture that was sufficiently neutral as to be accepted readily by both the majority Chechens and Georgians, and the minority Russians, all of whom wanted an end to conflict.

Supporters of The Island in Ireland were invited by my father to become settlers in Chechnya and to begin work to rebuild the shattered land. The Island would be behind them, as would Moscow, as negotiations between the Russians and Chechen rebels were on the rocks. Moscow offered us a free hand to solve the problem, whilst allowing the Russian government to take the credit so that they would perform well rather than badly at the polls. The Kremlin promised not even to mention The Island, whilst the Chechens simply saw us as a team of outside volunteers from Ireland who were willing to invest in their people in order to turn the place around.

Stoneman's theory introduces the concept of a flashpoint, that is to say a point at which a critical number of people will take up arms and use them aggressively. To illustrate, Northern Ireland had in the 1970s a lower flashpoint than the Irish Republic. The flashpoint is, however, not the same as the point at which arms are simply taken and left in a mothballed state. Arms may exist, but so long as they are never used the flashpoint will not be reached. Such a system may be said to be stable and, as you will have learnt from Deming, there is no need to tamper with a stable system.

In Chechnya our priority was first to raise the flashpoint and then to decommission the arms, strictly in that order, with the help of people from a place where the flashpoint had already been successfully raised, Northern Ireland.

As our power in the world grows, it is anticipated that we will acquire a greater ability to raise flashpoints. Neither the soldier nor the terrorist has a place in a civilised society. The soldier, by his presence, will be forever a legitimate target for the terrorist, who is in turn an outlaw. Similarly the lawman who wears the minority's colours in the majority's force contributes to a lowering of the flashpoint by virtue of providing a service to that which is being opposed. Where orange officers, in an orange force, police orange streets there can still be harmony, but where green or orange officers, in an orange force, police green streets the flashpoint will go down and there will be a discord. Green streets cannot be expected to respect orange law. They need green law and green law enforcers.

In Chechnya in the seventies we assumed that the zero-sum game that existed was the consequence of the prevailing system of majority rule in a minority state, just as it had been in twentieth-century Ulster. We assumed the existence of a sizeable prejudiced minority, that arms were freely available, and that the flashpoint had been breached. We then applied Deming's theory which told us that where there was disharmony the root cause was likely to be the system rather than the people and, therefore, we had to all work together to improve the system. This being the case, the system upon which we had to work was the nature of government from Moscow, and the question that we had to ask was 'did we really have to have red laws policed by red officers on sky blue pink streets?' The answer clearly was no.

Today, uniquely in the capitalist world, Chechnya is policed by the Greencoats. Everyone has accepted a modified form of Irish law and a modified form of The Island faith, which demands tolerance from all sides. Guns were banned and a full programme of cooperation instituted, with vastly increased rates of pay for all those who participated. Unemployment was reduced to zero. Then, we gradually merged the Irish law with a combination of different laws in different areas. Russian law was retained in some areas, for example, but importantly people were given the freedom to choose the laws which they wanted at community level. So we have, in effect, different laws for different people. Simple, isn't it? Worth working for, isn't it?

Ladies and gentlemen, I commend to you The Golden Harp, a careful blend of old and new, a tolerable gap between rich and poor, and no gap eventually with Non-Capitalist Economics. Pride in one's culture, joy in work and harmony when being played. It's a commitment to excellence that will endure forever.

Enjoy the film and the buffet."

Chapter Fourteen
Searching for Sawicki

Three days later.

Gary and the others had arrived at the ice rink for their training. This time, however, the training had a new element. With her now familiar whistle Jobine summoned them to the centre of the rink.

"Today," she said, "I am going to introduce you to something new".

As she spoke a harness dropped as if by magic from above and landed in her hands.

"It's known as flying, and what you will all need to be able to do before you leave here is to be able to perfect a routine that involves not just skating but elevation also. The Kamchatskiy trainers require me to train you in this, although your particular routine for Carnival will not feature the harness. Had you been on course for a place with Kamchatskiy Aerospace or Kamchatskiy Maritime then it would.

First of all you need to become accustomed to strapping yourselves into it, and then taking small steps from the ice so as to become airborne. So I will ask each of you in turn to strap yourselves in and begin to experience the sensation."

Jobine then demonstrated to the set how to attach the straps around their waists and then to attempt a small bunny hop to provide sufficient spring to enable the skater to part from the ice so as to reach a height of about three feet before completing a simple turn in the air and returning with a neat touchdown.

"The touchdown is very important," stressed Jobine. "The landing should be soft and with a straight free leg extension. You will need to get used to this for a while before we start to increase the height and the complexity of moves."

Claudia was the first to try. Jobine helped her to adjust the straps so that they were tight and offered minimal discomfort. Then she took three small steps on her toe-picks using the first two to gain speed before using the third to acquire height. Then the harness took over, providing her with the necessary assistance to complete a single rotation.

"Keep your head up as you come back down," Jobine urged.

Claudia gave a slight shriek as she completed the rotation, not quite sure at first when to prepare her skating leg for placement back on the ice. She completed the landing, however, sufficiently well to gain a quiet "well done" from Jobine.

The others attempted the same one by one with varying degrees of success. Then the height was increased and a somersault introduced. Then a variation was added which allowed for an immediate return to the air following a single touchdown. It was not long, however, before the inevitable disorientation and nausea effects became apparent for all of the setmates, as height and speed were increased and positions varied from the simple upright posture which they had assumed at the start.

"Don't worry too much," Jobine said as the setmates predictably complained of sickness and disorientation, almost to the point of collapse in Gary's case. "I know none of you are used to this but the discomfort will subside, trust me."

"Good show," said Jobine, applauding as Gary eventually completed the troublesome somersault. "Now we will do it again, but with increased momentum so that it will look a whole lot better."

"It's not very good, is it?" Gary remarked as he slowly

completed the movement once more. "I feel as if I'm going to be sick if I try that again."

"We will build on this exercise week by week," she explained. "We will experiment with different rhythms and get you performing a greater variety of movements whilst in the air. I now have to tell you that when you return to your cottage Joanie has something special for you, so I will now call time on today's lesson and let you get back so you can hear her television message."

*

When the set returned to the cottage the setmates immediately congregated around the television to await The PM's announcement.

"Setmates," she said. "It now gives me great pleasure to inform you that the holograms from your family and friends have been compiled and will be beamed to you shortly. I therefore call Claudia to the hologram suite."

They cheered as Claudia departed to the back room. The others waited until she returned, calling Michael through. Gary followed Connie.

The small back room contained a small stage and a single seat. Onto the stage were projected the three-dimensional images of Gary's parents.

"Gary, we are so pleased for you," said his father. "As soon as you had left we knew instantly what had happened and that you had received the prestigious Queen's Ticket."

"The embassy called an hour later," his mother continued. "They told us that you had been summoned by Her Majesty Queen Katie of Kamchatka, and your father said that he did know of the special place where you were to be taken, although he didn't know exactly where it was. They also told us that you would be joining the skaters of the Kamchatskiy Auto Company and going on tour after you had completed your training."

"The embassy assured us that nobody ever turns down an invitation from Queen Katie, and that she has many supporters in Britain as elsewhere," his father added. "We have been advised not to disclose our knowledge to others, but have been assured that the Kamchatkan authorities will take good care of you. There is no reason to disbelieve them, but of course we would like to see you if only in two dimensions. We are therefore sending this message via the British embassy hologram link to Petropavlovsk, who have assured us that we will have a confidential link to you through them."

"We all wish you well," said his mother. "We have seen pictures of you with your setmates, and are under no illusion that everyone is very contented in this place, wherever it is that you are. Anyway we are glad that we have seen you and that you are in the best of health."

As the images faded a voice issued the instructions to return a message.

"To return your message, stand on the white circle in front of the stage".

Gary duly stood on the spot.

"Hello, Mum and Dad. I have received your message in fab 3D and thank you. You are right everyone is very contented here. I have a great partner and am adjusting to life in a set of twelve which is great. Everyone works together here and it is like living in a dream. Today we learnt flying on ice, which was great. We have had some interesting challenges and there are more to come, but they don't worry us because nobody ever fails them, as long as we try, which everyone invariably does. The place is a really beautiful island, magical and full of mystique. It is also the birthplace of the most fantastic revolution that is happening in the world today.

We have dined with The Queen and she even acted as tour guide for us around the very first Non-Olympic stadium, which to our astonishment is nearly seventy years old. The Prime Minister, no less, is educating us personally on how to adapt to life in the new society. I thank you for your birthday gifts and look forward to spending some time with you next year. I will probably be married by then."

"Hello," said Connie briefly as she sneaked into the background for a second.

"That is my future wife, or principal, as partners are known here. I'm sure you will like her. We are going to the Jeweller's tomorrow to choose a wedding ring. I can't believe how my life has been transformed through this place. The only unanswered question so far is who sent me the Ticket. Perhaps all will be revealed in the end. Goodbye for now."

Gary then returned to the set and called Graca through.

"So, how did it go?" Claudia asked.

"Great. It was a relief to see my parents again."

"I think we all feel a bit like that. Most of us have been worried that there would be people back home that would be worried about us fearing the worst rather than the best. I was just surprised at how quickly our folks knew exactly what had happened to us. I'm glad to know now that nobody is worrying at all."

"By the way, Connie, what's that thing that I have to go to tomorrow at the hospital? Is it some kind of medical? You went last week, didn't you?" Gary asked her.

"Yeah," said Connie. "It's a bit more than just a medical though. It's a complete brain profiling operation and it takes about an hour to undergo the scan in The Dream Machine as they call it. Apparently it's an experimental device that can induce dreaming and measure subsequent activity in various regions of the brain. It then comes up with your very own personalised brain profile. I've never been through anything like it before. You need to be there for ten o'clock so I guess the Kammie will be round for you at about quarter to. You should be out by lunchtime, wondering what on earth you have just gone through, but

171

there is nothing to fear. It's not painful or anything, just peculiar, and quite interesting, I thought."

*

The next day as Gary sat in the waiting room he pondered what this so-called profiling was going to entail. He was in there for about five minutes before The Island Doctor, and Chief Medical Officer for the Clifford Centre for Brain Research, called him through into the theatre where his assistant was waiting. She held a visor in her hand, whilst beside her and in front of him was The Dream Machine, a long white cylindrical unit to which various wires were attached and connected to an array of viewing apparatus.

"Do sit down," said the tall, slim and slightly balding man. "I am Dr Adrian Schultz. Welcome to The Clifford Centre for Brain Research, one of the most advanced brain scanning centres in the world. It takes its name, of course, from our Founder Clifford, The Scientist, whom you know about already and who was a keen pioneer in the field of human brain research, as well as being a highly talented engineer and aviator.

The machine that you see in front of you is the world's most advanced brain analysis unit, which combines the technology of several types of former brain scanning units into one compound unit. Technically it is an electroencephalogram or EEG, a functional magnetic resonance imaging unit, or MRI, a positron emission tomography unit, or PET, and a magnetoencephalography unit or MEG. It is also a very sophisticated inducer of complex mental states. By combining each of these technologies into one singular piece of equipment it is possible to exploit the advantages of each of them with good effect, with each technology serving to amplify the others enabling resolution to be detected right down to the single cellular level. It is an extremely accurate monitor of brain activity by anyone's standards.

With this machine we are able to broaden our sphere of brain research further than ever before and aim very soon to make brain damage a thing of the past. Thanks to advanced brain profiling, we are now able to pinpoint exactly the region or regions of the brain that correspond with an individual's symptoms and correct them with microrobots which can enter and repair the affected tissue with minute implants which effectively plaster over the defect and remedy it. Stem cell research and projects such as the human genome have helped in this, as has the more modern science of microrobotic bioengineering.

An eminent scientist and compatriot of Clifford Hebden, Dr Masaki Sawicki, who was recruited for The Island by the engineers Endo and Kai, was particularly expert in the field of microbotics and developed a number of solutions for detecting and repairing damaged tissue in the human brain. It was he who developed, with the help of Clifford Hebden, the first prototype of the machine that you now see and that you will soon be entering. It was also he who first postulated about the existence of a trio of specific cells in the human brain, notably the receptor or R cell, the suicide or S cell and the transmitter or T cell each of which is believed to have a very special role in the brain. So convinced was he of the existence of the S cell, that effectively has the power to shut down the brain completely when subject to a certain stimulus, that he devoted much of his later life searching for it. He never found what he was looking for, but such was his devotion to the pursuit of this discovery that the S cell, for which we are still searching, was later named after him.

The term Sawicki has now been broadened to refer to any problem that involves a search for something which cannot be observed or otherwise pinpointed. In terms of brain research a Sawicki search is a search for an otherwise undiscovered cell or group of cells with a suspected or unidentified role. For example, we suspect that the R, S and T cells, when acting in unison, can have the effect potentially of shutting down the brain and thus killing it in the event of a fatality, such as a stroke or heart attack of a high magnitude. In particular the S cell, is believed to be responsible for a considerable number of unexplained deaths in infants by becoming activated in error at a time shortly after its formation. The R cell, on the other hand, is believed to have supernatural capabilities and is thought to be responsive to unidentifiable inputs, as for example in psychics. Likewise the T cell has the role of a master and is the only cell that has the power to activate the S cell. In a near fatal situation it is thought that the T cell can throw control back to other cells prompting the brain to go into recovery mode, which may or may not be completed fully.

When it comes to mapping the brain, we know that we are still at the Christopher Columbus stage, but at least it is a beginning and something upon which we can build. Already we are being able to track, in each individual, the manner in which control is passed from one brain region to another in response to certain stimuli, and pinpoint which cell batches are responsible for example for changes of mood, and for certain behavioural traits such as aggression, generation of ideas, and determination to complete a particular task by controlling one's own brain state, something which we will be asking you to do later with this magnificent box of tricks that you see here.

Now, I expect you are wondering what we have in store for you?"

"Yes," Gary said, nodding.

"So I will now explain. Shortly I will ask you to lie on the trolley and put on the visor, which my good assistant will strap around your head, along with the headphones that will supply oral inputs to match the visual. A painless injection will also be given both to stimulate relaxation and to supply the mild radioactive properties that are needed for the PET instrumentation to be activated. When all of this has been done, and you are comfortably in place, we will start the machine and the trolley will enter the capsule.

Once inside the capsule you will descend through the four stages of sleep into the fifth, which is referred to as rapid eye movement or REM sleep. It is in this fifth stage that what we commonly understand as dreaming takes place. In this stage the brain is capable of making decisions as if in the conscious world, and, until a few years ago, it was believed that this stage was the limit of our sleeping capabilities. Then, at the turn of the century, here at the Clifford Centre, I, with the aid of some Russian experts, managed to prove that there was indeed a sixth level of sleep, which had been suspected, but never proved, to exist. This sixth stage, which our machine has now been adapted to induce, is referred to as the superconducting state, so named because in this state there is not only a capacity for dreaming, but also a heightened sensitivity to external inputs, which is far less marked in the ordinary REM. This is believed to occur as, just as with supercooled materials, ions begin to flow far more freely as a result of the totally relaxed condition into which neurons or brain receptors are immersed. As with REM it is a transitory state. It is difficult to hold for more than a few minutes at a time, but the results have been startling. We now have evidence, stronger than ever before, that the R, S and T combination of cells does exist, and although we have so far been unable to pinpoint just exactly where they are, we are narrowing down the permutations month by month. Soon we will find Sawicki, and with it just maybe find a long-awaited cure for those mysterious infant deaths that cause so much heartbreak and pain when they occur, as well as explaining why death in other cases occurs the way that it does as far as the brain is concerned.

I will now ask you to lie down please, place the visor around your head, and present your left arm for injection."

Gary followed the instructions and became instantly tranquillised. After one minute the machine was turned on and he disappeared into it. The Doctor then stepped toward the input device.

"Input synchronised," said his lady assistant.

"Go," said The Doctor.

"Output synchronised".

"Go."

Gary was now in a dream world, except that, unlike in a normal dream, this dream could be influenced by the program that had been inserted into the machine.

A flash of light and a crack of thunder greeted Gary as he entered the world of Sawicki. A blurred image slowly became clearer, and there was rain that looked and felt as if for all the world that it were real. The image that was depicted was that of the crucifixion, with the recognisable image of Christ as the central figure on the cross betwixt two other unrecognisable figures.

"Oh Lord, why hast thou forsaken me," came the voice from the central cross.

This was followed by a direct oral input from The Doctor, which was as if delivered hypnotically from the direct input line.

"I want you to imagine that you are at one with the figure on the crucifix," he said. "Think of Christ's work and what he did for the world, the sacrifice, the question that is being asked, and the desire to be at one with God. Feel yourself entering the presence of the scene. Let the thoughts flood out."

"Believe in me and you shall not perish, but shall pass through me into everlasting life, for I am the Truth, the Way and the Life".

With this the program played on the subject's Christian convictions, and it was inevitable that Gary's subconscious response would be naturally Christian in its composition. The assistant stood by the output screens as they began to deliver their wave and point results plotted against time. The wave output showed the electrical EEG display whilst the point output showed the location display of relative cell activity on a three-dimensional map of the brain.

"Note here the standard alpha rhythm, backed up by the weaker theta rhythm," said The Doctor to his assistant – who was one of several being trained by him – pointing to the pattern on the EEG screen. "And just appearing we see the shadow delta rhythm. At the moment the subject is not conscious of them. We will see how well he can control them later. Then you will be able to calculate the power factor of the brain, that is to say, how well this particular brain can control its own modes of relaxation. Joanie needs to know this for her report to Kamchatskiy."

Dr Schultz then returned to the input side of the machine.

"Why has the Lord forsaken Christ?" he continued. "To send him to a better world perhaps? A world of kinder, more receptive souls perhaps?"

The image receded.

"Note the change of rhythm," The Doctor explained to his assistant. "There's a distinct change of mood here and the point sensors should show a transfer of cell activity to match. See if you can place the efficiency of this transfer on that chart I showed you last week. Different brains exhibit different transfer coefficients or 'schalters' as we call them. These show how well a brain can switch control from one cell region to another under different conditions, which is related to the T cell that we are seeking to find."

Back in Gary's world an image of starlight appeared. Before him was nothing but outer space. Then, a tiny speck appeared which grew steadily brighter. Gradually it came closer, dwarfing the stars around it. Soon he was able to make out the image of a winged angel descending toward him. Slowly, it reached out to touch him. Its touch felt strange, almost magic, invoking inner feelings of comfort and desire, yet two more emotions that The Doctor was eager to monitor the physiological profiles of.

The angel carried him upward, providing a sensation of flying, not too unlike that which he had experienced for real on the rink the previous day, except that here there was clearly a fictitious context that would inevitably be reflected in the brain wave patterns. Nevertheless the sensation provided a clear link between fantasy and reality as far as the brain was concerned. The Dream Machine was sufficiently sophisticated to induce a brain to play tricks on itself.

The angel provided a subtle mechanism by which to manipulate the subject's emotions. First it was wondrous, providing an exciting, magical touch sensation. Then there was the similarity with the previous day's real experiences. Then, excitement shifted toward a sense of protection as he was carried through space through gas clouds and meteorite storms. Each shift represented a different facet of one's mind, with a consequent change in brain activity that was detectable.

Flying gave way to floating followed by a feeling of hurtling toward the Earth. Then sinking became the dominant sensation, with a mild fear element built in, along with apprehension as to what was now going to occur. This part of the program introduced uncertainty and The Doctor was keen to observe what effect this had on the human brains that he was studying. Again, some brains would exhibit a greater degree of robustness than others, a fact which could be used when seeking to train or employ an individual in a particular way.

After about ten seconds the sinking stopped. Then there was nothing. All of a sudden the brain was faced with confusion. With a completely neutral input it had to think of something to do itself, but it couldn't. It had adapted to a supplied input to the point that in this superconducting mode it needed another supplied input in order to avoid moving up a level to REM. The program, however, did not intend this, so The Doctor intervened.

"You are entering a new world now, Gary," came The Doctor's voice. "Can you think of a name for it? It's a new and wondrous place."

"Goldenworld," Gary murmured, still hypnotised by the machine, as the colour gold was fed in and a small gold object rotated in the centre of his plane of vision.

"Goldenworld. Yes, that's a nice name," continued the voice. "Think of Goldenworld. Fix it in your mind as a place that is everything that you want it to be."

The Doctor then turned to his assistant and pointed to the EEG output screen.

"Now, I want you to keep a close eye on those alpha rhythms. By focusing on his imaginary Goldenworld our subject should be able to maintain his relaxed state. If he relaxes sufficiently he will be able to complete the exercise that our machine will create for him. If, however, he should become distracted and therefore fail to control his relaxation, then we will see a drift. I want you to watch for and record any drift that you observe and calculate its magnitude using the vector analyser. In the old days a subject merely controlled the motion of a model electric train by doing this, but that was a simple stop or start system. Now we are able not just to measure whether a brain is under control, but also the extent and efficiency of that control, as well as the susceptibility to various distracters."

Gary's vision was now focused on a rotating three-dimensional gold hexagon that grew steadily larger over a period of about a minute.

"There it is, Gary," said the voice. "There is Goldenworld. You can steer yourself towards it. Just think spiritually and you will be home and dry. The temporal world is behind. The spiritual world awaits. Reach out for the spirits, Gary. Align your mind with them and they will be with you. As you relax you will become as one with the spirits."

Briefly he saw the angel again, and it spoke to him in a soft voice repeatedly calling "Goldenworld". The angel was specifically tailored to offer a fantasy love to its subjects, helping to aid relaxation. The angel touched him, so forging a link between contrived relaxation and a mental steering toward the hollow centre of the hexagon as it floated in space.

Once he was on course the machine introduced the first of its distracters in the form of high-pitched noises or bleeps, which the subject had to learn to ignore. At first these blew Gary completely off course to a point where the hexagon almost disappeared from his view. The program, however, was designed in every case to allow an opportunity for correction and restoration of the course. It would even help the subject to do so, as it provided an output reading showing the amount of restoring relaxation energy that was needed.

"Think of the spirits. Ignore the distracters," came the voice again.

High-pitched whistles gave way to odours of various kinds, each one of which was designed to disrupt the thought pattern. This time, however, it was the sense of smell rather than sound that was under scrutiny. After that flashing lights were used to momentarily disturb the visual input of the hexagon, and finally, small electric impulses through the hands, which tested the resilience to touch inputs. After each distracter Gary had to restore the alpha rhythms, with assistance from the angel if necessary. Every time control had to be restored to that cellular combination that was responsible for maintaining the vision.

Subconsciously, Gary was being taught how to control his alpha rhythms. In each case Gary learned how to control the drift as it occurred. He soon found that it was a technique that could be mastered.

As Gary steered himself through the centre of the hexagon, the sensations that were delivered to him changed. The effects of different kinds of music were monitored in the latter stages of the steering operation. Some music was positive, enhancing the alpha rhythms, whilst other pieces gave a negative effect. The relative effects of the different pieces, however, varied between subjects and this was noted.

Eventually Gary felt himself being absorbed by the hexagon, as if passing into a honeycomb. Then he was sliding through it, as if being squeezed through by its slippery walls. The sensation was one of warmth and tightness. To the brain it was a simulation of a kind of birth process, designed at least to an extent to activate and monitor the activity of parts of the brain that were formed very early on. The stimulation was such that these childhood and pre-birth cells could, although not necessarily would, spill out a series of electrical waves that were the very essence of a human time signature.

For eight minutes the waves were induced with the brain's memory temporarily fooled into believing that it had gone back to a much earlier period in its development. Cells which were once active, but had fallen into disuse, were revived. For these eight minutes the brain believed that it was re-enacting its babyhood and its child-type wave motions were studied with interest, for here were infant time signature waves emanating from an otherwise mature mind.

Peach-coloured lava plumes concluded the eight-minute journey along the Goldenworld canal. Then there was a brilliant flash of light and a loud bang, which shook the brain out of its temporary mode, ready to receive another superconducting input. For a moment there was darkness. Then a very different image appeared, one that was somewhat more familiar. It was that of an open-plan office, with various people standing and working at computer terminals.

Thoughts of a grand masterplan to change the world were induced by the machine such that the brain would be encouraged to spill ideas out should it be sensitive to this particular input. The machine would then measure the nature and extent of the response.

Visual inputs followed in the form of key words and phrases such as 'systems thinking', 'process improvement', 'improve the process of birth', and 'improve the process of death'. Each successive input was designed to invoke a response from the brain.

"Note the spikes that you see here," The Doctor said to his assistant. "That should prove to Joanie and the Kamchatskiy management that we have made a good choice in investing in this person".

After about a dozen visual inputs had been applied, a man in a dark suit, who looked rather similar to Dr Schultz, appeared to him. He pointed to the screen beside him on which was displayed a scene in which a number of protesters were chanting, clearly dissatisfied.

"We want to live forever," came a voice.

"Eternal life – you promised, now deliver," came another.

"Hey, thingy, give us back our souls," shouted a third.

"Well, you can hear what they are telling you," said the man, Dr Schultz feeding in the voice-over. "What do you think we should do about it?"

"Were they promised eternal life?" Gary instinctively asked in his mind.

"Note the code classification of this response to the instinct test," said The Doctor to his assistant.

"Yes," responded the man in the dream. "They were."

"Then can we deliver?" replied the subdued Gary.

"No, but we know someone who can. What's more, so do they. You saw Him a while ago. Trouble is they don't seem to want to listen. Improvement is not top of their list. Neither is listening. They want us to just give them eternal life as of right. Even the Holy Lord has a right to expect a fair deal before conceding anything. The question is should we give them something or not. The last thing we gave them was the chance to invent the contraceptive pill and some use they made of that. Since then the world has gone down not up."

"What about throwing in a new cure for some disease, perhaps. That wouldn't do any harm, would it?"

"It wouldn't change their thinking though. They would just be back tomorrow with all the protests that you see here. No, unless someone comes up with a Breakthrough solution I'm not interested. What they need is the stick rather than the carrot. If they do not start teaching the next generation about the value of cooperation then they will deserve all that they get from climate change. Those who want eternal life will have to earn it, others must perish. Do you agree?"

"It could be done fairly. After all a lot of good souls are going to waste."

"Ah, waste, is that what you think it is about?"

"Most certainly," said Gary.

"Then we must move on. We will leave the protesters for now. Let them sit and think for a bit. Now, what do you make of this character?"

The crucifixion scene returned to him.

"A very barbaric event."

"Barbaric, yes, but do you think that it was wasteful".

"Definitely," said Gary.

"Think about the question 'why hast Thou forsaken me'," said the man. "What if the Holy Lord had a more important place for Christ to be? Imagine that this place was somewhere where people would actually listen more and be guided far more effectively as a result of His presence and activity. Then tell me if you can be absolutely certain that the whole thing was wasteful."

Gary couldn't answer. Now doubt had become introduced into the brain wave pattern.

"Watch those tiny dissipating currents," said The Doctor, back in the real world. "They're a bit like eddy currents and they appear whenever there is doubt or apprehension on the part of the subject. They signify caution and danger. They aren't necessarily bad, but in excess they can impair judgment. Subjects need to know how to control these, but it's much harder to learn this than the simple alpha wave control that we looked at earlier. But it can be done in a very strong subject. No, there are a few more of these currents than we would like with this subject, but it's not enough to be a cause of failure. We will just have to advise Joanie that a bit more training will be needed to remove the tendency for doubt and anxiety to creep in during the course of problem solving, but I think we can close the program now."

The machine stopped and Gary awoke.

"Congratulations," said Dr Schultz. "Nothing painful at all, was there?"

"Not at all," said Gary. "That was just an absolutely remarkable experience."

"I tell you, this box of tricks is remarkable. It is the most incredible piece of kit and the amount of information that it gives us about a person's personality and make up is quite fantastic. We know, for example, exactly how to fine-tune a person's training and how to maintain an individual's contentment, something which is very important to our government. Now, I suppose you would like to know how well you did?"

"Of course," said Gary.

"Well, we have identified those regions of the brain which remained active throughout and those areas which became active at different points in the program. The scan is continuous, like a moving picture, but we have taken one or two snapshots in interesting places.

We have compared the results with others and I can say that we have managed to obtain an aggregate changeover locus of a sort as control is passed from one cell combination to another, which is consistent to a degree between subjects. We have also calculated a three-dimensional hunting criterion, which when aggregated should lead us closer to the elusive R, S and T cell combination. The hunting criterion is so named because it is part of a converging series of numbers which we believe will prove conclusively that the Sawicki cell combination does actually exist.

A particularly useful measurement has been that of the deviation from a fix mean created by the so-called distracters. Each distracter was designed to make a group of cells active which was different from the original fix. We measured the shift back to the fix mean each time you restored your imaginary flight path in line with the golden hexagon. The fix mean dictated the correct flight path or Glide Path as we call it.

Another interesting result of recent years has also been that when the same test has been applied to individuals with thinking patterns that are less aligned with our own, we find a statistical variation associated with the restoration from the distracters. The conclusion is that the human species is, in fact, working to two fundamentally different programs of brain activity, and that this could be highly significant to the evolutionary process. The two are necessarily conflicting and it is believed that the human species is in the process of sub-dividing into two. There is the old model which has existed for centuries with its various racial strands, and the new form, which will be differentiated by the dominance of certain cellular regions of the brain and certain locus patterns.

As for the Sawicki cluster itself, that remains both a theory and a mystery. It could be that the location or locations are different in each person and that nature does not intend us to find it even if we can prove that it exists. There are no clues yet as to the shape of any one of the three cluster cells. We can only presume that they all have the appearance of any ordinary brain cell. Your results, of course, add one more piece to the jigsaw."

Chapter Fifteen
One Party Democracy

The first of October at four o'clock.

Gary and the others had just returned from the ice rink and were sitting together in the living room. That morning they had received an interim report of their progress from Mitsumoto-san on their study assignments.

"We are now halfway through the course," said Carl, checking through the list of completed assignments. "We have completed so far eight assignments and have eight more to complete. We have just completed Innovation and Creativity, before that we did Management of Best Practice, Automotive Manufacture theory and practice, Testing and Quality Control, Information Technology and Robotic Assembly, Graphic Art and Design, Management of Resources and Management of Operations. The next module and set of lectures are on The Theory of Systems, but that doesn't have to be completed until the 20th of November. Mitsumoto-san will no doubt give us more details nearer the time as to what we have to do."

"So what's left after that?" asked Jose.

"We still have to complete Knowledge Management, Marketing and Public Relations Management, Maintenance and Reliability, Housekeeping, Administration, Organisational Development and Technical Auditing.

"Fine," said Anne. "So we are all up to date, including our ongoing health and safety updates?"

"Everything is done and Mitsumoto-san has submitted his interim report on us to Joanie who is by all accounts pleased with our progress."

"So now we just wait for her broadcast at five?" said Lars.

"Well, we have all read Eric Fallon's book on the electoral system, *One Party Democracy*," said Claudia. "All we can do now is wait for The PM to demonstrate to us how the theory works in practice."

"It will be interesting to see how it works," said Gary. "A single candidate standing for a single party with votes that each citizen has to earn as opposed to simply having."

"In today's *Island Times* the front page reads 'Sets must rise to challenge as Joanie lays down gauntlet'," explained Connie. "According to the headlines she 'will not be handing out ballot papers like confetti this year' and 'expects all sets to present high quality and well thought out questions that will result in positive suggestions to help her to improve the way in which she governs'."

"What else does it say," Michael asked.

"It goes on to say that she has let it be known that apathy on the part of any of her citizens is something that will not be accepted," Connie continued.

"Sounds stern stuff from our normally mild mannered Prime Minister," commented Graca.

"It is," said Connie. "She says that it is an issue that she will address firmly in adherence with The Queen's wishes. She says that sets must rise to the challenge of eliminating apathy by justifying their right to vote on November fifth. Only when she is completely satisfied that all sets have presented credible and realistic ideas for improvement by way of thorough questioning that allows her to declare a total absence of apathy throughout the community will she permit voting to begin."

At five o'clock they assembled around the television as Joanie had instructed, and, on cue, it switched itself on.

"Good afternoon, good citizens," she said, broadcasting

from the Great Dome. "As you all know, every year on The Island I am required by the rules of One Party Democracy to submit myself for re-election by all citizens. Procedure requires that whilst only one party and one candidate may stand for office, the candidate so selected must secure unanimous support from all members of the community. The candidate is permitted under such procedure to set their own target for turnout and vote on the part of the electorate. Should the targets be reached then the candidate is duly elected for another year. Should it not be reached the Island Council, which represents all of The Island territories, may intervene and demand either a new target and a re-run of the ballot, or that an alternative candidate be tried, who must then poll better than the original, otherwise the original will be re-elected by default. Such a method allows for a replacement of a candidate who proves to be unpopular.

No MP in our community wishes to lose face in an election and so all will usually set for themselves an ambitious target that, if met, will indicate a pretty high level of popularity. Targets of over 90 per cent tend to be normal these days. I am not going to be the exception to the rule, other than to go that little bit further and set myself the target of 100 per cent. It's unusual, it's ambitious, but I feel I owe it to everyone to return only if every citizen is satisfied with my performance, as well as every citizen being worthy of having a casting vote. It should be noted that when a citizen earns the right to vote, by virtue of making a contribution to the continual improvement of our society, he or she is under no obligation to cast it unless completely satisfied with the performance of the candidate.

In setting this target – and it is my target, nobody else has set it for me – I feel that if returned to office I will be able to feel certain that I have the total support of everyone here for the duties and tasks which I am required to undertake. Likewise I trust that all of you will play your part in making our society and our country better by expressing concerns and questioning issues which you believe to be important. Only through this can an MP, in a state which practices true One Party Democracy, gain a satisfactory indication of public opinion and an ability to prioritise opportunities for improvement.

Our good Founder Eric conceived this version of One Party Democracy following years of experience of studying political systems throughout the world and analysing their strengths and weaknesses. His conclusion was that one party systems were potentially superior to multi-party ones because they require everyone to work together toward a single objective, as opposed to having opposing priorities with competition between parties serving to encourage electioneering rather than good management. One party systems had, however, hitherto proven themselves to be dictatorial and autocratic, with internal struggles for power that resulted in unpopular and unfair regimes that took no account of people's hopes and preferences. Therefore, just as Leo argued that a new economic system was needed for the world, so Eric argued that a completely new political model was needed also to support it, free from the usual corruption that typified practically all regimes of the world, whether single party or multi-party.

With the help of the other Founders, Eric managed to make his revolutionary political system a reality, and took great pride in seeing it start to function effectively, having created the first virtually corruption free political system in the world. The key, of course, was to impose the opposite requirement for a one party state than that which was normal in the world, namely that all citizens be required to effectively speak out against systems and processes that were in need of improvement, rather than having such views suppressed, and thereafter requiring that all issues raised be acted upon and be seen to be acted upon by those in charge. Where there were conflicts of interest consensus solutions had to be arrived at by relevant parties. The need for change had to be recognised. Opportunities for improvement, both Breakthrough and Incremental, always had to be considered and these invariably come from the people, not from bureaucrats in remote offices.

In order to make this system function effectively it requires the participation of everybody. We therefore set aside a period of time every year during which people are expected to consider and examine critically the systems which operate around them. As a result of this thought each set is required by law to submit a question to their elected representative, in this case me, which will have a direct bearing on the improvement of our society. In turn the elected representative is expected to supply an answer. When all of the questions have been received and meet the required standard for submissions, each person will be supplied with a ballot paper which he or she may then cast or not cast for the candidate. When all of the answers have been given, you, the people, must decide if you feel that I am up to the job.

The next time you will see me will be on Halloween, which is a public holiday throughout The Island territories and is when all councils are dissolved pending the election result. The days between Halloween and November fifth are allocated to the assessment of questions and the preparation of answers. You should submit your questions to the Town Hall no later than noon on Halloween, which gives you thirty days to prepare. You should not delay in starting this exercise, but you should think your ideas out carefully before submitting them, and remember that it is a collective exercise. I will be watching you all to make sure that every member of every set participates actively and that the question that you submit is realised by consensus of the group as a whole. It is not about who can shout the loudest or pushes their idea the hardest. So please all of you help me to realise my dream as I have realised yours. Help me to maintain the momentum of

Breakthrough and Incremental improvement for everyone. May the spirits of Deming and Juran be with you."

*

That evening the set began to brainstorm for ideas as to how to approach the challenge that Joanie had set.

"So, where do we begin?" asked Carl.

"What I would like to know is the extent to which the media can be trusted in this apparently Utopian society," replied Connie.

"And the extent to which they should be allowed to pursue people in public life," Anne added. "So far I have seen nothing to suggest that the media behaves any better here than in any other part of the world. Remember Sylvia on the train? She pretty much confessed that the media here was as biased as anywhere else and perfectly prepared to cover things up if it suited them."

"I think we should jot a few of these ideas down, then think about them and return to them again in a day or two," suggested Michael.

"I'll get a pad," said Claudia.

"We could ask what is being done to improve the accuracy of reporting," Jose suggested. "Then we don't have to approach the subject in an accusative way that could be construed as antagonistic."

"True," said Carl. "If we make a submission that presumes that The Island media is corrupt without having any evidence I don't think that The PM would be very pleased. This will certainly teach us how to learn to be diplomatic."

"I noticed that she mentioned losing face," said Terry. "That is the first time I have heard her say that. It doesn't surprise me given how influential the Japanese were in setting up this place."

"Okay, well we could ask something about the media," said Yvonne. "But what about other things such as health, education and the environment. Those are always topical areas in any political discussion. They certainly are in Australia and I expect they are here also."

"Yes," said Graca. "But do we want to ask a question that is necessarily topical. After all other sets will probably be thinking along those lines, and I'm sure Joanie would appreciate something a bit more original."

"That's a good point," acknowledged Connie. "Judging by Eric's book, duplication of questions is not encouraged, unless it is indicative of a matter that is clearly of widespread concern amongst a particular community, but I can't see how this is the case here. I think we should have something based on a common theme, but which is also original and different from other sets. Gary, come on, we need to hear from you too. Joanie says this has to involve everybody."

"Perhaps the issue of spare time could be addressed?" he suggested.

"What do you have in mind?" asked Lars.

"Well, does everyone have enough? Does she feel that some people have too much relative to others, and if so, would she take steps to redress the balance? Does she feel that she is sometimes working a little too much?"

"That could certainly be likely," answered Elena. "Especially when a Prime Minister is devoting at least half of her time educating 240 aspiring skating stars."

"So, what do you suggest?" asked Connie.

"We could ask her whether she feels that the balance between work and leisure could be improved".

"What about you, Terry?"

"Elena, what do you think?" Connie asked.

"I'd like to know if there is anything of which our Prime Minister is afraid, and if there is anything we could do to make her less afraid."

"Michael?"

"I think we should ask her if she would be prepared to tell us openly about some of her problems so that we can all put our heads together to help her to solve them."

193

"Is she confident enough in others to be able to talk openly about her problems?" Claudia added as she jotted down the various suggestions.

"We would have to be careful how we phrased that question also," said Lars. "Personally I would like us to focus more on results and ask her just exactly how much of what she has promised in the past has actually been delivered. After all we have seen no evidence here as elsewhere to show that our leaders actually do keep to their promises and to what extent."

"I agree," added Gary. "I would like to ask her if she could maybe give us a few examples of things she has promised and actually delivered."

"How about asking her what she thinks about improving life and death?" suggested Elena.

"Well we've got some ideas to start with," said Carl. "Maybe tomorrow we can come up with a few more."

*

During the next few days the sets networked and talked through their ideas with each other, which helped to remove the problem of coincidental duplication of questions, which all agreed was not desirable. Gary's set, however, had been the only one to mention the life and death idea, and it received encouragement from the others. Gary's set therefore agreed to develop this theme further for their question, leaving the other sets to concentrate on the other suggestions. The Cat and Fiddle provided a popular meeting point for the various sets to come together in order to exchange ideas.

The following week the set returned to the Clifford Institute in order to examine the scientific evidence that had been gathered on the subject. Dr Schultz was only too pleased to spare an hour of his time to assist them.

"Good morning, how lovely to see you all again," he said, greeting them for their appointment the following

Tuesday. "So you want to know what we know about death, the final mystery?"

"Indeed we do," said Anne.

"Well, I can recommend a few good books and papers that our scientists have written," said The Doctor. "As you know we have this theory of the suicide cell in the brain, but evidence is far from conclusive. What exactly are you keen to find out?"

"We were thinking along the lines of increasing life expectancy," Lars explained. "Lots of people believe now that there are scientists in the world who can make people live longer and stay younger for longer by retarding the ageing process, but they are sworn to secrecy because they know that if anyone were to release the technology it would cause havoc because of the way in which the capitalist system operates. Yet, with Non-Capitalist Economics and our stable process of population regeneration we see no reason why such technology, if it exists, should not be made more widely available, at least quietly within our slow revolutionary process. As a true expert in your field we feel that you, more than anyone else, would be likely to know if this technology exists, and if so, whether it is not scientists but politicians who are impeding its availability."

"Well," said Dr Schultz. "This is not exactly within my field of expertise, but I can certainly say that techniques do exist which can prolong the ageing process, although there is no cure as such for old age. You are right that it is politicians who are the obstacle, but they themselves have a problem in that once such technology is disclosed there is likely to be an explosion in demand which could have all sorts of serious repercussions. In particular, it would be something that rich people and criminals would seek to obtain by all kinds of illicit means. This, of course, could be very damaging to the world, and so they are quite right to suppress such things at least for the time being. I do know that there have been some terrible cases recently in some parts of the world in which the brains of old, wealthy, influential and bad people have been rejuvenated and transplanted into much younger bodies with varying degrees of success. Scientists such as myself obviously deplore these practices, which are largely a consequence of modern technology advancing at a far faster pace than social sciences like politics and economics. The Island condemns these practices, but that is not to say that we condemn the principle of increased life expectancy. What is it that you were thinking of asking The PM?"

"We were going to ask her if she would be prepared to take measures to help to drive out the fear associated with ageing by improving access to the technology which exists to counter it, and to commit more resources to that end and to improving the technology itself," Carl explained.

"Well, it is certainly a noble question to put and it certainly won't disgrace you in your quest to receive your ballot paper. I would definitely be prepared to endorse your submission. I can say that a lot of this kind of information is still strictly confidential within scientific as well as Island circles. The techniques are also still largely experimental in nature and have yet to be proven for their reliability. I do wish you well in your endeavours, though, for I know that in the long term such techniques could be of real benefit to the world and should not be kept under wraps forever.

As for the knowledge that you seek I can refer you to some of our published work that has been provisionally cleared for release for limited circulation within The Island and its territories. I wish you well and will of course be watching the election as ever with great interest. Do feel free to look around the Institute."

Upstairs in the exhibition hall the setmates cast their eyes around the various exhibits, which included models, diagrams and texts most of which were dedicated to the fields of neuroscience and brain research. A large three-dimensional brain hologram stood encased in the centre of the hall, with push buttons which, when pressed, would illuminate a small cluster or region of brain cells responsible for a particular function. The lights in the hall could be dimmed by pushing a special button, which then permitted a tiny point of light to shine where current estimates suggested that the elusive Sawicki cells may lie. The set pondered over this for a while before moving on.

"I suppose what we are doing is a bit like searching for Sawicki," Connie remarked. "Here we are looking for clues to something which we strongly suspect exists, a key to extended life for all, yet cannot somehow pinpoint. But I know it's there, it has to be, just as I was sure back home that The Island existed. It was just a question of discovering it."

Another exhibit was a large atlas of the brain that was constantly being updated. Just like an atlas of the world shows mountain ranges, rivers and deserts, this showed details of folds and ranges of the cortex and other recognised brain regions, each with their own technical names and functions. Some, such as the hippocampus, were features that had been known about for many years. Others had been discovered somewhat more recently, such as the castle neuron, which took its name from the manner in which it controlled other neurons through its portcullis or drawbridge axon, which served to allow or restrict electrical inputs to its neighbouring house neurons.

A small virtual reality cinema at one end of the hall invited visitors the opportunity to embark on a 'Fantastic Journey' inside a graphically produced simulation of a human brain.

"That's worth an hour of anyone's time," said Anne.

Animated animal and insect brains were depicted diagrammatically along one half wall of the hall, with descriptive comparisons made between each. Then, the human genome was presented and, crucially, a section that was devoted to cell regeneration.

"I think this could be what we have been looking for," remarked Connie.

"What's that?" Gary asked.

"Stem cells. The building blocks of life," Connie continued, scrutinising the diagrams of the various cells. "Every type of every cell in a human body, including brain cells, can be perfectly recreated and produced to order. Only capitalism stands in the way of cell regeneration becoming a quite normal and acceptable part of everyday life. Definitely a life-saver."

"I suppose we should be grateful to Dr Schultz for allowing us to see it," said Graca. "The text even calls it the Sawicki of yesteryear."

"What is?" asked Gary.

"The stem cell," answered Graca.

"I think I will note some of these references," said Claudia, scrutinising the text. "Then we can go to Commander and see the fine detail, or at least as much of it as has been declassified for Island use."

"I can understand why, looking at all of this, The Island is concerned only to maintain a small and controlled trickle output of information about the true capabilities of this sort of technology," said Connie. "There must be some concern, as with The Island itself, that if this revolution in technology were to occur too quickly the whole concept could become horribly misused, just like those ghastly transplants that The Doctor mentioned."

"I shuddered when I heard that," Elena confessed.

"So did I," said Terry. "To think that the knowledge associated with being able to execute complete brain rejuvenation and transplants has led to a black market in brainless teenage bodies with soaring rates of kidnapping is unfortunately a harsh reflection of human depravity in the twenty-second century."

*

Halloween morning after breakfast.

"The costumes have arrived," said Anne, as she signed for a large box at the door.

Lars and Carl carried the box into the living room where Claudia opened it.

"They're all named," she said.

The set gathered round and took the garments that had been tailored for them.

The setmates tried on the costumes, which were of witches, warlocks and ghouls, complete with makeup. Then, they returned to the issue of the election question, which had to be submitted by noon. From the window they noticed other sets making their way to the Town Hall.

Clad in their costumes staff and setmates hurriedly finished their last minute business before the shutdown. In the centre of the Town Square preparations were already underway, as a huge black cauldron was being erected hanging from metal supports that reached to a height of some thirty feet above Leo's Lake. Standing from inside the cauldron was a chair, which rose some ten feet above it, mounted on a pole, such that it could descend into it. Beneath it logs had been placed on a large circular steel pontoon. When dusk came the whole scene would spring into life.

"So, are we all satisfied with the wording of our question?" asked Anne.

"I think so, we have been through it enough times," answered Lars.

"Then if we are all satisfied that we have done our best, I will make the submission to the Council."

On her way out she collected a copy of *The Island Times* from a pile that had been placed on a table before returning to Angel.

"What do the papers say?" Connie asked.

"Headlines say Halloween festivities promise to be the best yet. Then it says Prime Minister stands by her word to accept nothing less than 100 per cent at the polls otherwise she will stand down."

"Well, everyone's behind her," said Carl. "She must stand some chance. Everybody thinks she's fantastic."

199

"Of course, we all love Joanie, don't we?" said Claudia, raising her arms in support.

"Yes," said all the others in unison.

"Joanie forever," said Jose, waving his arms above his head.

Back in her Dome Joanie chuckled as she viewed them briefly before passing on to another set.

"The paper also explains the arrangements for polling day," Anne continued. "The election takes place at The Town Hall on November fifth. Ballot papers will be issued at the end of questioning, which is usually complete by three o'clock. Staff will have their question session in the morning in Government House. For the rest it will be outside, weather permitting, by the Stone Boat after lunch. The declaration will be announced at the grand bonfire and fireworks display, which will take place in the East Garden of the Royal Palace at eight. A shuttle train service will operate from six onwards. Tonight's events will commence at sunset, which by my reckoning at this time of year will be at about 6 p.m."

*

At six the crowd gathered in the Town Square. A subtle combination of red and orange lights beneath the giant cauldron simulated the effect of a fire burning brightly beneath. Around it on Leo's Lake floated about twenty turnip lanterns each on a circular polystyrene base. On the stone wall surrounding the Lake a larger number of unlit lanterns stood, whilst at the end of the wall was a wooden slate upon which were written the words:

'These lanterns are a gift from the senior citizens of The Island. They are for participants to light up and place into the water around the cauldron along with a prayer for your friends and loved ones, for our most noble King and Queen, and for the successful return to office of our most honourable Prime Minister who has given us so much and been an inspiration to us all.'

High above the cauldron, seated in the chair at the top of the protruding pole, was Joanie, dressed in her ceremonial good witch robes of blue and gold, The Island logo prominently displayed on her cloak. She had the privilege of looking down on the throng below where the women were dressed as witches, clasping broomsticks, and the men were dressed either as wizards, complete with conical hats and magic wands, or ghouls, with silvery grey hair and werewolf-like hands. Gary was one of the latter.

As Anne was preparing to light a lantern on behalf of her set, she was joined by The Janitor, a slim woman of about fifty-five, who also took a lantern and taper.

"Isn't she gorgeous," The Janitor said, as she gazed up at Joanie, who responded with a wave. "It's her day of course, and so nice to see her dressed in her magic outfit."

"And I do hope she gets re-elected," The Janitor added.

"What makes you think that she won't?" asked Carl.

"Well, 100 per cent turnout, 100 per cent of the vote, all genuine, no coercion, no corruption. I don't think any candidate in the world has ever managed that, not even here. And it's by no means certain that she will manage it, not because anyone doesn't want to see her back in charge, it's just that the slightest hitch could prevent it. Last year, for example, she set herself a 99 per cent target which she easily met, but there was one vote not cast because one elderly lady, unfortunately, died before she could cast her vote. It wasn't expected, and it didn't make any difference to the result, but if such a thing were to happen this year, it would affect the result. So I am lighting my lantern and praying that it does not. Hopefully you will do the same."

For about five minutes the crowd stood talking and exchanging greetings. Then, the chattering simmered as The Reverend appeared as an orange wizard, beating his drum to summon people to attention as he led the procession. The

Queen followed him in her open-topped royal Kammie, dressed in white as the good fairy, accompanied by The King as Merlin, The Queen Mother as a brightly-dressed fairy godmother, and the two young children as green elves, their bright colours contrasting with the dark ones of the setmates and staff. The Concierge, dressed as the green wizard, and The Chancellor as the yellow wizard, brought up the rear in a standard two-seater Kammie. The crowd stood back as the procession made its way to face The Colonnade. There it stopped, and The Concierge got out and ascended the steps of The Colonnade so that he could address the crowd. The Chancellor followed him and stood at his side.

"Welcome," shouted The Concierge. "Three cheers for The Prime Minister."

The call prompted the usual three 'hip, hip hoorays'.

"Wonderful," The Concierge replied. "Now we just want it a to be a little bit louder, so that Joanie can hear you loud and clear all on her own way upon high. Let her know that she is going to come out of this election, not only duly elected, but also with a world record, of which she can be justly proud."

The cheering was repeated, this time fractionally louder.

"Tonight is Halloween," The Concierge continued. "The night when all spooks, wizards, witches, warlocks, ghouls and gremlins come out into the night, and when all things that frighten you come out into the open ready to be dealt with one by one. It is also that time of year when you, the people, have your chance to express your views and say what you think of us. It is also a time of celebration and feasting, a holiday, granted to us by the pioneer of our One Party Democracy, our dear Founder Eric Fallon. We celebrate, ladies and gentlemen, a system that brings us freedom and prosperity without rivalry, bitterness and corruption, and spares us from the squandering of precious resources that ensues as sides locked in opposition struggle to secure power. This is because, ladies and gentlemen, in our society those in charge do not seek power. What they seek is good management and the welfare of the people they serve. For here, politics is history. We are run by technicians, not politicians, and our wonderful first lady, Joan Carmichael, and others like her, are likewise technicians, trained and experienced to do the job that needs to be done, not trained to fight elections and defeat opponents."

The Reverend gave a single beat of his drum and the crowd applauded, the setmates following the staff members' cue.

"The cauldron, which is the centrepiece of our festivities, is a concept which owes its existence to a staff suggestion which we received a few years ago with the aim of making this event more interesting and entertaining than it used to be. It has since been copied in other Island territories so you should not be surprised if you see a copy of it when you go to Kamchatka.

Above the cauldron, perched upon high, we see a woman who leads by example and whom we know cares passionately about each and every one of us. We must now respond in kind by telling her, in no uncertain terms, that we, like her, will not glibly accept things as they are just because life is comfortable. Nor will we fall victim to the temptation of change for change's sake. For we know what we must do. What must we do?"

"Progress. Progress. Progress," shouted the staff members, urging the setmates to repeat the words after them as The Reverend beat his drum three times.

"Indeed we must. So, in a few moments I shall wave my magic wand, and then I will ask our very own Island folk group, Ten A Penny, to begin playing, as I now have pleasure in declaring The Island Election for 2107 officially open."

The crowd cheered and The Reverend beat his drum repeatedly as blasts of mist shot up from within the cauldron, temporarily obscuring Joanie each time. Then the music began, 'carried away by a moonlight shadow'. The crowd danced rhythmically to the beat, Island staff leading the way for the others to join in. Then, after about two minutes, Joanie began to descend slowly until she eventually sank out of view, leaving just the cauldron with mist which simply overflowed as opposed to being blasted.

After that the various stands began to serve punch, popcorn and other delights. Gary and the others passed the hot dog stand and were duly served with vegetarian hot dogs.

Further on they passed a table by Leo's Lake upon which were laid piles of small sticks of 2107 Election rock. Setmates helped themselves, as they ate and made merry for about half an hour. Then the band stopped for a well-earned break as magicians, jugglers, clowns and men on stilts showed off their skills, whilst at the same time The Queen and the other royals joined the throng, as ever, exchanging greetings with as many people as possible.

For the first time Gary shook hands with King Neville.

"So, how are you finding The Island? A bit different from where you were before?"

"A lot different," Gary replied.

"All enjoying it I hope as well as learning?" The King then asked to the complete set.

"It is absolutely fabulous," replied Yvonne "It's like living in a dream. I don't know how we can thank The Queen enough."

"Oh, it's very simple," said the King. "Just vote for Joanie on November fifth. That is all that she asks."

"But how do we know that our question will be accepted?" asked Carl.

"Oh it will be. You need have no fears about that. Otherwise one of my advisers would have been in touch with you. Enjoy the party."

"Thank you Your Majesty," the setmates said as The King moved on.

About twenty minutes passed. Then, there was a strange screeching sound, almost like the sound of a wild animal, but with a slight whistling tone. The people froze, their eyes drawn toward The Great Dome. As they stared up the two ornamental golden eagles on The Dome separated opening up a segment of its roof. Then, from it, emerged what appeared to be an illuminated witch mounted on a broomstick, complete with black cat. Using its legs to become airborne it then flew with the aid of its mighty steel wings. It circled overhead before flying out over the coast so that everyone could stand back and admire the object.

"It's The Eagle," Jobine called out to the set, as she waved and approached them from the Gloriette, dressed as a skating phantom on roller skates."

There were a few cries of "Wow" from the setmates as they gazed at the great bird, which circled around for about ten minutes before it returned to its base, prompting spontaneous applause from the crowd. A short display of fireworks then brought the evening festivities to a close before The Night Watchman, dressed as the man in black, made his customary appearance as a hint to everyone that the show was over, at least for the time being.

*

Election Day arrived and at three o'clock all of the setmates assembled in normal dress on the lawn of the Training Centre facing the Stone Boat where The PM sat, accompanied by her Concierge. The Concierge opened proceedings:

"In accordance with the law of One Party Democracy I now declare the forum open. I will briefly outline official procedure, which is as follows. The nominated representative of each set shall put forward their set's question, exactly as submitted. When called that representative shall rise and read out the question which has been agreed. The candidate shall then answer the question, with the right to reply being

205

reserved for the representative. A short dialogue only between the representative and the candidate may follow, which I, as returning officer, have the authority to terminate. I now call upon Antonio Rodriguez to present our first question."

The Brazilian man presently rose to his feet.

"Will you ensure that children will always be able to choose their school, and that no school will refuse a child if they are oversubscribed?" He asked.

"A school cannot refuse a child a place simply because it is oversubscribed," Joanie answered. "They must make room and any of our MPs would argue the case for any school that is in such a position to be given whatever resources it needs in order to cater for any excess demand. The right to freedom of choice with regard to a child's education is a basic right for all children within our territories. Next."

"Mr. Anton Praznowski."

A tall Russian gent rose to his feet.

"Madam Prime Minister, will you assure us that you will do all that you can to ensure that Russia, with the help of The Island, will maintain its commitment to improving the world's environment?"

"The communists inflicted great damage on the environment in the twentieth century and work is still ongoing to rectify this. That said, as you know, Russia has, with our help achieved the greatest rate of environmental improvement in recent years and Non-Capitalist Economics has helped greatly. We will continue to press for capitalist countries outside Russia to match at least the Russian rate of improvement so that we can reverse the decline worldwide. You still have your hand raised."

"Yes, because our set believes that The Island's measures do not go far enough. Do you feel that more action should be taken against those countries with the worst records? After all, it would be good for everyone, wouldn't it?"

"Both Russia and The Island are, at present, limited as to how far they can intervene internationally, but I do accept

206

that the world is changing and that the situation could change in the next decade or so. With the new sovereignty of nations concept, which I know you have researched, and that I will continue to press for, the days will soon be numbered for governments that do not fulfil their duty to practice and enforce good environmental practice, as they could find themselves being bought out by governments that do. It is the next stage of globalisation. Next."

"Miss Delia Fremse."

"We cannot uninvent nuclear weapons," declared the Danish girl. "So they are still a danger to the world. What do you think can be done to reduce the danger and what are you personally prepared to do?"

"I accept that we cannot uninvent these horrific weapons of mass destruction, but we can try to remove the incentives for people to want to either build more or use the ones that already exist. My belief is that by improving the quality of life for people all over the world, and by keeping our 200-year revolution that our Founders started seventy years ago on course, I think that we can put into play a form of obsolescent drift. Then, eventually, these weapons should just simply vanish into history. You don't seem satisfied."

"In the meantime how serious do you believe the danger is of our dreams being shattered by our supposedly nuclear free state being held to ransom by an enemy?"

"Of course there is a danger, but I do not think that the danger is very great. Our people exist throughout the world and I have every confidence that our grapevine would warn us of any impending threat in the unlikely event that one existed. Not only that, our power to retaliate economically is very strong. We could, if we wished, supply any market for any product at zero cost in money terms, and all countries know that this is a very great weapon of ours should we ever be forced to use it."

"Mr. Barnes Brigham."

"Good health is our right," a South African man asserted.

"And from time to time everyone needs good healthcare. Should you be re-elected can you assure us that everyone will receive the healthcare that they need, and that reliability will continue to improve?"

"We have a slightly different approach to healthcare than other countries. Our philosophy is that harm to one is harm to the whole. Thus, when it comes to healthcare room will always be found and resources provided. Economics is not a consideration, only the ability to provide. Of course, no one can ever guarantee that every operation or treatment will be 100 per cent successful, but we do guarantee not just to match, but to exceed, the highest standards that currently exist in the world today. This goes for all aspects of the service and I can say that we will always be driven by our desire to continually improve the system rather than by targets. We benchmark our health service against that of every country and are proud of our achievements. As you will have seen from Commander, our hospitals have the appearance of top class hotels relative to those in capitalist countries, and our doctors and nurses will always have access to the world's finest training and resources. Next."

"Miss Marie Lafarge."

"To what extent do you support or otherwise the action by an Island truck driver in agreeing to accept a consignment of lambs destined for slaughter from a lorry hijacked by Russian animal rights activists in Magadan, and then subsequently driving them over the border in northern Kamchatka and taking them to a sheep farm there?" asked the French girl.

"I know a lot of you read about this in *The Island Times* last month, and I know that most of you feel strongly that it was wrong of my officials to reprimand the driver for this, and to serve on him a Declaration of Deviance with an accompanying sentence of three months of Directed Labour. The problem was that, although what he did was right to many people, he acted against international law, because he was outside our territory when he committed the offence. This caused embarrassment to the Russian authorities, as well as requiring us to compensate the farmer who, of course lost his revenue. I know you feel for the animals as I do, but you have to understand that it is simply not our right to interfere with the affairs of territories that are not our own in this kind of way. Technically, his actions amounted to theft and therefore he had to accept the punishment, which, incidentally, he was happy to do. Next."

"Miss Lei Tan"

A 26-year-old Filipino girl rose.

"Prime Minister. Can you assure us that the issue of child abuse is being satisfactorily addressed in The Island's territories?"

"Yes, now I would like to commend your set for the excellent research that you have conducted in this area. You obviously looked back at our records and discovered that some years ago a man was expelled from The Island by the then Queen Mary for alleged improper conduct towards certain minors. This proved that even this our wonderful Island can sometimes have its problems. However, in answer to your question, I do feel that we are addressing it satisfactorily. I say that because, although there have been cases of child abuse in The Island territories, the occurrences are rare and the level of severity minor relative to other nations.

The expulsion happened before I became Prime Minister. When I took office I instigated a programme, through The Self-policing State, in which children volunteer to help the authorities to control the problem and mitigate its effects, working with offenders in many cases before the offences are committed. In other words we adopt a philosophy of prevention rather than cure, and it does work, if only partially. These brave children act as befrienders to those who feel that they need the befriending, bringing about a controlled set of circumstances. Potential offenders who accept the terms and conditions laid down by the rules can remain within the law, and this has greatly reduced the number of cases of child abuse coming to court. Our brave band of children help to make these rules so they, between them, decide what is acceptable and what is not. I am proud to say that they are very effective at what they do, and proud, having defused many potentially harmful situations. I will continue to support them. Next."

"Mr. Andros Katriatis."

"Do you feel that The Island's media is fair and accurate in its reporting?" asked a Greek gent.

"The Island media tends to be a bit of a discreet entity, as you know. Reporting is honest and open, but, as with all media organisations, there are limits as to what can and will be reported. Occasionally some items do have to be censored in the interests of the community. We can't tell everyone everything. I know that in your research you looked closely into the reporting of the demonstrations in northern Kamchatka, and expressed dismay at the Greencoats who turned away the little girl who wanted to cross the border into Island territory. Some of this reporting was, I accept, suppressed, and we told our reporter that some photographs should not be printed as they could distort the truth, conveying the wrong impression to the outside world about The Island. Some scenes turned ugly and I kindly requested the media not to publish photographs of the riots nor of the combined actions of the Greencoats and the Russian police in controlling the crowd. The Russian journalists thankfully responded in kind. There were casualties, I accept that, and I have to share in the responsibility for that, but sometimes we have to be firm to prevent a situation that could be even worse. I know your set really felt for the little girl and her family, who were highlighted by our reporter Ms Smith, and I sympathise, but I'm sure that you can understand that we had to do what we did otherwise there could have been anarchy. We can absorb new towns only at the rate at which we can buy up the land and buildings and finance our tax liabilities, and wherever the border is placed there will always be those who will find themselves on the other side of it. I see you want to speak again."

"Yes. Don't you think that this situation could get out of hand soon?"

"No I don't think that because we have a very good understanding with the Russian authorities, who will use whatever force they deem fit to keep those who belong on their side of the divide to stay on their side, and as long as they do both sides can suppress reporting on the issue. It is unfortunate that we have some very poor towns close to our border and that those who live there are aware of the stark contrast between their towns and the ones on our side that have been absorbed by The Island and therefore have been converted to Non-Capitalist Economics. It is a fact that our Greencoats have fired warning shots to deter those who feel that they can sneak across undetected, and they have been informed that even if they do manage to get across they will be handed over straight away to the Russian authorities. It sounds harsh, but believe me it is the least worst option. Next."

"Miss Anne Clancy."

Anne rose.

"Will you take steps to drive out the fear of ageing by urging your MPs to provide improved access to the technology currently available for life extension and for more resources to be committed to the improvement of this technology in the interests of the community?"

"This subject has been debated in the Kamchatkan Parliament on several occasions and there has been a broad consensus to allow improved accessibility to what technology there is. Most people accept that this technology is in its infancy despite prolonged efforts to make it a reality. Progress is being made, but we all have to accept that it is slow, and that it is more likely that it will be your children rather than yourselves who will reap the benefits. We do owe it to the next generation to create a world with some of these benefits in place, but they will have to understand that should there be such a thing as life extension in this century it will certainly not be granted purely for play without a return of some sort for the community. I will do my best to put these measures in place. Next."

The questioning continued until all twenty sets had presented their questions. Then The Concierge brought the session to a close:

"Thank you. That concludes the formal part of today's proceedings. Let's now hear a big round of applause for Joan Carmichael, Prime Minister of The Island and its territories. I will now ask you to file past The Deming Memorial and to collect your ballot papers from the table beside it. You may then cast them or not, as you wish, at The Town Hall. My good friend The Reverend is already there and will tick your names off as you collect your papers."

With just 240 votes left to be cast the process was relatively quick.

*

As evening came the Kammies began to ferry staff and setmates to the station for the train that was to take them to the Royal Palace. The train halted at the Palace Gates station at the foot of the East Garden, where tents and marquees had been erected. At the other end of the Garden a large bonfire had been constructed next to a clear area where fireworks had been prepared. As at Halloween, stands had been placed for the provision of vegetarian hot dogs, crepes, vegetarian kebabs, bubble and squeak, and an assortment of sweet and savoury snacks. Long candlelit tables with punchbowls and salad had been set up on the lawn in the centre of the Garden, the weather still just about pleasantly warm. Nearest The Palace was the gold marquee, where The

Queen, her family, The Prime Minister, and other senior staff members of The Island would dine. A few yards from it was the somewhat larger blue marquee, which housed the same brass band that had played earlier at the Colonnade, and had a floor in front that had been laid down for dancing.

Joanie and the five royals, arrived in the royal coach, dressed in their best evening wear, with The Chancellor, Concierge and Reverend following behind in the Landau. Inconspicuously Sylvia was waiting to take a few pictures. When they were seated and all of the guests had arrived, The Concierge prepared to address the audience from the stand that had been placed outside the gold marquee.

"Ladies and gentlemen," he said. "As returning officer it gives me great pleasure tonight to declare the result of the seventieth Island leadership election. I hereby declare that the percentage of votes issued on behalf of the candidate, Joan Carmichael, Prime Minister of the Island and its territories is as follows: 100 per cent. I also declare that the number of votes cast in favour of the same Joan Carmichael is as follows: 100 per cent. I therefore declare that the said Joan Carmichael has been duly elected to serve as Prime Minister of The Island and its territories for a further year."

A loud spontaneous cheer then rang out.

"Yes, ladies and gentlemen, good citizens of The Island, she did it. We now have, officially, for the first time anywhere in the world, 100 percent votes issued and 100 per cent votes cast in favour of a single candidate, without coercion or corruption. In that regard I would like to thank our international observers, led by our trusted reporter Sylvia Smith, who can be satisfied that this is indeed a genuine world record. Now we can all stand proud and say that we have all played a part in this process, and be proud that we alone have the world's most popular leader, the one and only irreplaceable, Joanie."

He held her hand high as the crowd cheered again and she prepared to speak.

"Well, I counted them all out and I counted them all back. Fellow citizens. Good friends. True friends. I would like to thank all of you from the bottom of my heart. This world record is my dream come true, and it pleases me that just as, hopefully, Her Majesty and I have been able to make your dreams come true by bringing you here, so you have repaid in full by securing this most special re-election. I see I have just been passed a copy of tomorrow's *Island Times*, hot off the press, with the headlines 'It's Official, It's One Hundred Per Cent at Seventieth Election'. I will, of course endeavour to serve you all as in the past, my dear constituents, and all of the territories of The Island as its leader and political representative. I am proud to have the confidence of all of Her Majesty's ministers, as well as the continued confidence and respect of all of our citizens and supporters worldwide, who, like myself, continue to dream of making the world a better and safer place, and, slowly, we are getting there."

The crowd cheered again.

"We are all winners here tonight," she continued. "We stand united as one. Before today you had not chosen me nor I you, but thanks to our One Party Democracy we can all speak with one voice. It gives our Government a power, a strength and a popularity that cannot be matched. As in other aspects of life, The Island leads the way, ahead of every other nation, and you can all feel proud to be a part of it on this our beautiful Island of Dreams. I thank, as ever, my loyal and faithful staff for all of their hard work over the past year, and of course, Her Majesty The Queen, His Majesty The King, and The Queen Mother, for their devotion and dedication to all of our loyal subjects in our territories and beyond. Ladies and gentlemen, Your Majesties, Your Royal Highnesses, I promise to serve you well. I will now ask you all to enjoy the rest of this night. Eat, drink and be merry, and I love you all. Let the display commence."

The bonfire lit spontaneously and fireworks were released into the night sky. Catherine wheels mixed with gold and silver sprays, and sparklers were handed out to the setmates, who were invited to approach close to the fire where potatoes were baking, free for the taking along with various fillings. Rockets and roman candles shot up providing a colourful display that lasted for about twenty minutes. At the end an array of golden fireworks displayed The Island logo of Saturn on an illuminated blue background, underneath which was the message 'The Island of Dreams – 70 years leading the world'.

The sets mingled together as the band played and the floor of the ballroom marquee was opened for dancing. As the wine flowed the setmates, who had by now got to know each other quite well in this somewhat closed community, were able to become just that little bit more intimate, but in a civilised and respectful fashion, quite unlike the environment that Gary had left behind some seven months earlier.

The Queen and Prime Minister made a point of mixing with the crowd as the evening wore on, taking care to shake hands and circulate with everyone, thanking them individually for their support.

At half past ten the familiar whistle of the locomotive Prince told setmates that it would soon be time for them to board the train back to The Town, with The Chancellor and The Concierge providing a gentle cue.

215

Chapter Sixteen
Christmas Lights

One month later.

Gary and the others were working late in the afternoon at the rink where Jobine was teaching them some new lifts now that they had become more confident in attempting them.

"Lifts help to teach you how to develop complete confidence in your fellow setmates," Jobine asserted. "There is a wide variety of lifts that you are likely to encounter with the Kamchatskiy trainers so it's as well to be familiar with the basic ones. Some, like the straight-arm lift and the frog lift, are couple lifts. Others, such as the shuttle lift that you will be using in your Carnival routine, are designed to involve the whole set. The shuttle lift is one that involves switching or shuttling partners as it is performed. Some of the others involve rotating as the partners are lifted, whilst others, like the spinning lotus, involve a turning action once the girl has been lifted into a lotus position, and passing of the girls round in a circle. However, as the shuttle lift is going to be your centrepiece, and all sets must have a centrepiece, we will try to perfect that one with the others practised just sufficiently for the Kamchatskiy trainers to be satisfied that you have a working knowledge of them.

I can tell you that your lifting capability has to be improved considerably if you are going to achieve the standard that the Kamchatskiy trainers are going to expect by Mardi Gras. However, I also need to get you used to working with the car as prop."

The display model of the new executive Kamchatskiy, The Silver Shadow, was presently driven onto the ice.

"This is what you are going to be working with," she explained. "It's smaller than the real-life model, with dimensions that have been specially tailored to allow lifts like the shuttle lift to be performed above it. In order to perform it I need the six men and three girls. I will start with Anne, Connie and Graca. Yvonne I have a special role for you that I will explain later. Now I want two men each to lift one girl by the feet and shoulders so that she clears the roof of the car by half a metre. I then want you to stand in a line so that all three girls are suspended over the roof of the car. I then want the girls to be interchanged between you starting with the rear end girl and the centre girl. The rear girl passes under the centre girl as the first two partnerships are switched. Then it will be the turn of the front end girl who will pass under the new centre girl so as to finish in centre position. When you have had a few goes I will change the girls around so that each gets to practice the move from every starting position. By the time we reach Carnival Night you need to be able to make this complex lift look effortless."

The first three girls did as Jobine asked and they were all lifted successfully into position. It was when the interchanging started that the trouble began. Arms flapped and legs kicked as the changeovers faltered repeatedly. Jobine knew, however, that the shuttle lift was going to be a real challenge for the setmates, and that she was going to have to have patience as she had had in the past, so she did her best to be encouraging.

"Not bad for a first attempt," she said as she swapped the first three girls for the second, who predictably didn't fare much better. "Come on lads now you have practised with the first three girls already. It's all about timing. If you time yourselves correctly you will be able to make it."

She put her hands over her face when the boys managed to drop Claudia feet first onto the roof of the Kamchatskiy.

"Never mind," she said calmly. "You can allow yourselves one mistake. At least nobody was hurt. Try again."

They repeated the move and this time they just about completed it, although it was slow and cumbersome and would never have fitted to the timing of the music.

"Do you think that we will ever be able to manage that?" Carl asked Jobine at the end of the session.

"In a few weeks I'm sure," she replied. "A lot of it is just nerves, and a case of persisting and not giving up. Once you can interchange the girls consistently then we can look at getting the lift sequence fully choreographed."

By the time the set had finished at the rink the winter sun had already set over The Island. As the set returned to Angel the Christmas lights were turned on, brightening up the scene, with a distinctive Santa and reindeer flashing so as to bring life to The Colonnade. A large Christmas tree had been placed at the far end of the Leo's Lake nearest The Gloriette whilst other Christmas themed illuminations had been placed around it.

"Pretty lights," Claudia commented, rubbing her hands together as a slightly chilly breeze now rolled in from the sea under the clearing skies.

"Yes," replied Anne. "That reminds me. We must collect our Christmas vouchers tomorrow from The House of Cards. Eleven vouchers each the manager said to use as we wish on special gifts from the Christmas section."

"What if somebody wants to make a special gift, to another set for example?" Gary asked.

"I think you can requisition special gifts over the allowances," said Connie. "As long as they are just a few the system will tolerate it. The vouchers are specifically designed for the set to use so that we all get to give and receive the same number of gifts to each other. That way nobody gets left out I suppose."

"Yes, the Government here is obviously very keen to see that no one becomes marginalised," Michael added.

*

The next day after breakfast the set made the finishing touches to the Christmas decorations that Joanie had provided for them. Then Anne keyed in to Commander to check their messages.

"That's good," she said.

"What's that?" asked Lars.

"Jobine has sent us a message saying that she has completed the editing of the music for our skating routine. Hang on, there's something from The Prime Minister."

When she said this the setmates quickly gathered round.

"What does it say?" asked Carl.

Anne read the message.

"On New Year's Day, The Island will host its annual fun and games contest, Games Without Frontieres, for all of the finalists from the Island territories. You can see examples of the games on your consoles. To help keep the tradition alive all sets are asked devise their own original game for the event, which will be held on ice at the Non-Olympic Stadium. So whether it be leaping polar bears, dancing penguins or ice and fire, get your creative caps on and start dreaming up the weird and wonderful for our annual day of thrills and spills. Submissions should be made to The Chancellor in the Great Dome no later than noon one week from now."

At the rink Jobine was waiting for them on the ice, with the car placed in the centre.

"You have listened to your edited music?"

They nodded.

"Great," said Jobine. "Now we can use it to complete the choreography."

They listened together to the track.

"So, let's see how it goes on the ice working with the car as prop. I did say that I had a special role for Yvonne."

Yvonne looked at her quizically as she beckoned her to

approach her and then asked her to perch herself on the bonnet of the Kamchatskiy.

"You look very suggestive on that bonnet," laughed Elena.

"She does," added Jobine. "And that's where I want the routine to start, with Yvonne looking sexy on the bonnet whilst the rest of you admire her. Then the dancing will begin. You have eight seconds of intro. Then you need to be ready for the Silver Shadow piece to begin. Yvonne you will be dressed in silver for the part of Silver Shadow."

They took their positions.

"The beginning needs to be snappy," Jobine emphasised. "You could start by all holding hands, except Yvonne who will start on the bonnet. Then you need some catchy little moves to get the audience focused. Remember, it's your car, and you want everyone to be interested in it."

The set continued to work out their moves one by one, as they took the music section by section. Small turns and lifts were integrated together into the formation dance interspersed between static poses prior to the introduction of the shuttle lift.

"It needs to flow smoothly," Jobine called to them. "And you need to stay perfectly matched. Two or three of you are not in time and not coordinated with the others. Try again."

The set changed the sequence of moves about four times before Jobine was eventually satisfied that they had a routine that was adequate to work with as a composition that would form the basis of their first demonstration performance.

"You have just under three months left in which to get it perfected," Jobine reminded them. "Along with all the other things. I can see I'm going to have to increase your training schedule."

When they returned to their cottage their schedule was already waiting for them. From now on they had to put in a minimum of twenty hours of ice time per week rather than the current fifteen, in addition to continuing with the study modules and lectures for Mitsumoto-san. The schedule was intentionally intensive as Christmas approached, with up to four sets being taught on the ice simultaneously, but that was not to say that Joanie intended sets to miss out on Christmas cheer and festivities. On the contrary, her desire was that this Christmas on The Island of Dreams would be the most memorable of their lives for the setmates. A carefully constructed programme of Christmas shows and parties were therefore laid on so that all sets could enjoy entertaining nights out and happy times together. After all, this was a once in a lifetime experience.

The sets skated by day and relaxed by night, allowing for a couple of hours of study in between. The lectures were spaced out slightly more to allow for the increased ice time, and some morning sessions started slightly later during the Advent season so that setmates could relax a little more in the evenings.

*

One week later Joanie was ready to receive the submissions for the New Year Games Without Frontiers contest. Gary's set was the last to submit, which prompted her to activate her screen and view Gary's set as the setmates finalised their submission.

"Everybody loved the penguins last year," said Lars.

"I know," said Anne. "But it's been done to death recently, just like the polar bears and the sledges. All of the archive footage shows that."

"No, we can't have sledges, or skaters in reindeer outfits, and we definitely don't want to duplicate any ideas from the other sets," said Connie.

"Well, as we are the last set to submit we can at least view all of the others' submissions now. We need to hurry up and decide though because it's now twenty past eleven and it has to be in by noon."

"I think we should go with Connie's idea of having ten snow maidens being rescued by elves," suggested Graca. "No other set has come up with that."

"I agree," said Jose.

"And me," said Yvonne.

"Then we are all agreed we will submit Connie's snow maiden game?" said Anne.

The set nodded.

"I must say I'm looking forward to looking at all these wonderful games," The Chancellor said. "I have a feeling this will be our best grand final of Games Without Frontieres yet. It gets better every year and everybody loves it."

"The teams take it all very seriously," Joanie said, smiling. "But it's so nice to see competition made fun, which is why Queen Mary resurrected the concept that was popular in Europe in the 1960s and 70s and decided to adopt it as an Island tradition on that otherwise redundant Non-Olympic Stadium of ours. So, has the council been briefed for the appraisal of the twenty games?"

"Yes Ma'am," said The Chancellor.

"Good. Because it looks as if Anne Clancy is about to make her way to The Town Hall."

*

Christmas Eve arrived and all sets had been given the day off to complete their last-minute shopping from the Christmas catalogue and to prepare their Christmas night feast. Other than that the day was given over to relaxation with other sets in the bars where Christmas savouries and snacks were served, with vegetarian turkey, stuffing and cranberry top of the list, along with other alternatives such as mushroom vol au vent, potted shrimps and a variety of fish. The festive gluhwein was popular, as were the obligatory mince pies, mini Christmas puddings, Christmas cake and iced stollen.

Staff and setmates mingled together sharing experiences, with staff keen to find out informally from all of the new recruits just exactly what they thought of The Island and its philosophy in the ninth month of their stay.

"You're all celebrities now," came the constant message from the staff.

They tried their luck in The House of Cards at a variety of games including bar billiards, poker, roulette, and various games of skill which offered the possibility of winning various token prizes. In this respect The Island was not totally devoid of gambling. It just didn't offer huge rewards or the possibility of losing a fortune, as was the case under capitalism.

Then it was back to Angel and a chance to admire the Christmas lights once more before getting ready for the evening feast of Christmas fare complete with vegetarian turkey, which they all helped to prepare. Then the presents were laid around the tree, ready for opening the following day.

Joanie, still at work, observed each of the sets in turn.

"It's pleasing to see that in every case the sets are all working well as teams. That's the true Island spirit," Joanie said to The Chancellor. "Now we must prepare for the Midnight Mass, and what comes afterwards."

"Of course Ma'am."

*

At half-past eleven the church bells chimed, summoning staff and setmates alike to the Island church, which was, like all other churches in the Island territories, divided into a main service area, complete with pulpit and pews, and several side areas each dedicated to a specific religion or belief, the emphasis being on combining and respecting as many recognised faiths of the world as possible.

A single chime of the church bell served to indicate that the initial prayer period was over and that the main service was about to begin. The Reverend lit a candle beside the Nativity Scene that had been constructed by The Island's senior citizens and was toward one side of the main altar. The main altar meanwhile was devoid of the religious connotations that usually characterised altars. For, whilst there was religious décor in the various religious chambers of the building, the main altar intentionally did not favour any specific religion. Instead it was a plain marble altar that had at its centrepiece a brass statuette not of the Virgin Mary, but of the Founder Mary of The Island Faith. It was a large church, with enough space for the entire Island to be enclosed within it at any one time. Not that that happened, except on this one night.

The congregation took its place in the long rows of pews that had been laid out. When The PM, royals and senior staff were seated in the reserved front row, The Reverend commenced the short service.

"Welcome all of you to this our annual Midnight Mass service. We are a fine church and a fine community, and I am pleased tonight to welcome you all to it. As you know, we are a religion with a difference, and behind me is the person whom we all must thank for it's existence, the true life-saver herself our good Founder Mary. I say she is a saviour of life for it was her who brought to us the unique philosophy of religious tolerance and understanding that we enjoy today, and that has become so instrumental in our objective of achieving world peace.

We therefore pray this night for hope that throughout the world through her and her thinking, all religions may be liberated and born anew so that they can be practised throughout the world without fear. Her dream is our dream, that Christmas should be enjoyed by everyone, of whatever faith and in whatever land, and no more should religious dogma be used as a smokescreen for politics.

Lord in thy Mercy."

"Hear our prayer," responded the congregation.

"Let us pray for all those who, unlike ourselves, are still suffering from the effects of religious dogma, for all of those who have been killed and maimed as a result of it, and for those for whom these times are sad rather than happy. Let us pray for all of those whose hopes have been dashed, and for whom dreams have not been realised.

Let us pray also for those who are sick at this time, and for those who may need special comfort. Let us pray also for the continued success of our steady revolution, that it may continue to bring great benefit to the world, and succeed in its long-term objectives.

Let us pray especially for the good health of our noble Queen, and for her happiness and prosperity in the coming year whatever it may bring. We pray for the strength of character of whoever she may choose as her Prince Regent, and that as our leader he will prove to be a worthy King when his great moment of crowning shall come.

Lord in thy Mercy."

"Hear our prayer."

"Let us also give thanks on this happy day, for our Prime Minister, for her wise governance, and for the unending joy that she has brought to us. We pray that in the year ahead she will be able to continue her good work, and, with the help of her ministers, will be able to continue with the excellent management of our Island and its territories. We must also congratulate her again for her well-deserved world-beating election victory, which could only happen on The Island of Dreams.

I now ask that we pray for each other as our setmates embark on a new stage in their lives. We hope that in every case each one of you will go forth in the name of God to lead happy and fulfilling lives in your new land, free from the shackles of capitalism, and able to serve to the best of your ability and potential.

You all learnt here about the spiritual concept of The Golden Harp. Keep it in your minds as we enter a new year of hope and prosperity and as we pray for the continued success of my dear friend and colleague, Patrick O'Rourke, in his endeavours in Chechnya and elsewhere so that he might continue to lead and achieve further the wonderful transformation that he and his brave compatriots have engineered to such great effect.

Accept these prayers O Gracious Lord we beseech thee.

Lord in thy Mercy."

"Hear our prayer."

A selection of carols followed, sung by the choir of The Karaginsky School. Then, with the service over the setmates walked back to their cottages. Joanie and the royals took the royal Kammie. Joanie disembarked at The Great Dome where she took her seat and pressed the button that released The Eagle, that mechanical bird which stood ten feet high and was housed in the roof of The Dome.

The roof opened and the bird shot out. The setmates gazed upward as its now recognisable screeching forced attention from the people below. Overhead it flew, as it had done at Halloween, except this time it was illuminated with reindeer pulling Santa's sleigh. It circled overhead for about ten minutes before returning to The Dome from which it had emerged. This time, however, the roof did not close. The iron bird merely perched upon its launching bar, its wings gently folded.

It was not until the entire Island was asleep that the wondrous invention flew out again, but this time more quietly. There was no screeching or sound of any kind, although the illuminations were still lit.

At about 1 a.m., as Gary and Connie slept, a rustling sound was heard.

"What's that?" whispered Gary.

"What?" asked Connie.

"Didn't you hear it?"

The sound came again.

"Yes, I heard it. It's downstairs. I'll go and take a look."

Everything appeared normal, until a slight rustle drew their attention to the large ornamental fireplace at the far corner of the living room, into which a Christmas stocking had been dropped. Connie looked out of the window as the others rushed down.

"Oh my God," said Claudia quickly, smiling as she looked out also.

What she saw was the Eagle flying from cottage to cottage, then settling on each rooftop whilst a man dressed as Father Christmas stuffed the filled stockings through a special opening in each one.

"Hmm. Who do we know who comes out into The Town in the dead of night?" said Connie, as she and Graca watched a stocking being poked down one of the specially adapted chimneys of one of the neighbouring cottages.

"It's The Night Watchman," Graca replied. "He's riding on the back of that amazing bird."

"I bet he has some fun doing that every year," said Gary.

*

On Christmas morning the set enjoyed a light breakfast before setting to the task of opening the presents which they had 'purchased' for each other with their vouchers. Then, there were the surprise gifts that each setmate had been given courtesy of Joanie's Christmas stocking.

"Each one of these has a name on it, so you can see which ones are yours," said Anne.

The surprise presents were mostly Island souvenirs identified by Joanie and her staff. There were, for example, items of jewellery, for the girls, hats and scarves for the men, and general gifts such as Island tablemats and coasters, and souvenir platinum badges for each setmate, with The Island logo and each setmate's personal name engraved upon them along with the words 'Class of 2107'. There was a special six-inch high golden globe of Saturn which stood upright on a blue john base, and signed photographs of Queen Katie and The Prime Minister. The intention behind these gifts was clearly to help to give lasting memories of The Island experience, which were unique to those who had had the rare honour of being trained on The Island of Dreams. These gifts were not the type that could be requisitioned with vouchers.

The gifts that the setmates had obtained for each other by contrast were not generally souvenirs, but gifts that were more typical of Christmas. Such items as watches, luxury food items, vintage Island bottled Two's Company wine, commemorative bottles of Prince Regent lager, Number Six stout, sportswear, leather goods, golf balls and various items of clothing such as suits, jackets, blouses and coats. Here the emphasis was on functionality rather than nostalgia.

The set was booked in for Christmas lunch at The Training Centre where the retirees had taken some considerable time and trouble to serve up a feast to remember for all of the setmates in four sittings. Gary's set, as they were representing Kamchatskiy Auto, were in the first sitting.

The retirees, like everyone on The Island, took great pride in their work, ever-mindful of the teaching of W. Edwards Deming, to which they were all devoted. By three o'clock all of the sittings were complete and all setmates assembled in their cottages to listen to The Queen, as she delivered her annual Christmas message from The Island to its territories.

The setmates congregated around the television in accordance with the time-honoured British custom which The Island monarch had adopted since the time of Queen Justine. The Island flag introduced the broadcast, accompanied with the national anthem of The Island, 'I vow to thee my Island', sung by The Island's very own King Kenneth male voice choir.

On the screen Queen Katie appeared not on The Island, but at Buckingham Palace in London, where she mingled with other monarchs at a state reception. She shook hands with all of them, exchanging greetings. This had clearly taken place well before Christmas. Then, she delivered her speech from her own Royal Palace.

"Loyal subjects," she said. "It gives me great pleasure to address you today as your Queen. It is an honour for me, and I thought I would begin by showing a short scene that came as a great and pleasant surprise to me as well as to many others to whom I have spoken. I was both pleased and surprised this year to be the first Island monarch ever to have been invited to a state occasion at Buckingham Palace. There I had the unique privilege of being introduced to various heads of state from around the world. The welcome and respect that I received was unprecedented, and the messages I received were even more unprecedented.

The message that came from these people was one of great hope, being told by many of them that all of the monarchs from around the world were now looking to The Island to give their institutions fresh hope in troubled times. I was astounded to hear that some of them were actually looking to me to bring about new and sustained change to the world, and that they believed that as the world's youngest and newest monarch I would be positioned to make advances in times when they could not. I was, they said, the only monarch left that was actively participating in a revolution, and that I was uniquely placed to appeal to the younger generation and to steer them in the direction of good practice both in work and family life.

I was moved to have been invited as the guest of honour at this event, and yet more moved when many of these much older and established people stated that they hoped to learn from me and The Island's example. This was something which I never expected. Of course all of the world's monarchs today know of The Island and what we are about. They know that we have a long-standing aim to be a force for good in the world, but until I spoke to them I was never quite sure what other monarchies actually thought of us. Now I can truly say that whilst many politicians, who have achieved power generally as a result of winning a competitive and often corrupt election, may not have our best interests at heart, we do have some true friends and allies amongst the world's royal families. They do, without question, believe in us, and, furthermore, are not afraid to say so. To be told that I was a young bright shining star on the world stage was a comment that truly touched my heart. On hearing that I immediately promised that I would relay the message and all of their kind wishes to all of my subjects in Kamchatka and elsewhere.

I was told at the same event that it was not always easy being a monarch. Most these days are constrained by elected governments that do not deserve to be elected. I was then again surprised when quietly, over dinner, I was told how other monarchs wished that they were in my shoes, having such a wonderful Government, Prime Minister, and friends with whom I was able to work and effect decisions. I had no idea that the world's kings, queens, princes and princesses were thinking along these lines, and it shows that the world is changing. They are constrained in areas where I am strangely free. The lack of competition and capitalism in our society gives us an overwhelming advantage.

This advantage, as I said to our hosts, was hard won and is not God-given. It comes only from the help and support of our people, and I made it known that my people, rather than any personal fortune or wealth, were my greatest asset. Unlike other monarchs, I do not have a fortune, but then, with support such as I have from my people, I do not need one. What I had, and they did not, was a better way of managing the world. They knew it, and they respected it. What was more, some of them made it known that they wanted it. I said in return that I was more than happy to help anyone and everyone in royal circles who is keen to learn and apply more of our theory and practice. To be told that my popularity amongst my people as a monarch was greatly envied by certain other monarchs was, to me, a revelation.

That brings me to the question of the sovereignty of nations, which has been a talking point recently with all world leaders. The difference between sovereignty and ownership is becoming much less clearly defined. As The Island has proved, it is possible now to have ownership and governance of a territory without necessarily having sovereignty. Sovereignty can remain constant, yet the sovereign as such can be different and linked to ownership. That is the unique position in which I, as Queen of Kamchatka, find myself. The Falkland Islands, for example, are the sovereign territory of the United Kingdom, and therefore fall under the territory of the British monarchy, but in reality the ownership of the territory falls under The Island, as does the newly acquired territory of Tierra del Fuego. The new arrangement naturally places myself as joint head of state for both territories.

I once thought that such an arrangement could lead to great conflict, but in fact it has created unity, with all of the world's monarchies wishing me well in my new role. Even the Government of Argentina has wished me well, as through me The Falklands have now been joined with Argentina, but not in a way that anyone would once have imagined.

Elsewhere in the world The Island continues to be a force for good. In Chechnya, for example, new schools and hospitals are being built and crime is down by a factor of ten on last year, making it now one of the world's safest regions outside Island territory. Then there are the very poorest areas of the world where our activists are busily at work building new reservoirs and transforming transport systems so that people in some of the most deprived regions can start to have safe and healthy lives in pleasant surroundings. Earlier this year I met some of these people and saw for myself just what had been improved, for example in Zimbabwe, Rwanda and Somalia."

The Queen was then shown talking to the Island-sponsored engineers who were working on the irrigation and building schemes, showing the before and after results.

"And this is all funded through Non-Capitalist Economics," The Queen said to one engineer.

"All through Non-Capitalist Economics," he confirmed.

Then she turned to the still unresolved issue of landmines, and was seen walking with a soldier along a remote piece of Somalian coastline.

"I am not the first member of a royal family to draw attention to this issue," The Queen said. "But it's still a problem."

"It's still a problem," replied the soldier. "It's outlawed but it's still practised. Your help has been invaluable in helping to eradicate it. Once people are well fed and contented the incentives are much reduced, and the people then respect those who are giving them lives that are worth living."

"Do your people see us as peacemakers?" asked The Queen.

"Without a doubt," the soldier answered.

"We wish we could do more," said The Queen, returning to her broadcast. "But even our powers are limited. The key issue is how to do as much as possible with as little as possible, and, above all, to strip out waste from the system so that as many people as possible benefit. I told the monarchs in London that it is not as difficult as it looks to achieve dramatic results just so long as resources are channelled directly to where they are most needed, with careful thought and application, and not diverted through costly and unnecessary administration systems.

My final message to you for this year is to ask that each and every one of you continue to play your part in helping to support and comfort each other, and to give special help to those most in need. In this it may help to remember the teachings of William Edwards Deming and to, as he taught us, work constantly to improve the system.

As your Queen I wish you all a very happy Christmas and contentment in the coming year."

"Some tea and then we can join the carol singing," Anne suggested.

The Karaginsky School Choir led the singing in The Square, where staff and setmates joined together in celebration, along with Sylvia, who took her obligatory photographs for *The Island Times*.

At the end of the singing the Eagle made one more flypast as dusk fell, circling overhead for ten minutes, with both its Christmas illuminations and its passenger from the previous night. Santa waved, his image just about discernable in the twilight. Then, it was off to The Cat and Fiddle for wine, sandwiches, and some games of chess with The Reverend and Concierge on hand to give a few tips.

*

On Boxing Day the set had decided to go skiing, as fresh artificial snow had been laid down so as to create the ideal piste. Santa's grotto had been decorated for the occasion, with Nativity scenes and all things festive. The children of The Island had made these, along with ice sculptures of Father Christmas, The Prime Minister, The Chancellor, The Queen and her parents, all made in ice and carefully preserved in the cool chamber.

The skiing was a welcome change and challenge for the set as they braved the downhill and the slalom. Other sets also tried their skills, with help from The Island's skiing instructor Sheena, principal to The Concierge. Then, by way of a change, they took their chances on the four-person bobsleigh which zoomed its way down the ice channel that ran parallel to the ski slope as far as the next cable-car stop. This was new to the setmates and definitely an experience.

Bitten by the winter sports bug, the setmates continued to make the most of the facilities that were provided for the next few days, and Joanie was happy to allow these days of relaxation during the festive season. The royal family and The PM even joined in, The Queen inviting sets to join them for curling in the East Garden, where the site which had been used for the bonfire and firework display had now been used to provide a curling rink.

In the evenings The Cat and Fiddle and The House of Cards extended the holiday atmosphere as special food and drink was provided relieving setmates from the usual requirement to prepare their own evening fare. In The Cat and Fiddle the visitors could relax and party with the setmates, pulling crackers, telling jokes and enjoying the odd dance as the band played a medley of ballroom favourites.

The evening of 30th December ended for Gary's set in the snooker room of The House of Cards where they played for a while against Hamish's set. Two tables were free so the girls played on one table and the men on the other until the game was complete.

"Right down to the last black," her friend Angie from Kamchatskiy Aerospace said to Anne. "But someone has to win."

"Great game though," said Connie as they shook hands. "We lost, but where would we be without competition?"

Then, with closing time approaching, it was time just for one short walk around The Square with the other set to talk and admire the Christmas lights.

Chapter Seventeen
Games without Frontiers

New Year's Eve for Gary's set began with a round of golf on The Island's championship golf course, which was on the west side of the island, just north of the secluded West Garden and private beach of The Royal Palace. It was the ideal chance for Gary to try out his now rusty golfing skills, whilst the course, which was managed by The Queen's gardener, provided clubs. That man of many talents, The Concierge, a keen golfer, was on hand to provide private tuition to the setmates to help them to improve their game.

"Keep your eye on the ball and try not to stab at it when you strike," he advised Gary on the practice ground. "And Anne try to flex your legs a little more, and keep your left shoulder in line with the direction in which you want to aim."

With the half hour of tuition complete they commenced their round in couples, having had a mini-draw earlier at breakfast to determine who would be paired with whom. The result was three girls paired with each other, and three men paired with each other.

The course was a challenging links course, with a prevailing light westerly breeze. Joanie and the Queen regularly invited Government officials and heads of state to play there on state visits, as some of the photographs in the clubhouse indicated.

"I think we just had to play this course," said Anne as she struck her tee shot to the par three sixth. "I couldn't have left The Island without."

"I like some of the names they give to the holes," remarked Connie, with whom Anne was paired. "This one, for example, is called The Prisoner, because of the way the bunkers surround and guard the green. I see the seventh is called The Two Rivers because of the two rivers that cross the fairway. According to Patrick you never know quite how to play it. It's quite a difficult par four."

The par-five twelfth proved to be difficult for the set to negotiate, the tee shot over the bay catching a few of them out and requiring them to be three off the tee.

"The wind keeps catching the ball and driving it into the water," Gary said to Carl.

"Never mind. I'm not doing much better," said Carl. "I have taken four just to reach the fairway."

Terry and Lars meanwhile found the sand traps and burn on the fourteenth equally troublesome, with rusty putting giving them both double bogeys. Only the two girls Elena and Yvonne managed to stay under par within their handicap.

"So, you two must be the winners," said The Concierge, back at the clubhouse. "Congratulations. So now I think it's time for a drink. Now, Gary I know you like Number Six Stout, so I will go and pull one from the bar. And for Yvonne, for you I will pull a half litre of this year's commemorative lager, Prince Regent, so you can be the first to try the new draught, and for those who like wine I will bring a couple of bottles of Two's Company."

Gary and the others looked awhile at some of the photographs.

"Isn't that the King of Spain?" Claudia asked The Concierge.

"Yes, playing with Queen Katie last year," he replied. "He's played this course a few times. And he always curses when his ball lands in the sea or one of those deep bunkers that takes him no end of shots to get out of. He assures our Queen he will get his own back when he invites her to play on one of his courses. Not that I think he will beat her. She's very good."

"And who can we attribute that to?" laughed Jose.

The Concierge said nothing, but just grinned back as if it were a question that needed no answer.

"So, are you all ready for the fun and games tomorrow?" he asked.

"Oh I think that will be great fun," replied Connie. "Seeing all those hilarious games played out in costume. I can't wait to see what that snow-maiden game is going to look like."

"It will all be televised you know," answered The Concierge. "Everyone watching in The Island territories will see your game."

In the evening the setmates piled into The Cat and Fiddle where a ceilidh had been arranged with The Island's folk band Ten A Penny on hand to play a variety of Scottish jigs, reels and strathspeys as evening fare was served. At nine, a vegetarian haggis was piped in by The Night Watchman, who was dressed in his finest Glengarry tartan. The royals, The PM, Chancellor, Concierge, Reverend and Jobine joined the setmates for the celebration. Sylvia naturally also had a place and was on hand to take photographs, which she invited the setmates to keep as souvenirs. Then, at midnight they all assembled in The Square ready for The Bell Tower clock to ring in the New Year. The setmates circled Leo's Lake, joining hands for the traditional 'Auld Lang Syne'. Fireworks then lit up the night sky before the roof of The Great Dome opened and The Eagle made one last flight, with the message 'Happy New Year' prominently displayed over its wings.

*

The following afternoon the cable cars were filled to capacity as they shuttled staff, setmates and some lucky fans of the visiting teams up to The Non-Olympic Stadium ready to watch the eight visiting teams that had made through to the final of 'Games without Frontiers' to battle it out to win the honour of being crowned Games Without Frontiers champions for 2108. Setmates would also have the pleasure of seeing the games that they had invented performed by the teams. The materials and props had been flown in and assembled in advance ready for the contest, which was jointly hosted by The Concierge and Chancellor. In the stands setmates and staff watched on, joined by invited guests from the winning towns. Joanie, The Queen and the royal set filled the royal enclosure.

"Welcome citizens to Games Without Frontiers," The Chancellor hailed. "The friendly games where competition becomes everything and nothing, where laughter abounds, and where everything turns out well in the end. You know the rules I'm sure. We have eight teams who play a total of twenty games. On any one of them they can play their joker, which will automatically double their score. For each game the winner receives eight points, then seven, then six and so on."

"My good friend The Reverend becomes our trusted referee," The Concierge continued. "And a lovely lady by the name of Jobine will be on hand to start each game with a blow on her magic whistle, and look after the scoreboard."

"So without further ado, let's meet the teams," said The Chancellor. "Open the portcullis."

The portcullis at the centre of the arena on the cable-car side opened and the teams skated into the stadium as The Island band played.

"So now we have our wonderful finalists from our eight heats," The Chancellor continued. "Please welcome the best eight teams from The Aleutians, The Falklands, Kamchatka North, Kamchatka Central, Kamchatka South, Sakhalin North, Sakhalin South and The Kuril Islands."

The visitors skated around until all of them had entered. Then the band stopped.

"Thank you, my friend," said The Concierge. "Now as you all know, this is the grand final, with the best scoring sides from each of the eight Island territories. In this special show we have a total of twenty games based on a Christmas and New Year theme, each of which is devised by one of the twenty sets that Her Majesty Queen Katie invited here as an opportunity to transform their lives. Now The Chancellor will introduce the first game."

"As you can see," The Chancellor continued. "There are eight Christmas angels each on the end of a jib who have to quickly levitate themselves using the toe-picks of their skates. Once aloft they have to stay there for as long as possible. As the time progresses the jib becomes heavier as the ice block that weighs it down melts over a column of steam and the angels have to flap their wings in order to prevent themselves from falling back to earth. It's a lovely game and it is the competitor who can stay aloft the longest that will win the eight points for their team. On Jobine's whistle, three, two, one, go."

On hearing the whistle the angels rose with the all-important push from their toe-picks, rising high and remaining there for as long as they could. It was a test of stamina as the counterbalancing mechanism on the jibs gradually made it increasingly difficult to remain aloft.

Gary's set, like the other sets, had reserved places such that they would have a good view of the game that they had invented, in this case game eleven.

"I wonder which set came up with that," said Anne, commenting on the first game, which was not too far from game eleven.

"I think that was Marie's set," answered Terry. "They researched the origins of 'Games without Frontiers' and went into the archives right back to 1982 and got the idea for this wonderful game from the very last European version of *'Jeux sans Frontieres'*. They then adapted it for this event. Quite clever, I thought."

"I'm looking forward to seeing what they make of our game," said Claudia.

The games used a set of standard props with additional features. There was laughter and cheers as the teams scrambled for coins in Christmas puddings, leapt over pontoons dressed as mince pies, decorated Christmas trees in outfits that gradually inflated as opposing teammates turned wheels, chased turkeys around the ice, pulled sleighs full of presents dressed as reindeers, and generally had fun playing crazy games in outrageous costumes in a stadium that had been transformed into a winter wonderland for what was now its sole purpose.

Presently game eleven came around and The Chancellor introduced it:

"So to game eleven. Here we see ten snow maidens trapped on ice floes. They have to be rescued by elves who have to battle their way through a polystyrene barrier. They then have to negotiate an obstacle course. Their opponents will try to stop them from getting along by blowing snow at them, throwing snowballs at them and finally spraying them with a jet of water."

The Chancellor paused for a moment, struggling to control his laughter.

"The first elf to rescue their team's snow maiden and skate back to base with her will be declared the winner."

Jobine prepared to blow her whistle, but was temporarily stopped by The Chancellor.

"What is this?" he said, as he was approached by two competitors holding a shield with the letters KS printed on it. "Do I see the Kamchatka South joker?"

The Chancellor shook the competitors' hands and wished them luck. Then Jobine did blow her whistle and the game was underway, Gary and his setmates now adopting the Kamchatka South team and cheering them on, given that they had selected their game for their joker.

The Kamchatka South elf was quick off the mark, making it through to the glacier first, but as the snow came down and the snowballs were thrown he was soon caught up. He was, however, a fast skater and he was soon past the obstacles. He skated quickly past the water jet aimed at him by The Aleutians girl. Swiftly he grabbed his snow maiden from the raised pontoon, carried her over his shoulder and rushed back three seconds ahead of his Kamchatka North rival. The gamble had paid off and Gary and the others rose to their feet to cheer their adopted hero.

"Sixteen points from our game," Anne said excitedly as they watched Jobine press her magic button that saw their score rise.

Then it was quickly on to the next game, and so it continued until it was time for the final game, which was on a New Year theme and against the clock.

"So to our finale," The Concierge declared. "And it's all on the last game to decide whether the Games Without Frontiers champion of champions for 2108 will be Kamchatka North, Kamchatka South or Sakhalin South. Any one of the three could win. One man from each team has to skate as fast as he can in the harness, get airborne and fly through the air like grease lightning to the top of Big Ben which is set at half-past eleven. He then needs to wind the hands on, but as soon as he lands at the top three games from opposing teams will begin to try to wind the hands back from within the clock. The man at the top then has to unwind a rope and hoist up his five teammates so they can join him at the top and begin to wind the clock forward using a handle at the top. When both the long hand and the short hand reach twelve the clock will chime signifying the end of the game. Last year we had people chiming bells twelve times after skating along a thin ice beam. This year it is altogether a much more elaborate and demanding game. Teams, get ready. On the Jobine's whistle three, two, one, go."

The eight teams battled it out, and the fans cheered as the men in harnesses zoomed toward the clock faces before quickly unwinding the rope for the eagerly awaiting team-mates who were waiting at the bottom whilst the opposition frantically attempted to wind in the opposite direction in order to try to turn back the clock. Of course eventually the five men would succeed in winding the clock forward, with their superior strength and gearing, but it was a closely fought contest. One by one the chimes sounded until eventually the final whistle sounded with The Falklands and The Kuril Islands unfortunately failing to complete the game. Gary and the others continued to cheer their adopted Kamchatka South, but in the end it was Kamchatka North that was victorious, just shading Kamchatka South out of the points.

"Well, better luck next year," said Connie, as they watched the Kamchatka North captain receive the coveted trophy from Queen Katie, and his team completed its lap of honour, shaking hands first with Kamchatka South, then with the other teams.

"A gallant contest, conducted as ever in a wonderful spirit," said The Queen. "Now it's all over for another year and this lovely stadium will once more become a silent museum piece until it is brought to life once more on New Year's Day 2110 as there will be no games next year. But the spirit of Games Without Frontiers lives on. I thank you all for the laughter and cheer that you have given us."

Chapter Eighteen
Carnival on Ice

For the remainder of January, Jobine worked the setmates hard, determined to maximise their potential before they were finally handed over to their employers. For Gary and the others this meant a yet more intensive training schedule on the ice, as the set prepared for the Mardi Gras Carnival.

"I need this to be right for Carnival," Jobine asserted on the morning of February 4th. "First, the company routine for your year, which you will skate alongside the four other sets with whom you will be working when you join Kamchatskiy Auto. This is an original set pattern Paso Doble routine, the steps and choreography of which will be common to you five sets, and it is always skated to the company anthem of 'Viva Kamchatskiy', which is itself, as you know, cloned from the ever popular 'Viva Espana'."

Jobine reached for her mobile phone, and a few seconds later the Silver Shadow prop car was driven onto the ice.

"Now we will see what this Paso Doble is made of. Tomorrow I will watch you performing it alongside the other four sets. Only one set will be performing this on Carnival night, but all five sets must be able to skate it to exactly the same standard. There are no lifts in the company dance. It is just the Paso Doble steps that I have already taught you, together with some polished arm and head movements. What I want to see is six couples skating in unison maintaining a fixed distance apart just as we practised way back. When I blow my whistle I want you to take your positions at fixed distances around the car, and I want all of your body lines matching exactly, frozen in the waltz hold, heads slightly offset."

The music started and the set duly performed the dance for its stipulated three minutes.

"Cross rolls crisper Gary," shouted Jobine. "And Elena, your body-line must match those of the others, you're still slightly askew going round those corners. Remember you need the lilt as you go round the front and back of the prop and you must match your opposite number at the other end as you go round. We need perfect symmetry here."

At the end she summoned the set together again and shook her head.

"I have told you a thousand times," she yelled. "You must gain a consistent momentum around the ends to carry you round to the other side. There is a very pronounced rise and fall there as the choctaws take you round, and it is a Paso Doble rhythm so your arm raises must be firm and definite, and no gaps in hold. Timing is important here and yours is out. Try again."

The dance was repeated.

"Right," said Jobine. "Arm movements and turns better, but the dance holds need to be closer. It's still too much like you're on a dance interval skating with friends. This is your life now. It's a career. You will be touring in a few months time. Try again."

Jobine made the set perform this routine a total of eleven times before she moved on to the other Kamchatskiy routine, Silver Shadow, which was unique to them. This was a much more complicated affair, lasting for a full minute longer and incorporating a number of eye-catching lifts, in particular their centrepiece, the elaborate shuttle lift, and poses on the bonnet of the car at the beginning and end, which Yvonne had to master in addition to the routine as a whole.

"You have just two more weeks to perfect this routine ready for Carnival," said Jobine. "Your synchronisation needs to be 100 per cent better and the lifts absolutely in unison."

The set performed the routine once through, then again, and again, until they had performed it a total of five times. By now, however, the strain was beginning to show.

"I can't go on. I can't go on," said Yvonne tearfully at the end of the fifth run through.

The others came over to console her along with Jobine.

"Yvonne. Look. I know you're tired as we all are," said Jobine. "But you only get to do this once, and I know you can do it, and I know you want to do this, don't you?"

"Come on," said Carl. "You know we were all promised a better life when we came here, not an easier life."

She nodded and rose to her feet, the hug from Carl serving to give her the confidence that she needed.

"You're right I must pull myself together," she said. "We must go on."

They continued for another ten minutes until Jobine herself could see that there was little point in continuing yet further with a now exhausted set of recruits. Instead she requested a meeting with Joanie.

Back at the cottage the set watched as Jobine crossed The Square and ascended the steps that led from The Colonnade to The Dome.

"She's going to the Great Dome," Connie whispered as they watched her climb the steps.

"It's my fault. I know it is," said Yvonne, her tears reappearing as Lars consoled her.

"It's not your fault," he said. "We are all responsible together. That's one of the first things Island citizens are taught. You're as strong as the rest of us and nobody is ever going to say anything different, certainly not Jobine or Joanie. That routine is difficult, anyone will tell you that, and even the best skating partnerships get tested to the limit occasionally. I bet the other sets are going through exactly the same thing."

Criticism of the set was not, however, the reason why Jobine had decided to visit the PM.

"Do you think I'm pushing some of these sets too hard?" Jobine asked, after describing what had occurred.

"Not at all," said Joanie. "After all I am the one that asked you to do it. Sometimes to get the best out of people you have to raise the boundaries of self-expectation. All of the sets will emerge stronger for it."

"One of the setmates admitted we promised them a better life, not an easier one."

"Of course. We aren't here just to make life a pleasure-cruise. We are here to give people rewarding opportunities and a new life. I think you are doing a great job with these sets. Her Majesty is delighted with what you have achieved so far and so am I. No other trainer in the world could do what you have done.

No. You're doing just fine, and so are they. Carnival will be an absolute treat this year. It's always the case at this time of year, when sets are necessarily pushed that little bit harder that we will get the odd breakdown, but that does not mean either that the person is weak or that the coaching is wrong. It is just a normal part of working together."

"Do you think I should be a bit softer tomorrow?"

"No," Joanie replied. "That you must not do, otherwise the setmates will suspect that they are to blame, and we can't have that creeping in. No, you must continue to work them to their limits from now till the end. They will all respect you for it, believe me."

"Thank you Joanie. I don't know where I would be without you."

"Any time. The door is always open."

*

Shrove Tuesday was the first of the two Carnival days. As was customary the Flower Girls placed flowers on the windowsills of all of the cottages to symbolise the start of Mardi Gras. Then the costumes arrived, the set having been instructed to try these on to ensure that the tailoring had been correct, before the dress rehearsal that afternoon.

At two o'clock, the five Kamchatskiy Auto sets arrived at the rink to perform their routines once more through before the evening show, which would be presented to an invited audience that would include the PM, the royal family, and senior Island staff, as well as the directors of the four Kamchatskiy companies and the twenty Kamchatskiy trainers who, each year, were The Queen's guests of honour.

For Gary and the others the great day had finally arrived when they would present their display for the first time. It was the culmination of eleven months of dedicated work and practise.

Jobine summoned the setmates to the centre of the rink as she clutched a small black bag containing four coloured balls and a black ball. She blew her whistle and everyone stopped chattering.

"Right," she said. "One member of each set draws a ball from the bag. The set that draws the black ball gets to perform the Kamchatskiy Auto company dance for 2108. This will be the first time that it will have been performed before a public audience. I know that you would all like to perform it, but, to be fair, only one set can have the honour and you all have a one-in-five chance."

As it happened it was the French girl Marie who plucked the black ball from Jobine's old cloth bag.

"Looks like your set will be doing it," Jobine said to her as she could hardly believe her luck. "So you might as well take your positions. This means of course that you will be the last set to perform the demonstration dance."

Marie and her setmates duly took their positions around the Kamchatskiy prop and performed the new Kamchatskiy Auto version of 'Viva Kamchatskiy', which attracted a good round of applause from the others.

"That was well done," said Jobine. "I won't complain at that. That was good basic solid ice dancing performed as well as anyone could."

The main routines, however, were a different matter entirely. Jobine, always seeking perfection, tried hard not to shake her head as five difficult four-minute-long routines were performed well, albeit with small errors that were apparent to her, but not necessarily to anyone else. Inside she felt that she was responsible for these, even though the routines were sound and polished, but the dress rehearsal was a time for confidence building rather than the shaking of heads. She therefore refrained from the negative and instead delivered a pat on the back to each of the setmates, knowing that at this point she could do no more other than to ensure that all of her performers were sufficiently relaxed and confident to be able to perform to the very best of their abilities. Afterwards she would then hope, rather than assume, that the Kamchatskiy trainers would be satisfied with a job well done.

"That looks really fabulous," she said to Gary's set, seeking to enhance the setmates' morale. "Far better than a few weeks ago. It flows well and the transitions between moves are good. Whatever will be will be with the shuttle lift. I've tested you with it. You've shown that you can cope with it and I'm sure you will tonight. Yvonne, you're a star."

With the dress rehearsal over, the setmates studied the itinerary for the evening's events. The event itself would start at half past seven and continue until half past nine. There would be an opening number from the pupils of The Karaginsky School. Then the Kamchatskiy Auto prop, the scale model of the executive Silver Shadow, would be driven onto the ice and Marie's set would then perform the company dance. Afterwards the five Kamchatskiy Auto sets would perform their demonstration dances, the draw having placed Gary's set fourth in the order of performance. A resurface would follow with a fifteen-minute interval after which the five Kamchatskiy Maritime sets would perform.

*

Evening came and the ice rink was filled to capacity. The Queen was in attendance with the rest of her family, her parents and her younger brother and sister. Joanie was seated with them in the royal enclosure with their guests, the directors of Kamchatskiy Auto, Kamchatskiy Aerospace, Kamchatskiy Maritime and Kamchatskiy Logistics. Below them, at ice level, the twenty Kamchatskiy ice trainers sat, each in coloured training suits, red for Kamchatskiy Auto, white for Kamchatskiy Aerospace, blue for Kamchatskiy Maritime and green for Kamchatskiy Logistics. It followed that after the handover from The Island each set would be assigned one trainer from their respective company. Jobine sat in the centre, the visitors smiling and chatting amiably with her.

When everyone was seated and the first of the skaters were ready the PM rose to her feet.

"Welcome, ladies and gentlemen, distinguished guests, to The Island of Dreams," she began. "The place where each year Her Majesty Queen Katie fixes it for 240 people from outside The Island territories to change their lives forever and live the dream of becoming skating celebrities under the wing of the world's greatest transportation company, The Kamchatskiy Corporation. For the last eleven months our new recruits have had fun, learnt about a new way of living, new economic and political systems, advanced management skills and, on top of this, worked hard and given their all to perform for you to night. Thanks to our resident skating coach, Jobine, the finest ice dance trainer in the world, the miracle continues and for the eleventh year we have transformed 240 hobby skaters into true ice dancers. I ask that you applaud our fine setmates as we welcome them formally into our society and into our great company."

The audience applauded as Joanie paused.

"They have learnt everything about our social order, everything about management and everything about skating that Her Majesty's ministers have stipulated that they should know. Now it is down to you, the management of Kamchatskiy, to adopt these fine people so that they might give lifelong service to your company in its four divisions. I'm sure that they will not disappoint.

Soon you will see for yourselves the excellence of their capabilities. First, however, it gives me great pleasure, in keeping with Island tradition, to welcome a team of skaters from this year's invited school to perform the opening number for Carnival on Ice 2108. Ladies and gentlemen, distinguished guests, please give a special Island of Dreams welcome to the up and coming skaters of The Karaginsky School."

As the lights dimmed, two dozen skaters in their early teens stepped onto the ice. They were dressed as skeletons, their black leotard suits reflecting the phosphorescent bone outlines against the ultra violet. Then the music of Saint Saens' 'Dance Macabre' echoed around the rink.

The music fired the skaters into action with running and leaping and turns in the air. Various single and double jumps served together with intricate turns and spins to symbolise the releasing of wild spirits into the night and the bringing of death to life. Excellent solo ice dancing blended with high class free skating to give the exhibition a special essence that was rare to see. Then, as the music softened, the spirits quietened and the light gradually returned synthesising the dawn by which they were tamed. Slowly, one by one, they swayed and fell in a withering style as they dropped to rest.

The audience applauded as the performers rose and bowed.

"Thank you very much, Karaginsky Young Skaters," said Joanie. "They have come a long way to be with us tonight and that was a real delight to watch. You have trained hard to bring us that and it was great."

The smiles on the children's faces said it all. For them it was a dream come true to have the chance to perform in front of their Queen and Prime Minister as well as to visit The Island of Dreams, the birthplace of the economic and political system that had brought freedom from the misery of capitalism for them and others like them. There were even a few tears as they watched the royal family stand to applaud them. When the applauding had died down Joanie continued:

"It now gives me great pleasure to introduce to you the first of our five sets representing Kamchatskiy Auto. As is customary this set will begin by unveiling this year's Kamchatskiy Auto company dance, as devised by the five Kamchatskiy Auto trainers, to the company's anthem 'Viva Kamchatskiy'. Ladies and gentlemen, distinguished guests, please welcome them."

As the children left the ice the Kamchatskiy Silver Shadow prop was driven onto the ice and parked in the centre of the rink. Marie and her eleven setmates, dressed in Kamchatskiy Auto's glossy red uniform, then took their positions around it.

"The music please," said Joanie when she could see that they were ready to start.

The Paso Doble rhythm then rang out prompting a swift start to the dance, which was devoid of lifts or jumps, but demanded basic ice dancing steps in hold, cleanly executed. This performance would then provide the Kamchatskiy trainers with a first impression as to how well Jobine had succeeded in ensuring that they had mastered the basics to a supreme level of consistency. The evidence provided showed, naturally, that these setmates could really dance on ice. They were fast, smooth, and fully expressed the character of the Paso Doble in time to the music. In addition their pattern was perfectly symmetrical around the prop, and the couples were perfectly in unison with each other, two aspects that the Kamchatskiy Auto trainers, with their high expectations, were keen to observe.

At the end of the three-minute routine, Joanie rose to her feet and clapped, prompting the audience to do the same.

"Ladies and gentlemen, distinguished guests, the all-new Kamchatskiy Auto company dance for 2108. 'Viva Kamchatskiy' Auto version, beautifully skated. We salute you. We will welcome this set back when they perform their demonstration dance."

As she looked down to ice level, Joanie noticed the applause from the Kamchatskiy Auto trainers, and especially at one male trainer whose level of enthusiasm was decidedly greater than the others. This told her that he was more than satisfied with what would obviously be his set.

"Next, specially for the Japanese market, a big welcome for our first demonstration dance of 2108. This will be skated to the music of 'Japanese Medley' by one of my favourite modern music groups, Super Shogun."

As the setmates left the ice the first set to demonstrate stepped out dressed in their Japanese outfits, kimonos for the girls, Samurai warrior outfits for the men. Gentle chords of authentic Japanese koto music began the routine, the highlight of which was a rooftop lift that involved three men lifting a lady from three equidistant points at the same time. Each lady then laid back to link with the opposite lady to form three spokes of a wheel over the roof of the prop. Meanwhile the other three couples danced Japanese-style in the opposite direction to the turning wheel. Then, after a minute, they dismantled quickly and the directions and the roles were reversed. They danced perfectly in time to the music that became increasingly lively as it progressed, with the spinning lotus lifts, like the ones that Jobine had taught Gary's set, used to create an impressive finale to the routine. Quite clearly Jobine had biased her training with this set to favour the ability to combine difficult lifts with quick changes of position, as distinct from assembling and manipulating a single difficult lift over a sustained period of time, as was the case with Gary's set.

The next routine was very different and, again, contrasting in skill content. This time the skaters simulated the actions of croupiers and their assistants in a modestly satirical and cryptically cynical depiction of the world of capitalism in general and gambling in particular. The men mimed the actions of the croupiers spinning the roulette before lifting the girls straight upwards and turning them as they held the additional props, consisting of a rectangular tablet that they were able to hold up with their hands at the girl opposite. The electronic tablets enabled cards to be flicked exactly in time to the music as they held their positions at six evenly spaced points on either side of the car. The lifts were turning lifts, but when the cards were flicked the turning motion was quickly arrested, providing evidence of a specific skill that Gary and the others immediately identified.

"That is a superb lift," Yvonne remarked to her setmates, who sat at ice level towards the top end of the rink. "Did you see how well that turning lift was checked?"

"They can do it clockwise and anticlockwise as well," Elena added.

"Its absolutely brilliant," Anne whispered to herself.

"I'm looking at the head positions of the girls as they are lifted," continued Carl. "The girls' heads are all totally straight, the ascent was totally straight and they are looking firmly at the one opposite for exactly four beats whilst they flick the cards. Then they come down, all do a perfectly synchronised toe loop, and are perfectly placed for the next lift in the next position. Talk about right first time every time. Jobine has really gone to town on that with them."

"We have our high point too," Michael reminded them.

"You know I think there is a little bit of internal competition going on between those five Kamchatskiy Auto trainers," said Connie, as she observed the fact that after both of the first two performances one particular trainer cheered more than the others.

"Oh?" said Gary.

"Yes. There are five trainers, right?"

"Right."

"They all work together, but don't you detect that by the way each of them responds to each of the performances they are in fact trying each to outdo the others? When one trainer cheers more than the others it must be because that is going to be that trainer's adopted set."

"You might be right there," said Carl. "But it's clear that they all want the performances to be exemplary."

"That's for sure," Connie replied. "But it shows that internal competition is far from dead in a society that prides itself in supposedly eliminating it. There is clearly some satisfaction for the trainers in adopting a particular set and seeing it do something that distinguishes it positively from the others."

"I wonder which one we will get?" Anne asked.

"I think it will be that small fair-haired lady on the end of the row next to the Kamchatskiy Aerospace trainers," Terry answered, as he pointed to the lady who had applauded, but so far not cheered excessively, at the other performances, as well as studying her position relative to the other trainers, and noting the sequence of the higher cheering levels.

There was now just one more set to perform before Gary's set would be ready to take to the ice. Gary and the others knew that this set had worked especially hard on their showpiece maypole lift, which was their equivalent of the shuttle lift that had given Gary and the others, and particularly Yvonne, so much difficulty. Joanie presently introduced them:

"Now, ladies and gentlemen, distinguished guests, it gives me great pleasure to introduce our third Kamchatskiy set, the very special toys from our magical Island toybox, skating to the music of 'The Maypole Dance' by the ever popular Russian band Toytown."

In this routine, toys were brought to life by a fairy who descended from above by means of a harness, then became detached from it and subsequently became part of a vibrant scene. The maypole lift formed and reformed over the roof of the Kamchatskiy, such that each man took hold of one of the girls' feet and lifted her. She then laid back with her hands raised so she could link with the girl opposite. The whole formation then turned clockwise until it had completed four revolutions around the car. This centrepiece was like a chorus figure, with the verses consisting of synchronised movements representative of the dolls, puppets and marionettes that their costumes depicted. After each verse the maypole reformed, turning faster and faster as the routine progressed. The last verse took the form of a miming act designed to add variety and simulate fairground magic. Then, to finish, after the maypole lift had dismantled for the fifth time, the toys froze so as to provide the appearance of motionless toys waiting to be rewound.

When they had finished yet again there was the ecstatic applause of the audience and trainers with this time, predictably, a different trainer applauding and cheering more avidly than the others. Also, predictably, this trainer was not the small fair-haired lady.

As the setmates left the ice Gary's set prepared to step out to give the performance of their lives.

"Thank you skaters," said Joanie. "How did you like that?"

The audience cheered.

"A wonderful routine full of magic and charm. Now, to commemorate the launch of this fabulous new car, I will ask our fourth set to take to the ice to perform 'Silver Shadow', which has been specially composed for us by the Russian band, Silhouette.

Dressed in their silver catsuits, the setmates took their starting positions with Yvonne, the Silver Shadow, taking her place on the bonnet, and the others assuming various positions around the Kamchatskiy. Nerves were evident but not dominant, and no more apparent than they had been for the previous three sets, each of which they had seen manage to complete the tough routines that Jobine had choreographed for them with very few imperfections.

With Gary's set Jobine had placed the emphasis on maintaining a complex lift for a lengthy period of time, which required a high level of stamina. Yvonne, who had never been accustomed to being the centre of attention, suddenly found herself in a position where all eyes were upon her. She started on the bonnet, whilst the others began in fixed positions around the car. Then, when the music started she slid down and shadowed the other skaters with contrasting movements, as they all showed the trainers that they had a firm grasp of all of the standard single jumps, upright spins and step sequences comprising basic dance steps joined together with and without the aid of a partner. This continued for the first thirty seconds of the routine, before the six men lifted Connie, Claudia and Graca to form the shuttle that would be continuous for the next three minutes, with the girls being lifted so that one man held her shoulders and another her feet. They would then be interchanged such that the girl at the rear end changed first with the centre girl, passing under her, then with the front girl passing over her, and back again, to the centre position. Meanwhile a new girl was ready to join the line at the rear, so that eventually all of the girls would have participated in the shuttle.

It was fast, complicated and difficult to perform as it had to be sustained for a longer time than any of the lifts that the other sets had to perform, and indeed any lift that would normally be seen in a skating show. When they were not in the shuttle, the three skating girls had to return to the demanding solo skating in unison that Jobine had choreographed for them. This was the case for all of the girls except Yvonne, who, as the Silver Shadow, had her own special moves that had a higher degree of difficulty, but, at the same time, would earn the highest level of admiration from the trainers and the audience, making her stand out and feel special, which was something that Jobine had strived for as a matter of necessity to ensure that this particular setmate would not be lacking in confidence ever again. It was therefore the case that Yvonne's moves outside the shuttle, as well as the shuttle itself, would make or break the routine. She thus had to skate at a wider radius from the car than the others, which demanded more energy, and her step sequences were necessarily longer, more complex, and composed of harder elements. Once out of the shuttle she had to dominate the scene, almost overshadowing the shuttle itself. Like a phantom she had to be fast, furious and almost aggressive, completely outside her comfort zone, as well as perform every single step, jump, twizzle and spin excellently and consistently.

Three-and-a-half minutes into the routine the shuttle disbanded and the finale began in which all of the skaters except Yvonne joined together in a circle around the Kamchatskiy ready to lift and turn Yvonne before placing her gently onto the bonnet into the pose that she had had at the beginning.

Throughout the routine the entire set had to make the highly difficult appear like simplicity itself. In the shuttle one tiny error could make the entire movement collapse with no chance of recovery, as they had found in training. Jobine, however, had made sure that no such error was ever going to occur on her watch. In addition she had ensured that imperceptibly the body language of all of the setmates had improved immeasurably since they had begun their training eleven months earlier.

Throughout the routine Yvonne was focused on her task. Coolly and carefully she avoided the panic attack that she had feared. That had been drummed out of her weeks earlier. By the time this night had come she was ready to be lifted, swung round, thrown and shuttled. For her, and the others, fear was a thing of the past. The entire set showed off its talents with pride, determined, like the others, that they were worthy of wearing the Kamchatskiy badge and making the most of the opportunity that had been given to them to have the life and career that they cherished, and a year ago never dreamed that they would ever have. Once into the performance nerves were quickly replaced by a collective determination to at least match the other sets that were in the same position as themselves.

As the setmates bowed to the audience and to the trainers they could not help but notice the small fair-haired lady bouncing with delight on the trainers' bench, gesturing to them as if to confirm that it was she who would be their new trainer.

"What a performance," said Joanie. "The magnificent Silver Shadow, Kamchatskiy's finest to date, launched in spectacular style. Well done skaters, that was great. Now, let us welcome back onto the ice our first set, who had the honour of performing the company dance, to perform our fifth and final demonstration before the interval, skating to 'Robotic Manoeuvres' by British pop orchestra Ever Living."

"Wow, We've given our first performance for Kamchatskiy," Anne shouted as the setmates returned to their seats, hugging each other as they sat.

"Well, we didn't disgrace ourselves, did we?" said Gary. "Our turns were mostly clean, our changes of position all worked, nobody fell and we actually got that difficult lift right in the end."

"Only because Jobine pushed us," Carl reminded them. "She knew that she was going to have to really drive us to make sure that everything came off and that we all had enough confidence on the night to overcome any fear of failure. I give full credit to her."

"I agree," said Connie. "And Yvonne, you were brilliant. Aren't you glad now that all of that hard work has paid off?"

"I really enjoyed that. It was fantastic," Yvonne confessed.

"The satisfaction is indescribable. I can't believe how lucky I've been, and all through one man that I just happened to meet one day walking along a beach after a skating session."

Now Gary's set could relax a little as Marie's set, now changed from the glossy red Kamchatskiy Auto uniforms into robots, prepared to skate their piece, which had a style all of its own, intentionally mechanistic yet flowing as the skaters turned and interacted together as if they were one coordinated unit. They gestured to the car as well as to each other as if to communicate that they were at one with it. They maintained a deliberately rigid posture throughout performing like machines with a centrepiece of a clambering lift whereby the girls were not lifted but rather clambered over the backs of the men, insect-like, until a complex pyramidal lift formation had been assembled over the car, with three girls forming the base that supported another two, with the star, Marie, raised to the top. Her head then turned, like the head of an android that moved, like some alien being across the ice, becoming eventually detached from the prop so as to overshadow it. The girls then twisted and turned around one another simulating screwing and locking actions that gradually unwound the structure. The subtle partner changes demanded considerable concentration and, as with Gary's set's shuttle lift, this was a prolonged movement, which, also like the shuttle lift, could easily fall apart with one small error. There were no such errors though, Jobine had made sure of that, and all of the difficult turning, interlocking and crawling moves were performed impeccably.

"There's something different for you," Joanie commented at the end of the routine. "It has to be seen to be believed. Thank you skaters. That was a stunning way to conclude our five fabulous Kamchatskiy Auto demonstration dances. Great trainers of Kamchatskiy Auto, I present these five sets to you."

*

With the resurfacing of the ice came an opportunity for the Kamchatskiy Auto setmates to meet their respective trainers for the first time. The Usherette brought each of the setmates that had performed champagne and luxury cheese biscuits as the trainers came over to introduce themselves.

"I'm Rodnina Malenkov, pleased to meet you," said the short fair-haired lady to Gary's set as she shook the hands of the setmates. "We are going to get along famously. That was a lovely display of skating, and a three-minute long lift. I have never seen that before. Jobine raises the skill level every year. I have come to say that after the show I have arranged for you to meet my set from last year with whom you will mostly be working and training with on the tour. They are in the audience with all of the other setmates from last year. The Kammie will take you down to The Cat and Fiddle."

"Won't you be coming with us?" asked Jose.

"Alas no," said Rodnina. "All of the trainers have been invited to stay at The Royal Palace with the company directors, but we will get to talk a little bit more tomorrow. Today the Kamchatskiy Aerospace and Kamchatskiy Logistics sets were able to relax and watch. Tomorrow it is the other way around. The other setmates will give you an insight into what to expect next year though, and are probably better placed than me to explain it to you."

The remainder of the interval provided the skaters with an opportunity to remove their skates and outfits before taking their places to watch the five Kamchatskiy Maritime performances and their company dance to 'Viva Kamchatskiy'. For these demonstrations a scaled down replica of Kamchatskiy Maritime's latest yacht was unveiled as the prop around which the routines would be based.

The Kamchatskiy Maritime routines, unlike those of Kamchatskiy Auto, made use of special effects to augment the performances, such as computer-generated imagery that provided the audience with the illusion that the boat was actually moving as the skaters performed on and around it in a series of sea-based themes. Thus, there was swimming with dolphins, sailing to magical islands, a slow-tempo romance at sea, a comical sketch depicting life at sea, and a yacht race to finish. At the end the image of Ken, The Mariner and first King of The Island, was projected looking over The Stone Boat that the setmates had come to know so well, and which also served as the emblem for Kamchatskiy Maritime.

In these routines the lifts were somewhat simpler than those that had been performed by Kamchatskiy Auto, but to compensate for that elementary use of the harness had been incorporated into the routines. Kamchatskiy Maritime therefore used a mixture of lifts and harness moves so as to demonstrate that its sets had mastered both types of skill in equal proportions.

"Bravo. Bravo," Joanie said as the last routine ended. "A familiar face to us all. Much loved and much remembered."

*

After the show, at The Cat and Fiddle, Gary and the others met Donna from Switzerland, Gerry from Cardiff, Michelle from France, Ally from Toronto, Tara from Australia, Alexander from Croatia, Francesca and Manuel from Portugal, Maria from Greece, Juan from Ecuador, Rhianna from Inverness and Paolo from Italy.

"So, what's it like one year on?" Carl asked Rhianna.

"Unbelievable," she replied. "We have learnt such a lot going on tour, seeing the world and of course living our dream of being skating celebrities. The Kamchatskiy trainers expect a lot, but they know that with Jobine we have had the best grounding possible. Last year we really surprised ourselves with what we were able to accomplish. I expect you feel the same."

"Absolutely," Gary's set nodded.

"Your routine was very polished and no sign of nerves at all," added Maria. "And Yvonne, how did you manage to keep all of that up? So much energy."

"It's because Jobine is a genius," Yvonne replied. "She knows exactly when to drive a skater, exactly when not to drive, exactly how to give a skater confidence, and how to take away all of those nerves, which we all had."

"But didn't show on the night," answered Juan. "Yes, it was the same for us. And it has lasted. We don't get nervous at all with Rodnina. She's a bundle of fun, very easy to get along with even when she's pushing us to the limit, and she does, just like Jobine. Life's a bit more formal under the Kamchatskiy trainers, but the experience is fantastic."

"Also, before we came here we learnt that all of the current skating sets will get an extra year since there won't be any Queen's Tickets issued next year with the Royal Acclamation," said Ally.

"Royal Acclamation?" said Gary.

"The approval of The Prince Regent by The Queen's ministers," said Alexander. "That's the name that's given to the process."

"What about life in Kamchatka?" asked Lars. "What's that like?"

"Absolutely brilliant," replied Juan. "The people are so sincere. Nobody will ever do you down. There are so many interdependencies built into the system."

"When we arrived," continued Francesca. "We got a guided tour of the Parliament which was fascinating. They showed us the debating rooms and The Lab where Commander reigns supreme. Of course the master computer is only as reliable as the information that is fed into it, but it is incredible how every element of supply and demand is exactly balanced. There are thirty senior ministers and about another 570 MPs who are appointed by these ministers, prior to standing for election by the method that you will have learnt about. The senior ministers in theory report directly to The Queen and Prime Minister, but in practice The Queen and Prime Minister are really just symbolic characters. How else would they have the time to dedicate to us and this place? It is the thirty senior ministers who hold the real power. Ordinary Kamchatkans have all heard of The Island and what it has done to improve their lives, but that is usually the limit of their knowledge, unless they have been fortunate enough to have visited it, as a few have. Occasionally there are school visits, as with The Karaginsky School for example."

"We're still trying to get used to Non-Capitalist Economics," said Gary.

"That's no problem," Paolo explained. "It's easy to get used to. Once your requisitioning pattern is recognised and stays stable it just continues as a matter of course. Everything is carefully measured and used to make aggregate forecasts so that labour can be allocated accordingly. It's a wonderful tool Commander. There are so many things it can do, even running the country and managing the economy. The ministers just keep an eye on it and make sure that it does its job, highlighting inequalities when they occur and need rectification. You could say Commander is the real Prime Minister."

"Tara, you're from Australia," said Yvonne. "May I ask which part?"

"A place called Orange in New South Wales," she replied. "And you?"

"I'm from the Northern Territory, near Darwin."

"Don't tell me, you were given The Queen's Ticket by a blondish guy of about thirty, yes?"

"How did you guess?"

"Because I got mine from the same man. Last year the Defence Congress was in Sydney and he just happened to see me skating at Macquarie Ice Rink. I know he owns lots of land, though. He practically owns Bathurst Island

and Melville Island having invested his parent's fortune in them. He's not a particularly popular politician in Australia. Australians who are friends of The Island either buy or rent their homes on one or other of those islands. They will be an important strategic acquisition for The Queen, with a merging for the first time of Russian and Australian sovereignty. There's a lot of political as well as physical attraction between Aub and The Queen."

"And so The Island empire grows a little bit more," replied Michael.

"Absolutely," said Tara. "We are living in interesting times."

"Coming back to skating," said Elena. "How do people cope with things like injuries? Surely they must happen from time to time?"

"They do," said Gerry. "But fortunately our medical services are so advanced that things can be healed in minutes that used to take weeks or even months. The latest regenerative technology works wonders."

"Tell me, what are the houses like?" Claudia asked.

"Innovative in design, and spacious. Ours looks a bit like a small Scottish castle or manor house," Michelle explained, as she continued to describe their property in more detail.

Closing time approached.

"I think you'll find the best bit of your time here is still to come," Francesca told Anne. "But we cannot reveal it to you. Joanie would be very cross if we did, but you have got a really great surprise to come, I promise."

"Give us a clue," Claudia pleaded.

"No, no. No clues," replied Francesca. "Strictly forbidden."

"Where are you staying on The Island?" asked Lars.

Well, we're here for the show tomorrow so we can all watch our contemporaries from Kamchatskiy Aerospace and Kamchatskiy Logistics," Manuel explained. "As for where we are staying, we have rooms in Aldebaran, next to the lodge where the Karaginsky children are staying with their headmaster. There's a special train leaving at midnight to take us back."

*

The next day both sets were able to relax as they strolled along the beach and meet further with their trainers and their new contemporaries from the previous year's Kamchatskiy Maritime. It was a day of everyone getting to know everyone else in preparation for the times that lay ahead. It was also a time for reflection as each set knew that times on The Island were drawing to a close, albeit with happy memories that would last a lifetime.

It was now the turn of the Kamchatskiy Aerospace and Kamchatskiy Logistics trainers and directors to be entertained by Joanie in Government House, whilst Jobine presided over day two's dress rehearsals.

At 7.30 p.m., everyone took their seats to watch the concluding part of Carnival on Ice. This began with the displays from Kamchatskiy Aerospace, the prop for which was the all-new Hebden business jet, the Hebden Ten, again reduced in size, and mounted on a special platform so as to make it a workable prop for The Island's prestigious display of new skating talent.

As with the other companies the show began with the unveiling of the new company dance, still to the familiar Paso Doble rhythm of 'Viva Kamchatskiy'. The five demonstration performances then followed, this time with aviation and flight themes. Comical tweeting birds provided the first display, which was cheeky and eye-catching. This was then followed by a depiction of the tale of Icarus and Daedalus, and after the flight of the bumblebee with twelve bees buzzing around the jet, skydivers in formation and finally astronauts taking off to the moon and conducting a moonwalk, ready to usher in a new age of man in flight for the first real occasion since the Apollo moon landings of the 1960s.

There were comparatively few lifts in the Kamchatskiy Aerospace routines, but this was made up for by the fact that these sets demonstrated complete mastery of the harness. They therefore surpassed all of the others on this attribute, although, naturally, under Jobine the setmates had to have learnt to achieve a benchmark level of attainment in all of the skating skills that were generally required. It was simply that the bias was the reverse to that for the Kamchatskiy Auto sets.

With Kamchatskiy Logistics, the approach was different again. This time the theme was multimodal transport and instead of making use of one single prop the skaters had to work with one which rotated and moved, a giant unit that comprised of cranes and moving containers that symbolised the movement of goods from one transport mode to another.

The fact that the prop had moving parts required a very special combination of skills that integrated both lifts, and the use of the harness with the motion of the prop itself. Skaters had to be synchronised with its movements, giving the setmates again a distinguishing skill profile relative to the others. There were, as with Kamchatskiy Maritime, moderately difficult lifts combined with elementary use of the harness such that the girls could be placed on various parts of the moving machinery either by lifting or by use of the harness. Returning to the ice was then a skill in itself, utilising either a harness, or a lift down, or, in some cases, a specially timed drop from a part of the apparatus that had to be executed cleanly so that the entire routine flowed without interruption. This was definitely harder than it looked.

The routines covered ports of the world, railways of the world, the lifting and moving of goods, the world of the truck convoy, and express delivery of milk. The prop, unlike those of the others, was, with the aid of special effects, completely adaptable to each routine as various sections remained hidden until they were required. Some clever engineering and electronics enabled the prop to literally transform itself without manual intervention so as to be adaptable to every performance.

"Beat that if you can," Joanie declared at the end of the final performance before this extraordinary prop was quickly dismantled by the ice squad. "Now we are complete. All twenty sets have now performed for you, and we hope you will agree that they are now fully trained and equipped for stardom. Now, before we close our show I would like to give particular thanks to a remarkable woman without whom this fabulous event couldn't have been achieved. It is of course the one and only Jobine. She may not have any medals, nor have passed any tests, nor won any competitions, but her reputation as being the world's greatest ice dance trainer remains undisputed. I will now ask the youngest girl from The Karaginsky School Young Skaters to come up here and collect a bouquet of flowers from Her Majesty to present to Jobine in recognition of all of the tremendous work that she has done to make the dreams of these fine setmates become a reality."

Jobine rose to her feet among the Kamchatskiy Aerospace and Kamchatskiy Logistics trainers to accept the flowers. She could not conceal her tears as the audience gave her a standing ovation, cheering, clapping and whistling continuously in appreciation. Then she said a few touching words:

"I know I say this every year, but I would like to say to all of my wonderful setmates that I was once in your shoes. One day, some fifteen years ago, I was a skater in Amsterdam. I couldn't make the grade because I couldn't pass the tests, because nerves always got the better of me and in the end my age threatened to destroy my chances of doing the work that I loved. It was just by chance that I was spotted by Donald McIlroy, on the last day of his William of Orange tour, at the rink, just as I was about to give up hope. Little did I know that Patrick was in the ice rink bar secretly watching my every move. I have to thank them, because without them I would not be here doing what I love doing best, making skating dreams come true. Believe me, I am happier doing what I am doing and seeing the setmates achieve so much than ever I would have been in the skating world. So, please give them some applause."

The audience duly applauded as The Concierge stood briefly in the royal enclosure microphone in hand.

"It is true," he said. "She was a brilliant performer and as soon as Donald caught sight of her we knew we wanted her. We knew she would be superb for what we needed. It was only her nerves that stopped her, but it was enough to mean that in the skating world she was not going to make the top flight that she deserved. So we helped her to overcome her nerves and learn to train others. Her methods are unique and now her results are legendary. Jobine, nothing compares to you."

He handed the microphone back to Joanie.

"Ladies and gentlemen, distinguished guests, that almost concludes our Carnival on Ice for another year, but not quite. Each year we conclude our Carnival with a performance by one couple from The Karaginsky Young Skaters of the classic Bolero routine performed exactly as the legendary Jayne Torvill and Christopher Dean performed it at the 1984 Sarajevo Winter Olympics. It is a tradition that we have maintained here ever since our good Queen Justine gave her royal command that it should be performed by two children from an invited school to officially end Carnival. This year is no exception, so please welcome onto the ice Petra Constantin and Oleg Shelikova from The Karaginsky School."

The two sixteen-year-olds duly assumed their starting positions on the now clear ice ready to perform their carefully rehearsed 'Bolero'. Just as in Torvill and Dean's original, the routine started with the sway and lift for 28 seconds prior to the commencement of skating, reflecting the rules of ice dancing as they had been at the time, with the skating being of exactly four minutes duration. Every step and movement was performed exactly as in the original, with the same body lines preserved throughout. The performance ended with the carefully controlled fall after which the spotlights faded and the lights were finally out on the amazing one and only Carnival on Ice.

Chapter Nineteen
Prince Regent

One week later, at The Australian Defence Industry Annual Congress in Perth, Western Australia.

The delegates assembled promptly for the keynote address from Aub Ryman, Minister for Defence.

"Good morning, ladies and gents. You will be pleased to know that I will not go on for long. What I have to say to you will be swift and to the point. Furthermore, what I have to do cannot wait. So I will now outline what I propose to do.

I know many of you are expecting me to approve your budgets. This is despite what I have already told all of you, as well as the rest of this extraordinarily incompetent government, or what passes for a government, about the crisis that our defence industry now faces. As you know, I have made it known on several occasions now that the world is changing and faster than any of you can see. Like a load of blinkered bulls in a china shop you are expecting me to approve a policy that is not only outdated but foolhardy and dangerous for our country. You are wanting me to commit millions of dollars of the taxpayers' money to a plan that hasn't got a hope in hell of succeeding, and if I sign for it I will be held responsible. Ladies and gentlemen, no."

There were spontaneous groans and shakes of heads from the delegates.

"What does the idiot think he's doing?" whispered one delegate to another.

"Why doesn't the bloody fool just follow his whip and get on with it?" whispered another, exasperated.

Aub observed the reaction and continued.

"I know many of you have been trained merely to follow orders and that thinking comes second. I do not blame any of you for that, because it has been drummed into you for so many years that I expect the majority of you have lost count. However, I am not prepared to follow this course any longer. I will say again once and once only to you what I believe the right course of action is.

You all think, and believe, because that is what you have been told by those in authority, that the way forward for our defence industry is to invest in more tanks, more warplanes, more bombs, more missiles, more guns and more weapons, because you think nothing has changed. But you couldn't be more wrong. As I have said before, things are happening in the world that neither you nor anyone else in this haphazard regime are even aware of. You haven't seen it, but I have, and I know that this country needs to respond to it very quickly. The sovereignty of nations is disappearing. The entire concept of countries going to war in order to defend themselves is a thing of the past. Taking territory by force is a thing of the past. On the other hand, the displacement of governments that have proven themselves to be obsessed with holding onto power and managing their resources poorly, is a thing of the present. The days of internal wrangling and merely following orders in the hope of surviving at the expense of others are coming to an abrupt end.

You haven't listened before and I doubt you will listen now, but if you choose not to even at this late stage, then be it on your own heads. Don't be surprised if in a few years' time a large number of you don't have a job because somebody over you has decided to sell out, and they will. They have those sorts of minds and are certain to be tempted by some high offers from foreign quarters. The Japanese, the Russians, the Chinese, even the Germans are fancying their chances here. It may not happen overnight, but mark my words it will happen, and when it does I for one am determined to be on the winning side. There won't be a shot fired, nor a missile launched. It will be quiet, discreet, and done behind a little closed door that none of you even know about by people that you do not even know about.

Some revolutions are quick, some are slow. Unfortunately you have only been trained to recognise and respond to the fast type. The slow type that has been going on for the last seventy years has remained unseen by all but a select number of people who have come to understand its purpose and objectives over the decades. These people, of whom I am one, have found out, if only by accident, that there is a better way of managing the world than those which have existed hitherto. The Japanese learnt a bit about it early on, but not nearly enough. We have stayed in ignorance, believing 'she'll be right mate', which, in fact, amounts to pure ignorance on your parts."

"Oh, can't we get this buffoon out? He's useless," ranted one old general, within earshot of the speaker.

"You'll get your wish soon enough sir," said Aub, as he stared at the red-faced man. "The New Game is coming. In fact it is almost upon us. In place of wars and battles is coming the era of trading in sovereignties, by which and through which wars will soon be a thing of the past. Who wants war anyway? Who wins? Nobody really wins a war. Wars are merely ended by one side or the other. The days are numbered for those who believe in war in the conventional sense, and that means you unless you can accept the nature of the change that is unfolding.

Get ready for the New Game. Get ready to show that you are good managers who will manage the nation's and the world's resources wisely, and be ready to be more self-critical than ever before. Be wise to your own deficiencies and sub-optimisation. Be wise to the need for lifelong learning and the meaning of cooperation as W. Edwards Deming said way back in, what was it, the 1950s? Let people take pride in their work, and end the practice of making choices purely on the basis of price. This is the age of the quality practitioner, not the cowboys and the fools who want to cut corners in the false belief that they are saving money.

Now, as I know some of you are getting impatient..."

"You're telling me," puffed the old general.

"As I said, as some of you are getting impatient, I am going to announce to you that as of today I resign. Now, if you will excuse me I have work to do and a new life to get on with."

There was then a mixture of astonishment, surprise, and in some cases relief as he broke the news. As some, like the old general, smiled and whispered "Thank God for that", others were less sure, particularly the younger delegates, a few of whom shook their heads, knowing deep in their hearts that the minister probably was telling the truth and in fact it was the old guard whom they should fear. There was dissent in the ranks and arguments broke out amongst the delegates as Aub stepped down and made his way to the exit.

One or two of the delegates rose and chased after Aub as he walked briskly along the corridor to await his chauffeur.

"You can't walk out now, sir," one of them said to him.

"I just have," Aub replied.

"But think of your country."

"That's exactly what I am thinking of."

"Come on, you can't just walk off the job," said another.

"Can't I? Just watch."

"But you're the best we've got," said a third delegate.

"Best you ever will get."

"But your country needs you," said the first delegate again.

"My country's still got me. It's only you buggers who have just lost me."

"Some of us are loyal to you, you know that," said the second delegate.

"Yes, and I know who you are. You will be amply rewarded when the time comes."

Aub carried on walking until he reached the door to the hotel complex.

"Now he should be there ready and waiting," said Joanie, observing the entrance to the complex from within The Great Dome, her Chancellor by her side.

"I think you'll find it's all taken care of," The Chancellor replied.

The minister stepped into the awaiting Kamchatskiy, a brand new Silver Shadow.

"Where on earth is he going?" the second delegate asked the first.

"I don't know, but I rather think the clue might be in the car that just drove him away."

The car proceeded swiftly and quietly through the streets of Perth, passing through the northern suburb of Mirrabooka and on through Northbridge until it finally arrived at the airport.

"Good luck, Prince Regent," said the driver as he deposited his passenger at the terminal building.

The Prince did not stop at the check-in, but continued instead directly toward departure gate six. Joanie meanwhile followed his progress with the remote camera which Aub had placed carefully in the lock of his suitcase, just as she had ordered him to do the night before. He followed the pathway through the airport that she had prepared for him, allowing him to bypass airport security, until he had almost reached departure gate six. At that point he was approached by two security officials.

"Excuse me sir," one of them said to him. "You cannot go there. There are no flights from gate six today. I'm afraid you must return to airport security at once."

Fortunately Aub had the perfect response. He removed from his jacket pocket a small case containing the blue and gold hologram badge that Queen Katie had given to him the previous Christmas. This bore The Island logo, which international security officials had knowledge of. He flashed it at the security guards who instantly recognised its significance.

"I'm so sorry. This way Your Royal Highness," said one of the guards, who pointed the way toward The Queen's own Hebden Three that was parked discreetly by the gate.

Back in her Dome Joanie reached for her mobile phone.

"Can I have a close-up on that plane," she ordered to her Operations Manager, triggering a transfer from the camera in Aub's suitcase to that on the tail of the aircraft. "And make sure the pilot is ready for takeoff on cue and that he gets immediate clearance from the airport authorities. I will now inform The Queen that his presence on The Island is now imminent."

The plane took off and followed a westerly course until eventually reaching supersonic speed over the Indian Ocean, approximately one hundred miles north-west of Perth. The same hostess that had greeted Gary on his somewhat shorter flight to The Island greeted the sole passenger, first with a commemorative bottle of Prince Regent lager, The Prince noting his face embossed in gold on the label, then with a document for him to sign.

"Sir, Her Majesty kindly ask that you sign paper," said the petite Korean.

"Oh? What could that be for then? She knows who I am doesn't she?"

"Of course sir. But she need you to sign for plane. Queen want that you have it as a gift. From now on plane and pilot are at your command."

He scrutinised the form carefully and noted that it did indeed transfer ownership of the aircraft to him.

"What if I don't want to own the plane?"

"Then too bad. Queen will transfer it to you anyway."

"So the form is meaningless?"

"No. Form very important. It show Queen that you respect her wishes."

"I see. Then I suppose I had better sign it."

She offered him the pen and bowed her head. He noted the gesture, detecting that if he refused to sign the hostess would see it, rightly or wrongly, as a reflection upon her. He knew that, unlike with the budgets that he had been asked to approve a couple of hours earlier, he had to sign.

"Much obliged," said hostess Su Lin, whose name was written on her Island logo badge. "Now I bring menu. Su Lin think Your Royal Highness ready for lunch."

She returned a few seconds later and handed Aub the menu.

"Quite a choice," he remarked looking at the various fish and vegetarian options before making his choice.

"Prime Minister want that you have great flight to Island and will have everything ready for your arrival. If you look at screen you will see coachman preparing horses and royal coach."

The viewing screen was revealed allowing Aub to see for the first time the coachman carefully grooming the two black stallions that would pull the meticulously polished royal coach from the beach airstrip to The Town. Then Joanie appeared on the screen.

"Greetings Prince Regent," she said. "Her Majesty and I are so pleased that you have decided on this day to accept the new and great future that she has offered to you. You will know from our history what awaits you in the weeks and months ahead. You know that a lot will be expected of you, but we have every confidence that you are the man who can steer us forward. It is a decision that we know you will not regret, and we are honoured to have you. You are now officially Prince Regent, and the band may start to play."

The band started playing from the Colonnade as selected members of The Island's staff – led by The Reverend, who beat his drum loudly, followed by The Concierge – began to parade around the Town Square marching in time in military fashion in their ceremonial blue and gold uniforms.

Aub watched as those on parade turned their heads perfectly in unison and saluted as they passed the camera that would beam the image directly to his plane whilst Su Lin prepared his chosen meal of vegetable soup and lobster crepes. Gary and the others watched from their cottage.

"Oh it's started," said Anne. "The others are all joining."

"He's going to be here soon," added Connie. "The papers predicted that he would be here at three o' clock, but by the looks of things it is going to be a bit earlier than that."

As the plane entered South African airspace Joanie reached again for her mobile phone.

"Can you confirm that we have clearance from the Western Cape?" she asked as she observed the plane's progress on the map on her screen.

On board Su Lin updated The Prince Regent on the latest developments on The Island.

"Setmates have one more week," she said. "Then they will be leaving."

"That's good. At least I'll have the pleasure of meeting them. It will also be good to see the ones I sent there this year. It's a shame I'm just that bit too late for the Carnival on Ice. Then I could have met last year's as well. It will be a refreshing change though after the loons I've been cooked up with for the past five years."

"They are all eager to meet you. It has been so long since The Island has seen a royal acclamation. By the way Prime Minister also ask me to ask you if you have named an MP for the new constituency of Bathurst and Melville to serve in Kamchatka Parliament?"

"Tell her, certainly. It will be a man called Jacob Spence. He's very reliable and highly respected by all of our friends in Australia, and I think the Russians should take to him. I know The Queen has met him a couple of times when she visited my villa on Bathurst. Our friends also know that he will do everything to ensure that the quality of life improves throughout Australia. Something really does have to be done about the nation's beleaguered economy."

"Good. I make note. So I give you some in-flight entertainment. Highlights from this year's Carnival on Ice."

The plane touched down on the runway of The Island at 2.15 p.m. local time. The Prince said goodbye to Su Lin and thanked the pilot and copilot as he stepped out into the spring sunshine. As with Gary's arrival, once the plane was silent and the passenger had safely disembarked the coachman made his way toward the plane ready to transport in style the VIP to The Great Dome for his meeting with The Prime Minister.

As the carriage passed through The Triumphal Arch the crowd applauded from The Square. The Prince Regent was slightly surprised at the number of people, the entire Island, that had turned out to greet him, once Joanie had announced that His Royal Highness had landed. The Queen gazed down from the top of The Bell Tower where she stood alone, concealed, with her parents watching quietly from the steps of The Great Dome, ready to shake hands with The Prince. The throng then cheered as the carriage approached.

"Stand well back," The Chancellor ordered, as the carriage drew to a halt.

The cheering intensified as The Prince Regent stepped down from the carriage to a popstar-type greeting from setmates and staff alike. He was almost mobbed and was visibly overcome by his obvious immense popularity, which contrasted so markedly with the air of growing disapproval that he had left behind in Perth. He was showered with confetti as he made his way to the door of the Great Dome, which opened automatically as he approached. He shook hands with The King and Queen Mother as he entered and faced the seated Joanie. Then she rose ready to clasp his hands.

"Prince Regent, so good to meet you," she said. "After all this time it is really you, here on The Island. All the months of uncertainty are at last over. There is much to be done and I wish I was going to be here to see your great adventure."

"You're not?" said Aub.

"No. I thought you would have known. Now that you are here I have to resign and hand over all of my powers to The Queen's ministers who will, one by one, apply their tests to you prior to awarding their Royal Acclamation. When that has been done a new Prime Minister will be appointed from their ranks, whom you and The Queen must then approve. This is what our constitution demands, but I have had a wonderful six years here as Prime Minister, and it is only right that at some reasonable point I should stand down and hand over to someone else. I have been very privileged to have served in what some would say is the best job in the world.

It's not quite over for me yet, though. I still have the pleasure of showing you around the magical world of The Island over the next week, and, of course, have the honour of presenting you to Her Majesty The Queen. All has been made ready for you and I can assure you that all of my staff will do their very best to see that you are made welcome here and they will always be on hand to assist you. You already have more friends than you will ever know, and I know that you definitely will not regret making the decision that you did this morning. Your adventures are just beginning, and there is no doubt that you will have a very powerful and influential role in the future development of the world.

I listened to your brief speech in Perth this morning and felt so proud as you stood up and said no at last to those backward-thinking individuals. You will be your people's saviour in the end, mark my words. There is nothing more important that you could have done for Australia."

"Some will still see me as selling out to the Russians."

"There's no such thing as selling out, Prince. It is the others who will sell out when the bidding starts. You will be the man who will introduce Non-Capitalist Economics to the Australian people, and, when they see it working on Bathurst and Melville more will want it, and those old fogeys in the Australian Defence Committee will be where they belong, as footnotes in Australia's beleaguered past. So, come on Prince. Tell me how much you enjoyed this year's Carnival on Ice."

"I can't wait to get my skates on myself."

"Well, I can tell you that The Queen herself ordered her own personal maid to place a brand new pair of skates, tailored exactly to your foot measurements, on your bed in Samurai Cottage, and ice time has been set aside for you."

"With the setmates?"

"With or without. You choose. Jobine, our resident trainer is eager to meet you. Hopefully she will be able to help you and Katie to become the world's first true skating King and Queen. Now that Carnival is over and the setmates have only one more week left here I have asked that she allows them to relax a little now."

"Then they go to Kamchatskiy, right?"

"Right. But we will have a social night at the end of the week."

"I'd better get some practice in then. I'm very rusty compared to what I saw on the plane. I am pleased for all of the setmates, but especially for those from Australia to whom I have had the honour of handing over The Queen's precious tickets personally. Yvonne was fantastic compared to when I saw her skate in Darwin. I'm so glad that I found the perfect person to give that last ticket to. I was getting seriously worried about what I was going to do with it."

"Some tea, Your Royal Highness?" asked The Chancellor.

*

In the days ahead The Prince Regent made a point of visiting each of the twenty sets in person, showing himself to be the ordinary and somewhat humble man that he was. On the ice he took private instruction from Jobine and joined in with the setmates as they practised the range of simple social dances each night until the penultimate. The Queen joined them also from time to time, proving to them that she was no stranger to the ice. Her speed and flow across the ice was worthy of note, as were the variety of jumps, spins and twizzles that she showed off to her future principal.

On the sessions, The Prince Regent was very much the centre of attention. Then, when it was over, The Prince and The Queen would leave the rink together either by the royal coach or the royal train which took them to The Royal Palace. There the royal couple could spend at least some relaxing time together without the distraction of press cameras and prying eyes. It was at least a comfort for them to know that whilst all eyes were upon them, and *The Island Times*, with journalist Sylvia, was keen to report on their progress, the Royal Palace remained a place of sanctuary to all who were housed within. For, on The Island, the rich financial rewards for snooping reporters who could snatch inappropriate photographs and compile articles of marginal truth were nonexistent. Here the only desire was only for a blossoming romance that would lead subsequently to a royal wedding and a coronation.

Chapter Twenty
Going Underground

For their final night on The Island Joanie had arranged a fondue evening in the Training Centre at which all of the setmates and Island staff could meet together for one last time. Aub and The Queen also made an appearance, taking time to speak to everyone, wishing the setmates well in their new lives. As the stainless steel cauldrons of simmering cheese were wheeled in by royal chef Bob and The Usherette, The Chancellor played a lament gently upon the old organ which had been placed at the far end of the room.

For the setmates it was a time of farewells, goodbyes and thank-yous to all of the people who had taught and assisted them throughout the past year. In particular Mitsumoto-san and Jobine praised their efforts.

"It has been a joy to teach and work with you," said Mitsumoto-san to Gary's set. "Perhaps one day we will meet again. Now you know all about auto manufacture at Kamchatskiy. Now you must learn to put theory into practice."

"It has been a wonderful and memorable experience enhancing and developing your skating skills," Jobine added. "It has given me great pleasure helping to equip you with the skills and capabilities to join the fabulous elite of The Kamchatskiy Skaters. I know you will all go far and go on to have super careers."

"We naturally thank you also for giving us the wonderful training," said Anne to both of them. "To think that of all the people in the world we have been hand-picked is a truly amazing honour, and, like everyone else that has been given this most prestigious invitation, we have memories that we shall treasure forever."

"We will all miss this place," Elena added, a slight tear in her eye.

Joanie later came over to them, as she did with each of the other sets.

"You have had a great time I take it?" she said.

"Wonderful and unforgettable," Lars replied.

"We can't thank you enough for all that you have done," added Jose.

"Well. I can tell you that although this may be your last night on The Island, it is not over yet. You have your instructions for tomorrow?"

The set nodded.

"You will be pleased to know that you haven't quite seen the last of me yet."

"You'll be pleased to know that you haven't seen the back of me either," laughed the Concierge from behind, sipping a glass of red wine.

"Nor me," added the Reverend.

"So what is still to come?" Gary asked, mindful like the others about what Francesca had said.

"That's for us to know and you to find out," laughed Joanie. "But, like your time on The Island, it's something that I promise you will certainly remember. As we speak I can tell you that programmers and engineers are busily at work adding the final touches to our last surprise."

Aub and The Queen approached and shook hands with each of the setmates. Aub spoke notably to Yvonne.

"Glad you came?" he asked.

"Oh absolutely. It still just seems like a dream. I can't believe it."

"Don't worry. I feel a bit like that myself. You won't look back though. Nobody who comes here ever does. Oh, and by the way, I watched your routine on my flight here and it was so good it was unrecognisable from what I last saw of you in Australia. I know I couldn't have given that last ticket to a more worthy recipient, so very well done."

This praise from The Prince really touched her, to such a point that she just had to give The Prince a hug.

"Take care. You all have a great future ahead of you," added Queen Katie, letting go of Aub's hand for Yvonne's embrace.

"Thank you, Your Majesty for giving us this life-changing learning experience," Connie said, as she shook the royal hand for one last time.

Dr Schultz added his farewell to the set, along with The Night Watchman and The Deputy Prime Minister.

"Can't stay long as I have a lot of work to do tonight," said The Deputy PM. "But it's been lovely getting to know you".

"Likewise," said Claudia.

"Good luck," said Dr Schultz. "And well done on your achievements."

"We would say well done on yours," replied Graca.

"You'll be early to bed tonight, won't you?" laughed The Night Watchman. "You know you have a long day ahead tomorrow. But I do wish you well."

The sets mingled and exchanged views on their experiences, each still intrigued as to what Joanie's last surprise would be.

"One thing's for sure, we won't have long to wait," said Hamish, collecting a glass of wine from one of the circulating waitresses.

"What are your thoughts on leaving The Island?" Marie asked Terry.

"We are all going to miss The Island, but at least we will not miss each other."

"That's very true," said her Dutch principal.

"What has impressed you the most?" the Brazilian gent asked Claudia.

287

"The way in which everyone works together. Here, people think in terms of how they can each contribute to the whole, not just what they can get out of somebody else. It's a quantum leap in the way in which people think about the world and each other. And you?"

"I agree with you, but I have been especially surprised at how Joanie and her staff manage to get the most out of people. This place can only ever be a force for good in the world."

Presently The Chancellor stopped playing his soft lament. Joanie then made a few brief remarks.

"Well. That's it, apart from my one last surprise. I would like to say a big thank you to you all for being such hard working and dedicated learners. Tonight I especially thank The Queen's chef, Bob, and his team for keeping us so finely fed and watered."

Bob and his team of eight assistants bowed their heads.

"You are all model citizens in every respect," Joanie continued, "It's been a pleasure and a privilege to have been able to train and equip you for the tasks which lay ahead. I will be seeing you again very soon. Sleep well, and remember, don't be late for the train."

*

The train left promptly at ten o'clock the next morning. It was full to capacity as it left The Town station with all 240 setmates on board. Swiftly it steamed northwards through the now deserted stations of Sabfelt and Aldebaran. On board the setmates studied the instructions that Joanie had given them the previous morning.

"At The Cavern Station, proceed along the platform to the large steel door at the end and await further instructions," recited Connie.

"I expect it will make more sense when we get off the train," said Michael.

"Where on earth is The Cavern Station?" questioned Anne.

"As Joanie said, it's for her to know and for us to find out," Carl replied.

The train slowed down as it entered The Palace Gates station, but where ordinarily it would have come to a halt here, this time it did not, and for the first time the setmates travelled on a piece of track that had, until now, been sealed off. The train slowly rounded a bend before entering a tunnel that led deep into the mountainside. It then steamed on for a further eight minutes before finally coming to rest in an underground station named The Cavern where the tunnel ended. Now the mystery of this strange station was finally revealed.

The setmates followed The Usherette along the station's single platform to the large steel door at the far end. When all of the setmates were assembled in position the door opened to reveal a wide winding torchlit passageway. There then followed a long, winding walk that took some fifteen minutes.

"Does this ever end?" questioned Elena, excited and intrigued, after twelve minutes.

The passageway ended abruptly at another steel door. This then slid open to reveal a large circular chamber with another steel door opposite. Inside there were two long tables, one with tea, coffee and snacks placed upon it, the other with a total of 240 mortar boards and gowns. On the first table was a card upon which were written the words 'Put on your graduation outfits. Then rest awhile until called by the anthem'. A welcome water closet had also been provided.

This rest break lasted about twenty minutes, before the steel door on the far side of the chamber opened to reveal another winding passageway similar to the first, but somewhat shorter. As the setmates advanced the opening chords of Gustav Holst's 'Jupiter: The Bringer of Jollity'

289

were heard, quietly at first, then louder. The Island's national anthem 'I vow to thee my Island', cloned from 'I vow to thee my country' then rang out.

Together the 240 setmates marched along the 100-yard long tunnel which then opened out to reveal a large chamber with an oak door to the left and a pulpit to the right as one entered.. Facing the pulpit were two banks of pews separated by a red carpet. To the left of the pulpit was a long table with artefacts on it and a throne behind. On the other side of the pulpit was a smaller bank of pews, next to which was a black curtain, the significance of which was, at this point, unknown.

As the setmates entered The Usherette was ready to direct them to their various allotted positions. The setmates then began to fill the pews. Then, when they were all seated, a small group of masked adults followed from behind to take their places in the pews immediately to the right of the pulpit and beside the mysterious black curtain.

"Who are they?" and "What's behind that curtain?", the setmates whispered.

When the masked visitors were seated Joanie, The Chancellor, The Concierge and The Reverend took their places at the end of the front row of the left bank of pews facing the pulpit.

"Please be upstanding for Her Majesty The Queen," The Chancellor ordered.

The anthem then rang out again as The Queen entered, holding her head high as she strode along the red carpet to the throne, dressed in her finest ceremonial blue and gold robes.

"The assembly shall be seated," she announced as she took her place.

This provided the cue for Joanie to advance to the pulpit.

"Your Majesty. Your graduates are presented to you. These are the privileged individuals who have come here to live the dream that you made possible. These are the people who have been fortunate enough to have each received one of the 240 Tickets that you issued. They were hand-picked by our representatives in various countries, some of whom are now seated to my right, having been adjudged to have had what it takes. They have all now proven themselves worthy of the Kamchatskiy Celebrity Degree. They will each now play a part in helping to lead world reform in the new political economy.

These setmates have earned their right to be here. We have had fun and all enjoyed the past year, as well as working and studying in this special place. I now ask that you all stand behind our Queen as we pledge our allegiance to her. Setmates please say, we pledge our allegiance to you."

"We pledge our allegiance to you," the setmates responded.

"I will now ask Her Majesty to present to you the awards to which you are now entitled. In a few moments I will ask our newest citizens to file past Her Majesty to receive their certificates, personal files with some of their best moments carefully caught on camera, the coveted Island passport, and complimentary tickets to the next Non-Olympic Games. I will now ask my ever-faithful Chancellor to read out the names and for Sylvia to take snapshots of each setmate with their awards. When you have received your awards I will ask you to stand in line behind the black curtain that you see to my right beside The Friends of The Island's Benches. These good people are, by the way, some of The Queen's closest friends, whom many of you have to thank for your being here. They have been invited here specially to witness the graduation. Your parents and families will also be given a recording of this ceremony, of which they can be justly proud, since lives that otherwise were likely to have been grossly sub-optimised have now been guaranteed a great and glorious future at the forefront of the world's greatest ever revolution."

The music of 'Viva Kamchatskiy' played as the setmates filed past The Queen, Her Majesty wishing each and every one of her new subjects the very best for the future as she shook their hands and handed them each their awards. They were then guided by The Usherette to stand in line behind the black curtain. When they were all in line the music stopped and Joanie returned to the pulpit.

"Your Majesty, we thank you. That brings us to the end of today's formalities, but not the end of today, for I know that you are all asking what lies behind this magic curtain. I will now give you a clue, and that is to prepare for the longest journey of your lives, the trip of a lifetime. None of you are nervous, are you? You aren't afraid of anything are you?"

There were a few looks of astonishment from the setmates, hardly believing what some of them now suspected, that they were about to take a journey into space.

"No, of course not," she continued. "Island citizens are afraid of nothing. Kamchatskiy graduates are afraid of nothing. Fear has been driven out."

The setmates shook their heads in affirmation.

"You will love it, I promise," Joanie said as she pulled the lever that lifted the curtain. "The SGV or Space Going Vessel *Katie* is a fabulous ship. It will take off from here, orbit the Earth for three days at a distance of approximately 30,000 miles, then touch down into water in the North Pacific before gliding in seacat mode to Petropavlovsk Kamchatskiy just in time for your onward rail connection to your new houses. All aboard please."

The setmates then began to ascend the ramp that led on board. As they did they passed The Friends of The Island, who pulled back their masks and shook the hands of some of the setmates.

"Deirdre," Gary gasped as she turned her head towards him and shook his hand. "It was I who sent you The Queen's Ticket. Good luck Gary."

Chapter Twenty-One
Into Orbit

The craft was spear-shaped, with a distinctive bubble-shaped protrusion at the top of the front end that was carefully protected by two retractable re-entry shields.

Entering the spacecraft was not too dissimilar to entering a large aircraft, with a long straight ramp leading to a dedicated takeoff and landing seated area on the starboard side. Stewardesses directed each person to their allotted seats for take-off. Setmates naturally were seated in the main body of the take-off and landing section of the craft, with the first-class area beyond.

When everyone was in place the obligatory 'FASTEN SAFETY BELTS' sign became illuminated and the captain introduced himself.

"Good afternoon, ladies and gentlemen," came the man's voice. "I am Captain Vladimir Orkovsky and I am pleased to welcome you aboard the Kamchatskiy Aerospace Space Going Vessel SGV *Katie*. It is one of three sister ships, the oldest being the SGV Neville, and the newest the SGV Aub. The *Katie* is just over three years old and, like the others, was built by the Kamchatskiy Aerospace Space Division in Yuzhno Sakhalinsk and has a 100 per cent safety record.

As you know we are going into space. This is therefore no ordinary airline flight.

You will see from the plans that everyone is currently in the main shuttle capsule, which, in the event of an emergency on takeoff, or in space if there is time for everyone to reach it, is detachable from the rest of the craft and is designed to return safely to a suitable runway on Earth. Cabin crew will soon demonstrate the procedures for emergencies of this type, which broadly correspond to those of a conventional aircraft. Should the emergency occur in space directions will be given to assemble at an appropriate muster station, similar to those on ships. Small shuttles can then be used in the event of this capsule being damaged or inaccessible as a result of an accident.

Once we are safely in orbit around the Earth, the safety belt signs will be turned off and advice given when it is safe to proceed into the other parts of the craft and when the artificial gravity unit has been switched on. The workings of these units will be explained to you later. Should there be a failure in one or more elements of the gravity unit an alarm will sound and you should proceed at once either to this capsule, or to muster stations as directed if the fault is temporary. Instructions will then be given as to what you must do. It shouldn't happen, but you are kindly requested to study the safety procedures carefully whilst on board.

Hopefully our three-day voyage into space will pass off pleasantly, and the vessel will transform itself into seacat mode somewhere to the south of the Aleutians. For this you will return to this capsule for re-entry. The vessel will then continue to its dedicated terminal at Petropavlovsk Kamchatskiy, where you will then disembark.

I now ask that you sit back and relax as we prepare for takeoff for the trip of a lifetime that is normally reserved for millionaires. I say this as the SGVs are a nice little earner for The Island when in commercial use. So, the safety demonstration please."

A dull rumble followed, indicating that the main thrusters had now been activated. A short while later the whole craft tilted upwards and began to rise smoothly, the significant g-forces serving to remind everyone just exactly why it was vital to be seated and strapped firmly during the fifteen minute acceleration to a velocity of over 5,000 miles an hour.

At the end of its ascent the tilt of the vessel flattened and the 'FASTEN SAFETY BELTS' sign was turned off. Then the captain again addressed everyone on board.

"Ladies and gentlemen, I am pleased to report that our ascent has now stabilised and we are now on course for our parking orbit which we will reach in a little under six hours from now, when the Earth's gravitational field will act to hold us in place until we complete the burn that will propel us homeward.

In a few minutes the doors at the aft of this shuttle section will be opened allowing free entry into the main body of the SGV, which you are free to walk around for about an hour. Dinner will then be served in the Atrium, followed by an informative talk and some evening entertainment. We will then be asking all of our new setmates to attend the short marriage ceremony in The Wedding Chamber, after which there will be starlit dancing and an all-night bar for those who wish it. The sleeping quarters are on the deck below the Atrium and Wedding Chamber, and we suggest that you refer to the plans of the vessel so as to familiarise yourselves with the location of your own specific sleeping quarters. Some are on the port side of the vessel, others are on the starboard. Breakfast will be available in the Atrium from 8 a.m. Island time. The rest is holiday as if on a cruise ship."

The Atrium was a large open-plan area with a bar at one end and a dance floor in the centre. Its roof was of transparent super toughened plastic and convex, some twenty feet above the dancing area, and, with its shields retracted, afforded a perfect view of the heavens, completely free from all of the distortions and interference of the Earth's atmosphere. At the far end was a stage with a screen behind. A total of fifty tables each seating up to twelve people had been set covering the whole dance floor, with one larger and more ornate top table, where the senior Island staff and VIPs would sit, nearest the stage.

Inside Joanie, The Concierge and The Reverend again mixed with the new unmarried setmates. Children were also present, some of whom Gary recognised from his earlier experiences on The Island, which by now seemed a very distant place. Presently The Reverend approached Gary.

"So, what does it feel like being in space?" he asked him.

"It's a strange feeling, that seems almost unreal," replied Gary as he looked up at the transparent roof and observed the crystal clear view of the heavens. "All those prolonged g-forces and then this palace in the sky. What are the other SGVs like?"

"Well, the *Neville* is about the same size as this, but it's older and slower and has fewer facilities. It also carries fewer people and is heavier with bigger engines and a larger gravity unit. The *Aub* on the other hand is smaller and faster and can travel further, as far as the Moon and back, but again can't carry as many people as this craft. It has only just completed its maiden flight and will eventually be owned by the new King."

"Have you been on the others?"

"The *Neville* yes, the *Aub* no. These marriage ceremonies in space only began five years ago when the SGV *Neville* was built. Lots of people at the time were unsure if it would work. Nobody knew what to expect. Now it's as routine as going on a cruise."

"How often do these things fly?"

"This craft and the *Neville* usually take off three or four times a year, as there is no shortage of millionaires from around the world queuing up to buy tickets."

"Hello Gary, how are you?" Joanie asked as she approached his set.

"I was just telling him about the SGVs," said The Reverend.

"Great pieces of engineering," said Joanie. "Though nothing compared to Moonbase Alpha."

"Is that entirely Island owned?" Gary asked.

"Not entirely," said Joanie. "It's multinational, but The Island has the majority share in its ownership, which comes largely from our initial investment which no other nation was prepared to make. Other nations therefore effectively buy their rights from us. The Russians have helped us a lot though with their wealth of expertise, so we do a lot of concessionary exchanges with them. Unfortunately most of the capitalist countries have tended to see Moonbase Alpha as something far too ambitious and expensive to get involved with to any great extent. As well as that once the Russians became committed with us they have been keen to ensure that it is something between them and us, so the involvement of others has been kept to a minimum, but not so much as to prevent other countries from wanting to cooperate with us. At the end of next year we are hoping to launch a manned mission to Mars with a multinational crew from Moonbase Alpha, which I shall be overseeing, so I'm really looking forward to it."

"You'll never forget The Island though?"

"Nobody ever forgets The Island," she replied, knowing that the grapevine had told all of the setmates the news about The Prime Minister. "Once you have been there it becomes part of your life forever."

Joanie and the others continued to circulate as Gary rejoined his setmates who were ready to take their places for dinner. As on The Island the menu offered a combination of vegetarian and fish dishes.

"What's Moonfish?" asked Connie, glancing at the menu.

"I've heard of that," said Anne. "It's not actually a fish at all, but specially cultivated fish flesh, apparently indistinguishable in taste and appearance from normal fish, other than by a culinary expert. There are several types of Moonfish so it will be interesting to see what kind they serve up. Odd isn't it that the Moon already has its own food specialties before anyone has even properly lived there."

The service staff presently served the obligatory Two's Company sparkling wine to accompany the three-course meal. As the Moonfish arrived it soon became apparent that there was not one specific type of Moonfish but several.

"Looks like this has everything," commented Lars. "Salmon, cod, swordfish, bream, even a taster of deep fried squid Moonbase style."

"The food tastes good, albeit with a style all of its own," added Jose.

"To be sure a five-star hotel wouldn't present anything better," asserted Claudia.

After the meal, The Concierge rose from the top table and took to the stage where he prepared to give one more address.

"Ladies and gentlemen," he began, silencing the chattering. "Now that we have all sampled the culinary delights of Moonbase Alpha, I would like to have your attention for just one more time. It is interesting, I promise, as I'm going to show you some things in a moment that really are quite extraordinary. Before I do, however, I would like to welcome again the boys and girls of The Karaginsky School for their help in educating our new recruits. They are on the four sidetables either side of us. I think a round of applause is in order, both for them and for their headmaster Yuri Sentov, who hasn't just received a red card from his school governors, but joins us on this special night for something which neither he nor his school will ever forget."

The bearded man, who was seated at the top table, stood up and bowed. The audience then clapped before the Concierge continued.

"Tonight is a very special night for a number of reasons. It is special for, as in the past, our new recruits will soon be wedded as principals and secondaries and will henceforth become sets in their own right, before they take on their roles as skating stars for our four fine Kamchatskiy enterprises.

Tonight is also special because our trusted friend who has governed us so well over the last six years, has, as of today, been promoted to the post of Commander-in-Chief of Moonbase Alpha, which, although is not due to be opened formally until next year, has actually been almost fully operational for nearly a year. I naturally refer to the one and only Joanie Carmichael. I think a round of applause is in order here also, for a woman of exceptional talents, who has achieved so much for us."

The audience applauded again.

"She is, by the way, the first Prime Minister ever to be promoted in this way. In the past Prime Ministers have simply either resigned or retired. Never before has a higher post been either available or offered, but the post of Commander-in-Chief of a Moonbase has been ruled by Parliament to be such a post, requiring as it does the ultimate in technical and managerial expertise.

The appointment is timely, of course, for another special reason, and is that as of today, Her Majesty has announced her engagement to her chosen Prince Regent, Aub Ryman, formally Australian Minister of Defence, who, in just over a year will be crowned as our new Island King."

The audience applauded again.

"For these reasons alone tonight can be seen as a fine night of firsts, but there is more, and I mean much more. If you care to look at the screen behind me you will see some pictures of Moonbase Alpha, with its distinctive dark domes that allow light in, but not harmful cosmic rays. They are made of the same material as the atrium roof that you see above. I will now show you some pictures from Moonbase Alpha, and they are absolutely mindblowing.

Over the past two decades, The Island has despatched several probes, some to the very outer limits of the solar system. These have been successful in just about every respect. The world of astronomy has never had it so good. I will now share some of the information with you, as well as presenting as a gift to The Karaginsky School, a set of downloads which will allow you, Mr. Sentov, and your school to receive information directly from Alpha, which for the first time allows continuous streams of images to be received from the probes, so you can view and study action from the planets more or less as it happens.

I will begin with the most distant of the Island probes, and the oldest, Onegin 1, which currently orbits the planet Neptune. Downloads from it provide an insight into the density and exact composition of the atmosphere of Neptune, as well as radar maps of the planet's surface thanks to an atmospheric probe unit or A.P.U. that lives in suspension some 200 kilometres inside the cloud decks of this intriguing gas giant. The downloads allow schoolchildren to listen directly to the sounds of the upper atmosphere and measure variations in wind speed with depth, as well as temperature and pressure fluctuations. From these you will then be able to make your own computer-generated maps and become Neptunian weather forecasters.

Along with Onegin 1 comes Onegin 2, which last year was despatched from Onegin 1 to land on Neptune's largest moon Triton. Here you can see for the first time from the surface the mist-covered peaks and liquid ammonia lakes of this remote but fascinating world. If we are lucky we might even get to watch an ammonia geyser shoot its plume high into the dull purple sky above. This is because underground heat sources exist on Triton, which, now and again, create hot spots on the surface that quickly vaporise any localised liquid ammonia."

There was a pause as the plume of hot gas shot out for about ten seconds before the serenity returned.

"Moving in a bit closer, we have the Borodin probes which were launched to Saturn some fifteen years ago, and have now begun sending back high resolution images both of Saturn and of its largest moon, Titan. If you log on to Borodin 1 you will be able to view close-up images of Saturn and its spectacular ring system, about which we are learning new things all the time. Note the interesting braided ring, the F-ring, which defied scientific explanation for years. We now know that magnetic resonance plays a part in these formations and your pupils, Mr. Sentov, will soon be able to do their own calculations so as to explain just exactly why these rings are shaped as they are, and why the particles that comprise them display the remarkable patterns that they do. Small shepherd moons as they are called can also be seen meandering through the ring system creating interference effects that twist and bend the plane of the ring's particles, distorting their positions from the normal. The study of these has been especially useful as they have provided us with the basic theory for the invention of the gravity unit, which allows us to create and maintain Earth gravity within a small radius, such as on this vessel.

Logging on to Borodin 2 we see atmospheric probes that sit deep down, about 200 kilometres, in the atmosphere gathering measurements and producing images of vapour welling up from the interior as they race along propelled and energised by Saturn's powerful wind belts. Borodin 2 lets you watch it with your own eyes from the comfort of an armchair with its high-resolution cameras and sunken buoys that go with the flow, withstanding some of the highest temperatures and pressures of any scientific instruments ever made, and transmit some fabulous images of this fascinating world.

Borodin 3 lets you see the surface of Titan as it roams around in temperatures of around -170 degrees Centigrade, gathering and analysing samples of liquid ethane from its many rivers and lakes. These downloads will allow pupils to compare and contrast the weathering and erosion phenomena of Titan with those on Earth. A lovely geography lesson, you have to agree."

Mr. Sentov smiled as the whole audience sat and gazed in wonder as the images unfolded on the screen.

"For those who prefer to do a bit of touring, you could choose to log on to Borodin 4, which has an onboard camera that lets you observe close up the remaining satellites of Saturn. Note Iapetus, which is dark on one side and light on the other, as if someone has just thrown a paintball onto one side of it. Add to this Borodin 4a, which bores beneath the surface of the small icy moon Enceladus, seeking out water samples and examining them for signs of life. So far they have not been found here but of course they always might.

Now we're getting closer, and we're coming to the daddy of them all, Jupiter. Here we have a set of probes known as the Alexis Suite and these are, in my opinion, the most interesting of all. Alexis 1 hovers above The Great Red Spot and allows readings to be taken, for example, of the angular velocity of this huge whirling mass of nitrogenous material that continues to be drawn up from lower down.

Alexis 2 sits in the atmosphere at a depth of about one hundred kilometres where it gathers and transmits information at a temperature of just over minus 100 degrees Centigrade. These parameters were selected following the destruction of the very first atmospheric probe into Jupiter's atmosphere, which was launched from the Galileo Orbiter in July 1995 and succeeded in collecting data for 57 minutes.

We now know that the surface is releasing heat, like heating a pan full of soup until it boils and we can watch bubbles of gas and solids swirl around in a sea of hydrogenous liquid, as opposed to Saturn, which is merely simmering by comparison. The images are computer-generated by the way, compiled from powerful radio emissions from the probe capsule that penetrate through tens of thousands of miles of dense vapour and liquid before being reflected back, just as you would use to assess plate margins and underwater contours on Earth.

Above the boiling soup are dense, turbulent, dynamic wind and vapour belts, with thunder and lightening in the cloud decks that are thousands of times the strength of anything we can observe on Earth. You can see the flashes in the distance through the dense green fog that surrounds the suspended probe.

Contaminants of all kinds swirl around in hydrogen-rich clouds controlled by massive convection currents that feed the wind belts above. Alexis 2 has detected silicon as a component of granules, which, very occasionally, reach very high altitudes. Alexis 1 and Alexis 2 are an absolute must for chemistry students.

From the chemistry I will now turn to physics and Alexis 3, which focuses specifically on Jupiter's enormous magnetic field. The sheer figures involved make this a worthy subject of study. There is a hell of a lot of power involved and if ever we wanted access to an infinite supply of renewable energy we need look no further than Jupiter's magnetic field. A base on one of Jupiter's moons could well be a worthwhile investment if ever we needed to consider serious energy provision in space. At the moment Moonbase Alpha uses pure solar energy, which is sufficient for the Moon, but may not be for other more remote ventures.

For those interested in volcanoes I can recommend a log in to Alexis 4, which has been deployed on the surface of Io for the last three months. The Alexis Suite was launched seven years ago, but only now are these truly magnificent probes really showing us exactly what they are capable of. If you care to look at the screen you will be able to actually see the first ever volcanic eruption recorded from the surface of this, Jupiter's most geologically unstable moon."

Captivated, the audience watched as the eight-minute-long recording was played back allowing all to view the plumes of hot sulphurous gas and dust being sprayed into the abyss above, with magma gushing from hillside vents and flowing into solidifying lakes beneath.

"This probe can move about, using its finely tuned instruments both to measure seismic activity, and so predict when and where an eruption is likely to take place, and to look after its own safety. Logging in to Alexis 4 also allows students of geology to study the rock formations of Io, the stratification, and also the plate boundaries which are by far the most active anywhere in the solar system. With Alexis 4 we are much closer to understanding just exactly why this is so, and why this particular moon has proved to be so unlike any other.

Now, I did say tonight was a night of spectacular firsts, but if you think Alexis 4 is spectacular, you really have to take a look at Alexis 5, for this beauty of a probe has completely surpassed expectations following its landing on Europa six weeks ago. Europa, as you know, is a smooth, icy moon of Jupiter. It looks a little like a billiard ball, except for the strange streaks that run across the moon's surface. These we now understand to be long channels that have been cut as meteors have impacted on the smooth ice and sped across it for hundreds of miles before coming to rest. Beneath the surface, however, water, or what passes for it, has been found, and Alexis 5 has bored down through the mile thick ice cap into the murky depths underneath. There, what we have discovered with the aid of infrared photography has been absolutely stunning.

Alexis 5 operates in near darkness under the surface of Europa. It is self-propelled and should have sufficient power to continue its work for about two years, gradually making its way like a tiny submarine beneath the moon's surface. I will now show you one of the most fascinating things that I have ever seen. I can say that, apart from our elated scientists at our research station on Moonbase Alpha, we here are the first people ever to see these truly historic pictures. So, if you care to observe the screen I will do my best to explain what now seems to be almost certainly the first undisputed evidence ever uncovered of extraterrestial life."

The audience watched, spellbound, as the lights were dimmed and an image emerged of a dark and mysterious underwater cavern in which a dark shadowy object apparently hung motionless. The exact outline was unclear, but appeared fish-like against its cold dark surroundings, the only light for which was provided by the dim and distant black smokers that slowly released heat from deep within the moon's core. Slight movements of the object were evident with a trained eye. The image was continued for about two minutes before Patrick paused it.

"So, boys and girls, what do you think it is? Hands up if you think it's a fish."

The hands began to rise.

"About two-thirds of you think it's a fish. Okay, that boy at the front, what makes you sure that it's a fish?"

"Er, well, it sort of looks like a fish," the boy replied.

"But you're not sure are you?"

"Not 100 per cent."

"Not 100 per cent. No, neither are our experts. Hands up those who think it isn't a fish."

A couple of hands rose.

"Okay, why do you feel that it definitely isn't?" The Concierge asked, pointing to one of the girls.

"Because a fish would be swimming. That just looks like it could be a piece of dark matter in the water, maybe a rock or something, because it's quite close to the seabed."

"Well, we'll disprove that theory in a moment. The rest of you just don't know one way or the other? So, I will now continue the film and show you what happens when Alexis 5 fires an electrical pulse at the object."

There was a streak of light, which prompted a reaction from the object.

"As you can see the object jolted and moved unquestionably away from the probe, just as a fish would do under similar circumstances. For this reason our experts have concluded that this object has to be living. It could not possibly be a rock or other similar piece of inanimate material. They have therefore concluded that the object that we have witnessed is 'a fish-like creature', pictures of which will be sold by The Island to all of the world's news agencies tomorrow.

There are other things of interest too on Europa. The undersea vents, or black smokers, which erupt from time to time, are worth viewing. These provide a steady source of heat from the moon's interior, which is itself kept at an artificially high temperature due to the continual strains put upon it by that immense magnetic field of the parent planet, Jupiter.

So to Mars, just a stone's throw away really, and, of course the Leo probes, which continue to map the surface of the red planet, and to sift through layers of rock, sand and permafrost. The world was set alight a few years ago, as some of you may even have read and heard about well before you came here, when Leo 2, then to you a Russian probe that you would have been told was named after Leo Tolstoy, discovered what is almost certainly a fossil of some kind from a rock sample taken from close to the southern polar ice cap. The fossil is incomplete, but there is no doubting that it is indeed a fossil, indicating that at one time at least, there were primitive aquatic creatures there. The fossil itself is reminiscent of an ammonite, and has been dated at some two hundred million years, when the planet was undoubtedly warmer than today. Meanwhile the search continues for more and better examples.

Water has been found to exist in large quantities on Mars. The only trouble is we have to dig deep for it, but Leo 2 can do this and is continually seeking out water accumulations and analysing them for impurities, including possible life forms such as single-celled organisms. We have a print here showing what is almost certainly a single-celled structure living in Martian water. Leo 2 can also measure seismic activity and a continuous stream of data is being fed to Alpha that will allow your school to produce graphs so that we can further understand the geological nature of Mars.

Now, as some of you know there is a manned mission to Mars planned for launch next year from Moonbase Alpha. There have actually been plans for a manned mission to Mars for some years, but, until now, these have all been shelved, partly because of cost, and partly because of the huge logistical difficulties and risks involved. The construction of Moonbase Alpha has, however, revived interest in a manned mission, not least because the Moon is so much better a place to launch a spacecraft than the Earth. There are none of the problems associated with re-entry, and, with gravity only one-fifth what it is on Earth, a higher velocity can be achieved in a much shorter time, reducing the time taken to get to Mars from a minimum of six months to a minimum of two. This makes the whole concept so much more feasible than in the past.

We have had no shortage of volunteers to train for the mission. So far the plan is to send a team of three dozen people on a two-year long mission. If you care to look at the screen you can see the vessel, the SGV *Gagarin*, being assembled and tested for quality assurance. In this connection I thank our one and only Joanie Carmichael for supplying these and all the other pictures that we have seen tonight.

There's every material thing on the *Gagarin*, which is like a floating hotel. It will remain in space for a total of two years, with the crew taking it in turns to use shuttle craft to descend to specially selected landing sites on the planet's surface. Thanks to Leo 15, we now have landing sites with facilities to manufacture air and propellants for use on the surface. So, boys and girls, who can tell me the proportion of oxygen in the Martian atmosphere?"

Several hands rose.

"The girl at the front."

"About ten per cent".

"No. You're miles out."

"About two per cent," said one of the others.

"No. Any more guesses?"

"One per cent," shouted one of the boys.

"You're getting closer. It's actually about 0.15 per cent, which is not very much, but it is enough to be able to make air with the right sort of equipment, which the astronauts will take with them. Leo 16, which should touch down in another couple of months, also has some of the units, providing plenty of back up when the astronauts eventually arrive. They will remain on Mars for about eighteen months, until the Moon and Mars are once more in the correct alignment for the return journey.

So, what of the remaining planets? The King Kenneth probes to Uranus should be sending back images in another four months or so following their launch in September 2106. Then we have the Poulet 1 probe, which promises to be very exciting. Now you all know what a *poulet* is, don't you?"

"It's French for chicken," said one of the boys.

"It is. And do you know why we have called it that?"

A few heads shook.

"Well, its because it looks like a chicken, and it will take off from the Moon in December and fly to Mercury, where it will release lots of eggs containing worm-like instruments that will bury into the sands of Mercury and take samples for analysis so that schoolchildren all over the world can study the geology of this tiny, sunburnt planet. Special sensors on the instruments will tell them when it is safe to rise to the surface in the cool of the Mercurial night, and take images of the surface before burying themselves again so as to avoid the intense unprotected sunlight that sends surface temperatures soaring to over four hundred degrees centigrade. The graphics on the screen show how the probe will work. The mothership, the chicken, will act as a beacon, amplifying and relaying signals back to Alpha, once it has released its seven thousand or so eggs, some of which should statistically survive for up to twenty years, powered by heat absorbed from the ground.

On its way to Mercury, though, Poulet 1 will perform one more important task, as it bypasses Venus. At this point it will release two much larger and much stronger eggs that are ceramic, designed to withstand entry into the Venusian atmosphere, and conditions on the surface for up to a month. They will sample the local geology and atmosphere around the polar regions. The temperature by the way is about 470 degrees Centigrade, making it hotter than Mercury thanks to its runaway greenhouse effect, but it is uniform, that is to say the poles are not that much cooler than the equator and there aren't the extreme fluctuations that we see on Mercury. If you watch the screen you will see a simulation of what we hope will occur with the powerful cannons firing out the two capsules."

The simulation lasted about five minutes and showed first the release of Poulet 2 and Poulet 3 from Poulet 1, then their descent toward Venus, followed by their landings and subsequent rolling action as robust sensors then emerged like antennae ready to collect physical and chemical data for short periods at a time.

"I will now return to Moonbase Alpha and the magnificent observatory that has been constructed there. First though, can any of you tell me who this is?"

The face of a middle-aged man of oriental appearance now appeared and a couple of hands were raised.

"A couple of you seem to know. The girl at the front on the left."

"Is it Viktor Chenkov?"

"It is, yes, The Island scientist, and can you tell me what he is famous for? The boy at the back there."

"Didn't he discover Nemesis?"

"Well done. Now you all know. He discovered Nemesis, otherwise referred to as the Black Planet, because it is, as far as we are concerned, completely black. It does not reflect any light at all. He discovered it on 3rd October 2079, actually whilst looking for something else. From his small observatory on Sakhalin he made a series of observations looking for planets around other stars, and he found a few, or thought that he did. Then a recheck made him think twice as he compared his observations by those made by other astronomers. Further checking made him suspicious that at least a few of these so-called discoveries were not really discoveries at all, but in fact observations of the same object that had recurred on several occasions, leading observers to believe that they had detected a planet orbiting a star. He looked at the dates and times of these discoveries going back to the twentieth century and later confirmed his postulation by successfully predicting a sequence of stars that would dim appreciably at certain times.

Chenkov knew he was onto something, convinced that he had found not a planet of another star, but a very large distant body about one light year away that was drifting silently in space. We now know that this body is about five times the size of Jupiter and has about thirty-six times its mass. It reflects no light, which is why nobody could ever see it. It does, however, possess sufficient mass to enable it to perturb the orbits of the outer planets, particularly Uranus and Neptune, and to deflect comets, which would explain why one or two have apparently gone missing, like Brorsen's comet in 1879.

The latest theory is that the Black Planet could have once been part of the Sun, but around about the time that the solar system was forming it either broke off, or was ejected, from the Sun. Its huge mass, combined with a high velocity, then gave it sufficient momentum to almost escape the solar system, but not completely, so that the Sun still effectively holds it in a far distant orbit, you could say like a dead companion.

If you look at the screen now you will see the magnificent Clifford Observatory on Moonbase Alpha, which has a suite of fine telescopes of every kind, and permanently clear skies every night of the year. From here we can observe the Black Planet in more detail than ever before, and, indeed, in more detail than would ever be possible from the Earth. High magnifications of distant stars allow the Black Planet to be tracked across them, a bit like watching a transit of Mercury across the Sun. We can also predict where it will strike next and be ready for it so that it can be observed and viewed by schools.

With the latest technology, when you next return to school you should be able to do as I have done, and switch from one planet or moon to another at the touch of a button to view continuous images of things never before seen. With the help of space agencies around the world, The Island will make available a unique educational service, which will contribute greatly to our knowledge and understanding, and your school, Mr. Sentov, will be the first to receive it."

Mr. Sentov then stood to make a brief address.

"Words fail me," he said. "And the things I have witnessed tonight aren't just special, they are worldbeating and totally astounding. On behalf of the school, I have to thank you, your team, and of course Her Majesty and Ms Joanie Carmichael for what can only be described as making dreams come true yet again for our pupils. That tour of the planets was absolutely magnificent. I therefore ask that we all now put our hands together for a truly remarkable handful of individuals."

The audience stood to applaud. Then Concierge Patrick continued:

"That brings me to the next of tonight's highlights, and it is another first. Yes, for the first time, ladies and gentlemen, boys and girls, we have three sets of sixth formers from The Karaginsky School who are going to perform something quite unique, a new kind of dancing, known as space dancing. It has never been done before, and can only be done now thanks to that great twenty-second-century invention, the gravity unit, and in that connection boys and girls I now have another face for you to identify."

Another photograph of a middle-aged man appeared. This time no hands were raised.

"No takers? Well I can tell you that the man is Alexander Padrikov, an Island scientist who conducted experiments in 2090 involving the rotation of superconductors above an arrangement of powerful electromagnets. With this apparatus it was found that small objects experienced an apparent loss in weight of about two per cent. This was not a lot by modern standards, but it had never previously been observed let alone confirmed.

The poor treatment of other scientists around the world who had been conducting similar research led Padrikov to keep much of his work a secret. He therefore quietly researched the information of others, recreated the experiments and refined them.

As I said, the experiments created a weight reduction coefficient of just two per cent. On The Island scientists at the Clifford Institute knew that for space travel with full gravity compensation this figure needed to be increased to 100 per cent dissipated over an area of at least several square metres.

It took Island scientists ten years to eventually refine Padrikov's apparatus to the level of providing twenty per cent gravity compensation, and older literature refers to these units as Padrikov Units. Beyond this level, however, scientists knew that they were going to have to design and construct a far bigger piece of equipment and if money were a consideration it is doubtful that any such undertaking could have proved viable. Only The Island had both the means and the incentive to persist with the experimentation building ever larger and more elaborate contraptions.

I will now invite you to observe on the screen a simulation of a modern gravity unit in operation. These new machines bear little resemblance to the original

312

machines, which were, and still are, strictly gravity blockers rather than gravity creators. The first machine to produce 100 per cent gravity compensation was the unit on SGV *Neville*, which consists of three rotating superconducting plasma spheres suspended in a vacuum surrounded by a set of powerful electromagnets, which have the power to direct the resulting gravito-magnetic beam to a chosen target area some twelve metres above. Over the last five years the design has been improved, partly through improved materials science with the internal plasma, and partly through improved efficiency of the electromagnets, so that we now have rotating superconductors of half the original size, just ten metres in diameter rather than twenty, with twice the reliability and durability. As I said, if money were a consideration these machines just would never have seen the light of day. I won't say, Mr. Sentov, how many schools could be built for the cost of just one of these units. I will say though that the gravity unit is by far and away the most expensive piece of kit on board this spacecraft, and as little as a decade ago there were even Island scientists who were of the opinion that it really wasn't feasible to go above twenty per cent compensation, as even that needed at the time two extremely costly thirty metre diameter plasma spheres. At this point you may wish to compare the workings of the gravity unit with the natural gravitational characteristics of Saturn's shepherd moons which you saw earlier.

That now brings me back to the next item on tonight's agenda, the world's first ever space dance. Three sets of twelve sixth formers, who are going to be wedded tonight along with our setmates, are ready and waiting to delight you with their routine, and soon we will be tilting the gravity unit so that the upper reaches of the Atrium beneath the transparent dome, which allows us to see into space yet protects us from harmful cosmic rays, become gravity free. I will now hand over to our one and only charming Joanie, for one night only, to introduce our fine performers."

"Thank you Patrick," she said, rising to the stage. "Now you all enjoyed that didn't you boys and girls?"

The children cheered.

"You did, didn't you?"

There was then a louder cheer from the children's tables.

"So now for the entertainment. Last year, when I wrote to Mr. Sentov to invite his school to participate in the activities on The Island of Dreams, I suggested that three sets of sixth formers be invited to train on Sakhalin Island in Padrikov's original gravity blocker to produce a group of dances that could be performed in space. They would then travel with their school this year on the SGV *Katie* and perform their routines. Mr. Sentov said yes and now here they are to perform a one off group of dances of three minutes duration each based on a piece from Gustav Holst's *Planet Suite*, which next week will be broadcast on Russian television. Ladies and gentlemen, boys and girls, will you please welcome from The Karaginsky School, the one and only Space Dancers."

Six couples launched themselves from the balcony of the Atrium and began their routine floating beneath the twenty-metre wide transparent dome through which the stars in their bright constellations could be seen as never before. Their original interpretation of 'Jupiter, the Bringer of Jollity', integrated the majesty of the Island national anthem 'I vow to thee my Island' with the energy and vitality of the nymphs, portrayed by the girls, springing and performing somersaults with their new-found weightlessness. Agile and dressed in a silvery white they looped around the more darkly costumed gents, who utilised the more dominant chords of the piece, linking arms and forming intricate figures, until they eventually encircled the girls, who gathered into a ball and spun round wildly in the middle as a climax. Only the alteration of the angle of tilt of the gravity unit allowed the dancers to return to the sanctuary of the balcony from which they had made their entrance.

The next set presented a very different work of art. This time their chosen piece was 'Mercury, The Winged Messenger'. Here lots of short chords characterised the piece and the dancers utilised these to convey the idea of flying toward the heavens with messages passing to and fro as if in a relay. The girls were winged cupids that hovered at the top of the Atrium, looking first down at the messenger boys looping around each other below, transferring their baton prop hand-to-hand and foot-to-foot. Their complex whorls and chains culminated in their rise to the heavens with the independently performing angels raising their arms as if to draw them up to the spheres before they held each other and looked outward, opening their arms to the cosmos, poised to take their message further.

The last routine was 'Mars, The Bringer of War'. For this routine the six couples started suspended and facing one another in bright orange and red in a formation that portrayed the vision of two armies about to be locked into battle. A small quantity of red smoke added to the drama as the two sides charged into each other, flinging each other around before regrouping to wrestle and jostle with each other. The dance moves conveyed the concept of cyclical fighting and alternating victory for one side over the other as individual players were defeated only to come back and fight another day. The climax came when both sides collapsed inwardly to finish with a matrix of flat bodies suspended in mid-air that symbolised defeat for both sides. Only when the gravity unit was tilted slightly could the matrix be drawn to one side of the balcony to take its applause.

"Great stuff," said Joanie. "A big hand to all of our fine Space Dancers. Long may it live as a discipline of dancing in its own right. Dancing in space. I love it. Now, talking of love, we have just one more formality to complete and that is the marriage of Her Majesty's setmates. When the captain has reset the gravity unit to normal inclination, I will ask all of our new setmates to make their way to the Marriage Room, where The Usherette will ask each couple to collect their chosen wedding ring from her velvet covered tray. Following that the good Reverend will perform the short ceremony that will confer upon each their marriage as principals and secondaries in accordance with the Set Formation Act."

*

The setmates were ushered through from the Atrium to the small Marriage Room, outside which The Usherette stood behind a long table upon which was the rectangular velvet covered tray, upon which were placed the 120 specially crafted wedding rings that they had chosen from The Island Jeweller. Beside this was a list that displayed the order in which the sets were to enter the Marriage Room. This placed Gary's set fifth in order to enter to receive The Reverend's blessing.

The inside of the room was not as they had expected it to be, like a registry office or a small chapel. Instead it resembled an old-fashioned blacksmith's smithy, complete with horse shoes with an anvil at the centre where The Reverend stood, dressed as a blacksmith rather than a reverend, with an iron hammer.

"In the name of God the Father, Christ and the Holy Spirit," he declared. "I bless this set now and forever."

He then turned to each couple and asked each person to swear to the other.

"Do you take this person to be your lawful wedded principal, forsaking all others, for better or worse, until death shall part you?"

"I do," each replied.

When both man and woman had responded he struck the anvil with his hammer.

"I therefore declare you wedded as principals under the terms and conditions set out under the law of The Island and its territories. The husband may now kiss the bride and place the chosen ring upon her finger."

When this had been done he faced each couple again and asked them to swear again.

"I now ask you both, do you take these fellow setmates to be your lawful wedded secondaries and agree to be faithful to them alone, forsaking all others, for as long as you shall live, under the terms set out under the law of The Island and its territories?"

"We do," each couple replied.

"Then I hereby declare you as lawful wedded secondaries as prescribed by the above law."

He then struck the anvil again.

When all of the couples had sworn to both components of the Act he struck the anvil once more and turned to the complete set.

"It is now my honour to bestow upon you the right to be henceforth a set as prescribed by the law of The Island and its territories. Go forth in peace and serve The Lord."

The Concierge shook the hands of each couple as they left the Marriage Room ready for The Reverend to perform the next ceremony.

From the Marriage Room the setmates returned to the Atrium where the ballroom floor had been cleared and the Karaginsky pupils were already dancing to the music of a fine Wurlitzer organ that had risen from the stage, replacing the lectern and screen from earlier.

Gary and the others mixed with the pupils, congratulating the Space Dancers on their space dances, and taking the opportunity to dance with them under the stars that shone, light years away, through the large transparent dome above. Joanie watched on from a table on the balcony above, sipping a glass of red wine as she smiled, reminiscing over her past six years on The Island, a slight tear in her eye, whilst at the same time glancing at the manual in front of her, the cover of which displayed the words 'Moonbase Alpha. Supreme Commander: Roles and Responsibilities.'

For about an hour they danced before one by one they dispersed to their sleeping quarters. These contained a wooden four-poster bed, behind which was a porthole that offered a panoramic view of the Earth. Tired, but relaxed, Gary and Connie rested unclothed beneath the covers. They embraced. Then, with their marriage consummated, they kissed in the Earthlight. Then Gary turned to Connie and asked "What do those words in Russian mean that are carved above the bed?"

"And the meek shall inherit the Earth."